"Yolanda, I was in the airport in Atlanta, and I thought I saw him," Renee confessed.

"Him?" Yolanda probed gently.

"Him." Her bravado was fooling no one; this was obviously difficult. I just felt dizzy and queasy and sick to my very soul."

She went on to tell Yolanda all of the wonderful things that Andrew had arranged for her as a welcome-home surprise. Yolanda was once again impressed with the playful and sweet relationship that they were enjoying. She couldn't help but ask a pertinent question, though.

"Did you tell Andrew what you thought you saw at the airport?" Yolanda said quietly.

"No, I didn't," Renee said in an equally quiet voice. "I wasn't sure about what I had seen, and I didn't want to give it energy in any case. It all happened a long, long time ago. It's over. I have a new life and a new love and he can't touch any of that," she said confidently.

Yolanda let that statement settle and watched the determination on Renee's face. "One last thing, Renee, and then we will have some tea and relax. If you were to encounter Donovan Bailey, if you were to come face-to-face with him, how would you handle it?"

Without hesitation Renee answered, "I would try to kill him." She drew in a sharp breath as she realized what she had just uttered. *But I'm not taking it back.*

BOOK YOUR PLACE ON OUR WEBSITE AND MAKE THE ARABESQUE ROMANCE CONNECTION!

We've created a customized website just for our very special Arabesque readers, where you can get the inside scoop on everything that's going on with Arabesque romance novels.

When you come online, you'll have the exciting opportunity to:

- View covers of upcoming books

- Learn about our future publishing schedule (listed by publication month and author)

- Find out when your favorite authors will be visiting a city near you

- Search for and order backlist books

- Check out author bios and background information

- Send e-mail to your favorite authors

- Join us in weekly chats with authors, readers and other guests

- Get writing guidelines

- AND MUCH MORE!

Visit our website at
http://www.arabesquebooks.com

UNTIL THE END OF TIME

Melanie Schuster

ARABESQUE
BET
BOOKS

BET Publications, LLC
http://www.bet.com
http://www.arabesquebooks.com

Dedicated to Renee
Who graciously lent me her name
Though she bears no resemblance to the character
Other than being a person who knows the
True meaning of friendship . . .

ACKNOWLEDGMENTS

First, thanks to God for giving me the resources with which to fulfill a dream. And thanks to my family for encouraging me and believing in me.

To Frankie Ann Powell, thanks for just being you. Thanks also to my wonderful coworkers at Ameritech, your enthusiasm and support mean the world to me. To Janice Sims for friendship and for the wonderful title, to Brenda Woodbury for patience and understanding, to Danny Watley for continued friendship and for introducing me to the wonderful Marilyn Pearson . . . words aren't enough to express my gratitude.

To Mary Nicol at Barnes & Noble for the great event, Janet Martineau at the *Saginaw News* for the great article, to the readers who took the time and effort to let me know how much they enjoyed my work, a sincere thank you.

Another big thank you to Renee, who makes me feel like a star. Thank you for being my friend for so very long.

And as always, to Jamil: Thanks for your joy in my accomplishment, for being so proud of me and for being my one-man cheering section. Your presence in my life continues to be a true gift. Kiss Kamar for me!

Prologue

A somewhat familiar fragrance permeated the deep sleep of Andrew Cochran. He vaguely recognized it as the smell that women left behind in the bathroom after taking a shower—a warm, moist, sweet smell that was incredibly sexy to an eighteen year-old man. At least it was when it wasn't his sister's fragrance, and it could not have been hers—she had left the dormitory suite sometime before to put gas in the hoopty they shared and pick him up some breakfast. Yet the smell persisted and got even stronger when the bathroom door that joined the two bedrooms of his sister's suite opened.

"Bennie, I'm wearing your silver hoops, okay? I have that interview this morning and I want to look *très chic*. *Merci, mon amie!*" a voice said cheerfully.

Andrew's head was buried under the covers. He did not think it wise to answer the voice, which obviously thought that the lump in the bed was his twin sister, Benita.

Damn, that's a sexy voice, Andrew thought. Her voice was like a jazz legend's, rich and smoky. He could not resist peeking, and felt his heart stop. The woman who had blithely hailed his sister was picking up a pair of earrings from her dresser. She was wearing a pink towel carelessly wrapped around her body. The matching towel that wrapped her head was apparently wrapped too loosely, as she grabbed it with both hands. Unfortunately, the towel around her torso chose that moment to slip down to the floor, revealing her total nudity. Andrew's heart started pounding and he could not have spoken if his life depended on it. She was gorgeous!

She was tall, although not as tall as his sister. She had a fabulous figure, too—she had nice round hips, nice full breasts and legs that not only went on forever but were big and shapely, too. When she turned to go back into the bathroom, Andrew could not help noticing her tummy, which was rounded and smooth. Best of all, her skin was the flawless, smooth color of melted chocolate. Altogether, she was the most delectable thing Andrew had seen in his entire life.

He felt like the worst kind of voyeur in the world, but there was nothing short of instant blindness that would have made him close his eyes. Thank God she left the room. In what seemed like seconds, she was back, this time wearing pale lacy pink bikini panties that were somehow worse than total nudity. She was still chattering away to the long-gone Bennie, too, something about hair spray. She had taken the towel off her hair and Andrew could see that it was a healthy, shiny black, worn in a tight knot on the top of her head. It was severe, but it suited her, showing off her perfect features. She had a short, pointed nose, a mouth that curved in a sweet Cupid's bow and huge eyes that were remarkably golden, even in the dim light. The contrast with her skin was absolutely dynamite. Once again she disappeared into the bathroom.

Andrew considered slinking out of the room, which would be difficult, since he was well over six feet tall and not the most graceful person in the world. Plus, his observations had rendered him quite unable to move quickly due to a natural male response to a vital, lush feminine stimulus. His best move, he thought, would be to continue to hide until she got completely dressed and left. *God, I hope Bennie doesn't come back before she does. That poor girl would die of embarrassment.*

Unfortunately, the chocolate vision came back one more time, this time in a robe—*Thank you, Jesus*—a short, silky kimono of a robe, but at least she was covered. She had a gray suit on a hanger in one hand, and a red jacket with a black skirt dangling from the hanger in her other hand. "Okay, Bennie, this is the last time I'm bothering you this morning. Which one should I wear? The gray suit is very conservative and corporate, but the red and black is corporate and has a little savoir faire. Which shall it be?" she asked gaily.

Something evil possessed Andrew at that very moment—he had no idea what made him speak up, but he said, "I like the red. It will bring out your skin color much better."

The poor woman jumped straight in the air, screaming, at the same instant that the door flew open to reveal Bennie standing there with two cups of coffee and a bag of takeout from a local diner.

Bennie looked from her suitemate Renee Kemp to her twin brother and smiled gamely. "Well, I see you two have met," she said dryly.

One

"Benita, if you do not do something about that brother of yours, I am going to be forced to take drastic measures." Renee Kemp accompanied the ultimatum with a look that said she was not playing. Bennie tried not to smile, but it was difficult.

"Well, Renee, which one of my five brothers would that be?" she asked sweetly.

Renee rolled up a magazine and lightly whacked her best friend on the head with it. "Don't get cute! You know very well that I'm referring to your twin brother, the perennial thorn in my side, Andrew Bernard Cochran Junior. He needs to be restrained or lobotomized, whichever." Renee fairly spat the words, which meant that she was really steamed.

The two women were in the sitting room that adjoined Bennie's bedroom in the big house that they shared in the Indian Village section of Detroit. They had been friends since college and were as close as sisters, which is why Renee felt free to disparage Bennie's twin brother. Not that it would do any good—she and Andrew had not gotten along since the day Renee discovered him in Bennie's half of their dormitory suite. She swore to this day that he had seen her naked, a charge that he had denied for seventeen years. They had declared many truces over the years in deference to their love for Bennie, but with the best intentions in the world they could not get along for more than a week. Renee was just too much fun to tease, in Andrew's estimation. Bennie tried to be sympathetic, but it was difficult.

She looked at Renee, who was obviously pissed. "Well, what has he done this time?" she asked warily.

Renee turned her golden eyes to Bennie. "He has been sending me samples of Viagra in the mail. Samples and brochures, thank you very much," she hissed. "I do not have to tell you how funny that is not," she added.

Unfortunately, Bennie did think it was funny. She tried to control herself, but she started laughing, deep belly laughs, which had her convulsed with merriment within seconds.

Renee dated older men exclusively—very wealthy, well-connected men who were at least ten years her senior. Her escorts of choice were a never-ending source of hilarity to Andrew; he never seemed to run out of lame jokes to make at her escorts' expense. Even Renee had to admit that on some primitive level sending the information packets on impotence had a certain sly—albeit *crude*—wit about it, but she would never admit this. So she continued to try and look perturbed, although it was not easy with her friend rolling about, laughing like the proverbial hyena.

Renee had a great deal of practice in looking aloof. It was an expression that she had mastered after years of having her tender feelings trampled on by others. Renee's personality was often at odds with her appearance, and no wonder—it was an elaborately constructed thing. Renee was as complicated as one of those tiny ivory balls hand carved by Japanese artists that are actually a series of balls, one inside the other, each with its own intricate pattern.

She had learned over time that the best way for people to hurt you was for them to get to know you in some way. But she and Bennie had known each other for too many years to hide much. Now Renee waited patiently for her best friend to get over her fit of laughter. Bennie was one of the few people with whom Renee was really close.

Theirs was a friendship that Renee truly treasured. Although it was being tested this day.

Bennie finally regained control of herself. "Ne-ne, I am sorry. I'm sorry I laughed"—she gasped, wiping away the tears—"and I'm sorry that Andrew is being a jerk. Again. I'll have a little chat with him, but you know how that goes." Bennie sat up straight on the love seat and took a deep breath. "You know my brothers think of you as a sister. So I think it's just brotherly . . . you know, that makes him tease you so," she offered in a voice of conciliation.

Renee gave a ladylike snort. "Ain't gonna work, girlfriend. Andrew is your true brother and he treats you like gold. No, like *platinum* studded with diamonds. So don't hand me that sibling high jinks crap. None of your brothers would go to the lengths that Andrew does to plague me. He's just perverted, that's all. That man acts like I'm some kind of play toy for his amusement," she said. She was starting to get angry all over again.

"One day I'm going to have him just where I want him. And he will rue the day that he ever laid eyes on me," she vowed.

At the moment the culprit was bringing his long day to an end. Dr. Andrew Cochran was in his private office at his clinic, speaking rapidly into a small tape recorder, which would be used to transcribe his daily reports. A knock at the door caused him to look up and bid the caller to enter. It was his youngest brother, Adonis, who answered only to Donnie. Andrew was pleased to see his brother, although not necessarily surprised. He was close to all of his siblings, and often the only time he saw them was when they dropped by his office because his schedule was so full.

After exchanging greetings, Andrew said, "I know you did not come by here just to gaze on your older and wiser brother. What's up?"

Donnie picked up a small wooden maze from Andrew's

untidy desk and laughed as he shook it. "The jury is still out about the 'wiser' part. Listen, Adam and I are going down to the islands in a few weeks and we wondered if you would come along. You haven't had a vacation in, like, a thousand years, and the three of us haven't hung out in a while. How about it?" Adam was the Cochran brother next in age to Donnie.

Andrew hesitated for a moment. He was sorely tempted, but he shook his head in regret. "Can't do it, Donnie. I'm booked until June and then I go to Haiti with Medic International. That's going to be my vacation this year," he said.

Actually, it was his vacation every year. Andrew was a board-certified plastic surgeon who specialized in facial reconstruction. He was not the man to give one a prettier nose or to turn back the hands of time by removing unwanted wrinkles. Andrew Cochran specialized in hope. For burn victims, patients with congenital deformities and those suffering from disfiguring accidents, he was often the only man who could restore even a part of a person's normal life. Andrew was totally dedicated to his career. He had yet to marry, and in truth he had never made time for any really serious relationships. He worked very long hours at his clinic and at the hospitals where he had privileges. He also lectured and wrote articles that had been featured in a couple of medical journals.

Donnie sighed with real regret but could not resist pointing out, "You know, you need to have some kind of social life, too, man. I know you're a great doctor and your patients depend on you and all of that, but you've got to take some time for yourself. This is why you never got married and why you can't keep a woman. You work too much."

Andrew lifted his brows and stared at his brother with amusement. "And what makes you think I can't keep a woman? I've got plenty of women, hordes of 'em. There's a couple in the closet, and one under the very sofa you're sitting on. And they're all fine, too," he added with a yawn. "Stone foxes," he said tiredly.

Donnie had a smart rejoinder on the tip of his tongue, but the telephone interrupted his flow. It was Benita, touching base with Andrew.

"Don't tell me," he said, chuckling, "your little friend got a package in the mail that she wasn't too happy about, right?"

Bennie moaned with exasperation at Andrew's amusement.

"Yes, Bunchy, she did. And no, she is not happy about it. Although"—Bennie let out a guilty laugh—"it was pretty funny. But nevertheless, you have got to stop that! Can't my brother and my best friend get along for two minutes without me having to referee?"

Andrew took a deep breath. It was childish and he knew it, but it was so much fun at times. Still, he made a half-hearted promise to try and behave himself.

"So are we still on for tonight?" he asked, referring to his weekly dinner with his sister.

Bennie looked forward to the meal as much as Andrew did, but she had one stipulation.

"Yes, but either you cook, we get takeout or we eat out. I wouldn't show my face around here for a couple of days if I were you."

Andrew laughed. "Damn, is she that mad?"

"At least she says she is. You know that her hot button is her gentlemen callers. Anyway, are you willing to take that risk?"

Andrew decided that he was not. But he could not resist a parting shot. "Yeah, well, tell her if she doesn't want people getting her goat, she shouldn't let them know where she ties it up."

Donnie was looking at his brother with a big smile when he got off the phone. "So you're still picking on Renee, huh? Why do y'all go at each other like that? Can't you get along like adults?"

Andrew did not answer for a moment. The truth was way too complicated to try and explain. If he were to be completely honest, he would have to admit that there were indeed times when he wished that he had never heard the name Renee Kemp. He wished that his sister had found herself another suitemate altogether when she attended the University of Michigan; then, Andrew reasoned, he would have never even seen Renee, at least not the way he had when they were all college freshmen. It was a sight that he could never forget, and the recollection of it could even today precipitate the need for a cold shower. It was probably the immense impact of that first sighting that caused Andrew to pick on Renee so endlessly. That, and the fact that Renee bristled like a wet cat every time Andrew came near her. It was that as much as anything that kept him on her case, he had to admit it. Renee made no secret of the fact that she could barely stand him. The fact that his pulse jumped every time she came into a room was no one's business, he felt, but his own.

Finally Andrew answered Donnie. "I don't pick on Renee; she picks on *me*. I'm just trying to defend myself. You know she's madly in love with me and won't admit it."

"In love? With your old tired butt? Please! You gotta do better than that!" Donnie laughed. "Now if she was after me or Adam, the *fine* Cochrans, I could see that, but not you, Bunchy. Not with your nonpartying, nonplaying, workaholic self. You're way too out of it for someone like Renee."

Andrew threw a paperweight at his brother, which Donnie easily caught. "I party plenty," he said, defending himself. "And I'd watch the cracks about my looks since you look just like me."

Which was true. All of the Cochrans shared a decided similarity in features. They were all well over six feet. They shared with their sister, Benita, a golden caramel skin color and thick, wavy black hair that fairly gleamed with health and good grooming. Andrew also had what used to be referred to as "bedroom eyes," meaning that they were sexy, direct and inviting. In Andrew's case, they were also large and clear, with eyelashes that were unfairly long for a man. He had shiny thick eyebrows and a perfectly shaped mouth that would have looked almost feminine, had it not been for his thick black mustache. All the Cochran men, Andrew included, were big, handsome and pretty much irresistible to women. Except when it came to Renee.

Finally Andrew's hunger overrode his musings. "Let's go. I'm hungry and so is Bennie. So why don't you come with us to dinner? And since you're the youngest, you get to pay," he said with a grin.

Donnie agreed, adding, "Man, this is why you need a wife. We wouldn't be eating out and my money would stay in my wallet."

Continuing their amiable bickering, the two men left the clinic.

Bennie and Andrew need not have worried about a confrontation with Renee. She had a date that evening with one of her usual escorts. She had agreed to accompany Edwin Jackson to a play and a late supper afterward. As always, she took great care with her toilette, which was not symbolic of vanity but rather of years of insecurity. It was sometimes difficult for Renee to reconcile the reflection in the mirror with the image she held in her mind.

Renee jumped guiltily as Bennie entered her bedroom. She hated for anyone to catch her looking in the mirror. No one knew what she saw reflected in its depths. Bennie, however, knew pretty much what was on her friend's mind.

"Renee, you always do that. You can't stand for anyone to see you looking at yourself. In fact, I think you can't stand to look at your own reflection! After all this time, why is that?" Bennie asked her pointedly.

Renee narrowed her eyes at her friend. "Have I told you how much I dislike the caring, perceptive part of your personality?" she murmured. "Bennie, it's hard to explain. I look in my mirror and it's like looking into my past. I don't see what *you* see; I see what I remember," she admitted softly.

She would see a smooth, velvety complexion but would remember the savage acne that had led to years of unmerciful teasing from her peers. She would see the curvaceous body but remember the plump little preteen who was afraid to wear a bathing suit or even look at a second helping for fear of ridicule. She did not see the satiny seduction of her chocolate brown skin; she would see only the little black face that was so much darker than her sisters'. By one of those strange genetic quirks, Renee was the darkest member of her immediate family.

"It's really stupid, but I still remember that color thing. All my sisters are the same shade of medium brown, just like Daddy. My mother is darker, but not as dark as I am, even though she has these same ol' yellow eyes. Nope, I look just like my grandmother. Not that it's a bad thing; Big Momma was quite a belle in her day," Renee admitted.

"But people always made such a big thing out of it! 'Ooh, Pearlie Mae, where'd you get that little pickaninny from! Chile, you best to keep her out the sun or you won't find her come dark,' " Renee whined in a perfect imitation of the old ladies she despised in her youth. "I have to tell you, when I was a kid, you could call me anything and I would fight you, but call me black and I was *zoom!* in the house with a quickness. For some reason, it was just the most hurtful thing in the world to me. And I was the meanest little girl on Chateau Avenue, too! Nothing bothered me, except being called 'darky.'

"The family reunions were the very limit. I love my mother's family, but Lord, it was all I could do to get through that week of examination and comparison. 'Hmmph, Effie's child sho' got some big teeth! Unh, look how bowlegged that girl of Lula's is! And looky here at little Ree-nay! She just the spittin' image of Big Momma, ain't she?' " Renee shuddered delicately at the memory.

"You know, I was in college before I learned that spittin' image was the colloquial for 'spirit and image.' That sounds much nicer, don't you think? And I really am, you know. My grandmother was a pistol, you hear me? Big Momma was known for three things: her temper, her velvety black skin and her absolute refusal to take any mess off anyone, black or white, male or female. And she was a very, very sweet woman who made the best bread pudding you ever put in your mouth."

Renee sighed, remembering the gracious lady who was the stuff of legends in her part of the South. Her mouth turned up in a faint smile as she recalled her peppery grandmother. Big Momma kicked butt and took names, even in rural Mississippi. Even after Big Poppa had died, leaving her with a farm to run and children to raise, she stayed strong. *You wouldn't catch Big Momma whining over how dark she was or how mean people could be,* Renee thought shamefacedly. Big Momma was a woman in control of her fate, and Renee had indeed inherited that very trait. She lived it daily, as a matter of fact. But no one knew what she saw in her head when she looked in the mirror.

Renee turned to face Bennie and smiled wanly. "Did I ever tell you about my church obsession when I was a child? I loved to go to church, so much so that I couldn't wait for the regular service. There was a little Mennonite church across the street from us. The congregation was all white, of course. When my sisters were scrambling to get dressed to go to our regular AME service, I would sashay across the street just as big as day and plop myself right down with the rest of the folks," she said with a short laugh.

Bennie's eyes grew wide at this revelation and Renee continued as she slipped on her pantyhose. "These were some very nice, very quiet people and nobody ever said anything to me; they just accepted my presence," she recalled, shaking her head slightly.

"I would sit there quiet as a little mouse, just watching everything. But I would always look down at my legs sticking straight out on the pew. They were so *black!* Especially when I would look at the people around me. So black . . ." Her voice trailed off for a moment; then she straightened up with a smile.

"Don't get me wrong now. I would not give up one drop of melanin for anything. I love being the black berry with the sweet juice and all that goes with it! But there was a time when it was not a comfortable skin to be in, ya know?"

Bennie grabbed Renee and gave her a big hug. "Oh, darlin', you're just gorgeous. You have a perfect complexion and legs that bring tears to men's eyes. I have observed that very phenomenon, so don't deny it," Bennie said truthfully. "And you're just as beautiful on the inside, although not many people know that," she added shrewdly. "I also wish I could wear my hair like yours." She ended with a wistful sigh.

Renee wore her hair in a short, stylish cut, which framed her chocolate face to perfection. Bennie, on the other hand, was six-one to Renee's five-ten and was broad-shouldered and slim-hipped to boot and needed long hair to balance her body.

Renee looked in the mirror at Bennie's comment, admiring her sleek, shiny black hair. "Well, you know I have to show off the latest cuts. How would it look for a salon owner to have a bad hair day?" she asked rhetorically. "And you are not conning me into cutting your hair," she added pointedly, looking at Bennie's abundant locks.

Hastily changing the subject, Bennie admired Renee's outfit for the evening. Tonight she had decided to give poor Edwin a thrill by wearing an orange cashmere dress that was so vibrant in hue that it seemed drenched in gold. The dress not only accentuated every curve; it had a huge cowl neck that slipped invitingly over Renee's shoulders in a way that was guaranteed to drive a man crazy. It was, in fact, difficult to look at Renee without thinking about something really carnal, which was quite a paradox given Renee's cool demeanor. Dispassionately she turned to briefly inspect herself in her full-length mirror and decided that she was ready.

Bennie handed Renee a large pair of gold Sandy Baker earrings from her dresser. Renee put them on and added a touch of gloss to her lips, which were already wearing an alluring bronze lipstick. One more tiny dab of perfume behind her ear and she was done with her preparations. There was no sense in giving Edwin a heart attack; she enjoyed his company too much for that.

Bennie glanced at her watch and gasped. "Wow, look at the time. I'm meeting the 'Brother Who Shall Remain Nameless' for dinner. Have a good time with Edwin. Try not to hurt him," she added wickedly as she left Renee's suite. Renee wrinkled her nose at Bennie's retreating figure and went over to the window to check the weather before deciding on footwear. Spring in Detroit was a vicious affair—one never knew what the elements would do to challenge one.

Hearing the slight hiss of sleet, she decided to wear boots. There was no way she was messing up her good pumps in this weather. Besides, her legs looked darned good in the burnished brown designer boots. They had a three-inch heel and fit like silk hose, so she was quite sexy enough, thank you.

After Edwin arrived and helped her don her all-weather coat with the mink lining, he agreed completely. "My dear, you look lovely this evening." He inhaled her unique fragrance. "And you smell fantastic, as always," he added.

Renee favored him with a tiny smile—she did not want Edwin thinking that a little compliment like that would get him anywhere.

"Thank you, Edwin" was all she said, but with her incredible voice those few words were enough to get Edwin revved up for the evening. Renee was immediately ashamed of her irreverent thought; Edwin Jackson was a very nice man. He was six-one, well educated, soft spoken and gentlemanly. He was quite handsome, too, with medium brown skin and a debonair sprinkling of gray in his close-cropped hair. There was a little gray in his neatly trimmed beard and mustache, which increased his air of distinction. And even though he was in his early fifties, he had not let himself go. He was as trim of waist as a man twenty years younger, and Renee knew for a fact that he had great stamina—Edwin frequently played doubles tennis with her.

After Edwin seated her in his Lincoln Continental, Renee observed him closely as he went around the car to get in. She continued her scrutiny as he drove. Edwin was a contractor and land developer and had money by the buckets. He was amicably divorced and his two children had the decency to be adults who were out of college and lived in Texas. So it wasn't like she would have to put up with spoiled stepchildren underfoot, "baby mama drama" or an alimony income, were she and Edwin to become closer. He was attentive, entertaining and treated Renee with the delicacy normally reserved for a piece of Ming dynasty porcelain. So why didn't she feel anything more for the man? Edwin was like a pleasant habit, and that was all. He was as soothing as a cup of chamomile tea at the end of a harrowing day, and about as stimulating. Sometimes Renee wanted to slap herself for being the way that she was. Bennie was too kindhearted to say such a thing, but their friend Ceylon Simmons had volunteered her services many times.

Renee closed her eyes and could hear Ceylon's voice in her ear.

"Renee, darling, I don't mean to be ugly about this, but you are a contrary wench. There, I said it. The way you treat these poor men is disgraceful and you could use a good smack. And I happen to have a hand right here that isn't doing anything."

Renee had to stifle a giggle, recalling the last time she and Ceylon had a go-round regarding what Ceylon termed her heartless behavior. Even though Ceylon was mostly kidding, she never failed to point out that Renee was being unfair to her horde of admirers.

"But I don't lead anyone on," Renee would argue. "I don't promise them that I will be monogamous, or that our relationship will progress to anything other than what it is. It's not my fault that they persist," she would always say.

And it was perfectly true. Renee did not encourage men to make fools of themselves over her, but she certainly did not discourage their attention as long as it was the variety she favored, like tonight's date with Edwin. Theater and dinner, what could be nicer on a damp early-spring evening? From the look on Edwin's face, many things, apparently.

Edwin had been making small talk and clearing his throat for some time, indicating that he wanted to say something of great importance. Renee sighed and knew she would have to put the man out of his misery. She knew that another proposal of marriage was in the offing and the thought filled her with unease. Though it was irritating that Edwin kept asking her, she was not without feeling. She would let him down gently—as always—and gradually the relationship would resume its normal pleasant dimensions. Edwin would continue to wine her, dine her and present her with appropriate floral tributes and baubles; she would continue to allow him to do so.

She glanced at her companion across the table in the intimate and expensive little boîte that he had selected for her dining pleasure. Edwin was practically beside himself—he needed to get something off his chest in a hurry. Renee gave him a smile of encouragement, which could have been a mistake. Renee's smiles were noted for their infrequency and their beauty.

"Renee, you are so gorgeous. When you smile at me like that, it makes me want to . . . well, that smile of yours just does things to me," he said hoarsely.

Renee lowered her eyes and turned down the smile just a notch. There was no point in raising false hope in the poor man. Edwin went on with his declaration.

"Renee, you know that I am interested in remarrying. I have made no secret of the fact that I care for you very,

very much. I think that we make a good match in terms of our interests and our temperaments. I would certainly do everything in my power to make you happy. I simply cannot conceive of living the rest of my life without a partner, a wife with whom to share my life and to enjoy the finer things that I have managed to acquire."

Renee engrossed herself in tracing the pattern in the damask tablecloth while bracing herself for the closing argument. Despite her outward calm, she was getting more and more uncomfortable. She didn't ask for this, and it wasn't like she had not made her feelings perfectly plain to Edwin. Why did he persist in flinging himself at her like a doomed moth trying to mate with a lightbulb? She tried to pay attention to what he was saying.

"And so, it seems odd, but Muriel and I have been seeing each other for a couple of months now. It was kind of amazing how well we fit together after all this time. I mean, we have been divorced for quite a few years now. But I guess the old saying about how you never stop loving your first love is true. And I know that you have no interest in marriage at this time or ever, according to your own words, so . . ." Edwin had stopped looking anxious and started looking happy, which was contrary to all that Renee knew about the man. Maybe she should have listened more closely when he started speaking.

"Edwin, what exactly are you trying to tell me?" she asked in the precise, measured tone she reserved for people who were about to get royally reamed. Edwin was actually beaming by now.

"My former wife and I are getting remarried," Edwin said with a big silly smirk on his face. "I proposed last night and she did me the honor of accepting," he added.

Renee tried to tell herself that the reason for her inability to move had nothing to do with Edwin's announcement, but she knew better. *The old coot! I give him the pleasure of my company and this is how he repays me?* This and other savage thoughts raced through Renee's mind while she tried to compose herself.

Forcing her pretty mouth into a social smile, she said—warmly, she hoped—"Congratulations, Edwin. That is lovely news. And I do appreciate your telling me in person. It would have felt so odd to read it in the papers. You're so considerate," she said through a slightly clenched jaw.

Edwin, bless his thick head, did not see anything amiss with his behavior. He had a date with Renee and past experience had taught him that to break a date with her was to risk her considerable wrath. She was not the kind of woman to lose her temper, but what she did when she was riled was in many ways much worse. She could put you into a deep freeze with a glance; she was so tough that a man would still feel the chill days later. So he saw nothing wrong with having a last date while announcing his engagement.

They quickly left the restaurant and drove to Indian Village in what Edwin mistakenly believed was a companionable silence. It wasn't until he walked her to the door that he realized something was amiss. Renee turned to him with a variation of expression that he had never seen on her face before. It was a combination of siren and succubus, guaranteed to drive a man to the fiery brink of desire.

"Once again, Edwin, congratulations on your engagement. I hope you'll be very, very happy," she purred. And before he could respond, Renee grabbed him by the lapels and laid a kiss on him like nothing he had ever experienced in his life, certainly not with Renee. No, it was not one of her patented lip pecks; this was a long, sensual French kiss of the most erotic variety. It was over much too abruptly as Renee suddenly pulled away, leaving him breathless and wanting.

"Good-bye, Edwin," was all she said before slipping in the door.

Two

No sooner had the door closed behind her than Renee was consumed with guilt. *Why did I do that? That was just so sick and wrong!* she berated herself. Aretha, Bennie's huge black longhaired cat, seemed to agree with her. She sat on the stairs in the boxy shape that cats employ when they are observing humans. She always seemed to sense when some-one was up to something. Renee was not known as a cat lover, but she and Aretha were drawn to each other. When the two of them were alone, Renee talked to her like she was a person. Aretha always understood her, if no one else did. Renee hung her coat in the hall closet while she cursed her-self in French. Then she turned to the cat, who was waiting patiently for Renee to unburden herself.

"Well, if you're looking for an explanation, I can't give you one," Renee admitted as she picked up Aretha and car-ried her up to her suite of rooms on the third floor of the house. "Edwin—you remember him, the one with the beard—is a perfectly nice man. I just don't happen to be terribly interested in him. He's a wonderful dining com-panion, but I don't have any kind of abiding passion for him at all." She sat Aretha on the bed and began to un-dress. She removed the cashmere dress, shook it out carefully and hung it on one of the thickly padded hangers that she used to pamper her expensive clothes.

She removed her earrings and underwear, talking to Aretha all the while. "Well, he is getting married, thank you very much, and to his ex-wife, of all people. He makes this garbled announcement, and for some unknown and unknowable reason, I get this wave of . . . of . . . I don't know what the hell it was, to be honest. All I know is I was feeling much more than I should about the situation."

"About what situation?"

Bennie's voice floated in from her sitting room. Renee jumped guiltily and called out to her that she would be right out.

Renee slipped an expensive silk nightgown over her head and went into the bathroom to remove her makeup. She opened the door to the medicine cabinet and glanced at her daily affirmation, which she had put out of view—some things were too private to explain. In her neat block printing was the legend I AM THE PRIZE. Renee sniffed inelegantly as she looked at it and mumbled, "Damn right, I am."

She went into the sitting room and joined Bennie, who had made herself right at home with a tea tray containing a pot of Lapsang souchong tea and some Pepperidge Farm Bordeaux cookies, both of which Renee doted on. Renee was appreciative of the gesture, less so of the fact that Bennie went right back to her question like a bird dog.

"What situation were you talking about?" she asked mildly as she poured the tea.

"I don't suppose if I told you it was between Aretha and me, it would do any good, would it?" Renee parried.

"Nope. Unless you really don't want to tell me. You don't have to, of course; I was just curious," Bennie said disarmingly.

Renee sighed and told her the story of Edwin's engagement and her subsequent behavior at the front door. "For the life of me I do not understand why I am the least concerned over Edwin's middle-aged frolics. It's not my business; why should I care what he does and with whom? And why I decided to turn into Lady Marmalade at the very door of our home is beyond me. There must have been MSG in some of that food tonight," she said moodily.

Bennie looked carefully at her friend but did not say anything right away. "Well, we can always blame it on spring," she said neutrally. "A drastic change of seasons makes us all go a little mad."

They chatted for a while and Renee reminded Bennie that someone was coming to the salon/day spa in the morning for a preliminary interview. "We might be featured on television," Renee mused. "Or at least get a nice write-up in a national magazine. This reporter is Beth Thomas's sister-in-law, and she's this big-time freelancer with all kinds of connections. Beth just raved about the salon, so now she wants to come check it out," she said sleepily.

"Well, that's wonderful news, Renee. I'm going to turn in so that you can get up early and knock her socks off." Suiting action to words, Bennie bid Renee good-night and left with the tea tray.

Aretha remained behind as if to tuck Renee in. Renee yawned and looked at the fluffy black mass. "It was probably the full moon that did it," she murmured. Aretha did not answer; she merely stared at Renee with the feline equivalent of a knowing look. Renee settled in bed, fluffing her pillows and smoothing out her goose-down duvet. Looking at Aretha, she sighed.

"I'm sure that I'm gonna have to pay for what I did tonight. If no good deed goes unpunished, there's no telling what a scandalous move like that one will get me," she said ruefully.

Aretha walked over to her and butted her head affectionately before departing for the lower floor to join Bennie. Renee turned off the light and waited for sleep to arrive.

She was sure it would be a long time coming; she never could sleep when things were not settled in her mind, and she was far from settled right then. Despite her conversation with Bennie, she was still in turmoil over the events of the evening. Why had she given poor Edwin that big ol' slutty kiss? She knew very well that she did not want the man, but the idea of someone else having him was somehow galling to her. And why couldn't she seem to generate feelings, *normal* feelings, for Edwin or anyone else? Where had she gotten the idea that she was the Queen of Everything? Her face burned while she tried to forget her actions that night, or at least justify them.

Maybe it was the fact that Edwin had finally found her resistible that was so annoying. Who did he think he was, anyway? Even she had to admit that at almost twenty years her senior, Edwin was rather old for her. So he would rather remarry his first wife, who was roughly his age, than to continue to pursue her—a fine figure of a woman in her thirties. Well, there you have it; the man was obviously senile. He just didn't know—he should have asked somebody. *I am the prize,* she reminded herself, and fell asleep before she realized that a tiny tear was trickling down her cheek.

The next day, Renee was quite willing to chalk the whole incident up to PMS or indigestion. Her behavior on the previous night had been completely uncharacteristic, and so had the feelings that occasioned it. And since her actions had been so completely out of character, she obviously wasn't responsible for them. The whole thing had been a fluke of a very weird kind. A once-in-a-lifetime occurrence. And having successfully purged herself of any culpability in the matter, she put it out of her head entirely.

When she arrived at Urban Oasis, she was back to her normal self. She arrived extra early in deference to her guest. Although Urban Oasis was always immaculate, she wanted to have a few minutes to herself to make sure that everything was in order for the woman who was to interview her. And a few minutes was all she got, as Beth Thomas arrived not long after Renee. Beth was one of Renee's newest employees and the catalyst behind the interview.

Renee was in her small, private office when Beth tapped on the door and stuck her head in after Renee's greeting. Beth was tall, slim and a natural redhead, with the creamy complexion and green eyes that displayed her Irish heritage to advantage. She was a top-notch stylist and had brought a good clientele with her, as well as earning new clients with her considerable skill. Their admiration was mutual, as Renee felt lucky to have her and Beth felt lucky to work in one of the best salons in Detroit.

"Hi, Renee! We're a little bit early, but I thought I would get the coffee going and everything turned on while you and Sasha talked," she said by way of explanation.

Renee smiled in return. "No problem. Where is your sister-in-law?"

"She had to run to the ladies' room. She's pregnant again and she goes about every five minutes, I swear," said Beth, laughing.

"Oh, it's really funny, huh? Just wait until it happens to you," intoned a cheerful voice. A fashionably attired, exquisitely beautiful woman who was, by her very pregnant appearance, Beth's sister-in-law, joined Beth in the doorway.

Renee had to blink a couple of times to keep her surprise from flitting across her face. This woman was not only gorgeous, she was quite African American, something Beth had neglected to mention.

"Well, I'm going to get things rolling out here and I'll see you ladies later," Beth threw over her shoulder as she left the two women to chat.

Sasha's eyes brimmed with merriment as she made herself comfortable on the love seat situated in the office. "Don't tell me; let me guess—Beth did not mention the ethnic disparity of her brother's wife, did she?"

Disarmed by the woman's honesty, Renee was equally candid. "Nope, she didn't. And I've seen pictures of her niece and nephew and just always assumed, wrongly, that her *sister* was married to a black man. *Oops*"—she smiled—"my bad."

Sasha took no offense; she waved her hand airily as if to say it was a common mistake. "Beth is that rare kind of person who accepts people as they are. She and I are best friends as well as in-laws, and she just forgets that our ancestors are from opposite sides of the world." She accepted the cup of coffee Renee offered and adroitly changed the subject.

"Tell me about you and Urban Oasis. Beth tells me that you did this all on your own. I have to say I'm impressed. How did you get started?"

Renee was always happy to talk about her salon. "Well, first of all, I didn't do this by myself," she emphasized. "My best friend and roommate from college, Benita Cochran, is a partner in Urban Oasis. She was with me when I got the germ of the idea, and she has been by my side ever since, even though she doesn't participate in the day-to-day operations."

Sasha was intrigued. "When did you come up with the plan?" she asked, her eyes alit with curiosity.

"Well, it was a Saturday and Bennie and I were waiting, and waiting, and *waiting,* to get our hair blow-dried and curled. Our hairdresser at the time had perfected the art of shampooing you as soon as you walked in the door, slapping a deep conditioner on you and then letting you wait until hell froze over to get styled because she had overbooked," Renee said with a sigh.

"Ooh, girl, say no more! They do it because they know we'll sit there like sheep and wait for hours to get done, especially on the weekends! Who's going to go tearing out into the street with wet hair on a Saturday?" Sasha agreed animatedly.

Renee chuckled and said, "I almost did that day. I was about fit to be tied, and then I started looking around the shop and seeing all the people who were waiting, plus the people who were in styling chairs and trying to figure up how much money they were spending. I thought about how much money Bennie and I spent over the course of a month in just getting our hair done. And I realized that there was a lot of money to be made in this business. So I nudged Bennie, who was calmly doing a crossword puzzle, and I started talking money to her. And by the time we went to bed that night, we had made our plan.

"We decided to draw up a business plan for a spa/salon and go to beauty school in order to learn how to do it right. Since Bennie has an M.B.A., as well as having grown up in the family radio business, it wasn't anything for us to figure out the most profitable way to do it. It just took a lot of research into what potential customers were looking for in a spa experience. So in a very short time, et voilà, Urban Oasis opened its doors and we haven't looked back."

The two women left the office so that Renee could give her an extensive tour of the salon. They started in the main reception area with the soothing jazz playing and the abundance of green plants that complemented the soothing green-and-peach color scheme. Renee had selected the colors carefully to be evocative of a place of nurturing and inner growth. Warmth and relaxation seemed to beckon from the very walls, as well as the calming scent of the aromatics used in aromatherapy.

From there they went into the larger lounge area that had a big-screen television and juice bar as well as comfortable chairs and sofas. Everything about Urban Oasis said comfort, style and elegance, from the cool green marble counters in the retail area to the employees' chic smocks and the snazzy green shampoo bowls in the salon area. There were other places to get one's hair done in Detroit, and other places for manicures, pedicures and various kinds of massages and body wraps, but no day spa had the kind of panache that Renee's salon boasted.

Sasha was more than impressed. "Renee, I am amazed that you have done so much in a relatively short period. Believe me, I have been to day spas all over the country and it takes years to establish what you have here in Detroit. You're quite the businesswoman," she praised.

"Considering the fact that I never intended to work in the beauty business, I think I came up with a concept that's working quite well," Renee acknowledged modestly. "It's actually kind of ironic when I think about it."

By now, the two women were back in Renee's office. Sasha leaned toward Renee with curiosity all over her face. "Well, *dish,* girl! Don't keep me in the dark here. Tell me the whole story," she demanded.

"Well," Renee said slowly, "I always wanted to be in television. My degree is in radio and television broadcasting, with a minor in French. I envisioned myself as a foreign correspondent, and I think I would have been very good indeed. I really loved what I was being trained to do, and I would have done everything I could to rise to the top," she admitted.

Renee sighed; she was getting to the sticky part of the story. For some reason she felt comfortable enough with Sasha to tell her about a rather painful part of her past.

"A couple of my college professors had tried to warn me before I got too entrenched in my major that I would find it difficult to work in television because I'm a minority female. That only made me dig in my heels and try harder to be the best, which I was. I'm not bragging, but I graduated number one in my major and very near the head of my class. Summa cum laude, all of that. I did really well in my externships and internships; I got great evaluations. But I did not get jobs," she said flatly.

"Oh, I managed to secure a couple of reporting jobs in Podunk stations in Ohio, but they led nowhere fast. I had the tools and the talent, but I was lacking the right color skin," she said without a trace of bitterness.

"When I graduated, there were lots of brothers and sisters being employed by stations large and small—for a while the combination of a white male anchor and a black female anchor was the height of fashion. If you didn't have a black chick on the six o'clock, you were just dead in the water! But the females had to be of the fair-skinned, long-haired variety or they would never make it onto the airwaves. No one was hiring the chocolate sisters to grace their news desk, regardless of their talent. And after a while I said to hell with it," Renee said quietly.

Sasha nodded and gave her a sardonic smile. "I feel you, girl. With me it was the weight. I have never been rail thin, never wanted to be. And despite the fact that I could out-report and outwrite half of the people on staff, my weight was always an issue." Sasha took a final swallow of her now tepid coffee and set her cup down before continuing.

"Well, my motto became 'Living well is the best revenge.' Life is too short to let people bully you over superficialities. I moved out to Seattle and hooked up with a college friend who had a friend who was starting a computer company. A few years later, we were all millionaires, including my college friend, who is now my husband. Now I write for fun and enjoy my family tremendously. And who knows? If I had succeeded in TV, I might not be where I am," she said happily.

Renee returned Sasha's smile with one of her own. There were a lot of similarities in their stories. Except for one critical difference, but that was something Renee never talked about. After a devastating and humiliating episode in Newark, New Jersey, Renee had made a couple of decisions. One was that no one would ever hurt her again. The other was that she would find a way of making an excellent living wherein she was the boss; she was never dancing to anyone's tune again. And Urban Oasis was proof that she could do it.

Entering the salon always gave Renee a sense of peace that she seldom found anywhere else. This was her world, and she was the queen of all she surveyed. Despite everything, she was making an extremely good living with her own creation, for which she was profoundly grateful. She and Sasha spent another hour firming up plans for Sasha to return with her camera crew, and they also penciled in a lunch date. Surprisingly, it was still quite early when Sasha left. Renee's morning crew was still coming in as Sasha bade Renee farewell.

Valerie, her day manager, arrived accompanied by two of her best stylists, Charlotte and Eva. The three women greeted her and immediately had to catch her up with the latest news—Charlotte was getting married.

Charlotte happily displayed a modest diamond in a modern setting and was blushing all over as she described the proposal. "It was so sweet," she said dreamily. "We were at Lafayette Coney Island, the place we first met. And I was having my usual Boston Cooler, and Lamont asked me to get him some more ketchup. When I came back from the counter, there was my ring, on the straw sticking out of my cooler." Charlotte looked lovingly at her ring and sighed. "Wasn't that romantic? I just love that man to death."

Everyone oohed and aahed over the ring, except Renee. She wasn't about to hurt Charlotte's feelings, but in her estimation that thing on her stylist's finger was an "i-mond"; it wanted to be a diamond when it grew up. And she wished some man would try to propose to her in a hot-dog stand. . . . The very thought of her putting her foot into such a place was ludicrous! Yes, there was no denying that Charlotte looked completely happy. *Well, to each her own,* Renee thought, and hoped that no one picked up on her less than positive vibes. She really did want Charlotte to be happy.

But Valerie, who had the kind of perception that amounted to second sight in these matters, noticed the carefully controlled expression on Renee's face and knew the reason for it. She said nothing until the two women were alone, however.

"I know what you're thinking," Valerie said confidently. She was inspecting her Autumn Haze–tinted hair in a mirror as she spoke. The very light auburn color was actually quite flattering to Valerie's sienna complexion while showing off the colorist's skill. Renee ignored her, pretending to study the previous day's balance sheet, but Valerie would not be denied. Leaning closer to Renee, she repeated her statement.

"I know what you were thinking while you were watching Charlotte," she insisted. Renee closed an eye as if to dare Valerie to continue.

"You wouldn't wear a small diamond like that even as a pinkie ring. And a man couldn't *get* you into a Coney Island joint and best not dare ask you to be his wife while on the premises, that's what you were thinking," Valerie said triumphantly. Before Renee could answer, she went right on. "But Charlotte's not like you, Renee. She wants a home and a family and a whole lot of children. She couldn't care less about the size of the ring—she loves Lamont so much he could have put a Ring Pop on her finger and she'd be just as happy as she is now. That's romance for you," she added sagely.

Renee shrugged and pretended to go on perusing the computer-generated ledger sheets in front of her. "You can call it romance if you like; I call it something else entirely. But if Charlotte is happy, there really isn't anything to discuss, now is there," she said dryly.

Valerie looked at Renee curiously before exiting her private office to finish preparing for the day ahead. "Don't you *want* romance in your life? I mean, the real hot, sexy, passionate stuff?"

Valerie did not stand on ceremony with Renee—they had worked together for some years and were as close as Renee allowed herself to be with her employees. Which is why Renee really did not mind answering her queries—in her slightly intrusive way Valerie had Renee's best interests at heart. Now she looked at Valerie almost coyly.

"And what makes you think that I *don't* have some hot, steamy passion going?" she asked archly.

Valerie snorted as she turned to leave the office. "Oh, please. That kind of stuff shows all over a woman's face. If you had it, we'd all know it. And you don't have it 'cause you don't want it, not 'cause you can't get it."

Renee was taken slightly aback. Valerie's grammar may have been slightly garbled, but her meaning was clear— Renee was leading a rather dry existence despite her assortment of beaux, and it showed. Renee immediately shook off Valerie's observation. *She doesn't know what she's talking about. "Shows," indeed.*

Irritatingly enough, though, she could not get Valerie's words out of her head. Renee found herself glancing in the mirror several times that day to ascertain whether or not she was looking like some dried-up, drawn spinster. Satisfied that she was not, she went about her day's work. By six that evening she was about done in. The afternoon shift would close up for the day, her evening manager was on board and Renee was in need of refreshment. On impulse, she decided to go by Carlo's. There was nothing like some fervent attention from one of her beaux to improve her mood, and Carlo was nothing but attentive.

Carlo Gianelli was another of Renee's steady dates, although she had only been dating him for about eight months. At forty-seven, he was the youngest of the men whom she saw on a regular basis, and he was arguably the sexiest. Carlo was six feet two inches of Italian virility from the top of his head to the bottom of his feet. He was the owner of several popular restaurants and bistros in Detroit and the nearby suburbs, and he was outgoing and gregarious, as his chosen profession would indicate. Although he was born in Italy, he had grown up all over Europe. His mother died in childbirth, and it had been just Carlo and his father, Dante Gianelli, the famous opera singer, until Dante had met Suzanne Foster, an African American diva singing for a season at La Scala.

They fell in love and married when Carlo was three. Suzanne was the only mother Carlo knew and he was devoted to her. He also had three younger sisters, who were the product of that marriage. He grew up surrounded by beautiful black women and made no secret that he adored them. The fact that he was so easy in her company was one of the reasons that Renee was drawn to Carlo; she felt that this was not a case of jungle fever but that he could really appreciate her as a woman. Furthermore, Carlo was a gentleman. A

man as good-looking as he could expect more than his share
of feminine attention, but Carlo never tried any cheap moves
on her, which she thoroughly appreciated.

This was the first time that Renee had ever just dropped
in at his midtown establishment, Carlo's, although he had
invited her to do so many times. She knew that he was
likely to be there, since it was his newest restaurant and re-
quired more of his attention. If he was there, fine; if not, it
would be equally fine—she would have a nice glass of
wine and then go home. And besides, she just looked too
good to go straight home. She was wearing a peach-
colored wrap dress made of silk jersey, and the way it
enhanced her body simply deserved to be seen. She owed
it to Carlo to brighten up his day, she thought. And sure
enough, he was there, standing behind the bar in the
lounge area and looking utterly delectable.

The restaurant that bore his name was intimate yet spacious. It was in a building that had been converted from a
warehouse to office space and condominiums. Carlo's
took up most of the first floor of the building and still had
the exposed brick interior walls and plank flooring. It was
simply decorated with black wooden chairs and tables that
seated small groups. The low-hanging fixtures with wine-
colored shades gave a soft, seductive glow. It was the
perfect setting for an intimate tryst. Renee mentally ap-
praised the premises as she made her way to the bar. It was
cozy, elegant and romantic, a pleasant surprise to the eye
and the ear. The music that played softly was the kind of
jazz that was perfect for fine dining by candlelight. Renee
approved heartily of his establishment.

Carlo had looked mildly surprised at seeing Renee enter
the restaurant, but that did not stop him from being his most
gracious. He seated her at the bar and proceeded to pour her
a glass of a very fine wine that he knew she favored. Renee
was slightly puzzled by his demeanor, though. She had
turned her head slightly to accommodate the soft kiss he normally pressed on her cheek, only to find that it was not

forthcoming. He did not seem uncomfortable with her presence, just less interested, which, of course, was impossible. Renee was not usually put in the position of ascertaining a man's continuing interest in her, but after her strange conversation with Valerie, she felt compelled to do so.

"Well, Carlo," she began, "I haven't heard from you lately. Have you been out of town?" This last remark had a slightly more pointed edge than she would have liked, but it was too late to take it back. Luckily, Carlo did not seem to notice.

"No, I've been right here," he answered cheerfully.

He went on to ask how she had been and made the kind of small talk that one makes with old high-school classmates. Renee was nonplussed, to say the least. He was not making any effort to get into her good graces, nor was he pressing for a date. What was up? she silently wondered. As if he could hear what she was thinking, Carlo gently informed her that he was seeing someone exclusively.

"I've actually known her for a couple of years, but she was dating someone else. Now that relationship is finally over, and I was able to persuade her to go out with me," Carlo said with a satisfied smile.

Renee could not help herself; the question came out before she could stop it. "How long have you been seeing this woman?" *God, is that my accusing voice?*

Again Carlo did not seem to notice. He was happy to tell her that they had been dating for about a month. It had been about a month since she and Carlo had done anything together, Renee reflected. *Now I know why,* she thought angrily. It did not occur to her that she could have easily called him, as he often invited her to do. She had always let him do all the calling, as she did with all her swains. She was feeling irrationally upset over Carlo's announcement, as though he had been toying with her. Suddenly his face lit up in a way she had not seen before.

"What a coincidence—there she is now," he said happily. Unable to stop herself, Renee turned her head to see a small, slender blond woman heading in their general direction.

Carlo quickly came from behind the bar and started walking to the front of the restaurant. He walked right past the small blonde until he reached a beautiful African American woman, who had something in her hands. She was wearing jeans and a bulky red sweater. Her hair was, even in the dim light, a mass of shiny, silky black curls that were obviously natural. And her skin was as dark as Renee's own. Renee had to admit that she was quite lovely, even though she was a rather large package. She was a big, healthy woman with lots of curves, and it was obvious that Carlo was enamored of each and every one of them.

Oh, hell, they're coming over here! Renee longed for an escape route, but there was none to be had. Carlo brought the woman over to Renee and introduced them.

"Renee, this is Angela," he said in a caressing voice, never taking his eyes from the woman. "Angela, this is Renee."

Angela smiled, revealing perfectly straight white teeth and deep dimples in both cheeks. She and Renee exchanged hellos; before they could go any further, Carlo interrupted.

"Cara, what are you doing here with no coat on? You could catch a cold. And I'm going to be at your place in a couple of hours anyway," he murmured.

Angela turned that one-hundred-watt smile on him and explained that she was bringing him her key, in case she was in the shower when he arrived. "And to bring you this," she added, giving him a sheaf of flowers wrapped in green florist paper. "A preview to your birthday celebration," she said sweetly.

Carlo inhaled the fragrance of the freesias and stargazer lilies before kissing her on the cheek. *"Cara,* you are so thoughtful," he said.

She touched his cheek and told him she had to run. Making the usual "nice to meet you" noises at Renee, she waved at them both and started to leave. Carlo watched her for a moment and then went to catch up with her; it was as if he could not bear to let her out of his sight. And indeed, he kissed her quickly and passionately at the door and walked her out to make sure she got into her car safely.

Renee didn't know whether to wind her fanny or scratch her watch. She was too stunned to get up and leave during the little performance, plus she had to admit she was fascinated in some bizarre way. What she had witnessed was not some little show that Carlo had put on for her benefit—it was some of that hot, steamy stuff that Valerie had been yammering about earlier. Was this what she had been missing, and did she really want any of it? And why hadn't Carlo tried to have any of it with her, anyway?

Her turmoil was written across her face as though tattooed there. Her much vaunted self-control and aloofness had fled south, at least for the moment. Carlo could not ignore her obvious discomfiture on his return to the bar. Being a straightforward kind of man, he commented on it.

"Renee, if I didn't know better, I'd say that you seem a little upset that I have a committed relationship with Angela. And I know that couldn't be the case because you have no interest in me other than as a casual dining companion. Yet, I am sensing a little pique," he said kindly.

Renee took a long sip of wine before answering. "I wouldn't say that 'pique' is a good word for what I'm feeling. I am simply not used to being dumped so unceremoniously. And certainly not in the presence of the person who supplanted me in someone's affections. That's going to take a bit of getting used to," she said bitchily. She couldn't believe what she had blurted out, but there was obviously no going back. She angrily snatched her Dooney & Bourke handbag from the bar and was about to get off the bar stool in a big hurry when Carlo stopped her.

"Renee, what's this all about? In all the time that we've been seeing each other, you never indicated any kind of interest in me. You never once called me, you never accepted my invitations to drop by, and you were certainly not interested in having a physical relationship with me. Now you're acting like you're deeply wounded because I'm seeing someone else. What's the deal?" he asked in his most reasonable tone.

It was the very neutrality of his voice that was so annoying to Renee. Instead of answering his questions, she chose to zero in on one comment.

"Yes, well, the first time I take you up on your offer to 'drop by,' you see what I get. It's quite obvious that you were just using me because you couldn't have Miss What's-her-name, and I don't appreciate it in the least," she said unfairly. She knew she was way off base, but she had put her feet on the slippery slope to stupidity and could not seem to get off before sliding straight to the bottom. Carlo, however, was not going to let her embarrass herself further.

"Renee, we're obviously not going to see eye to eye on this, at least not tonight. I hate to leave you, but as you no doubt overheard, it's my birthday and I have a celebration planned. Take care of yourself." With a slight bow he left her to stew.

It felt as though hot needles were being shoved behind her eyes. How could so much go so wrong so quickly? And not just tonight's debacle; last night was still etched in her subconscious. In the space of two days, she had been cast aside by two of her gentlemen friends. As if that wasn't bad enough, she had been kicked to the curb for one woman who was almost twenty years her senior and another woman who was at least a size 18. Maybe a size 20, who knew? All she knew was she had to get home—and quickly—before more evil befell her. Snatching her coat from the rack, where Carlo had hung it up, Renee got the hell out of Dodge.

Three

Andrew was absolutely exhausted. He had spent most of the day in surgery, working on an eight-year-old boy who would be in his care for years to come. The child had been burned over his upper body with third-degree burns, which had taken months to heal and would require years of restorative surgery in order to create a semblance of a normal face. For Andrew, the worst part of the ordeal was that the child's father had set him on fire, supposedly to show the boy's mother, his ex-wife, how much he wanted them back. It was no consolation to Andrew that the man had also killed himself.

"Benita, I hope that asshole is burning in hell as we speak," Andrew confessed. He was sprawled on the couch in the basement rec room of Bennie's house, where he often took refuge after a day like the one he had experienced. He had a bottle of cola in his hand, but he wasn't drinking it. He set the bottle down on the table next to the couch and rubbed his hand across his brow. That he was in anguish was plain by the furrows in his forehead and the tension around his mouth.

Bennie did not censure him for his profanity, because she knew how deeply he cared about his patients and how much he loved children.

"Andrew, you know you're going to make a wonderful father someday. It's why you are so compassionate about your patients."

Andrew ignored her words and continued to talk about the brave little boy. "The thing is, Bennie, I will have to continue to operate on him for years because he is still growing. In order to accommodate his growth, every so often I have to go back in with my little scalpel and rearrange him, in addition to trying to give him a nose and ears and a mouth so people won't make his life more of a hell than it is." Andrew's eyes were moist with emotion. "And all because his bastard of a father was a certifiable nutcase. Life sucks, Benita. It really does."

Bennie put her arms around her twin and held him. "But, Andrew, this little guy has something that will get him through all this. He has you. You're going to take the best possible care of him, and in the end he will have a much, much better life because of your skill. You are blessed to be able to give him that, you know."

Andrew patted his sister on the back and pulled away from her. "I am *trained* to give him this kind of care, Bennie, not blessed. My expertise is the result of about ten very expensive years of schooling; it's not a gift from God. Please don't tell me you're beginning to believe what you read about me," he said with a look of comic distress.

"I love my work but I'm not that different from the guy who works on your Jaguar. This is what I was interested in and this is what I trained to do. And that's it," he added with finality. "Other than that, I am just your average guy who gets tired, gets lonely, and," he said reflectively as he rubbed his stomach, "gets hungry. Got anything to eat?"

They went up the stairs to the kitchen, arriving there just when Renee blew in the back door, looking like "Damn it, I'll bite you." Anyone else would have taken that as a cue to leave her alone, but in the mood Andrew was in, she looked like fair game. He didn't start on her immediately, but he looked her over carefully to zero in on something that would rile her and possibly make her laugh. Despite his seeming insistence on making her life miserable, it would have pained Andrew greatly to make her really unhappy. And she definitely looked out of sorts tonight.

However, she also looked delectable in her sexy peach dress. Andrew watched her closely as she went to the refrigerator and extracted a bottle of mineral water. She and Bennie chatted quietly while she reached for a glass. As she raised her arm to take a stemmed goblet from the top shelf, her body stretched in a way that sent alarms all over Andrew. *Damn, she's sexy.* It wasn't the first time that he had thought such a thing, certainly, but tonight was the first time in a long time that a wave of sexual urgency had engulfed him so swiftly. He swallowed hard and tried to focus on something other than the shape of Renee's derriere, her full, firm thighs and those enticing calves, which were displayed so beautifully.

The phone rang, causing Bennie to pause in her perusal of the refrigerator. "Hello, Clay," she said happily.

It was her new male interest, a man she had met the previous month and who seemed to be equally as interested in her. Andrew knew she would be on the telephone for some time, so he chose the coward's way out and beat a hasty retreat. Before he did so, though, he could not resist. Turning to Renee, who was sitting on a tall stool by the work island in the center of the kitchen, he told her to let Bennie know he had changed his mind about eating.

"Tell her I'll call her later, okay?"

Renee nodded absently. Andrew took advantage of her state to lean over and whisper, "You know, you look good enough to eat in that dress." Then he leaned even closer. Renee gasped softly in surprise but did not move until Andrew had left, whistling. She was still motionless a few minutes later when Bennie walked in.

"Where'd Bunchy go?" she asked, looking around the room.

"He left. He said he'd call you," Renee replied.

Bennie looked at her friend again. "Why do you have that strange look on your face?" she inquired.

Finally Renee looked directly at Bennie. "Because Andrew told me I looked good enough to eat. And then he *licked* me," she answered. At Bennie's shocked look, Renee repeated her statement. "He licked me. Just a little lick, right on the cheek."

Renee finally stood and turned to leave the room, taking the glass of mineral water with her. She looked at Bennie once more before she left the room and said, "I don't know what's wrong with your brother, but I'll bet it has a long name."

Like the good friend that she was, Bennie waited until Renee had gone up the stairs before she burst out laughing.

Bennie was not at all surprised when Renee came into her room later that night. She knew her friend well enough to know when something was bothering her. So when Renee showed up in her doorway, bearing a tray with a split of wine and two flutes, Bennie was more or less expecting her. She took the tray from Renee's hands while Renee made herself comfortable on the end of the bed. Renee accepted the glass that Bennie held out to her and stared morosely at its contents without speaking. Bennie decided that it must be really bad—Renee was many things, but never reticent.

"Okay, spill it. Whatever it is can't be that bad," Bennie said consolingly.

Renee looked at Bennie with a mixture of sadness and defiance on her face. "It's bad enough," she mumbled. "I have been dumped again. That's right, me, the original Miss Thing has been dumped. Twice in one week. On consecutive days, no less. How ya like them apples," she finished drolly.

Bennie demanded details, which Renee supplied grudgingly but thoroughly, leaving nothing out.

"So there you have it. First Edwin, he of the retractable spine, decides to go back to his ex-wife, a woman who is two decades my senior. Then Carlo, the Sicilian snake, takes up with this plus-sized model look-alike. What is the point of dieting and exercising like a madwoman if the big chicks are going to get all the men? I ask you!"

Renee ended her tirade with a large gulp of wine, then heaved a deep sigh, which turned into a miserable little hiccup. It was a sign of how bent she was that she made a crack about Angela's weight, something she would never have done had she been in her right mind. Bennie decided to derail her train of righteous indignation before it left the station.

"Now, Renee, let's be honest. You weren't in love with either of those men. You barely acknowledge their existence most of the time. So it's not like you can sue anybody for alienation of affection. When you have several escorts, it's to be expected that you'll lose interest and move on, or they will. Why are you wasting your energy on this? They were your *dates,* not your boyfriends," Bennie said fairly.

Renee scowled like a five-year-old and tried to get Bennie to see that she had been treated badly by the scoundrels in question. Bennie would not back down, though.

"Renee, what I don't understand is why you settle for these kinds of relationships. There are some very nice men out there, men with whom you could have a wonderful, meaningful relationship. But you never want more than a steady escort. Why is that?" Bennie pressed.

This was certainly not the first time that they had had this conversation, and Renee feared it would not be the last. She always dreaded this point because there was no simple answer. She tried turning the tables on her friend.

"Well, Bennie, why do *you* want more? Why are you so interested in this Clay Deveraux person all of a sudden?" Bennie's face immediately turned soft and dreamy, as did her voice.

"Clay is *exciting,* Renee. He's smart and handsome and ambitious and accomplished and adorable. He's also very, very sexy. *Very.* And yes, I want more. I want a lot— marriage, children, family, house, dog, the whole enchilada. I loved being married. If Gilbert had lived, we would've had four children by now, at least. I still miss him, you know. I miss his friendship, his company, his laughter; I miss everything about him. I miss being married to him. I'm not going to kid you; I loved that closeness and I want it again." Bennie took Renee's flute along with her own and rinsed them in the bathroom sink.

"And you know what, Renee? I think you want it, too. But you just won't admit it," Bennie said. She flopped across the bed on her stomach and rolled over on one side to survey Renee's face.

Renee tried to don her usual mask of indifference, but it was not possible with Bennie, who knew almost everything there was to know about her. Renee sighed deeply and pretended to look at her fingernails. Bennie tried again to get Renee to talk.

"C'mon, you can't tell me that all you want out of life is a series of dates with handsome men who are terrified of you," Bennie teased.

Renee smiled wanly and tried to go along with the joke. "And what's wrong with that? Sounds like a perfect life to me," she said with a laugh that sounded phony even to her. She sighed again and then admitted something she never thought she would own up to.

"I'm not as heartless as I seem, Bennie. I think sometimes, sure, yeah, why not get married. Then I go home and see my sisters and those idiots they're hitched to and I get the nervous trembles. Then I look at my mother and think about what Daddy did . . . and . . . I think, no way in hell am I going out like that." Renee rose from the foot of the bed and started fiddling with various objects on Bennie's dressing table. Revealing her innermost thoughts always made her fidgety.

Bennie looked at her friend with sympathy. "Ne-ne, I know that you don't have the best impression of marriage, but just remember two things. Number one, that's somebody else's reality. That's their life and it doesn't have to be yours. It *won't* be yours because you are a totally different person with totally different expectations and ideals. And number two"—Bennie sat up to make sure Renee was listening—"nobody says you have to get *married,* for heaven's sake. But you owe it to yourself to fall in love."

Renee spun around from the dressing table and looked at her friend as though she had suggested parasailing nude on the Detroit River. Bennie held her ground, though.

"Yes, indeedy, that's just what you need. A hot, steamy, passionate, messy love affair. It'll make a new woman out of you, I guarantee it," avowed Bennie.

Renee continued to look at her friend as if she had lost her mind; then a sly smile spread over her face. "So, is that what you're doing with this Clay Deveraux?" she asked archly. To her surprise, Bennie did not deny it but smiled a very private and lovely smile.

"Damn skippy," was all she said in reply.

Renee did not deny the truth of what Bennie was saying, nor did she reveal what she was feeling. She led the conversation to other matters quite adroitly, up to and including Andrew's behavior. Bennie had a suggestion for that, too.

"You know Andrew likes you. All my family adores you—they think of you like one of the family. Just give him back as good as he gives you. I've been telling you that for years. If he thinks he can get to you, he will. And he sees right through that air of sophistication of yours. You have to get down and dirty with him and he'll back off," Bennie advised.

"Oh, so I should have licked him back today?" said Renee with amusement.

Bennie laughed and said, "Well, it would have given him something to think about, that's for sure."

Renee was too weary to laugh, but she did give Bennie a weak smile before going off to her own room. Forget giving Andrew something to think about, Renee had plenty on her mind.

* * *

For the next few weeks Renee managed to maintain an outward semblance of normalcy. Her day-to-day appearance and demeanor did not portray the unsettled feelings that were roiling within. The defection of two of her minor beaux was yesterday's news; she was quite over that. As Bennie had pointed out, it wasn't as though she was enamored of them in any real way. The thing that was causing Renee to spend a lot of time in deep thought was the idea that Bennie had tossed at her about falling in love. The idea was not nearly as repellent as it had been in the past, and that might also be due to her friend's influence. Bennie was certainly taking her own advice.

Initially Renee had only seen a picture of the man whom Bennie was so impressed with, and frankly, it had frightened her. She had seen a grainy reproduction of an old newspaper picture of a skinny man with braids and a virtual scimitar of a nose. When Bennie met him in person, she insisted that he was quite good-looking, something that Renee had seen for herself when she went with Bennie to Chicago. Bennie had attended some kind of media conference, where she renewed her acquaintance with the man, and Renee had met him in person at last. He was absolutely gorgeous, and furthermore, he was totally smitten with Bennie. So much so that he was visiting her in Detroit for Memorial Day weekend.

Renee had a chance to observe them closely before the huge cookout that Bennie's father, Benny Cochran, threw every Memorial Day. They were sweet and tender with one another and obviously thrilled to be together. Any fool could see that they were well on their way to true love. Maybe it was the fact that her best friend was poised on the precipice of something big that made Renee so interested in passion all of a sudden. Bennie was, after all, one of the most levelheaded people that Renee had ever known and she was floating along in a rosy haze of bliss. Even when Bennie was dating her first husband, Gilbert, she didn't have a glow like the one she wore now. That, more than anything, made an impression on Renee because she knew how deeply Bennie had loved Gilbert and how devastated she had been when he died.

And maybe her wavering had something to do with the fact that her current beau was boring her to tears. Marshall Fuller was tall, well built, handsome and intelligent. He was retired from the army—a four-star general, at that— and was courteous and gentlemanly. He owned several bed-and-breakfast inns, including two in the northern part of Michigan. He played a good game of tennis, was an avid horseman and enjoyed traveling; all of which scored very high on Renee's lists of things to look for in a companion. He simply had no sense of humor that Renee could discern. That had not been a problem in the past, but for some reason, it was more and more annoying to Renee. The man never seemed to laugh at anything.

Today, as they entered the huge, beautifully landscaped backyard of the Palmer Park home of Bennie's father, his lack of humor was all the more apparent. Bennie's nieces and nephews caught sight of Renee and immediately made a beeline for her, calling her by her customary name within their ranks: "Uncle Renee! Uncle Renee!" Bennie's youngest nephew had started calling Renee that when he was first able to talk and no one could shake him of the habit. Even now, at age four, little Drew insisted that Renee was his "Uncle Renee," even though he understood what an aunt was and how aunts differed from uncles.

Renee found it charming, especially since he was her godchild. She might have found it less charming if she knew that Drew's godfather, Andrew, was the one who kept telling him that Renee was Uncle Renee. In one of his random attempts to rile Renee, he had inadvertently created a family joke, one that Marshall did not get and could not abide. When Drew persisted in calling Renee "Uncle," his two brothers and his three cousins all joined in.

Every time Marshall was around, though, it irritated him to no end. He brought it up again as he and Renee were seated at a long table under the big white tent in the back-yard.

"Renee, I fail to understand why those children persist in calling you 'Uncle.' It's disrespectful and silly," he said.

Renee gave him a long look from behind her sunglasses. As they were extra dark, she could give him a good assessment without his realizing it. On the surface Marshall was the perfect escort. But at the moment he was wearing an expression that could best be described as peevish, which was too bad. Renee was simply not in the mood to tolerate much in the way of drama today.

It was bad enough that Bennie had that "hunka-hunka burnin' love" Clay at her side, like he was welded there, but the ever-merry Andrew had struck again. After greeting Marshall with a warm handshake, he had waited until he was alone with Renee. In a whisper that no one else could hear, he said, "I thought that was your dad for a minute, but Mr. Kemp doesn't have that much gray hair."

It was his version of hilarity, since he had in fact met her father on several occasions. Renee had endured that with the clenched jaw of the martyr, refusing to allow Andrew to get the best of her. And for once, Andrew had a date, albeit a most unsuitable one, in Renee's opinion.

She was short and busty and had the weave of life, something that did not escape Renee's expert eyes. Plus, whoever had put on her sculptured nails should have been shot—they were much too thick and long. Altogether, Renee thought she was a bit on the cheap side, even for Andrew. But why she was even concerned about Andrew's love life was unexplainable—why did she care what he did with his spare time?

Even when LaKeisha, for that was her name, asked where Renee got her contact lenses, she remained calm. She gave her usual answer, "From God, dear," although she wasn't sure that LaKeisha was bright enough to understand what she meant. For the most part Renee was calm and unruffled, but an undercurrent of irritation remained. And Marshall was unknowingly stirring it up with his grumpiness.

Renee decided to avoid possible cross words by busying Marshall. He always seemed happier when he was fussing over her. "Marshall dear, could you get me something to drink? I'm terribly thirsty," she said sweetly. Unfortunately, Drew heard her remark, and like the devoted little godson that he was, he dashed off to get Uncle Renee some punch.

"I'll get it for you," he called as he sped off. He was back quickly, both grubby hands clutching a large glass of punch that was a little too full for him to carry. And before anyone could come to his aid, he stumbled in his eagerness and the contents of the glass spilled out all over Marshall's spiffy white pants. A look of complete horror transformed Marshall's face.

In seconds Renee was on her knees, scooping up Drew as the tears of mortification gushed out of his big eyes. "Are you all right, honey lamb?" she crooned. She set him on his feet to make sure that he had no scratches or cuts from his tumble.

"I-I-I'm s-s-s-sor-r-ry, Uncle Renee!" he wailed. "I didn' mean to spill it on that man!" Renee took Drew on her lap and kissed his tears away.

"Oh, honey lamb, Uncle Renee knows that and so does Mr. Marshall," she said, narrowing her eyes at Marshall and daring him to say otherwise. "Mr. Marshall is just going to go change his pants and come back to pick me up so we can go up north. Unless he would rather go by himself," she ended with a very fake smile directed right at Marshall.

By this time Drew's mother, Faye, became aware of what was going on and came to collect her offspring. She apologized to Renee, who brushed it off as unnecessary.

"You all forget that I have nieces and nephews, too. This kind of thing is in the job description of a small child. It's what they do," she said with a smile.

Faye had to agree. "But you know, Drew absolutely

adores you. If he thought you were angry with him, he would have been heartbroken."

Renee leaned over to give the sticky sweetie one more kiss so he knew that she was still his best girl. Which is when Faye noticed that there was quite a bit of punch on the leg of Renee's silk Capri pants.

"Renee, I don't know if that will come out, but you'd better try to spot it a little," she said, fretting.

Renee cast a casual glance and agreed, although she was pretty sure they would be a lost cause. She went into the house with Faye and Drew, who promptly usurped the powder room on the first floor. The caterers in the kitchen looked at her like "I dare you to try and use this sink," so she went upstairs to the guest bathroom. She went into the walk-through linen-closet-cum-dressing-area that separated the two guest bedrooms and was about to get a hand towel to begin her ministrations when she was distracted by a noise from one of the bedrooms. The door was ajar, so she peeked in and was turned into stone by what she saw.

Standing in the middle of the bedroom was Dr. Andrew Cochran; dripping wet from the shower, he wore nothing but drops of moisture.

Four

For a long moment Renee could not have breathed if her life depended on it. Nor could she tear her eyes away. Renee had certainly seen naked men before, but nothing like the one in the next room. Andrew was . . . he was . . . well . . . *beautiful*. No other word could do him justice. Renee had always known that Andrew was tall and well made; that much was obvious with his clothes on. But she had never paid attention to how muscular and well shaped his legs were, or how firm and muscular his thighs were, and she had certainly seen him in shorts many, many times. She had never noticed how broad his shoulders were and how nicely muscled his back was, and surely she had seen him shirtless before, in a basketball game or swimming. And his backside just defied description other than "perfect."

Andrew picked up his cell phone off the dresser and began punching in numbers with his back still facing Renee, who couldn't have, *wouldn't* have, moved if her life depended on it. She was too awash in a sea of sensation for conscious thought. Even when he began speaking into the phone and moving in a way that indicated that he might turn around, Renee did not move. And he *did* turn around and she *did* look.

Great googly moo! He was magnificent in every way from head to toe. His chest was broad and muscular and tapered into a hard waist. His hips were narrow and moved fluidly with a grace that reeked of sensuality. He had just enough hair on his chest to look really sexy and it trailed away in a fine line that led down to his most masculine region. And Renee saw it all, every single inch of his powerful manhood as natural as you please. She could feel her chest expanding and her breasts getting tight. Her knees were weakening, but she could not look away, not for all the Coach bags in the Somerset Collection.

It was dreadfully hot in the dressing area, although the heat seemed to be coming from inside of her. Renee was finding it more and more difficult to breathe; she started clutching at the towel rack frantically, thinking that she might faint.

Just then, Andrew stretched, causing his muscles to ripple in a truly spectacular way, which made Renee lose her grip on the towel rack and bump into the wall rather noisily. With eyebrows raised, Andrew turned his head toward the door.

"Is someone in there?" he asked. Crossing the room, he jerked the door fully open and found no one. "That's strange," he muttered. "I'm hearing things." He shrugged and was about to start getting dressed when he sniffed the air once, then twice. *That's Renee's perfume.* He would know that scent in his sleep. Getting dressed in record time, Andrew flew downstairs in search of her.

By the time Andrew emerged, Renee was seated as far away from the house as possible. She was once again wearing her sunglasses—this time to cover up any evidence of raging hormones—and was sipping ice water in an effort to cool the unfamiliar fire that was still smoldering. She was finally able to breathe properly, which was a huge relief. The tension that had threatened to explode just moments earlier was again at bay. Anyone looking at her would not have any way of knowing that she had just had her world turned upside down; at least she hoped that they wouldn't.

My, my, my. Who would have thought that Andrew Cochran, my perennial tormentor and nemesis, was a bronzed African god under his clothes? She hastily downed more ice water. The last thing she wanted to do was get heated up again, but somehow, the mere thought of him was enough to get her going.

Just then, Andrew spotted her, sitting by herself at a small table with a large goblet in front of her. She looked luscious and composed in some kind of orange-colored pants outfit; in fact, she looked wonderful. But Andrew was not about to let that stop him from getting a few answers out of her. He strode purposefully over to her table. "Where were you a few minutes ago?" he demanded.

"Here," she answered.

"Here, where?"

"At your father's house."

Andrew narrowed his eyes. This was going to get him nowhere. He sat down across from Renee and looked at her menacingly. "Were you inside or outside?"

"Yes," she answered in a suspiciously breathless voice.

"Did you go upstairs?"

"Mighta."

"Did you go in the bathroom?"

"Coulda."

Andrew counted to ten rapidly. Renee was not going to be forthcoming about this, not in the least.

"I was upstairs getting dressed after a shower and I distinctly heard someone in the dressing room. And I think that someone was you. And you are not explaining your whereabouts to my satisfaction. So," he said, reaching for her sunglasses, "where were you a few minutes ago?" He plucked the sunglasses from the bridge of her nose, hoping to reveal some inner truth in her expression. Instead, he got even more apprehensive.

Renee's beautiful golden eyes could look any number of ways. When she was angry, they were a dark, muddy bronze. When she was happy, they sparkled with bright green flecks. Now they looked totally different; they were warm and spangled with golden glints that he had never

seen. They looked soft and sweet, too, but her words be-
lied their appearance.

"Andrew, if I am to understand you, you are suggest-
ing that I hid in a dressing room and stared at your naked,
dripping wet body and that I am now evading that charge
by lying. Now, what kind of person would see another
person naked and not have the decency to avert their
gaze? And what kind of person would not own up to the
fact and apologize, rather than leave their unwitting victim in the limbo of not knowing whether they were being
spied on?" Renee sat back to watch the results of her
pronouncement and was thoroughly satisfied with the
results.

Andrew let each word sink in on him like a heavy
weight and was puce with embarrassment when she finished. Yes, he had seen every inch of Renee's lovely body,
and he had not given her a chance to run for cover by alerting her to his presence. And he had lied about it for
seventeen years. So now the tables were turned. Or were
they?

Andrew leaned forward to look at her more closely; he
prided himself on being able to ferret out a lie. But all he accomplished was to get a really good sniff of her fragrance,
the one that he had smelled upstairs. *She* was *up there!* Andrew knew he was not crazy, but he was prevented from
further comment by the arrival of his sister.

Bennie sensed nothing wrong as she joined the two of
them. She did notice a change in her brother's attire.
"Bunchy, weren't you wearing something else a little while
ago? And what happened to your date?" she asked.

Andrew nodded in confirmation, still not taking his
eyes off Renee. "Donnie brought those dumb dogs of his,
the way he always does, and they put their muddy feet all
over me. So I got my gym bag out of the car because I have
to run by the hospital"—he glanced at his watch—"like
now. And I took a quick shower, which may have been a
mistake," he said darkly as he rose to go. "And LaKeisha

is not my date; we were just . . . talking." He cast one more long look at Renee, which said he was not through with this discussion quite yet.

Bennie looked from her brother's retreating figure to Renee's smiling face, trying to figure out what was going on, as there was obviously something afoot. She said as much to Renee, who continued to smirk like the Cheshire cat.

"Well, Bennie, I think Andrew and I are finally even," was all she would say.

What Andrew thought of the situation was another kettle of fish entirely. He had tried, over the years, to divorce himself from the momentous first meeting with Renee. He knew on some subconscious level that to do otherwise was to court disaster. Epic, cataclysmic disaster was all that could come of thinking about the sight of Renee's beautiful, strong body completely devoid of clothing.

To think of that day was to think of how utterly desirable and sensuous she was, and that was something Andrew tried never to do, ever. To give in to those thoughts would be akin to bungee jumping into an active volcano; assuming that it could be done, he felt the chances of escaping without permanent bodily harm were extremely slim. The same could be said of a relationship with Renee.

For one thing, she couldn't stand him. And for another thing, he knew too well the effect she had on men. He had seen too many of them reduced to slack-jawed, drooling incompetents after what he referred to as her "Curse of the Spider Woman" treatment. Renee liked to have a man under her heel. Well, if not under her stilettos, then certainly at her whim. She definitely liked having them at her beck and call, and her army of admirers seemed to like being there. And that was an utter impossibility for Andrew.

When he was involved with a woman, it had to be fifty-fifty or there was no point to the relationship. Andrew had a great respect for and admiration of women; he would never try to dominate one or infantilize her. He just wanted to get as good as he gave, that was all. He knew from years of observation that would not be the case with Renee. What he did not know was why his thoughts kept turning to these matters anyway. For some reason he had not been able to get Renee out of his mind since the day that she saw—may have seen—him naked.

The memory of the incident still made him hot all over. It wasn't that he was unduly embarrassed by the situation; on the contrary, he got a perverse satisfaction out of the idea that Renee had beheld him in all his glory. He had nothing to be ashamed of, as far as his physique went. In a peculiar way the idea that she had seen him as nature made him was sexy, kind of erotic. But it was confusing nonetheless.

Why in the world was he having these thoughts about Renee? These were dangerous thoughts, very dangerous. No good could come of them at all. Which is why Andrew was rather surprised to find himself pulling into the parking lot of Urban Oasis. There were other places to get his hair cut—Bennie would do it for him gladly. Yet, here he was, about to walk into the lair of the beast.

Andrew had to laugh at the irony—he had been avoiding Renee like the plague for days, and without thinking he had rolled right up on her turf. "Meddle not in the affairs of dragons, for you are crunchy and good with ketchup," he muttered to himself as he parked his Bentley. It was with great relief that he noted the absence of Renee's Mercedes. *Good, she's not here. I get to live.* His relief vanished like the last rib at a family reunion when he entered the reception area to find her standing behind the desk with the telephone in her hand.

She did not notice him right away as she was checking the appointment book for a customer. After marking off the appropriate time for the right stylist, she raised her long lashes to greet the new arrival. Without missing a beat she purred, "Andrew. How nice to see you. Have you an appointment today?"

Andrew swallowed hard. Was it his imagination or had she put an odd inflection on the "nice to see you"?

"No, I don't have an appointment. I was hoping someone could work me in," he admitted sheepishly. Renee's smile got even more feline and feminine.

"Well, why don't you come over here and let me take care of you? I've never had the pleasure of styling you," she said sweetly. She strolled around the counter to take his arm and show him to the area she customarily used for styling her very few, very exclusive clients. It was hard to say who was the more astounded—Andrew or Renee's staff. Under normal circumstances Renee did not take walk-ins. And under no circumstances would she have volunteered to cut Andrew's hair—his throat, maybe, but not his hair. The normal hum of conversation died to near silence as Renee hung up Andrew's suit coat and prepared to drape him with a cutting cape. Luckily for all concerned, Renee noticed nothing amiss in the salon, and rather quickly people gathered their wits and went back to work.

Renee's surprise viewing of Andrew in the buff had a residual effect on her that was unexpected yet rather enjoyable. Besides the obvious feeling of having something on him for once, she seemed to have a surfeit of joie de vivre. An air of happy mischief hovered about her, which caused more than one person to look at her askance. She was so high-spirited at work that gossip was rampant that the boss had a new beau. And the fact that she was in such a good mood made them believe that he was not one of her usual AARP denizens, either. Of course, Andrew's presence just confirmed everyone's suspicions—this must be the mystery man who had their boss purring all day long. He had to be the one—they certainly looked like they belonged together.

Andrew was trying to relax and enjoy the process of getting his hair cut, but the level of apprehension that Renee aroused in him made it impossible. It wasn't that she was being hostile or unpleasant; on the contrary, she was being sweet, which was infinitely more unnerving. She acted as though they were the best of friends as she undid the top button on his shirt, removed his tie and turned his collar in. Chatting all the while, she put a small towel around his neck and then draped him with a silky cape to protect his clothing from hair. She had at least one hand on him at all times, almost but not quite caressing his neck or clasping his shoulder.

The apprehension at last went away, only to be replaced by something much worse—desire. Andrew was profoundly glad that the cape covered him almost to his knees because the proximity of Renee's body and the soft fragrance that emanated from her warmth was driving him mad. When she put both hands into his thick, wavy hair and lightly massaged his scalp, he was ready to leap out of the hydraulic chair. He forced himself to sit still and submit to her ministrations.

"Andrew, you have beautiful hair," Renee murmured. "All you Cochrans do, darn it. If y'all weren't so nice, I'd be jealous. All this beautiful hair on a man—there is no justice," she went on, oblivious to Andrew's growing discomfort. Finally done with her massage, she turned him to face the mirror. Looking at their reflection in the mirror, she asked him how he wanted it cut.

"Short. Very short," he emphasized. Renee raised an eyebrow as if to ask why and he hastened to explain. "I'm going to Haiti in a few days for my annual stint with Medic International. I don't want to have to think about grooming matters at all. I'll probably come back with a beard, too," he said carelessly.

Renee was surprised at his words. She knew that Andrew went overseas for every vacation to do medical missionary work, but she had not realized that it was that time of year already.

"Well, you know Dad's big retirement celebration is in August and I wanted to go and come back well before then so I can help Bennie get it arranged. So this was the best time," he explained.

Renee quickly and expertly cut his hair close to his scalp as requested. As she was giving him a precision finish, she asked when he was leaving and was stunned at the feeling of disquiet she got when told that he was leaving on Sunday.

"Sunday? But this is Thursday," she said reproachfully. "Why would you wait until now to tell me you're leaving?" A hot blush surged up her neck as she realized what she was saying. Luckily, Andrew was so entranced with the feel of her hands on his body that he did not notice the urgency in her voice.

"I'm sorry. I guess I forgot to mention it," he said ruefully.

To cover her embarrassment, Renee asked him if he would like a shampoo, something to which he agreed immediately. Renee expertly removed the cutting cape and replaced it with a shampoo cape, brushing all the tiny hairs away as she did so. She led him to the shampoo bowls and proceeded to give him the most heavenly scalp massage he had ever received. The feel of her fingers coupled with the smell of the fragrant shampoo was wonderful. When he opened his eyes and saw Renee's luscious bosom suspended over his face while she reached for some conditioner, it was almost his undoing. He was holding on to his self-control with the grip of death—one more delightful surprise like that and he would not be responsible. Finally the torture was over.

He was sitting in the styling chair with his hair freshly cut, shampooed and toweled dry, finished with a nimble stroking of Renee's fingers with a light touch of pomade. She had brushed him off, dusted his neck lightly with imported talcum powder and rearranged his shirt collar. She even retied his tie for him.

"There. You're all done and you look very handsome, if I do say so myself," Renee said approvingly.

"I don't know about the handsome part, but I do like my

haircut," he said. "How much is my tab?" To his surprise, Renee refused any payment.

"It's my treat," she said. Andrew took the opportunity to turn the tables on her.

"Well then, please allow me to take you to dinner. It's the least I can do for such professional work," he said.

Renee agreed at once. Somehow an impromptu dinner with Andrew sounded like just the thing to her. "You'll have to take me home first, though. I walked here."

Andrew looked concerned. "Is your car in the shop?" he asked.

It wasn't anything dire like that—Renee liked walking the three miles from Indian Village to the salon on Jefferson to get exercise—she did it all spring and summer and most of the fall. Light dawned for Andrew.

"So that's why . . ." He stopped, aware that he was about to reveal the fact that he thought she wasn't there when he arrived. At Renee's look of puzzlement he finished with a partial lie, a very tiny one. "That's why you have such great legs."

Renee raised her eyebrow as if to say, "I know you're bluffing, but I'm going to let you slide," but remained silent. Bidding her still astounded staff good evening, she and Andrew left to have their very first dinner alone together.

After a brief stop at the house in Indian Village so that Renee could freshen up and change clothes, Andrew had taken her to a nice restaurant that featured delicious food and equally tasty jazz. If Andrew had been thinking more clearly, he might have imagined the evening would be uncomfortable, full of awkward silences and pauses. On the contrary, it was a lovely evening, full of pleasant surprises. Renee and Andrew were both relaxed and equally determined to be charming good company for the other. If Andrew had not known better, he would have sworn that Renee was actually flirting with him at times. He would look up to find her looking at him with an expression that he would have called fond if it had been anyone but Renee. But he knew her too well for that.

For her part, Renee was magnificently surprised at how at ease she felt with Andrew. It was the first time in all their years of acquaintance that she was not tensed in wait for one of his barbed remarks or outrageous jokes at her expense. And even if he had pulled one of his pranks on her, she knew she would ultimately have the upper hand. There was just something about seeing someone in the altogether that made the person seem so much more human and accessible. Nudity was a great equalizer, she thought. She no longer felt like Andrew had some dirty little secret to hold over her head—she had the same one on him. Not that it was a dirty secret—in an odd way it was rather sweet.

She had seen Andrew in his most natural, most vulnerable state; the memory of it was not a cause for ridicule, not at all. In point of fact, it was incredibly sexy and Renee would have been less than truthful if she had not admitted to herself that she would do it again. Yes, she would. If given the opportunity to gaze at this handsome man in all his naked glory again, she would do it, and the Devil take the hindmost. Renee had not quite analyzed what the logic of that kind of thinking meant. All she knew was that for some reason she felt freer than she had in years, and she was enjoying it. It was ironic that Andrew was the unwitting cause of her liberation.

Renee was unaware that she was glowing like a thousand fireflies or she might have attempted to tone it down a bit. It didn't really matter, though, because Andrew was also being his most charming.

"Renee, this is the nicest evening I have had in a long time. Why haven't we ever done this before?" Renee opened her mouth to speak, but Andrew answered his own question. "Oh, I forgot. You can't stand me, that's why." He tried to look hurt, but the smile in his eyes gave him away. Renee wasn't going to let him get away with that, though.

"Oh, no you don't. You're the one that can't stand *me!*

You have never missed an opportunity to pick on me, not once in seventeen years. So don't even go there, Andrew Bernard Cochran Junior. Don't even try it," Renee said quickly, but she, too, was smiling.

They continued to tease each other while Andrew paid the bill, and they walked out to his car, still sniping at each other, but gently, with amusement and not malice. They made the short trip back to the house relatively quickly—there wasn't much traffic. Andrew opened the car door for Renee and walked her up to the back door. They were so accustomed to each other that it was perfectly natural for him to come in for a few minutes, which he did unhesitatingly.

Andrew asked when Bennie would be home, only to be told that she was in Atlanta visiting Clay. Andrew's brows knit together briefly, which Renee assumed meant that he did not approve of Clay for some reason. She was about to express the idea that Clay was a worthy partner for his sister when he spoke.

"You're going to be all alone in this big house? I don't know if I like that idea," he said. "Are you sure you'll be okay by yourself?" Renee was touched by his concern. Coming from anyone else, those words would seem like a big come-on, but she knew that Andrew was sincerely interested in her well-being. She assured him that she would be fine.

"This is a very safe area, you know. There's a private security patrol, plus we have an alarm system. And I have Aretha, the watch cat, to alert me to prowlers," she said, smiling. As if she had heard her name, Aretha sauntered into the kitchen, where Andrew and Renee were standing, and flopped on the floor as if her legs had suddenly vanished. Andrew looked at the large, inert pile of black fur and raised a brow.

"Oh, yeah, she's right on the case. Come on, let me check all these doors and windows for you," he said, taking Renee by the hand.

Over Renee's protests, he checked every entrance and window on the first floor to make sure they were locked.

He repeated his actions on the second floor and was about to go to the third floor, where Renee's rooms were, when she stopped him.

"Andrew, if anyone gets on the third floor, they would have to be airborne," she reminded him. "Now, how about some iced tea or wine or something?"

He reluctantly agreed to tea and followed her downstairs. He hadn't given up on her personal safety, though. "You know, Donnie or Adam can come over and stay here until Bennie gets back," he said worriedly. "You don't have to stay here alone. In fact, I can stay in The Outhouse until I leave on Sunday."

Renee gave him a sweet smile that was full of amusement as she poured large glasses of iced tea and arranged a sprig of fresh mint in each one. "Andrew, I'm really touched that you are so concerned for my safety, but I'll be fine. I've stayed here before all by my lonesome and nothing happened. Now let's go into the living room and listen to a little music, okay?"

Andrew sighed. It was apparent that he was not going to win, so he pretended to bow to Renee's judgment. He was a little surprised at himself as he followed Renee into the living room. When had he become so protective of her? He never would have let any harm come to her at any time, but for some reason he had this sudden sense of responsibility toward her, like she was some delicate flower that he had to safeguard. Nothing could have been further from the truth—could it? He looked at Renee, who was oblivious to his scrutiny as she selected some CDs.

Before going to dinner, she had changed into a pink linen sleeveless dress with deeply cut armholes that exposed her firm, rounded shoulders. The collar of the dress was turned up toward her face and framed her dark beauty. The rosy pink color of the dress was perfect with her dark skin and matched the sexy little mules she wore on her long, slender feet. Many dark-skinned women were afraid to wear soft or bright colors, but not Renee. She had an unerring eye for what would look exquisite on her and she always looked like a million bucks. And she always smelled terrific. Before he could stop himself, Andrew blurted these observations.

"Renee, you are one of the best-dressed women I have ever known. Anything you put on looks good on you," he said admiringly. Renee was taken aback momentarily but managed to rally. She joined Andrew, who was sprawled on one end of the sofa.

"Well, thank you, Andrew. I think that's the first time you've ever paid me a compliment," she said honestly. Andrew smiled.

"I said you looked good enough to eat not too long ago," he reminded her.

Renee blushed at the memory and pointed out to him that he was not being complimentary on that occasion. "You just did that to pick at me. You *licked* me, if I recall," she said mildly.

Andrew just continued to smile lazily at her. "I wasn't licking you. I was *tasting* you. I always thought you would taste just like chocolate, and you do."

Renee's long lashes blinked slowly. She was suddenly very warm, even though the temperature in the room was quite comfortable. Furthermore, she seemed to have goose bumps. The sound of Andrew's voice, the caress of his simple, well-chosen words, and the sight of him stretched across the sofa had combined to give Renee an odd rush. She was trying to think of something witty and sophisticated to say when he spoke again.

"Ever since the first time I saw you, I wanted to know what you would taste like," he admitted.

Renee leaned back against the pillowed sofa. At last the truth would come out. "You *were* looking at me that day, weren't you?" she accused.

Andrew sat up to answer her.

"Yes, I looked. *Hell yes,* I looked. I was eighteen years old and horny as a mink, and you were the most incredible thing

I had ever seen in my life. I *looked,"* he said fervently. Before she could speak, he went on. "I know it was sick and voyeuristic and I have wanted to beg your pardon hundreds of times, but for some reason I thought if I pretended it never happened, you wouldn't have to be embarrassed about it. I know that's the logic of an eighteen-year-old and I know it's stupid, but that's all I had to go on at the time," he said passionately.

"Do you forgive me? I mean, can we be friends now? I really am sorry, you know." Andrew finally stopped speaking long enough to let Renee get a word in edgewise. He couldn't tell what she was thinking because she was completely still and wore a surprisingly neutral expression.

Suddenly she smiled radiantly. "Andrew, that was such a sweet apology I couldn't possibly turn it down," she began. "Although, I have to confess that I might have at one time. But since I really was in that dressing room . . . and I really did see you au naturel . . . I have a much better understanding of your perspective," she murmured while looking him directly in the eyes.

Andrew's mouth opened slightly as he registered what Renee just uttered. "You sneak. I knew that was you—I smelled your perfume! So you did cop a peek at me! I feel so violated," he said dramatically, laughing all the while.

Renee was laughing, too, but she had to correct him. "Oh, no, honey, I got a good *long* look—it was no peek, believe me." She blushed and covered her mouth as she realized what she just said, but it was too late. Andrew started laughing again, totally shameless.

"That's 'cause you liked what you saw, the same way I did. This is too funny," he said. He stood and pulled Renee to her feet with him. He wrapped his long arms around her and gave her a tight squeeze. Renee made a little sound of surprise. Andrew immediately released her. "Did I hurt you?" he asked anxiously.

Renee never took her eyes from him as she shook her head. "No, you didn't. You just never hugged me before.

All your brothers have, but not you," she said honestly. Andrew smiled his relief and hugged her again.

"That's because they're not scared of you—you didn't have it in for them," he teased. He kept one arm around her shoulder and looked at his watch. "I have to be at the clinic early tomorrow, so I should go. Want to do something before I leave for Haiti on Sunday?"

Renee agreed unhesitatingly as they walked to the back door. Andrew said he would call her the next day with details. Then he kissed her, a quick, warm, wet kiss, and reminded her to lock the door and enable the alarm.

"I should have Donnie bring over Jordan and Pippen at least," he said, referring to his brother's golden retrievers. Renee laughed as she pushed him out the door.

"Oh, please, those two run from Aretha. How are they supposed to protect me?"

Andrew conceded her point. "But you be extra careful, you hear me? Now that you're not trying to put a contract out on me, I kinda want to keep you around," he said with a wink. He kissed her once more and left.

Renee quickly locked the door, securing the dead bolt and punching in the alarm system code. She touched her lips lightly where Andrew's hot, sweet ones had just been and gave in to the mild panic that was gripping her. *What in the world happened here? And how am I going to deal with it?* She looked over at Aretha, who was observing her discomfort with typical feline curiosity.

"Ooh, Aretha. What am I getting myself into now?" Renee whispered. Aretha had no answer for her other than a soft meow.

Five

It would have been apparent to anyone who knew her that Renee was not herself. And the woman sitting across from her had known her for some time. In fact, she knew her better than many people. Yolanda Williams was an acquaintance of long standing. She was a gifted and compassionate psychologist and had been seeing Renee as a patient for over a year. She had taken Renee over some very rocky ground in the past months, and the changes that she had seen recently were very positive. Yolanda had been on a much-needed vacation for the past three weeks, and she and Renee had a lot of catching up to do.

Renee sighed deeply and dramatically. She put the back of her left wrist to her forehead and intoned theatrically, "So much has gone on, I don't know where to begin." She immediately dropped the pose, but Yolanda knew there was something underlying her friend's histrionics.

"Well, tell all, dear. That's what I'm here for. What's been happening over the past few weeks?" Yolanda's dark, clever eyes scanned Renee's face. Despite her edginess, she seemed energized and refreshed, which was in itself a good sign. The tale she told lent credence to the same idea.

"Well," Renee said slowly, "I saw a naked man. And my, what a man he was." Before Yolanda could react, Renee had recounted for her the entire scenario of her encounter with Andrew and its aftermath. As good therapists do, Yolanda asked Renee how she felt about the incident.

Renee answered her honestly, in her own inimitable fashion. "Yolanda, you remember the *Little Rascals?*" Seeing her nod, Renee went on. "You remember the episode where there was the Wild Man from Borneo, who kept saying, 'Yum-yum, eat 'em up'? Well, that pretty much describes how I felt when I saw Mr. Andrew. *Yum-yum, eat him up!* Ooh, he was . . . delicious; that's about the only way I can describe him," she finished, fanning herself lightly with one hand.

Despite Renee's discomfiture, Yolanda was thrilled with her revelation. "Good for you, Renee! This is a big, big step for you! I can remember not too long ago when it would have been impossible for you to have those kinds of feelings for a man. This is definitely progress," she enthused. Renee tried not to look too pleased at Yolanda's words, but a fleeting look of accomplishment crossed her face.

She waited for Yolanda to get used to her first news before dropping her bombshell. "Yeah, well that's not all—he kissed me, too. Several times. *Real* kisses, too, I might add." Yolanda all but applauded as she begged for details. Renee sighed and obliged her with everything that had transpired between her and Andrew.

After their first dinner had gone so well and they had shared a brief but sweet kiss, Renee had nervously awaited their next rendezvous. She did not have long to wait, as Andrew took her to Chene Park the next night for a jazz concert under the stars. He had taken her to a charming little café for an early supper before the concert, and he suggested that they go to his apartment for dessert. Renee was feeling so mellow and relaxed after their nice evening that she agreed with no reservations. She had never been to Andrew's abode and was more than a little curious.

Andrew's hobby was fixing up old houses. Among those

he owned was a recently completed brick duplex. He was living in half and rented the other half to a fellow doctor. It was an imposing two-story building in a gentrified area not too far from Indian Village. Renee was immediately impressed, both by the immaculate exterior and the nicely decorated interior of the house. It had highly polished wood floors and all the woodwork was in its natural state, which she adored. Renee hated painted wood and told Andrew so. He admitted having to strip it all when he bought the place, but he agreed that it was worth the effort and expense.

The rooms were furnished simply and elegantly, with family photos and expensive artwork abounding. Nothing was out of place or extreme; everything was stylish, peaceful and unpretentious, much like the man she was coming to really know. The centerpiece of the living room was a baby grand piano, which surprised Renee. She had forgotten that Andrew played. When he returned to the living room with a tray bearing coffee and mocha cheesecake, she commented on the piano.

"Oh, yeah. I took lessons for years. My mother was the first person to teach Bennie and me and after that we took lessons. Bennie also plays the flute, but she probably never told you that." Renee's brow had puckered, trying vainly to recall whether she knew. Renee was notoriously poor at details. Bennie would have known the answer to a question like that about her—Bennie never forgot anything about a person, Renee thought guiltily.

She and Andrew drank their coffee and enjoyed the delicious cheesecake in relative silence. Then Andrew rose and went to the piano. He sat down and played "Maiden Voyage" for Renee, again surprising her. He was not just a passable player; he was very, very skilled. She remarked on the fact and he shrugged off her praise.

"I think we all get it from our mother. She was a very talented pianist and singer. She could have easily been a concert pianist, if she had not preferred being a wife and mother," he said. He started playing "Clair de Lune" very softly, commenting that it was one of his mother's favorite pieces. "After our mother died, Bennie made sure that we all kept up with our lessons. She knew that it would have pleased our mother very much. She even got Donnie started when he was about three. First she taught him, then he started taking lessons." He played without speaking for a few minutes.

"You know, Renee, I wish you could have known my mother," he said softly. "She was a wonderful person. She was sweet, smart, talented and very loving. Bennie is a lot like her," he finished.

For some reason Renee felt small and uncomfortable when he said that. Yes, Bennie was world-class wonderful and there was no way she could compete with that. Bennie was practically a saint and Renee felt like a lesser demon in comparison. In a small voice she said, "I'm nothing like your sister, Andrew. I'm not the same kind of woman that she is at all."

Andrew's answer to that was to stop playing the piano and come back to sit next to Renee on the sofa. "So? Why in the world would I want a woman that's just like Bennie? That's kinda nasty, when you think about it. I mean, damn, that's my sister! Yechhh!" he said, drawing away from Renee with a truly comical grimace on his face. "That's just sick and wrong! They have jails for people like that!"

Renee punched at his arm, but she was laughing as she did it. "You know what I mean, you loon! I am not going to dignify this further by discussion," she said tartly.

Andrew's expression had changed totally and he was no longer paying any attention to her words. Without speaking he drew her into his arms and kissed her. At first it was soft and gentle, so she could pull away if she wanted to. When she didn't, he settled back on the sofa and began a leisurely exploration of her mouth with his lips and tongue, leaving tiny bursts of fire wherever he touched her. Renee had been too stunned to move at first, but she began to return his sweet passion with her own. Andrew's lips were firm and soft and sweet, and the feel of his velvety mustache was simply amazing. When he finally pulled away, she was dizzy and dreamy-eyed, which probably accounted for what happened next.

"Renee," Andrew said softly. "Sweet Renee. Now that we've proven we can be alone and not kill each other, I think we should start dating when I come back from Haiti. Real dating, not friendly, once-in-a-while stuff; I mean the real thing," he said firmly and persuasively.

And Renee, her eyes glittering with golden sparks, just nodded and agreed before sinking back into his arms for another one of those mind-boggling kisses. "Anything you say, Andrew," she murmured before tasting his lips again.

This time Yolanda really did applaud, to Renee's chagrin. "Isn't that against the Hippocratic oath or something?" she asked grumpily. Yolanda was not put off by Renee's demeanor in the least.

"Renee, I am applauding because this is a momentous event for you! Not too long ago you thought you would never be able to have a normal physical relationship with a man, and now you are taking the first steps in that direction. This is some remarkable progress, my dear." Yolanda was beaming, but Renee was not so sure.

"I don't know about all this, Yolanda. First of all, it's Andrew Cochran, my best friend's twin brother. I have known him for seventeen years and we have fought almost weekly for all of those years," she began. Yolanda had an answer for that, naturally.

"A large part of your animosity toward Andrew stemmed from the fact that you were always convinced that he had seen you nude, which gave him a tremendous advantage in the relationship. You have always felt vulnerable to him and were, therefore, always defensive with him. The fact that you were able at long last to turn the situation around and get the upper hand has allowed the two of you to meet each other on a common ground as friends. And you cannot tell me that during the past seventeen years you have never seen him as anything other than an irritant, can you?"

Renee had to admit that she could easily see the good side of Andrew. She knew him to be immensely brilliant in his chosen profession, that he gave of his time tirelessly and that he was unstinting in the affection that he gave to his family. She had actually never heard him say a cross word to anyone and he had a wonderful, albeit twisted, sense of humor, especially when it came to her. Yes, she had to admit that there were many qualities to admire about Andrew. Especially since he was handsome, sexy and a delectable kisser. But that was not the least of Renee's concerns.

"Okay, Yolanda, I have never found Andrew totally repulsive, not at all. But it's not just the fact that he and I have this history that's bothering me," she admitted, turning troubled eyes to Yolanda. "I know that this is one of the things that we have been working toward in this therapy, but now that it's at my doorstep, I don't know whether I can actually open the door," she said softly.

Yolanda nodded her head in sympathy and understanding. "Considering what happened to you, it is quite normal for you to be this apprehensive. After an ordeal like the one you went through, you have every reason and every right to be wary of having a physical relationship with a man. But you knew within yourself that you wanted to have a normal relationship, which is one of the reasons you went into therapy.

"You did not want your past to control your future anymore and you began the long process of working through your pain. You are making tremendous progress, Renee. The fact that you are experiencing physical desire for a man is a very good, very positive sign. And you are experiencing attraction for Andrew, are you not?"

Renee sighed. *Attraction. Such a tepid, nondescript*

word for what I'm feeling. But it will suffice. "Yes," she said quietly. "I am very attracted to Andrew."

Yolanda pressed a little more. "So he is now in Haiti, where he will be for a few weeks. And how did you two leave things?"

This time Renee smiled.

After spending Thursday and Friday nights together, she and Andrew had been together all day Saturday, running errands and picking up things he needed to take on his trip that he had forgotten. Then they had gone to his brother Alan's house for a cookout, a family tradition whenever Andrew was about to take one of his overseas trips. The only person missing was Bennie, who was still in Atlanta, but she called to tell her twin good-bye.

No one had noticed that Renee and Andrew had come together and were leaving together, so they were able to avoid a lot of questions about their fledgling relationship. The next morning, Renee had driven him to the airport and had insisted on walking him right up to his gate. He was joined by two other doctors from the same medical missionary group. Everything was fine until it was time to actually say good-bye to Andrew. For some reason Renee's eyes had filled with hot tears, which she was too surprised to try and hide.

Andrew hadn't even tried to make a joke about it, either, which endeared him to Renee even more. He just kissed them away and reminded her that he would be back very soon. "I can't promise that I'll write, because we are really busy over there. And calling is difficult. But I'll be thinking about you every day, and I'll miss you," he said sincerely.

Renee had felt something inside her begin to melt, and when he lowered his head to hers for a good-bye kiss, she was just gone. She stood there like a besotted teenager until the plane had taken off, even though she couldn't see him. And like a truly lovestruck girl, she had actually shed a few

tears until she realized what she was doing. She was the
prize! What was she doing standing in Detroit Metro with
tears running down her face over Andrew Cochran, of all
people? The man had obviously put a spell on her. She tried
unsuccessfully to shrug the whole incident off.

She thought about nothing else all the rest of the day—
in fact, all the days that had passed until she could get to
her appointment with Yolanda. And now Yolanda was
telling her that all this emotional turmoil was a good thing
and that she was making progress. Which she supposed
that she was—it was just that she felt so vulnerable, so
naked, for want of a better word. She felt like she was in
one of those dreams where you were walking along in your
underwear on a crowded city street or that you were at
work without a stitch on. She finished her story with those
very words and looked to Yolanda for comfort.

Yolanda did not let her down, either. Leaning forward,
she took one of Renee's hands and clasped it firmly.
"Renee, of course you feel vulnerable and exposed. This is
no small thing for you. It's taken a lot of hard work and
courage for you to get as far as you have. You are doing
just fine. The feelings you have are perfectly normal, believe me. Just keep working at it the way you have and let
things unfold. There's a lot of strength in you, Renee.
You're going to have the happy ending that you want because you're brave enough to fight for it."

Renee did not completely share Yolanda's optimism, but
she was willing, for now, to take a chance. What could she
possibly lose?

Despite Yolanda's encouragement, Renee was a bundle
of nerves. She could not get rid of an anxious, giddy feeling that plagued her daily. She hadn't felt like this since
college! There was a reason that she maintained the kind

of relationships that she had. They were neat, orderly and controllable. None of the benign older men who were allowed in her circle did this to her. No matter how rich, how handsome or how attentive, not a one of them could stir her the way Andrew had. The feelings that he brought to the surface without even trying were heady, exciting and definitely sexy. Just remembering what Andrew looked like naked, coupled with those hot kisses, was enough to make the small of her back tingle and turn moist at the same time. Not to mention other places.

It had gotten so bad that Renee had to consciously limit the amount of time she spent thinking about Andrew. Even so, she was prone to take little mental side trips every so often. Valerie had an uncanny way of knowing just when Renee had drifted away and would often tease her.

"Okay, what's his name? Who is the mystery man that has you all caught up, hmmm? Who is it?" Valerie would demand, only to get an enigmatic smile from Renee.

That in itself was a huge change—the acerbic, businesslike Renee had taken a backseat to a Renee who was quicker to smile, more eager to laugh and definitely less intimidating than her predecessor. Everyone remarked on the change, except Bennie, who had never thought of her friend in those uncomplimentary terms anyway.

The hardest thing for Renee other than admitting to herself that she was counting the days until Andrew returned was not saying a word to Bennie. She did not want her friend to get in the middle of an ugly situation if things did not work out with her and Andrew. She also was just not ready to reveal that she had this kind of interest in her best friend's brother—it seemed so like an ingenue or something. Besides, who said there was anything to actually tell Bennie? Andrew had said that he wanted to start dating when he got home. What was *dating,* for heaven's sake? Although she knew in her heart what he probably meant, it was hard to get her head around that idea.

Andrew was young, virile, sexy and magnificent. Dating

did not mean what it meant to her middle-aged admirers. It would not mean taking Renee where she wanted to go when she wanted to go there, nor would it mean catering to her every whim and rewarding her with trinkets for allowing them to spend time with her. Dating to Andrew would mean something totally different, something along the lines of "Let's do what you want one day, and do what I want the next. And let's have sex and plenty of it." *Yow.*

At the moment Renee was scrunched up on her chaise longue having monster cramps. The thought of a totally new kind of relationship with a totally different kind of man made her leap to her feet, causing momentary dizziness. The door to her sitting room was open and she could hear Bennie singing and talking to Aretha. She decided to join her friend—maybe Bennie could shed some light on a few things.

"Aretha, please get out of there. I am not sending you to Atlanta, no matter how much you flirt with Clay," Bennie said absentmindedly. She was cutting wrapping paper while Aretha was staking out a box as her personal territory, daring anyone to try and remove her from her new domain. Renee came in and sat on the love seat in Bennie's sitting room.

"And just what are you doing?" she asked, although it was plain that Bennie was wrapping a present for Clay.

Bennie confirmed that yes, she was sending Clay a present.

"Why?" demanded Renee. "Is it his birthday or something?"

Bennie admitted that it was not his birthday or any other special event, she just wanted to send him something because she loved him. She said it proudly, too, like it was just the greatest thing in the world. Renee looked at her carefully. Bennie looked wonderful, but then she always did. Renee had to admit, though, that in these days of Clay Deveraux, Bennie had an extra beauty, a glow that came from within. She was a good-natured person in any case, but these days she was positively angelic. It was almost sickening. Renee could not resist getting to the heart of a few things.

"I have to ask, why are you sending him something? Shouldn't he be sending you something?" She tried not to sound petty, but it was unavoidable. Bennie did not point that out, however. She was gracious and honest in her answer.

"Renee, I like to give gifts, you know that. And I especially like to give Clay things because he is so special to me. It's not about who gave whom what or anything like that. And if it was, I have a lot of catch-up to do. Do you know how much Judith Leiber bags cost, for instance? And when I bought those earrings in Atlanta, he bought me the matching necklace and bracelet as a surprise. And they were like four times the cost of the earrings, which were not cheap, by any means. I'll have to take you to Skippy Musket the next time we're in Atlanta," she added as she dumped Aretha out of the box.

Blowing the cat hair away, Bennie continued, "I know you're not supposed to tell men how you feel about them or show them a lot of affection or buy them presents—I've read those *How to Catch a Man* books and I just think they're stupid. Well, maybe stupid is a strong word, but they are just not for me. I knew Gilbert was the right man for me because I never had to hold back with him. I could be as smart as I wanted, and do or say anything around him because he loved me just as I am. And I can do the same with Clay for the same reason."

Bennie busied herself with wrapping the books she had purchased for Clay while Renee mulled over what she had said. In theory, she supposed Bennie was right. Her late husband, Gilbert, was certainly mad for her, and Clay seemed to be following in the same pattern. But Renee could not resist probing a little further.

"Okay, I'm playing devil's advocate here. Suppose, just suppose, that things don't work out with you and Clay. How are you going to reclaim that part of yourself that you gave to him? How do you get yourself back?" Renee asked softly.

Bennie gave Renee her full attention then. "I don't think you do," she said honestly. "Even I'm not that big a Pollyanna—I think that you do give a part of yourself away when you love someone. But even if it doesn't 'work out' between Clay and me, I don't *want* that part back. It's a gift that I give to him, just like these books of poetry that I bought him—one of which is erotic Japanese haiku, just so you know. It is his gift that I give freely and I don't want it back."

Renee was amazed. Bennie was truly light-years ahead of her in the love game. Either that or she was too far-gone over Clay to be sensible. Renee had to point out, once again, that it was Bennie who was the prize. Bennie went right back to her wrapping.

"Renee, I understand in theory why you say that. I understand that it means that you are worthy of being loved, that you are a treasure and a rare jewel and all of that. I am not trying to discount those feelings. But, honey, I don't *want* to be a prize. I don't think of myself in those terms and I don't think of Clay in those terms. Our relationship, what we have together, that's my prize. Quiet as it's kept, I want to be a wife and a mother. That, to me, would be a real prize." Bennie looked at Renee's astounded expression and laughed out loud.

"Yes, I said it and I meant it. So put that in your pipe and smoke it, sister," she said happily, and laughed contentedly again.

Renee, for once, was stunned into silence. Either the whole world was going mad or she needed desperately to get a new perspective on life. Or at least a new affirmation, because the old one seemed a little outdated, even though it had served its purpose. There had been a time when she desperately needed to feel that she was worthy of love and respect. There had been a time when she needed something strong and defining to cling to, and the affirmation had served that purpose. But maybe it was time to let it go and find a new definition for Renee.

And maybe, just maybe, a new relationship with Andrew would help bring that about. Renee felt that same pleasurable yet frightening tremor ripple over her body as she thought about exciting new possibilities. Saying a hasty good-bye to Bennie and Aretha, Renee scooted back upstairs to count the days until Andrew would be back home. She might not be ready to swim in the deep end just yet, but she was darned if she was going to keep wading in the shallows.

Six

"Would you care for more tea, Mrs. Hasenpfeffer?"

"I would love some, Mrs. Rutabaga, thank you so much," the gracious lady said, extending her tiny cup for more of the lemonade that Renee was pouring from a china teapot. Bennie's niece Lillian was having a tea party in the backyard with Bennie and Renee as her guests. Periodically they would have a special "Girls' Day" just for Lillian, who was not only the youngest of the middle Cochran brother's children but the only girl.

So Bennie and Renee would take her on outings away from the boys, have a special sleepover for her and play dress up with outlandish costumes and mad hats, as they were now doing.

Lillian was ravishing in a black feather boa, white opera gloves and a huge pink hat adorned with purple and fuchsia flowers. Bennie was similarly attired, with a rhinestone tiara and a lavender bed jacket lavished with lace; she also boasted a wealth of beads of the Fishbone's variety. Fishbone's was a trendy restaurant that specialized in New Orleans–style cuisine, right down to the traditional Mardi Gras beads used as souvenirs. And Renee was way over the top in a pair of bejeweled cat eye sunglasses with a beaded neck chain, leopard-spotted Capri pants, a huge straw hat and cork wedge heeled sandals. She also affected a Norma Desmond facade for all it was worth. Everything was "dah-hling" and "but-of-*course*," much to Lillian's delight. Altogether, it was a charming group frolicking in the backyard of Bennie's house, at least that's what Andrew thought when he rounded the corner.

"Well, do you ladies think you can spare a cup of tea for a thirsty traveler?" he asked in an amused voice. Bennie and Lillian immediately ran to him and hugged him hard. Renee stood there frozen—he wasn't supposed to be back until the next day. *And here I am, ready for my damn close-up,* she fretted. It didn't seem to matter, though, as Andrew was looking at her like she had hung the moon or something else miraculous and wonderful. It was all she could do not to give him her own hug, for she was so glad to see him.

He looked dashing, although a little tired. The stress of the past few weeks showed clearly, yet he still had a healthy glow about him. And a beard—as he had threatened, he had not done much in the way of grooming while away. It suited him in a way. While Bennie and Lillian were chattering away, Renee found herself walking toward him, her eyes locked on his. She had to touch him, just a little, to make sure he was really there. Andrew had not moved. It was as though he were holding his breath until she reached his side. Renee had gotten just close enough to touch his hand when Lillian spoke.

"Who is that? Where did she come from?"

Following Lillian's gaze, Renee turned to see a tiny, pale woman with a cascade of brown hair walking around the corner of the house as if she belonged there. She was smiling broadly and waving happily at Andrew.

"Oh, isn't she adorable! I'm Dana Pierson, honey. Your uncle Andrew brought me here. We were in Haiti together," she said confidently.

Three pairs of eyes, two almost black and one golden, turned to Andrew for confirmation. It was quite obvious that he had erred somewhere to judge by the looks he was getting from his twin, his niece and his . . . whatever Renee was. The fact that he was slightly jet-lagged did not help

Andrew's power of speech: he was reduced to the universal male cry for help.

"What?" he asked plaintively.

It wasn't as damning as it looked, by any means. Dana Pierson was a television journalist doing a story on the Medic International and had been covering the site where Andrew was working as well as other locations. When Andrew's tour was over, they ended up on the same flight home. Dana's cousin was getting married in Detroit and she was participating in the wedding. She had rented a car at the airport and offered to drop Andrew off, which seemed like a good thing. After all, no one was expecting him until the next day and he did not want to inconvenience anyone. Although from the looks he was getting, he would have done well to wake them all up at midnight and drag them to Romulus, where Detroit Metropolitan Airport was located.

After the introductions and explanations were over, everything, more or less, returned to normal. Bennie was just a bit chagrined at having been caught cavorting by a stranger. Lillian did not take to strange women, period. She had no real use for most women outside her own family, another result of having two brothers and lots of boy cousins. Renee, however, was ready to raise hell and put a chunk in it.

She could not have possibly cared less about the fact that they were having a child's party. But she did resent, for some reason, Andrew's unexpected appearance. She had another scenario planned, one that she had discussed for weeks with Yolanda. She knew just what she would wear, how she would smell, and how she would act. She had been anticipating his return with an eagerness that she had not allowed herself to feel for years and years, and just look at what had happened. Showing up out of the blue was bad enough. But to drag that woman along was just the very limit. Renee felt like a Roman candle had replaced her head—if someone had set a match to her, she would have spiraled off in fiery circles of rage. And if she landed on that little snip, so much the better.

Andrew was bone tired and thoroughly sick of the garrulous Dana's incessant conversation. All he wanted at the moment was a hot shower and a cool bed. But he wasn't so tired that he did not recognize an angry woman when he saw one. Renee's cheeks were full of wind and he ought to know—he had caused that condition more times than he could remember. What he did not understand was why she was in such a snit. She had barely stayed around for the introductions and explanations; she had disappeared into the house without saying a word to him. After a suitable interval Andrew followed Renee into the house, where she was making a great, noisy show of cleaning up the dishes from their impromptu party.

Andrew came up behind her and slipped his arms around her waist. "You didn't say hello to me," he accused softly. Renee did not turn around.

"Hello, Andrew, nice to see you, hope you had a wonderful trip," she rattled off in a monotone.

Andrew was undaunted. He turned her around and planted a big kiss on her forehead, followed by one on each cheek and one on the mouth. "I've been missing you like crazy and this is the best you can do in the way of a greeting? I'm crushed, Renee, I really am," he said. He tried to sound light and amused, but a tiny bit of real hurt crept into his voice.

Renee looked up at him and a slight smile flickered over her face. "Well, I really had another welcome-home in mind," she admitted. "One that involved just the two of us. And a really nice kiss, like this," she cooed, touching her lips to his. The first contact was feather soft and sent a current of electricity rocketing through them both. In seconds a sweet kiss had turned into a deep, sensual mating that spoke volumes. It would have gone on and on, had it not been for the entrance of Lillian.

"Ooh, you're kissin'. Why are you kissin'? Are you gettin' married? Is he your *boyfriend?*" she asked Renee.

Turning to Andrew, she asked, "Do you *love* her? Is she your *girlfriend?*" Lillian was obviously quite taken with the idea.

Andrew hastily handed Lillian some French coins from his pocket. He customarily brought home foreign currency for his niece and nephews. "Okay, Shorty, this is our little secret, okay? Just you and me and Uncle Renee. We're just going to keep this among ourselves, okay?"

Lillian was so enchanted with the odd-looking coins that she agreed immediately. Renee was relieved, both because the kissing had stopped and because Andrew had bought Lillian's silence. She was not ready for a public debut of their relationship until it really was a relationship and not some bizarre flirtation. And the kissing was so hot that she would have done something really crazy right in the kitchen if Lillian had not burst in on them.

Tina arrived at about that time to collect Lillian. Hearing her mother's voice made Lillian dash out of the kitchen, leaving Andrew and Renee alone again. Andrew immediately moved back to Renee, reaching for her with an unmistakable gleam in his eye.

"Okay. Now, where were we? I think you were going to tell me why you were being so standoffish outside and how much you missed me while I was away. Then I'm going to tell you what we're going to be doing tonight, and tomorrow night, and the next night," he said confidently.

Before Renee could answer, the back door opened once again. "Well, here you are, Andrew. I was wondering where you had gotten off to!"

It was the ever-perky Dana, one of the main reasons for Renee's disposition. Renee immediately got very still and quiet, always a bad sign. Andrew sensed her distance immediately but couldn't fathom the reason for it. Then Dana started chattering away again.

"Well, Andrew, I really have to dash. There's a shower for my cousin Deirdre that I must attend today. And the rehearsal dinner is Friday, but of course you know that." Turning to Renee, she added that Andrew was escorting her to the wedding the next Saturday. "You're welcome to tag along if you like," she added condescendingly.

Renee surprised even herself when she unhesitatingly agreed. "Thanks, I'd love to," she said in the phoniest voice she could muster.

Renee excused herself, but not before hearing Dana say that Tina had invited her to the family party on Sunday to celebrate Andrew's return. She wasn't looking at Andrew or she would have seen the look of stark horror that crossed his face when Dana announced her news. By this time Renee had crossed the dining room and was heading for the main stairway. She stomped up the stairs to her suite of rooms and began taking off her clothes for a nice, cooling shower.

She put on her favorite summer robe, a long pink-and-white seersucker one that tied at the waist and had a huge white portrait collar and deep white cuffs. She was sitting at her dressing table, angrily brushing her hair, when Andrew burst into her room without even knocking.

"Why aren't you downstairs with your little playmate?" Renee said nastily.

Andrew was mystified. "Who, Lillian?" he asked. Renee snorted indelicately.

"No, I mean Safari Barbie, that's who," she continued in the same voice. "She's probably wondering where you are."

Andrew finally got it. He was tired and unaccustomed to seeing this side of Renee, but he finally got it—she was *jealous!* Why she was jealous of that airheaded woman, he would never know, but she was definitely being territorial and he loved it. With a great sigh of happiness he threw himself across Renee's bed.

"Dana has gone and Tina is about to take me home. I was hoping that you would do me that favor, but I see you aren't exactly dressed for the occasion. So how about one more little kiss before I get out of here," he said with a huge yawn.

Renee tried to look aloof, but it was difficult. He looked

too sweet and sleepy. "Okay, one kiss, but from a standing position," she insisted.

Andrew was tickled by that proviso. "You find me hard to resist, don't you? You think something will happen if we're lying down, don't you?" Without waiting for a response he rose to his full, magnificent height and stretched. "Any other time you would be right, but I am too tired for that now. Even though you look pretty cute." He leered at her.

Renee looked down and realized that she was in her robe, but before she could get flustered, Andrew read her thoughts and forestalled any embarrassment on her part.

"Don't forget, we have no secrets—we've seen each other naked, remember?" He tilted her head back and got one more sweet, sinful kiss before leaving. "I'm going to sleep as long as possible; then I'll call you. Maybe we can think of something to do to celebrate, okay?"

Renee nodded and watched him leave. Then she immediately hopped into a cold shower. Every time Andrew touched her, it was like being immersed in a volcano of passion. The slightest contact made her skin heat up, and when his lips touched hers, vibrations like harp music would set her body to trembling. That new beard he was sporting seemed to intensify the effect. She relived the feel of its velvety softness against her skin and her knees actually buckled. "Lawdy, Lawdy, what is a girl to do?" she said aloud. When she realized that the cold shower was not going to do a thing for her, she gave up and stepped out of the shower stall. It was going to be a long, hot summer for sure—it was just July and she had no idea how she was going to handle the heat. *And I don't mean the damned barometric pressure, either. I mean Hurricane Andrew. Ummph.*

Andrew was so wiped out that he slept the rest of the day and night. When he finally came back to consciousness, it was Sunday morning. He glanced at his bedside clock, wondering if he was too late for church. When it was apparent that only a superhuman effort would get him there on time, he yawned and lay down again. A smile spread across his face as he remembered the events of the previous day. His homecoming had not gone precisely as planned, but what in life ever did? As far as he was concerned, it was a complete success because he now had irrefutable proof that Renee was far from indifferent to him. She had actually gotten jealous on his behalf.

He had known her for seventeen years and had seen her with a variety of men during that time span and he had not once seen her display anything but amused tolerance for a man—never passion, not ardor and certainly not any undue concern over where their attention might be wandering. He had always thought of Renee as being a little cold and aloof, but it was obvious that she was capable of warmth and affection. What other little surprises did she have in store for him? Suddenly he couldn't wait to find out more.

While he was entering her phone number into the handset, he thought about the conversation he had with his sister-in-law Tina on the way to his house on the previous day. Tina was completely innocent, of course; she had no way of knowing that she was inviting disaster when she impulsively asked Dana Pierson to join the family for dinner. Andrew tried tactfully to suggest that Tina not be so forthcoming in the future.

"Well, Andrew, I had brought up the dinner right in front of the woman; I couldn't very well not ask her to come, could I? Besides, I thought she was, you know, *with* you. I thought I was being polite. So what if she's not your date? It's not like you're dating someone else right now—what's the problem?"

Andrew was at a loss to explain, but Lillian was happy to inform her mother that Uncle Andrew did indeed have a girlfriend. Tina's mouth dropped open and she was about to make inquiries, but Lillian put a dainty, grubby finger to her tiny lips. "But I can't tell who it is. It's a *secret*."

Luckily, they had reached Andrew's house by then and further conversation was postponed.

Renee answered the telephone within two rings. Andrew settled back into his pillows with a huge smile on his face. He already loved Renee's sexy voice, and the fact that he could gain access to it with ease was gratifying. He used to have to needle her to get her to say something other than hello; now he could just pick up the phone.

"Good morning, Renee. I'm sorry I didn't call last night, but I didn't wake up until about fifteen minutes ago. Am I forgiven?" he asked.

"Of course. I hope you're well rested. I take it you won't be joining us at church?" she said, making it a statement rather than a question.

Andrew agreed that he would not; he was still in bed. "But I'll see you at Tina and Andre's after church. Say a prayer for me." He yawned before saying his good-bye and hanging up. He lay there for a few more minutes, warmed by his brief conversation. Renee sounded as interested and eager as he felt. This was going to be a wonderful relationship, of that he was sure.

Renee hung up the phone and stared at it like it was going to do a little dance or something. The sound of Andrew's voice was enough to get her motor running, a motor that hadn't been revved up in years. This was going to be a dangerous relationship; she could just feel it in her bones. There was something about Andrew that was too compelling, too sexy and too lovable to be resisted. For the first time in a long, long, *long* time, Renee could feel herself getting in over her head, something that had not happened since she was in college.

She snapped out of her reverie long enough to make sure that she had her purse and gloves. Unlike the overtired Andrew, she was going to church that morning. She was really quite glad that Andrew had not called her the previous night;

there was no telling what kind of mischief she might have gotten into. Instead, she had sought refuge at Tina and Andre's house, ostensibly to help Tina with the food for the day's dinner, but in reality she was hiding out. Plus, Clay had shown up at the house and Renee did not relish being a third wheel. There was little chance of that, given the size of the house and the relative privacy she enjoyed on the third floor, but still, she knew that Clay and Bennie needed to be alone.

Clay's arrival had reminded Renee that besides being Andrew's homecoming, it was Bennie's birthday. Renee was terrible at remembering birthdays. Bennie had never once forgotten Renee's birthday in the entire time that they had known each other—Renee had not once remembered Bennie's. She always made it up to her with a present and a card, but she had never prepared ahead of time the way Bennie did. And since it was Bennie's birthday, it was also Andrew's birthday—that's how these things worked with twins. Well, for once, Renee was prepared. It was a last-minute preparation, but it was still impressive, given her track record.

She scooted out to the Somerset Collection and purchased a beautiful silk kimono patterned in peonies to replace the one that Bennie had somehow ruined on one of her trips to Atlanta. It wasn't torn or anything, but it was full of grass stains, which Bennie would not explain and about which Renee did not want to speculate. The new one was quite lovely, though, and Bennie would be thrilled. She also purchased one of Bennie's favorite scents in the form of eau de toilette, bath gel and body lotion. In that accord she and Bennie were as one. They loved fragrance, wore it daily and could not get enough of it.

After her trip to Somerset, Renee headed over to one of those dreadful mega-size music discount stores that drove her mad. She was lucky enough to locate a salesperson of great knowledge and indeterminate gender. With the spiked hair and the pierced ears, lip, nose and eyebrow, Renee wasn't sure what the person was, but he/she served her admirably. Andrew liked all kinds of music, but he had a particular passion for jazz. Renee and her little helper assembled a nice collection of music for Andrew, including the complete works of Miles Davis. It was just personal enough, she felt. She had never actually given Andrew a present before.

Renee was not used to giving presents to men at all, other than her father and her brothers-in-law. And she sadly reflected that she hadn't given too much to her father in recent years. Since he had upped and left her mother some years before, Renee's contacts with him were sporadic and uncomfortable. Renee had been Daddy's girl, too, so his defection had hurt doubly, even though she was an adult when it occurred. When she thought about her mother and how painfully empty her life had become after her father's defection, she would invariably tense up. This was one of the very reasons that she was the way she was in relationships, due to the cold, stark fear of being abandoned the way her mother had been.

Standing in the card section of Target, Renee wanted to slap herself silly. She and Yolanda had been working on these issues for so long, and she was about to lose it in Target because she had bought a few CDs for a nice man. She found herself repeating some of Yolanda's words of wisdom to keep her in the moment.

"It is her life, not yours. Every story does not have a sad ending or a happy one. You write your own ending. Each situation is different. You deserve happiness," she murmured. And out of the blue came another thought. "Andrew would never, ever hurt me," she said aloud. It was absurd to be having startling flashes of insight in a discount store. Renee realized it didn't matter when the knowledge came, as long as it got there.

The combination welcome-home and birthday party qualified as a complete success, except for the grating presence of Dana Pierson. At least, that was Andrew's opinion. The woman was fast on her way to becoming a pest. In a burst of prescience Andrew had cornered his younger brother Adam and asked him to perform a huge favor. The two men were in the side yard of the huge house occupied by their brother Andre and his wife, Tina.

"Adam, please keep this woman off me today. No matter what you have to do, stay between the two of us, okay? Use all of your so-called charm and keep her occupied," Andrew pleaded.

Adam was vastly amused. He was the next-to-youngest Cochran brother and derived the standard amount of entertainment from his brother's romantic life. Although Andrew didn't currently have a romantic life that Adam knew of, so he didn't see what the big deal was.

"Okay, so she's this reporter that you won't see too much of anyway, she lives in California. So what's the problem?" he asked. "I'm not saying I won't do it, I just want to know why I am being forced to prostitute myself in this manner," he finished grandly.

It was a mark of how serious Andrew was that he did not even pay attention to the prostitute comment. He was totally honest with Adam. "It's because I don't want her up in my face making Renee uncomfortable. They didn't take to each other too well, for one thing, and Dana has the wrong idea about me, for another. I have no interest in her at all."

Adam was too stunned to speak for a moment. "You . . . and *Renee*? Renee Kemp? The same Renee that you have been fighting with for years? *That* Renee?"

Andrew nodded. "Yes, that Renee. And I'd appreciate it if you kept your mouth shut. We're just kind of keeping it between us for right now."

"I don't know, Bunchy; that's a mighty big secret to keep. I mean, this is some fascinating news, bro. If word of this got out, it'd make for some good gossip for weeks and weeks," he mused.

Andrew squinted at Adam. "I might've known you couldn't be trusted. What do you want, you opportunist?"

Adam pretended to think for a moment. Then, as if it had just occurred to him, he snapped his fingers and said brightly, "The use of your car. One week for blocking Dana, and one week for keeping my mouth shut."

Andrew groaned, because he knew it would mean that he would be driving Adam's Range Rover for two weeks. As an architect and builder, Adam needed something roomy to carry around loads of necessary tools. As a Cochran, he needed to do it with style. Unfortunately, the style and beauty of the SUV was lost in the fact that it rode as though it was on the plains of the Serengeti, where it belonged. Andrew hated it. He was about to start bargaining anew when Donnie, their youngest brother, joined them.

Adam seized the advantage by jumping in with both feet.

"Donnie, guess what? Andrew is letting me use his car for two weeks. Isn't that nice of him?" he asked innocently.

Donnie looked from brother to brother. "What's he got on you, man? You should have come to me—I'd have only kept it for a week."

Andrew shook his head in despair and started around the corner of the house. "Just do what I asked you to do and there won't be any trouble." Adam just laughed his butt off, to Donnie's mystification.

And due to everyone's best efforts, there were very few rough spots. It was a most congenial group that convened in the beautifully arranged backyard setting. It was mostly immediate family—Big Benny Cochran, his lovely fiancée, Martha, Bennie and Clay, and Alan and Andre, the other Cochran twins, and their wives and children. Renee rounded out the group, with Donnie and Adam. Donnie had a date, Aneesah. Other than that, the only person without a family connection was Dana. She was not the least bit shy about it, either. Renee did not revise her Safari Barbie assessment of Miss Dana one iota when she showed up in an animal print short set and the variety of laced sandal that used to be in vogue some years before. They were apparently making a comeback.

Renee, on the other hand, was cool and lovely in a constructed sundress that bared her shoulders and back while revealing only a hint of cleavage. It was an unusual shade of jade green, and the tight bodice flowed smoothly down to her hips before flaring out into a full skirt that was almost ankle length. The straps met behind her neck in a bow that was as feminine as it was sexy. Andrew tortured himself all afternoon by imagining the bow coming loose in his hand. She also had on a pair of little mules with French heels, the kind that accentuated her ankles and drove Andrew mad. And she smelled divine, as usual.

Renee was looking luscious enough to distract Andrew from the food, which was quite a feat. He was a dedicated omnivore, as was the rest of his family. He would eat everything, although that was not difficult with the array of appetizing dishes that were served. There was grilled chicken and smoked brisket, as well as fresh green beans cooked Southern style with onions and new potatoes. There was also potato salad and coleslaw, as well as fruit salad and sliced tomatoes. Andrew was particularly partial to the fried corn and coleslaw, both of which Renee had made. He said as much to her, surprising her with his knowledge of her cooking.

"Yours just tastes different, that's all. Nobody makes it quite the way you do," he said honestly.

Renee was touched that he had noticed. She was a good country cook when she got in the kitchen, which wasn't often. The look of gratitude and satisfaction on Andrew's face gave her the notion that cooking more often might not be a bad habit to cultivate.

Dana did her best to monopolize Andrew's attention, but she was failing miserably. Not only was Adam running interference as promised, but Andrew had eyes only for Renee. At every opportunity he was cornering her in the kitchen or the sun porch or some other secluded place trying to kiss her. It was silly—sweet and overheated in the way of a teenage romance. Renee kept laughing and pushing him away, but every time his hands or lips connected with her body, she would fairly sizzle. Thankfully, no one seemed to notice their frequent absences, except eagle-eyed Dana.

If Adam had been truly interested in Dana, he would have found her distraction annoying. Adam was as tall and handsome as the rest of his brothers, and downright sexy with his hair in a long ponytail. He was arguably the most creative of the Cochrans and certainly the most avant-garde in appearance. But Dana was not interested. She had apparently set her cap for Andrew and was not about to take no for an answer. She finally managed to break away from Adam and insinuate herself into a position at the table where Renee and Andrew were playing cards with Aneesah and Donnie.

Donnie made the forgivable but regrettable mistake of asking Dana what she did for a living, and Dana was happy to regale them with tale after tale of her glamorous life. Renee gritted her teeth silently and tried to ignore the woman. But Dana wasn't having it. After having told every "Dana Pierson, Girl Reporter" story she could come up with, she turned to Renee and asked her what she did for a living. Renee looked at her through her dark glasses, which she had hastily put on so that her disdain would not be visible. Dana knew perfectly well that she owned Urban Oasis—Renee had heard Bennie telling her so the previous day. What was she trying to prove? After Renee referenced the spa, she got her answer.

Dana leaned forward and conspiratorially touched Andrew's arm. "Well, you two are just polar opposites, aren't you? I mean, Andrew rebuilds people's faces and gives them a whole new life, and you give them a temporary illusion of beauty. Isn't that ironic?" she trilled.

Renee could feel a slow burning starting in her chest and it had nothing to do with indigestion. Out-and-out rudeness was a difficult thing to deal with. On the one hand, she did not want to whack the woman in front of witnesses. On the other, she wasn't good at the kind of polished retort that Bennie would use—Bennie could rip a person's legs off verbally and they would smile and say thank you when she was done. Renee was opening her mouth to reply when Faye, Alan's wife, came over to tell them that the cake was being brought out. *Saved by a pound cake* was all Renee could think. She knew beyond a shadow of a doubt that if she had spoken her mind, little Miss Safari Barbie would have been as dead as if she had been attacked by a jungle predator.

After blowing out the token two candles on the cake and opening presents, Andrew was ready to call it a day. He loved his family dearly and was truly pleased with the party, but he wanted to be alone with Renee. He waited until he saw her heading into the kitchen with an empty pitcher and followed her.

"Meet me at my house in about an hour? Please?" He breathed into her ear as he kissed her along her neck.

All the tension of the Dana incident eased as she felt his soft lips on her nape. "Well"—she pretended to think about it—"I guess I could manage to stop by in a while." She lowered her lashes and smiled.

"An hour?" he repeated, kissing her temple.

"Half hour," she whispered. "Maybe fifteen minutes if you keep doing that."

And once again they were kissing wildly, this time observed by three inquisitive sets of eyes.

Lillian turned to her brothers with a look of satisfaction. "I tol' you. They *were* kissin'. They're in love, but it's a *secret.*"

Seven

Out of the mouths of babes often come the most profound truths. Renee wasn't ready to give her relationship with Andrew a name, but it was certainly fulfilling. What had transpired the day of the party at his duplex was the true beginning of whatever was going on between them. Renee had arrived at Andrew's home bearing another gift, this time a homemade pound cake. Andrew was particularly passionate about pound cake in general and Renee's specifically. When she made the cake for the party, she had made another one just for him. She presented it to him with a flourish and a bottle of champagne for them to enjoy later.

Andrew was moved by the sweet gesture, but then again, he had been moved by the entire day. He told Renee that it was the nicest birthday that he could remember, and it was because she was celebrating it with him. The simple words put a huge smile on her face, one that she did not bother to disguise. Maybe it was because of their long history or because of all her hard work with Yolanda, but Renee was finding it very easy to connect with Andrew. They went to sit out on the deck that he had built in the back of the duplex.

The huge deck offered a lot of privacy, since there was a high partition between the two back doors. So each tenant had an opportunity to relax and enjoy a portion of the nicely kept backyard without worrying about disturbing or being disturbed by a neighbor. Andrew seldom used the yard, due to his overcommitted schedule, so this was a rare treat for him. Plus, his tenant was out of town, which made it all the nicer. It was just he and Renee with his new CDs playing softly and the sweet summer evening surrounding them. They were sitting side by side in a huge Adirondack-style recliner, which was extremely comfortable as well as intimate. Andrew was playing with Renee's hand, enjoying the feel of her long, cool fingers entwined with his.

"I want to ask you a question about something that's probably none of my business," he said. "In fact, I know it's not my business, but I want to know the answer anyway. Is that offensive?"

Renee was feeling so mellow that she just shrugged. "Go ahead and ask. If I don't want to tell you, I won't," was all she said.

Andrew plunged ahead. "Okay, then, I got the impression that you were not comfortable around Dana. You know me well enough to know that I would have no lasting interest in someone like that, so it's kind of hard for me to believe that you were jealous, flattering though that may be." He paused to wince, since Renee elbowed him sharply just about then.

"What I want to know, Renee, is what was going on in that convoluted little mind of yours regarding Dana?" Andrew asked curiously.

Renee sighed briefly. Normally she would have told him that he was full of it and refused to answer such a demeaning question, but for some reason she was willing to discuss it with him.

"Okay, Andrew, since you asked, I'll tell you. I didn't like Dana—not at all—but not because of you, at least not completely. I despised her because she has my dream job, the one I went to school to study for and the one that I couldn't get because I don't look like her," Renee said frankly.

She went on to explain how she had graduated with honors and done everything possible to be the best reporter in the business, but she wasn't considered marketable because of her appearance. "That's what it all boiled down to—I wasn't cute enough to be on television," Renee finished ruefully. "And when you came sauntering home with Miss Paper Bag Perfection on your arm—well, it was just a bit much to take."

Andrew was silent for a moment while he took it all in. There was definitely more to Renee than met the eye. When he finally could speak, he said words that came straight from his heart.

"Renee, I hope you realize that you are way beyond cute. You're exactly what God had in mind when he invented beauty," Andrew said, pulling her closer to him. "I think it's terrible that you were victimized by that kind of prejudice, but you certainly didn't let it keep you down. You have a great career, you know. You're so smart and talented that you could do anything you chose to do and do it well," he added.

Renee was warmed by his words, but she could not resist pointing out that the lovely Dana had a different take on the situation. "According to her, all I do is paint people up for a few hours. And compared to what you do, it really is insignificant," she said honestly. "I mean, there is no comparison between running a spa for pampered women and giving a person a chance at a normal life."

Andrew shook Renee slightly to emphasize his next words. "There shouldn't be any comparison! Look at my family—we each do something different. Andre and Alan practice law, Bennie writes and runs the radio stations, Donnie's in marketing and Adam is an architect. Does that mean that I'm somehow a god because I chose to study medicine? No, it means that we are each lucky enough to pursue careers that we find interesting. And I have to admit that I don't find news reporting to be that edifying," he added.

Renee looked shocked while Andrew expounded on the theme of media hype and overload and the impossibility of finding honest, unbiased reporting. They debated amicably for a while and Renee admitted that what she really missed was the opportunity to travel. She had to agree with Andrew on the larger picture, which was that news reporting was not the noble endeavor it was at one time—it seemed more like a circus. Which brought Renee back to what she felt was a very salient point—if he was so *not* crazy about Dana, why was he accompanying her to a wedding?

Andrew looked bemused and confessed that he did not know. "I don't remember her asking me, although she might have on the plane when I was half asleep. All I know is that somehow I agreed to go, I guess, so I can't back out of it. You are still going, aren't you?" he demanded with a hint of panic in his voice.

Renee demurred for a moment before committing to being there on the following Saturday. "After her charming invitation to 'tag along,' how could I not? Besides, if she lays a paw on you, her little butt is mine," Renee growled.

Andrew was delighted with her answer. "You know, she had a lot of nerve making a crack about your spa," he remarked. " 'Cause that woman owes a lot to a surgeon's knife."

Renee was delighted with that information, but even more delighted when all conversation stopped and a different form of communication started. There was no pressure, just promise and sweetness and fire in the kisses that she and Andrew exchanged. The fact that she was boiling inside was no one's concern but her own, she felt.

She did have to share the news with Yolanda, though. Yolanda knew immediately that something was up with Renee as soon as she floated into her office. Yolanda worked out of her home in a large brownstone house. Part of the first level had been converted into office space for her clients, but it still retained the warmth and charm of a home. The deeply cushioned sofa and love seat had seen many breakthroughs and breakdowns in their day. The pumpkin-colored walls with the deep green and brick red accents of the pillows and area rugs made the space feel like a safe haven.

And it had been a haven for Renee for many months now, something for which she was profoundly grateful—so grateful, in fact, that she brought Yolanda a nice bouquet of wildflowers. Yolanda was pleasantly surprised by Renee's impulsive gesture. Renee was truly blossoming, she thought. In the not too distant past, it would have never occurred to Renee to do something like that "just because." And now, without even thinking about it, she had done something sweet and generous for fun. The changes did not stop with the gesture, either. Renee was positively glowing and eager to talk about the events of the past week or so.

"Yolanda, Yolanda. It's just like that George Gershwin song—'How Long Has This Been Going On?' I have been having fun, actual fun with a man. With *the* man, with Andrew Cochran, of all people. I feel like I'm sixteen again. No, better than sixteen, because my skin is clear and I don't have a curfew." She sighed happily.

Yolanda gave her a smile to encourage further discussion. Renee told her about Andrew coming home early, about Safari Barbie and their frank discussion on her reaction to Dana and so on. Yolanda was particularly interested in that aspect of their talk.

"So did you feel any real jealousy toward Dana as a woman? Was all your rancor due to the fact that she, as you put it, has your job?" Yolanda asked quietly.

Renee did not have to hesitate on that one. "Well, I have never dealt with jealousy well. I am not one who likes a crowded playing field. In fact, I prefer it if the field is fixed in my favor, to be honest," she said ruefully. "I guess it stems from when I was chubby and I had bad skin. I was not about to put myself in a position to have to compete with another woman. When I went out with a boy, I had to be the only one or there was no go.

"Which is probably the reason I started dating older men after . . . well, you know. Much older men who were fascinated by me were the only ones I would date. I was sure I could keep their attention because they were, let's say . . . *thrilled* to have a younger woman on their arm." Renee stopped and sighed reflectively.

"That's not terribly nice, but it is accurate. But I have to say that despite the obvious physical difference between me and Dana, I was not the least worried about her being able to get her hooks into Andrew. Isn't that amazing?" She turned her eyes to Yolanda to gauge her reaction. But before Yolanda could speak, Renee had to fill her in on the most telling part of the adventure, the long-dreaded wedding of Dana's cousin Deirdre.

Two days before the big event, Renee had just escorted one of her private clients to the discreet side entrance of Urban Oasis when she realized she had a visitor. Dana was standing in the reception area of the salon wearing a little Miu-Miu summer frock looking, to Renee, like a lost teenager. Renee was wearing some comfortable Prada flats and a chic DKNY shirt and trousers that made her look cool, comfortable and in charge, which, of course, she was.

"Dana, how . . . odd to see you. Is there something I can do for you?" Renee asked politely.

Dana looked Rene up and down. "Well, I was just in the neighborhood, so I decided to stop by to say hello. You are still coming to the wedding, aren't you?" she asked breezily.

Renee was equally breezy in her reply. "Oh, yes, I certainly am. How could I refuse such a gracious invitation, after all? I'm so looking forward to it."

"So are Andrew and I," confided Dana. "It's going to be such fun for us to be together that night. After what we shared in Haiti . . . well, you know that kind of passion just does not disappear. We are so looking forward to rekindling it. He's been so busy this week, just getting back and all, but that will all be over this weekend." She practically purred.

She winked at Renee and turned to leave, but not before reminding Renee that it was a *formal* wedding.

Renee stared at Dana's retreating figure. *I think the little wench just told me how to dress,* she mused. Instead of getting angry, Renee got a huge smile on her face. This was going to be fun. Big fun.

Renee decided not to attend the wedding, just the reception. It was tacky enough to be going to a wedding to settle a score; she wasn't going to compound her sins by gawking at strangers taking vows. Regardless of what she felt about marriage in general, it was someone else's special day and she was going to be as discreet as possible. Up to a point, that was. While she was getting dressed, she reflected on her decision to attend. She had to admit that it had gone beyond her irritation at "Dana Pierson, Girl Reporter" and had segued into some kind of validation of self. That little ocher witch actually thought that she could intimidate Renee "Miss Thing" Kemp with her store-bought boobs and expensively weaved hair. Maybe she could have, in Renee's youth. No question, after the Newark debacle when Renee was lost, lonely and hiding out, she could have; but not now and certainly not tonight.

Renee took an extra long time in the tub that evening. She adored her claw-footed bathtub because she could fill it up to her shoulders and luxuriate in bubbles as long as she liked. Finally, thoroughly scented with Annick Goutal bath gel, she came out of the tub, lightly patted herself dry and creamed and lotioned her body with the same scent. Renee brushed her glossy black hair off her forehead to draw attention to her face. She applied a bare minimum of makeup with the exception of mascara to bring out her fabulous eyes.

She sprayed on a cloud of Annick Goutal, slipped on her dress and a pair of scandalous Dolce & Gabbana evening sandals that were little more than glittering wisps on three-inch heels. Renee surveyed herself in her three-way full-length mirror. Her one accessory was a theatrical pair of vintage earrings. They were constructed of crystal beads and

a delicate fan of pink feathers and were outrageously feminine. They had belonged to Renee's aunt who was once a
dancer at the legendary Cotton Club in Harlem. With a satisfied nod to her reflection, Renee picked up her tiny
evening bag and turned off the lights before leaving. *Fasten
your seat belts,* she thought. *It's going to be a bumpy ride.*

Renee walked toward Andrew with the air of a queen allowing homage to be paid her. She had a slightly amused
expression, due to the ripple of activity that seemed to follow in her wake. Indeed, there was an odd moment when
two waiters collided after discovering that her dress had no
back whatsoever. Luckily, only a few glasses actually broke
and most of them were not filled at the time. Renee was totally unrepentant, though. When she reached Andrew, she
merely smiled. "Let's see, chaos, panic and disorder. I think
my work here is done," she said with amusement.

Andrew was overcome by admiration. "Damn, you look
beautiful. Absolutely gorgeous." He kissed her on both
cheeks and walked around her, giving a low wolf whistle
when he saw the back of her dress. "Hot damn! Where did
you get this dress from, Renee?"

Rene raised an eyebrow. She was not about to tell him
that the dress had come from his sister's closet. Bennie had
the dress made to let Clay know that she meant business
and it had worked admirably for her, so Renee decided to
see if the charm would hold. It apparently had, because
Andrew was looking at her like she was the only woman
in the known universe. The only thing that was better than
the enraptured look on Andrew's face was the look of dis-
may that riddled little Dana's countenance.

When the bridal party finally arrived and was situated
at the enormous head table, Dana had craned her head
frantically trying to locate Andrew. When she finally
found him seated with Renee, her stomach actually turned
over. Andrew was wearing the unmistakable look of a man

deeply smitten, and Dana was at least bright enough to realize that the look was not for her. As soon as was humanly possible, she hustled over to their table to break up their little clinch. Dana was also wearing pink, as was the rest of the bridal party. Unhappily, it was not the subtle, sensuous pastel of Renee's frock. Hers was the resounding, bilious hue most often seen in bottles of Pepto-Bismol, and it was presented in taffeta and ruffles, no less. Deirdre, it seemed, adhered to the thinking that the bridesmaid should never look as good as the bride. The frightening antebellum outfits she chose for her attendants made sure of that.

Dana was not to be denied, however. She did everything short of throwing herself into Andrew's lap to get his attention, all to no avail. For her part, Renee was sweetly gracious, which seemed to enrage Dana. Every time Renee would attempt to engage her in conversation, Dana would snap and snarl, giving her all the charm of a rabid schnauzer. This amused Renee very much, which was like splashing kerosene on a barbecue. Every polite comment just set Dana off again. Much of this byplay was lost on Andrew, who was too busy drooling over Renee to pay Dana's antics any attention. Finally Dana resorted to international subterfuge, which was a huge mistake on her part.

Leaning over to Renee, Dana hissed at her in French. "You are a great big cow with the face of a dog. You look like a slut in that dress and you're way too black to be wearing pink, you tramp." Dana was unaware that her face had taken on an ugly red hue, which was really nasty-looking with the pink *shmatte* from hell.

Renee's face took on a look of total bemusement. She did not even bother to raise her voice when she responded to Dana. "You are a very pathetic and strange woman. You would do well to wipe the foam off your mouth and tuck in that bra strap because you are making a fool of yourself. And the next time you want to go to battle, bring weapons other than your wit and charm because you are pitifully unarmed," she said in perfect French. Dana's mouth fell open with shock.

By now, even Andrew knew that something was amiss and decided a discreet retreat was in order. He stood, bowed to the table, pulled out Renee's chair and escorted her out, trying very hard not to laugh as he did so. They made it almost all the way to valet parking before he let loose.

"Damn, that was fun. I would have paid to see that. Renee, you are better than guerrilla theater." He sighed as he wiped away tears of laughter. "My place or yours?" he added as they waited for their cars to be brought around.

Renee looked over at Yolanda and was bashfully pleased at Yolanda's look of total admiration. After a moment of silence Yolanda actually rose and gave Renee a bow before giving her a hand.

"Brava, Renee, Brava! What a lot of ground you have covered! I am so very pleased. You have taken some tremendous steps lately. You have allowed a man of your age to befriend you, to show admiration and desire and you have been able to reciprocate that desire," Yolanda said, counting off Renee's triumphs on her fingertips.

"You were able to discuss a very meaningful and painful part of your past and you were able to confront a romantic rival with panache and wit. Two years ago, none of this would have happened, Renee. Even a year ago, these things would simply not have been possible. You are making wonderful progress," Yolanda said warmly. She stopped talking long enough to really look at Renee, who was looking slightly uncomfortable; she wasn't basking in the aura of approval that Yolanda was creating.

"Okay, Renee, what's going on in that clever little mind of yours? You don't seem to be as thrilled as I am with all your progress." Yolanda tilted her head into a listening pose to encourage Renee to speak.

As was her habit, Renee stood and started fidgeting

around the office before answering. Yolanda was dead on the money when she recognized that Renee was not entirely happy with what had been going on in her life. Yes, she was having a ball with Andrew. Yes, it was free and easy and sweet and fun, but it was just a little bit too free and easy. Things just did not happen like that of their own accord, at least not in Renee's life. Things happened for her when she made them happen, when she was the one pulling the strings and writing the script. This was just too spontaneous and wonderful; something was bound to go wrong. And besides, where was it all going to end up? Renee finally turned to Yolanda with a face full of despair.

"Yolanda, suppose I'm just kidding myself. Suppose I'm never going to get past . . . you know. I think things are just going too fast, is all. I don't know if I'm ready for anything else," Renee whispered. "I don't know if I ever will be," she added.

She put down the carved African figurine she was clutching and finally wandered back over to the sofa, where she sat down, scrunching herself in the corner and barricading herself with a large throw pillow. She looked at Yolanda with huge, wanting eyes, silently pleading for redemption. Yolanda leaned forward and took her hands.

"Renee, rape is a terrible ordeal. The fact that you were raped by a colleague, someone you trusted and admired is even more shattering. Whether it happened ten days ago or ten years ago like yours is immaterial. There is no statute of limitations on how long you suffer from something like that." Yolanda tightened her grip on Renee's hands and continued to speak in a soothing voice.

"When you first came to me, it was because you said you were tired of being a victim. Tired of suffering in silence, right? You had carried that burden alone for so many years that you were finally worn out from it. You were done with the pain and you wanted to learn how to live again. Well, that's what you're doing right now. It's like learning how to ride a bicycle all over again. Right now, it's like you just took off the training wheels, but you still feel a little shaky. That's normal; that's understandable. But you will be able to ride that bike again—I truly believe that. Down the street, up the street and maybe around the block a time or two. And before you know it, you'll be training for a triathlon, girl. And I'll be cheering you on!"

Renee's eyes filled with tears of gratitude for Yolanda's comforting words. She always seemed to know what to say to keep her on the right path. She even laughed a little as she wiped away the tears. Bicycle riding, huh? Little did Yolanda know, Renee had once been the two-wheeled ten-speed champion of Chateau Avenue in Cleveland, Ohio. And if Yolanda believed in her, she could do it again, even with a slightly different context. She might even pop a wheelie or two before it was over.

Eight

Although Renee was poised on the brink of uncertainty, Andrew was having the time of his life. It seemed as though Renee had filled an empty hole that Andrew had not known existed. In some ways he rued the years they had wasted picking on each other like grade-school children; in other ways he was profoundly grateful that they had spent so many years being acquainted. There were so many things they knew about each other, so many things they understood. He knew that Renee was a demon tennis player, was good with children and loved old black-and-white movies, theater and the blues. He knew that she was allergic to lobster, adored jelly beans and would run screaming at the sight of any many-legged creature. He even knew about her penchant for counting her fingers when she was concentrating. She would touch her fingers to her thumb one at a time, starting with her pinkie and ending with her index finger. She would do this over and over again, as if to reassure herself that they were all still attached.

He adored all these little quirks because they were familiar and uniquely her. But even after knowing her for seventeen years, there were still aspects of Renee that were new and surprising. One day he was finishing his rounds at the Children's Hospital when he looked down the hall and thought he saw Renee. *Couldn't have been her,* he thought, but was moved to check it out. He sprinted down the corridor just in time to see a tall, shapely form round a corner and head purposefully for the nursery. Before he could catch her, she was inside and a colleague waylaid him. Breaking away as soon as possible, he went into the nursery and looked around. His eyes widened in shock and he stood completely still to observe.

Sitting in a large rocking chair, Renee was cuddling a tiny infant. Oblivious to everything around her except her tiny charge, Renee was rocking the fretful infant and humming a soft lullaby to calm the baby's nerves. How long he stood there, Andrew did not know, but one of the pediatric nurses spotted him and inquired if he needed any help.

"Hmm? Oh, no," Andrew said distractedly. "I just saw a friend of mine and I was kind of surprised, is all." The nurse followed his line of vision to Renee and smiled broadly.

"Oh, so you know Miss Kemp? Such a nice lady! She's been one of our rockers for about two years now. And she's one of our very best, too," the nurse added as she left Andrew standing there, still in shock.

Andrew knew that the problem of abandoned babies was growing, as was the influx of babies born with chemical addictions and other problems that would cause them to be detained in the hospital for extended periods. He also knew that there were volunteers who came in just to rock the babies and handle them so that they would have some semblance of normality in their lives. Touch therapy was crucial in the development of these infants and the volunteers were godsends. Andrew had no idea, though, that Renee was one of them. She had never mentioned the fact that she did volunteer work of any kind. He was totally touched by the sight of her, rocking away.

He was tactful enough to leave, but canny enough to just happen by the area when it was time for her to leave. He looked down at her with his best poker face and said something trite about how funny it was to run into her. Before she could put two and two together, he hastened to ask her to have dinner with him.

"I'll even let you pay," he joked lamely. Luckily, Renee was in a good mood.

"Okay, that would be a novelty at that. So what'll it be? White Castle? Mickey D's? You name it and it's yours." She grinned.

"Oh, damn, Renee, that's cold. But it's okay. I could go for some sliders," he said, using the local endearment for the horrid little square gut bombs from White Castle. "Just let me check on one patient and we're off."

Taking her arm with no self-consciousness at all, Andrew led her up to the surgical floor so that he could check on his favorite patient, a little boy named Harry. Harry was on his sixth operation to repair second- and third-degree burns, the result of an arson fire in which his father and brother had perished. Harry's mother had two other children at home and to say that life was difficult for them was an understatement. Andrew checked on Harry often because he was such a sweet, brave little boy who never complained. That evening Harry had a bit of a fever, though.

"Dr. Andy, could I have a Pepsi, please?" he asked plaintively. His little face was swathed in gauze, as were his hands and arms. Harry had bravely endured the surgeries and had years more to look forward to.

"Sure, you can have a Pepsi, kiddo," said Andrew. He turned to the nurse and requested that she bring the child one. Andrew could not help noticing that the woman turned beet red at the request. "Is there a problem, Nurse?"

"Well, no, not exactly. It's just that we don't stock Pepsi on the floors anymore. His family would have to get it from the vending machine because . . . We have fruit juice, though; I can get him some of that," she said quickly.

"That's what they said before." Harry sighed. "It's okay."

Andrew looked down at the boy's tiny figure lying in the antiseptic room and then at the nurse, who was wringing her hands in anxiety. Without a word he handed the nurse a dollar bill. "You'll have your Pepsi in a couple of minutes, kiddo. Now, you hang in there and Dr. Andy will be back tomorrow. And if you need anything else, you let the nurse know, okay?" Harry nodded happily and Andrew gave him a wink before leaving the room.

He walked right by Renee, who was patiently sitting in the visitors' area, and went behind the nurses' station to speak with the charge nurse. In clipped tones, with no words wasted, he let her know exactly what time it was.

"This is a fifty-dollar bill. You are to purchase as much Pepsi as this will buy. You are to keep it available for that child and whenever he wants one he can have it, do you understand me? Do not ever let me hear that one of my patients was denied something because it had to come out of a vending machine, or because some family member did not bring it. You have my pager, my cellular phone number, my answering service and my home telephone number, as well as several office numbers. Unless I am in surgery, I am always reachable. Always. Since the only kind of humanity that seems to be understood here is that which is on the chart, I am officially making it a part of my standing orders for this child. Do I make myself clear?"

Andrew had not raised his voice, but he was so cold and unyielding that the nurse feared for her life if she answered him. Dr. Cochran was always so easy to get along with; she had no idea how she was supposed to react. Luckily, he did not linger. Making a few notations on the chart, he carefully laid it down on the counter as if he could not trust himself not to throw it across the room. Abruptly he turned and left the area heading for the bank of elevators without looking back, not even for Renee.

When she realized that Andrew had forgotten her, Renee scrambled to her feet and took off after him. Ordinarily, she would have been madder than a wet hen, but she could see that something had affected Andrew deeply. In all the years she had known him, she had never seen Andrew so angry and it was clear that he was furious. She caught up to him at the elevators and touched his arm.

"Hey. Going my way?" was all she said. Andrew looked

down at her with a look of complete befuddlement, as if to say "What are you doing here?" Then he remembered that they were supposed to be having dinner together.

"Renee, I'm sorry. Tonight might not be such a good night after all," he began.

Renee put her arm through his and shook her head. "Oh, no you don't. Tonight is a perfect night for this." They got on the elevator and rode down to his office and collected his sport coat and briefcase, leaving his white coat behind. They did all this without saying a word, Renee because she had no idea what to say and Andrew because he was utterly spent. When they reached the parking lot, however, Renee's pragmatic good sense had kicked in. She took charge of the situation in her usual fashion.

"Okay, here's the deal. You go home and take a shower and get comfortable. By the time you get out of the shower, I will be there with dinner. You will relax and have a glass of wine while I set the table and then you will have a very relaxing evening with a first-rate companion." Without giving him a chance to answer, she pulled him down to her eye level and kissed him sweetly. "Thirty minutes, I'm walking in the door, so please let's not have a repeat of Memorial Day, okay?" She finally got a smile out of him.

Andrew looked down at Renee with affection and thanks. He was terribly glad for her presence, but he still tried a lame joke. "Yeah, but suppose I'm not dressed when you get there? Are you going to hide in a closet again or take advantage of me?" he drawled.

"Don't go there, Andy. You could not handle me tonight, trust me," Renee said dryly.

Andrew laughed, not realizing the wealth of truth in Renee's statement. Already feeling better, he got into his car and took off for home.

It was amazing what a difference a few hours could make. Now Andrew was relaxed, well fed and completely happy. Renee was true to her word and in about a half hour she had appeared at his duplex with a large carton that gave off an extremely enticing aroma. She had gone to a restaurant that specialized in home cooking for hapless yuppies and gotten a carryout meal of some of his favorite foods: roast chicken, mashed potatoes with a hint of garlic, fresh mixed vegetables and a green salad, plus a nice blueberry pie for dessert. She and Andrew both had a weakness for blueberries. She had even stopped off to get Breyers vanilla ice cream, the only commercially prepared ice cream that Andrew would consume. Andrew was overcome at her thoughtfulness. This was yet another surprising side of Renee.

Once she was able to get his blood sugar back to normal with a good meal and get his disposition back to its normal temperate range, she was ready to find out what had him so angry at the hospital. A favorite Michael Franks CD was playing softly in the background and Andrew was lying on his massive sofa with his head in Renee's lap. She was softly stroking his temples and massaging his scalp. He was practically purring with contentment when Renee started probing.

"Andrew. What got you so upset today, honey? I don't think it was just the incident with the Pepsi," she stated quietly. Andrew sighed deeply. With his eyes still closed, he began to speak.

"You're right, it wasn't just the thing about the Pepsi, although God knows I wish people would use common sense sometimes. Earlier today, I had a consultation with a young couple about their son. They have been waiting months for this appointment, because you know how backed up I am for new patients. And they wanted elective surgery, which I do not do. This couple—young, well-off—has a beautiful son, four years old. Absolutely beautiful child, perfectly healthy. The child has Down Syndrome, and he has the facial characteristics of a Down child. These people wanted me to surgically alter this child's face so that he wouldn't look like a retard anymore," Andrew finished sadly.

Renee was horrified. "Andy! Did they really say 'retard'?"

Andrew admitted that they had not. "But they may as well have said it. I was as calm as I could be, given the circumstances. I didn't cuss them out or throw them out of my office. I didn't even show them pictures of some of my most difficult cases and tell them to get their sorry asses to a church to pray for forgiveness for being so damned shallow and empty-headed. I explained that this was not the kind of work I did and suggested that they get another consultation from their original doctor.

"They admitted that their doctor had referred them to someone else, but they wanted me because I am the best. I told them that I did not think that this kind of surgery was in the best interest of the child and urged them to consider their options very carefully before doing anything rash. Then they left. And the sad thing, Renee, is that I think they genuinely do love their child. They were not deliberately being cruel and stupid; they have just bought into the whole idea of beauty like everyone else has. They really think that their child will be better off in life if he looks like something other than what he is—a sweet, healthy child with challenges." Andrew sighed again, and it seemed to come from the depths of his soul.

He sat up then and swung his legs around so that he was sitting next to Renee. He looked at her with a bleak expression and went on: "It was just bad timing that made me have to check on Harry after they left. When I saw that sweet little kid, and thought about how much pain he's in and how even after twelve surgeries he is going to look like a jigsaw puzzle, I just kind of lost it. These people want to buy a new face for their kid just because they can, and poor Harry couldn't even get a damned Pepsi. I snapped," he admitted.

"I just hope those nurses can forgive me," he mused. "You think flowers will do it, or should I treat them all to lunch?"

Renee was so flooded with emotion she could barely speak. "I think they'd like lunch a lot, Andy," she whispered. She locked her arms around his neck and just held on tight.

Renee was amazed at the feelings that she was experiencing. She had such affection for Andrew at that moment that she could hardly breathe. All she wanted was to take all of his pain away, just absorb it into her body so that he wouldn't feel it any more. They sat with their arms wrapped around each other for a long time, saying nothing. Gradually the warm and loving feelings turned into something else. It's hard to say who moved first, but their arms were no longer locked around each other, they were stroking each other with growing passion.

Renee's face was no longer buried in Andrew's neck; she was rubbing against his cheek. She loved the way his beard felt against her skin; she moaned softly and then sighed as he stroked it down her neck. Somehow she found herself in his lap and they were kissing with abandon. Renee's fingers were buried in his hair as their lips and tongues were dancing over each other in a wet swirl of sensation, which was simply amazing. She pulled away from his lips just long enough to sink her teeth gently into his lower lip and pull it into her mouth.

"You have the sweetest mouth in the world," she whispered, sighing, before kissing him again. Renee was absolutely lost. She could not ever remember feeling so much passion—she simply didn't think she was capable. And yet, in Andrew's arms she was on fire. Andrew seemed to know just how to hold her, just how to kiss her to make everything wonderful. Even when his long, clever hands slid from her waist and traveled up past her rib cage to her breasts, she didn't panic. Her breath came out in a soft burst of air and she sighed his name: "Andy . . ."

Even after her blouse was undone and he had his hands on the clasp of her bra, Renee did not react, except to move closer to his warm hands and his hot body. But when the clasp was undone and Andrew lowered his head to her breast, Renee started trembling all over. *Oh, my God, what am I doing?* she thought. Andrew immediately felt the change in her and raised his head, with a look of concern.

"Am I hurting you, Renee? Is this too soon, too fast, too anything?" he asked, baffled by the look on her face. She wasn't moving, wasn't speaking, and he had no idea what was wrong. She wasn't fighting him, but she wasn't exactly participating, either.

Just then, a beeper sounded. Renee was off his lap like a frog on a hot plate. Grabbing her Coach bag, she looked at the pager clipped to the strap. With every indication of relief she announced that it was her pager.

"It's the alarm company—something is wrong at Urban Oasis," she said hastily as she made a quick job of buttoning everything up. "I have to go meet the police, so I'll be going now. I'll talk to you later," she said as she made for the door.

Andrew's long arm braced the door shut and he looked at her as if she had lost all her reason. "Renee, it is late and you are not going down there alone. Are you crazy? I'm coming with you," he said in a tone that suggested she not argue.

Feebly she countered, "But, Andy, I do it all the time. Bennie and I both do, it's no big deal."

Andrew's brows lowered in a knot. "Well, it's a big damned deal now. And I will deal with Bennie later. Come on," he said roughly as he took her arm and led her out of the duplex.

It was a false alarm, as it always was. Someone had not turned off a panel of lights, which triggered a sensor in the overly alert alarm system. It knew that something was not as it should be and did its little job of alerting the alarm company, which signaled Renee as the first name on the call list. The nice young officer who met them at the door walked the premises with Renee to make sure nothing else was amiss, while Andrew made his own inspection. After the officer left, Renee turned to Andrew.

"See? I told you it was nothing. It happens fairly infrequently, but I can handle it when it does. It was strictly a nonevent," she said breezily.

"I don't care what you say, Renee. It's dangerous for you to be coming down here alone at night to meet a policeman. From now on, either I come or one of the other boys comes. Or you get yourself a security guard. If something happened to you, I would lose my damned mind, and that's a fact. Not to mention what Bennie and the rest of the family would do, or your family. Don't even think about attempting something like this again, do you hear me?"

Andrew looked so forbidding and serious, yet so utterly sweet and lovable, that all Renee could do was say, "Yes, Andy." He was really concerned about her! They stood in the middle of the reception area staring at each other, but Andrew was still basically glowering.

Renee knew just what would put him in a better frame of mind. She took his hand and offered him a tour of the spa. "I don't think you've seen everything around here," she began. "Let me show you the works."

She walked him through the various rooms in the spa, skipping the salon, which he had already seen. She showed him the various facial rooms, the areas for waxing and body wraps and the room just for pedicures. Then she took him into the massage room. "This is everybody's favorite room," she said in a low, sultry voice.

Andrew looked disinterestedly at the room—it looked like no big whoop to him. It was in the same soothing green as the other rooms, but it was hardly furnished at all. It just had three rather high tables that looked too tall for anything really useful. He was still pissed by the idea that Renee thought it sensible to come traipsing in the salon at all odd hours of the night. And his sister did the same. These women had no idea of personal safety, none at all.

Gruffly he said, "So what's the big deal? What kind of abuse goes on in here?" He didn't mean to sound so crabby, but this day was wearing on him.

Renee seemed to understand perfectly, though. She simply drew him into the room with a sweet smile on her face. "This is the massage room, honey. This is where you get all the knots and kinks and stress rubbed right out of you." Before Andrew could react, Renee had made him an offer he could not possibly refuse. "How about you take off that shirt and get up on that table and I give you a massage? And how about a Jacuzzi to follow?" she asked seductively.

Andrew was undressed almost before she finished speaking. True to her word, Renee gave a great massage. Andrew had no idea how tense he was until Renee's fingers started to release all the stiffness and tension from his knotted muscles. She had strong, capable hands, which seemed to know exactly how to find the source of the strain and get rid of it. He was in a state of complete bliss, thanks to her loving ministrations. He moaned his pleasure as her warm hands rubbed and stroked and massaged every inch of his strongly muscled back.

Renee was enjoying the massage every bit as much as Andrew. She loved the way his smooth caramel skin looked and felt, and she loved the perfect musculature of his back. His skin felt warm and supple under her hands and she knew that she was soothing him and driving him crazy at the same time. It was an intimate, erotic experience that she would not have believed possible until this very minute. Everything that she was giving Andrew, she was getting back, and more. The trembles, the hesitancy, the fear she had experienced earlier were all gone, at least for the moment.

She leaned over and whispered to Andrew, "Turn over." Without hesitation he did so and pulled her head down to his for another slow, sweet kiss. Renee managed to pull away from him and say breathlessly, "I'm not finished with your massage."

Andrew looked at her with a combination of desire and panic. "Damn, Renee, what else could you possibly do to me? You've turned me to mush as it is," he groaned.

Renee poured a few drops of massage oil in the middle of his chest and used the palms of both hands to smooth the oil across his nipples. At his shuddering sigh she smiled.

"Well, there's *that,* to begin with," she said. And she proceeded to show him exactly what else she could do to him that would further assist him in the relaxation process.

Andrew couldn't take any more and forced himself into a sitting position. He brought his legs down over the side of the table and locked Renee between them while he cupped her face with his hands for a kiss.

"Okay, that's enough! You're trying to kill me," he accused. "I know that's what you're doing, you're trying to pay me back for all those years when we didn't get along. But if I have to die at your hands, I'd rather it be in bed," he said softly, lowering his head to her willing lips.

Renee lost all conscious control of her body. She was perfectly willing to go wherever Andrew wanted to take her as long as she could keep feeling what she was feeling. It was wonderful. She was hot; she was cold; she was tingling all over and throbbing in places she had long forgotten about. She actually had her fingers at her own buttonholes, ready to offer herself totally to Andrew when the voice of reason in the form of an insistent, noisy pager interrupted. This time it was Andrew's, and if there was one thing a dedicated doctor could not do, it was ignore a page.

Andrew looked up at the ceiling and said, "Oh, Lord, just take me now and get it over with!" He hopped off the table in obvious discomfort due to a huge bulge in his pants and looked at Renee with great distress. All he could say was, "Damn."

He immediately put his arms around her and pulled her as close as he could get her. He cupped her derriere with his hands and let her feel firsthand how very much he did not want to let her go.

"Just one more kiss and then I'm taking you back to my place to get your car. This is not an omen. This is just . . . the life of a doctor, damn it." He kissed her as though he depended on her lips for sustenance, which at the moment he did. Abruptly he let her go and put on his shirt, never taking his eyes from hers. He grabbed her hand and they paused just long enough to reset the alarm before leaving.

They were back at his house in record time and he kissed her once more after she got into her Mercedes. "Soon, Renee. Very, very soon," was all he said. He watched her drive off and then got into the Bentley and took off for the hospital. All the way over, he tasted his lips with his sensitized tongue to see if any of Renee's sweetness remained.

Very *soon, or I am going to lose my mind,* he thought.

Nine

As Einstein explained in his theory of relativity, time is relative. A minute may not seem like a long time when you are next to a pretty woman, but if you are sitting on a hot stove, it seems like an eternity. And when you are a virile, sexy man with designs on an incredibly sensuous woman whom you have desired for seventeen years, *soon* can't come soon enough. After trying to get with Renee for several fruitless days, Andrew felt like the Spanish Inquisition was a day at the beach. He was being subjected to a form of torture that was much, much crueler.

It was just his bad luck that their little assignation came right before his father's retirement celebration. After fifty years in the radio business, Andrew Bernard Cochran Sr., known affectionately as Big Benny, was officially retiring. Andrew and his sister, with the help of the other siblings, had been planning a huge gala party to celebrate the event. To be fair, Bennie had done most of the planning and organizing, but Andrew had done what he could when he could. And now that the event was a mere day away, it was mandatory that his precious free time be spent in last-minute preparations. Thus, he could spend virtually no time with Renee, who was knee deep in the party planning with Bennie.

They saw each other, of course, and they had even concocted a logical reason why they were attending the event together. But it wasn't nearly enough for Andrew. Since the first time their lips met, all he wanted to do was spend two or three days doing nothing but making love to Renee. He was trying to take his time and be a gentleman about it, because he liked her as a friend and a person and he respected her. There was so much more to Renee than had ever met his eye that he was actually humbled at times. He had always thought of her as beautiful and smart and certainly sexy, but he was getting to know the sweet and sensitive person that she hid from public view.

He didn't want to rush her, but at the same time he felt like he was dying by degrees every time he touched her without consummating the relationship. He walked around as randy as a schoolboy most of the time. When he was in the same room with her, it was pure agony. He couldn't stop looking at her, wanting her and needing her. Like the present moment, for example.

They were in Bennie's basement—ostensibly tending to final details. Renee was busy checking the boxes of party favors; these would be placed on every chair in the ballroom. She was absorbed in her task and was not paying any real attention to Andrew, who was sprawled on the big leather sofa staring balefully at Renee. He glanced at an authentic lariat on the wall above the sofa and contemplated throwing a lasso over Renee's head. That would certainly get her attention.

Bennie had decorated the basement to look like a 1950s ranch house. Big Benny's love of Westerns, particularly the rare ones with African American stars, had influenced the decor. For a time all of the Cochrans had been mad for cowboy movies and all things western. There were several pictures displayed of all the children in cowboy regalia, which lent a sweetly nostalgic air to the room. At the moment, though, the kitschy charm of the area was lost on Andrew. All his attention was focused on Renee, who was counting objects in boxes and making notes and just generally ignoring him. Even Aretha, who was dogging her every step in case one of the boxes was for her, was ignoring him. Finally he couldn't take it anymore.

"What does a man have to do to get some attention around here?" he demanded.

Aretha and Renee both turned and looked at him as if he had lost his mind. Andrew noticed for the first time how much the two resembled each other, but thought it best not to bring it up. He repeated his question in a less querulous tone.

"How can I get you to stop that and come talk to me for a minute?" he asked nicely.

He looked so sweet and handsome Renee relented for a moment and went to sit with him on the sofa. She tried to look aloof but failed miserably as he immediately sat up and put his arms around her.

"Hey. Hey!" she protested. "We are supposed to be talking, not necking. I have to finish this inventory and you have to take it over to the Roostertail. And I have to get back to the Oasis—there are about five heads that I have to do, all of whom are members of your family, so . . . so . . ."

Her voice trailed off as Andrew found an effective means of stopping her recital. The feel of Andrew's lips on hers never failed to drive all conscious thought from Renee's mind. She couldn't think at all when he was kissing her, all she could do was respond to the touch of his lips, the demands of his tongue and the intoxicating passion that overtook her in his arms. When they finally broke apart, she was drugged with sensation and breathing hard. She couldn't open her eyes, even when Andrew started speaking to her.

"You know," he said hoarsely, "if I had any idea you could kiss like that when we were in college, I would have kidnapped you a long time ago. In fact, I think I'll kidnap you right now. Let's get out of here and go someplace where we can be alone. Like my bedroom."

Renee finally opened her eyes and gave him a look that almost stopped his heart. "Bennie would kill us both and you know it. We are going to be responsible adults and get this finished so that the party will go as planned tomorrow," she said firmly.

Of course, while she was saying this she was stroking Andrew's bottom lip with her forefinger, which was driving him crazy. He retaliated by drawing her finger into his mouth and sucking on it gently. Renee sighed softly and tried to pull her finger away. He held on for a few more seconds and then recaptured her lips. All of her resolve was swept away, until she heard Bennie calling her. They finally pulled away from each other and looked totally bereft as the contact ended. Renee jumped to her feet and looked over her shoulder at Andrew before going to see what Bennie needed.

"Don't forget where we left off," she said as she left.

Andrew fell back onto the sofa with a groan. Aretha ambled over to see what ailed him. She stood on her hind legs and pushed her elegantly feline face into his. Andrew reached out to scratch her between the ears, something that she adored.

"Bad timing, Aretha. Just bad timing, that's all," he said. *But not for much longer.*

Finally, finally, the day of the gala arrived. Renee was outwardly calm, but that was mostly for Bennie's benefit. She had never seen her friend so worked up over anything in her life. It was partially because of the sheer magnitude of the event, but mostly because she had invited Clay's whole family from Atlanta and she wanted to make the best possible impression. Renee was trying her best to act as though nothing out of the ordinary was happening, and she had pretty much convinced herself of that fallacy, too.

But it was foolish to try to pretend like this night was like any other. Big Benny Cochran was the toast of urban radio and had set so many precedents it was impossible to name them all. He had been in the business fifty glorious years and was finally retiring. Luminaries of show business, politics and big business were coming literally from all over the world to pay him homage. Bennie and Renee had worked like galley slaves putting everything together, and it was sure to be a wonderful night. And Renee was pretty sure that some other wonderful things would be happening that night, too, between her and Andrew.

She had selected her dress with the utmost care. She usually had her special clothes made by a wonderful dressmaker named Joyce who was a whiz with design and execution. Bennie, in fact, was wearing a Joyce creation that night. Renee had been inspired, however, when she saw a Randolph Duke gown in the Somerset Neiman Marcus. It was oyster white silk with a floor-length skirt and a halter bodice that was made entirely of pearls and crystal beads with tiny accents of gold here and there. Renee purchased the dress at once and had Joyce replace the long, straight skirt with a swirling knee-length one of silk chiffon. It gave the dress a fresh sexiness that was perfect for Renee.

With the dress she decided to wear her Dolce & Gabbana evening sandals that were mere straps of the thinnest pearlized leather. She considered not wearing jewelry, but decided to wear a pair of antique pearl drop earrings and a fabulous vintage bracelet of faux pearls and crystals. The only thing she needed was a purse, and that she could borrow from Bennie, who had a sizable collection of evening bags. Having laid out her attire to her satisfaction, she went downstairs to get a bag from Bennie. She managed to slip by the door of the room Bennie's aunt Ruth was sequestered in—Aunt Ruth was a wonderful woman, but long-winded.

She did stop at Ceylon Simmons's room to make sure that she was comfortable. As well as being a dear friend of both Bennie's and Renee's, Ceylon was part of the entertainment for the program that evening. Renee had barely had a chance to speak with Ceylon when she arrived, so she tapped on her door. Ceylon answered immediately, throwing the door open to admit Renee.

"Come on in, darlin'! Pull up a chair and let's talk, it's been way too long since I've seen you. What have you been up to?" she exclaimed in her warm, friendly way.

It was typical of Ceylon that she did not brag about her exploits, although she could have. Ceylon was hotter than the hottest star of a blazing comet. She was taking the world by storm with her amazing singing voice and her comedy. Ceylon, for all her fame and glory, was still as down-home and sweet as she had ever been. Fame had not changed her one iota.

She settled down to find out the latest goings-on in Renee's life with every indication of deep interest, an interest that was totally sincere. She cared about Bennie and Renee like they were her own sisters. That is one reason why Renee felt she could confide in Ceylon about the Andrew situation. The other reason was if she did not tell someone, she was going to burst.

"Ceylon, I am seeing someone new," Renee began.

Ceylon tried not to look disappointed, but this was old news to her. Renee caught her look and hurried on.

"No, Ceylon, this is different. He is my age, for one thing. I am dating him exclusively, for another. And we have known each other for some time. In fact, you know him, too," she teased.

Ceylon looked completely baffled, but before she could hazard a guess, Renee told her.

"Brace yourself. I am dating Andrew Bernard Cochran Junior," Renee said sweetly. "Surprise."

Ceylon's hazel eyes got huge and her mouth flew open.

"Oh-my-GOD! Finally! After all these years—I can't believe it!" she shrieked.

Now it was Renee's turn to look puzzled.

"What do you mean, 'after all these years'?"

"Oh, please, girl, Andrew has had a crush on you for

years, you know that!" Ceylon exclaimed. "Don't tell me you didn't realize that he was crazy about you!"

But it was evident from the look on Renee's face that it was news to her.

"Hmmph. Just as well, you would have just dogged him back in the day. Now you two are just right for each other." She sighed, clasping her hands. Ceylon was an incurable romantic.

"Well, don't just drop a bomb on me and then sit there, I need details. How, when, where and what does Bennie think? I'll bet she's just thrilled!"

Renee hastily explained that no one knew except Ceylon.

"We haven't told anyone because it's so new that we want to keep it private for as long as possible. And I certainly don't want Bennie to feel caught in the middle if things don't work out," Renee added.

Ceylon looked skeptical, but her expression turned approving as Renee explained the events that led up to their current situation.

"So you and Bennie have both found wonderful men at the same time. If I didn't love you heifers so much, I would be so jealous! What is Bennie's Clay like?" she asked.

"Oh, you'll meet him tonight. He's so perfect for her, it's ridiculous. And he is so fine you'll be begging him to let you meet his brothers. He has two or three of them, as a matter of fact," Renee told her, but Ceylon wasn't interested. She was too excited over Renee's news.

"I can't wait to see you two together tonight," Ceylon confessed. "You two are probably so beautiful together that it's sickening."

Renee just smiled and said nothing, but silently she agreed with Ceylon.

When she floated down the stairs later that evening, Andrew's reaction was all she could have hoped for. Bennie had just gone downstairs and knocked Clay's socks off with her stunning appearance, although Andrew was giving her grief. They were laughing at each other when

Renee appeared, and for once, Andrew had absolutely nothing to say. He simply stood and drank in every inch of Renee as if he were momentarily blinded to everything else in the world. He stood at the bottom of the main staircase, waiting for her. Luckily, Bennie and Clay were too absorbed in each other to pay them any attention. Renee didn't say anything; she merely took his tie from his fingers and proceeded to put it on him and tie it properly.

"Renee, you look . . . wonderful," Andrew said in a hoarse voice.

Renee just smiled. She was standing on the stairs so that she was eye level with Andrew. After she finished tying his tie, she ran her hands over his shoulders.

"You look quite handsome yourself, Andy," she finally said.

She continued to rest her hands on his shoulders and he slipped his hands around her waist. They stood there for the longest time, just staring into each other's eyes with quiet affection. What would have happened next is anyone's guess, but Ceylon chose that moment to come downstairs.

With a sigh of regret Renee took her hands from Andrew's shoulders and allowed him to escort her down the remaining stairs. They turned as one to greet Ceylon, whose eyes widened at the sight of them—they really did look wonderful together. After giving Andrew an effusive greeting and hug, she went into the living room to meet Clay.

Finally everyone was ready to leave, including Aunt Ruth and sundry Philadelphian cousins of the Cochrans'. Everyone piled into limousines, except Bennie and Clay, who wanted to be alone, and Renee and Andrew for the same reason. They got into Andrew's Bentley and followed Clay and Bennie in her Jaguar. Andrew took Renee's hand immediately and did not let it go for the rest of the night.

The only times that he was not holding her hand was when he was participating in the program honoring his father's retirement. Renee had to stifle sighs of admiration—he looked way too fine in his custom-tailored tuxedo. He was also a wonderful speaker and seemed perfectly at ease with talking in front of hundreds of people. Renee looked around the huge ballroom and decided that the event was as perfect as Bennie could have made it. Everything had a golden glow about it, from the soft indirect lighting to the candlelit centerpieces on every table. The gold lamé tablecloths with the ivory damask overlays were the perfect foils to the fragrant flower arrangements on every table. Thanks to the jazz stylings of Bennie's godfather, Bill "Bump" Williams, and his orchestra, the entire ambiance was that of a posh supper club from the 1940s, which was just what they were trying to invoke.

The entire evening was wonderful, especially when the speeches and testimonials were over and the dancing began. Andrew was an absolutely fantastic dancer. He was as graceful as he was tall and there was no dance that he could not do. From the electric slide to the merengue, he had them all down pat. And as for slow dancing, well, he was the most amazing partner Renee had ever had. They were hardly out of each other's arms all night.

"Andy, I had no idea that you could dance like this," Renee confessed.

"That's because you would never let me within ten feet of you at a social event. I love to dance. And I have always wanted to dance with you," he admitted.

Finally it became apparent that dancing was not going to substitute for what they really wanted, which was to be alone. They left as discreetly as possible and went directly to the house. Once there, it dawned on Renee that it might not be such a good idea to pursue anything with so many people underfoot. She was about to express this idea to Andrew when he covered her mouth with his. For several minutes all she could do was react to the feel of his hot, passionate lips on hers and the taste of his tongue as it wrapped around hers.

"I have been wanting to kiss that red lipstick off your mouth all night. Damn, that tastes good." He nearly moaned.

Renee stifled a moan of her own as she tried to gain control of the situation.

"Andy, I think we should, um, say good night. There are, like, fifty people staying here and they are all probably going to burst in here at once. Especially Aunt Ruth," she reminded him.

They had made it as far as the living room and were wrapped in each other's arms on the sofa. Andrew did not want to hear any voice of reason.

"So let's go to my house. Let's get the hell out of here, Renee. I want to be alone with you right now. For a long, long time, like all night," he growled.

Renee was touched and delighted by his frankness, but she did not see how she could just disappear and leave everything on Bennie's shoulders. Entertaining guests was hard work, especially when they had to make breakfast and keep them happy until it was time for a barbecue at Alan's house the next day. She tried to explain this to Andrew, but he did not want to hear it.

"Well, hell, Renee, if those old geezers of yours had to wait this long, they'd all be dead," he muttered.

Renee backed out of his arms as though he had morphed into a space alien.

"How dare you! What makes you think I was intimate with those men?" she hissed.

Andrew was not looking directly at her, or he would have seen the utter fury on her face.

"Well, if you weren't, they were bigger fools than I thought," he said thoughtlessly.

And those were the last words he spoke for some time, as Renee's left fist connected with his face.

"*You* are the biggest fool I ever met in my life, Andrew Cochran! Get the hell out of here!"

Before Andrew could form a response, she had leaped to her feet and dashed up the stairs.

Andrew slowly stood and looked in the direction that Renee had run.

"That didn't go as well as I planned," he said dryly.

Renee would have stayed in a rage all night, had it not been for two things. For one, after she had taken a shower to rid herself of Andrew's scent, she stormed downstairs for ice water, where she had encountered Bennie and Clay. They were now officially engaged. Renee had burst into tears of joy upon hearing the news, and she was awestruck at the exquisite yellow diamond ring that Clay had put on Bennie's finger. Renee was so thrilled with Bennie's obvious happiness that some of the anger ebbed away. The three of them had talked about wedding plans and Bennie's moving to Atlanta for a while and Renee had discreetly left them alone.

On the way up the stairs she had encountered Ceylon, who had come in search of her.

"Okay, you've kept me in suspense long enough! You and Andrew are perfect together," she gushed. "I want to know details. What did he say when he saw you, how much in love is he, when are you two getting hitched, tell me everything!" she wheedled as they strolled arm in arm up the wide stairs.

Renee sighed deeply and shrugged. "I hate to disappoint you, but he said I looked great, he couldn't possibly love me and we are never getting married. Ever," she said in a monotone.

By this time they were in Renee's sitting room, sitting at opposite ends of the cushy sofa that was upholstered in silvery gray raw silk. Everything was coordinated in pink and gray, including the carpet and draperies. The two women looked at each other, each wearing very telling expressions. Renee's was full of anger and Ceylon's was total confusion.

"Renee, come on now. Tell me what went wrong. I saw the two of you together and you looked absolutely beautiful! You couldn't stop looking at each other, especially Andrew. He never left your side for more than five minutes, and when he was away from you, his eyes were glued to you! I know you accuse me of being overly romantic, but that man is crazy about you! It's as plain as . . . as the size of my hips!" Ceylon exclaimed indignantly.

Renee chuckled a little at Ceylon's comparison. Ceylon was definitely full figured and shapely, and she was not in the least self-conscious about her figure. Why should she be? She was gorgeous and men found her irresistible. But she was not to be sidestepped. Leaning forward, she pressed Renee again.

"Okay, it's obvious that you two had a fight of some kind. What happened?"

Renee snorted. "Nothing happened. Andrew just thinks I am a skank whore, that's all." She gave the word its time-honored slang pronunciation of "ho."

Ceylon's eyes narrowed and her lips pursed. "I don't believe you just said that. You'd better explain the whole thing to me—and fast—before I go over there and kick his ass for you."

Renee explained the growing attraction between the two of them and how intent he was on fulfilling the passionate promises they had been making. She further explained that tonight was not the night, due to the crowded house and hostess obligations. Then she told Ceylon exactly what Andrew had said, and how she had slugged him.

"I mean, really! The nerve of him! Just because I date a man, or men, does not mean that I am having sex with them! What kind of assumption is that to make about a person, after all?" Renee turned angry, hurt eyes to Ceylon to get some support.

Ceylon's eyebrows had climbed to her hairline, practically, and the expression on her face was complicated, at best.

"Umm, Renee, dear heart?" Ceylon started gently. "I think it's a fairly normal assumption. Until this very moment I was operating under the same misapprehension as Andrew." She held up her hand to ward off the angry barrage that was about to explode from Renee. "Hold it right there. I am not saying that you are a hoochie-mama or a skank, and Andrew wasn't, either. But you are a very sexy and sophisticated woman who has had her pick of some very nice gentlemen. Sex is a lovely and important part of life—why wouldn't you have a sexual relationship with someone very special?" she asked gently.

Renee sprang up and started pacing, rearranging items on the small marquetry tables and needlessly fluffing the rose-and-peony pillows on the love seat.

"Come on and give me a facial," Ceylon said easily. "I haven't had one in I-don't-know-when, and you give the very best," she added.

As Ceylon had planned, once Renee was occupied with applying creams to her friend's skin, she was able to relax enough to talk. And the fact that Ceylon's eyes were closed made the words flow without hesitation.

"You know, I used to have a normal sex life," Renee confessed. "It wasn't the most prolific, to be sure, but I wasn't a prude or frigid or anything. I had one boyfriend from my senior year in high school through my freshman year of college. I had one boyfriend through college. And I had one after I graduated. You remember when I was living in Columbus, working at that crummy television station?"

Ceylon murmured an affirmative, which caused Renee to go on with her story.

"Well, I moved to Newark and took that job with the ABC affiliate there. I was the weekend anchor and spent all week long chasing stories like a big dog because I wanted to be the best. You have no idea how much I loved that job. I really thought I had a future there because the people were kind and supportive and no one was making stupid remarks about how I showed up on camera or anything. I was even getting fan letters! I was so sure that this was my big break." She sighed.

Renee paused to apply a steaming hot cloth to Ceylon's cream-covered skin. It was amazing, but talking to Ceylon was really helping. She didn't feel the gut-wrenching nausea that normally accompanied her memories of Newark. She was, in fact, eager to get it all out.

"There was a black anchorman at the station when I got there and he was the toast of the town. One of those pale pretty boys with the light brown curly hair, you know the type. And he was quite adequate in his job, too. He was smart and funny and just the nicest guy you could imagine. He was engaged to a really sweet girl; she was a schoolteacher or something. Anyway, he was kind of like a big brother to me. I have all sisters, you know, and Bennie's brothers are the closest things I have to male siblings. But I have always had a lot of male friends, guys that I just buddied around with, you know? And he was like that, too.

"We would sometimes have lunch together or go to a basketball game or just have a drink with everybody else at the station at happy hour and kick it around. Which is why I did not think twice about letting him take me home one night. My car wouldn't start and it was snowing and he offered me a lift and I said sure. He brought me home and came inside and we were just laughing and talking and having a good time. I had some leftover gumbo, I heated it up and he stayed for dinner. Just two old friends, you know?"

Renee sensed Ceylon's uneasiness and patted her shoulder.

"I'll spare you all the gory details. But yes, he did rape me. *Acquaintance* rape, they call it now. They didn't really have a name for it back then. At least I don't think they did; I'm not sure. One minute we were laughing and talking, not even flirting, mind you, just goofing around. And the next thing I know, he had thrown me onto the sofa and he's ripping . . . Well, you get the idea."

Renee's hands stayed busy, massaging and manipulating Ceylon's silken skin to improve the circulation. She ignored the tears that were sliding out of Ceylon's eyes.

"I was definitely traumatized, I have to admit it. He was so casual and cavalier about it—all he said afterward was, 'I know you've been wanting me, Renee, so quit pretending.' Then he used my towels and soap to clean himself up and left me lying there. He actually said that he would see me tomorrow!"

Now Renee could not ignore Ceylon's tears because she was shedding some of her own. She told Ceylon the rest of the story in short, clipped sentences—how she had gone to the emergency room and told them she was raped. How they acted like she was lying because there was no visible sign of trauma. She told how she had filed a police report, and how she had been humiliated and scoffed at, especially when she told them who her assailant was.

"Everyone's attitude was like I was too ugly for him to have assaulted. Why would he put his hands on me when he had that pretty little fiancée at home? You know something, that's one thing that still pisses me off—people act like rape is a crime of passion. It is a crime of *violence*. Sexual gratification is not the aim; it is punishment and domination. But everyone saw on the one hand a respected, admired member of the community, a handsome, acceptable man accused by a woman who was obviously not attractive enough to get her own man. A woman who was not smart enough to get a job on her own, so she had to try to ruin a black man's life in order to get ahead in her career."

Ceylon drew in a sharp, horrified breath and sat up. "Renee, that's terrible! People didn't actually say things like that to you! You were the victim, for God's sake!"

Renee looked at Ceylon solemnly. "Oh, honey, they said those things and much worse. In order to get out of Newark with my head intact, I quit my job and left in the dark of night, literally. I had gotten so much hate mail and threatening phone calls that I had no choice, or at least I thought I didn't. I really didn't have a choice about the job, either. The station manager made it plain to me that he didn't care what had happened: One highly visible light-skinned anchorman was worth two dozen little black gals like me. Oddly enough, he never actually said he did not believe me," she added thoughtfully.

"And yes, I was a victim then and I have been a victim

ever since. I tried to do the right thing then. I knew what you're supposed to do after a rape. Don't shower, don't change clothes. Go to a hospital as soon as possible, report the rape to the police—I did everything I was supposed to do and it all blew up in my face. I was treated like trash and I lost all respect for myself. So I refused to let anyone near me again. I never told my family or any of my friends. Not even Bennie," she said before Ceylon could ask. "At least not then.

"Gilbert was dying and she did not need to hear my sad story. I took myself to Boston and helped her all I could and just started my life over again. Of course, when I did tell her, after the fact, she was furious with me for not telling her sooner. I'd never seen her that mad and come to think of it, I haven't seen her that angry since," Renee said thoughtfully.

She wiped her fingers on a steaming hot towel and continued speaking. "Anyway, I made up my mind that no one was ever going to have me in that position again. I was going to call the shots from now on and no man was ever getting me in a place where I couldn't walk away clean. And to tell you the truth, the idea of sex terrified me to the point where I couldn't even think about it for years and years. Until recently, that is."

She told Ceylon about her therapy with Yolanda and how Andrew was the only man she had felt any desire for since the night of the rape. Then she smiled crookedly.

"And now he thinks I'm nuts," she said with a shaky laugh.

Ceylon embraced her warmly. "Dear heart, I am sure he thinks no such thing!" She stood back a moment and looked at Renee closely. "How hard did you hit him?"

"Pretty hard. As hard as I could, and you know I play tennis several times a week," Renee confessed.

"Well, he might think you're a *little* crazy. But when you explain things to him, he will understand," Ceylon said encouragingly.

"I hope you're right, because I do want to explain things to him. I have never been able to talk about it before, but I think he needs to know what kind of nutcase he is getting mixed up with. That's if he will speak to me at all," she said ruefully.

Ceylon hugged her again. "Oh, girl, you know I am never wrong about these things! You and he were meant to be together, just like Bennie and that yummy Clay. Where did that lucky heifer meet him, anyway?"

And before they knew it, they had talked until almost morning.

These two offices face onto Brighton Beach Avenue, almost directly beneath the elevated subway tracks. It is a rare day at their beachfront office that Renee doesn't see a rat or two darting across the cracked, uneven floor.

There was, for example, his behavior the day after the gala party. Renee had showered and dressed quickly—she had a mission. She put on a pair of tan cotton Comme des Garcons drawstring pants and a white cotton DKNY tank top. She strapped on a pair of snakeskin sandals and sprayed Annick Goutal liberally before going downstairs and slipping out the back door. She closed the door and turned around, coming face-to-face with Andrew, who was holding a huge bouquet of gerbera daisies, one of Renee's favorite flowers. She was speechless.

Ten

It was time for drastic measures, Renee decided. It was time to put her big plan into action. Things with Andrew could not have been going better and yet, she was ready to jump out of her skin. *Serves me right for picking the last gentleman on the planet to get involved with.* And Andrew was truly a gentleman in every sense of the word. Besides being mannerly, he was a very gentle and caring man.

There was, for example, his behavior the day after the gala party. Renee had showered and dressed quickly—she had a mission. She put on a pair of tan cotton Comme des Garcons drawstring pants and a white cotton DKNY tank top. She strapped on a pair of snakeskin sandals and sprayed Annick Goutal liberally before going downstairs and slipping out the back door. She closed the door and turned around, coming face-to-face with Andrew, who was holding a huge bouquet of gerbera daisies, one of Renee's favorite flowers. She was speechless.

"Don't hit me; I'm not armed," Andrew said quickly. "This is to apologize for my behavior last night. Renee, it was inexcusable. I had absolutely no right to say those things to you, no right whatsoever. Yes, I want to be with you more than you can possibly imagine, but that is no reason to say ugly things to you. I can't even claim that I was drunk, just made truly stupid by lust. I hope you don't hate me," he said quietly.

Renee felt both of her hands rise to her cheeks, which

were flaming hot by now. Andrew was attired very similarly to her, except that he had on a Gap T-shirt and Marithé & Girbaud khakis. He looked and smelled like he had been freshly laundered and hung out to dry in the sun. If she wasn't mistaken, there was the slightest swelling on his cheekbone where she had popped him one. He looked so sincere and adorable that she literally could not speak—the words just would not come out.

Andrew misinterpreted her gesture and sighed in defeat. He was about to place the flowers on the steps and leave when Renee found her voice.

"Oh, Andy, thank you," she breathed out. "I was just coming over to your house," she added.

Andrew was dumbstruck. "You were? Why?"

Renee leaned over and gave him a sweet little kiss where her fist had landed the night before. "For this. And to talk. There are some things I need to tell you, Andy."

After taking her lovely daisies into the house, she and Andrew left to go have breakfast. They went to one of his favorite places, a Coney Island joint on Jefferson. He looked at Renee anxiously before going in.

"Is this okay? I never asked you what you wanted to eat," he began.

Renee shrugged it off. "Please. I love diner food, quiet as it's kept. I know I act like the 'Queen of Everything,' but it's all for show. Well, most of it. *Some* of it," she amended.

They took a booth in the back of the small, spotlessly clean restaurant and chatted about this and that until their orders were taken and their coffee was served. Then Renee told him what she had told Ceylon the night before.

Renee was studying her coffee cup as she spoke, so she did not see the rage that built in him as she told him of her rape and subsequent betrayal by the system that was set up to protect her. When she finally did meet his eyes again, she was shocked at the fury contained in his face.

"Andy?" she said shakily. "It's okay, honey. It was a long time ago and I have finally put it behind me. Yolanda helped and you certainly helped. It's all over now, Andy."

Andrew was so filled with anger at the unknown man who had dared violate Renee that he couldn't really hear her soft voice.

"Renee, why didn't you tell someone? Why didn't you tell your family?" he asked bleakly. "Someone should have been there for you. *I* should have been there for you," he added.

Renee sighed. "You have met my mother. Sweet as she is, there is a real streak of 'That's what you get' that runs through her. She was never the type to dispense hugs and kisses when you fell down. It was always your fault, no matter what. My poor father would have had a heart attack. And I really didn't want anyone else to know. I already had a taste of how people would react, remember? There is so much guilt attached to the rape survivor. 'If only I hadn't—I should have done this or that—Why didn't I do this or that' . . . It's incredible. The only person I could have told was Bennie and the timing could not have been worse," she finished.

"What do you mean, the timing was bad?" asked Andrew.

Renee gently reminded him that his sister's husband was in the final stages of cancer when Renee's tragedy had occurred.

"Even I am not selfish enough to have expected Bennie to be able to cope with me and Gilbert at the same time. She knows about it now, of course, but it was after the fact. I finally got tired of suffering silently and torturing old men, and I got help. So now it's time for a new phase of my life to begin," she said calmly.

The food had come and she tucked into her western omelet with great appetite, although Andrew had lost his. He was quiet for most of the meal, although he did say with true regret that he wished that he had known what had happened. She placed her hand on his and stroked it gently.

"Andy, it's all over. What could you have possibly done, anyway?" she asked rhetorically.

"I would have broken his neck," Andrew said immediately. "Renee, do you think for a second that if my brothers and I had known that someone hurt you we would have let him live? Don't be crazy, woman. You'd be talking to me now through Plexiglas and chicken wire because I would have killed the bastard as sure as the world."

Having made that statement, he went back to moving his food around on his plate so that it would look like he was eating, but he was not. Finally they left and walked back to Andrew's car. They drove down Jefferson in silence and Renee said nothing when Andrew turned into Belle Isle, the huge public park that housed a botanical garden, among other things. They drove around for a few minutes until Andrew found a parking place near a grove of trees. He stopped the car and got out, coming around the car to open Renee's door. Before she could ask why they were on Belle Isle, he pulled her close to him and held her for a long time.

Then he bent his head to hers and kissed her—long, slow and sweet. While they were kissing, his hands were stroking her back and her arms as if to wipe away every bad memory she ever had. Finally he raised his head and then planted one more brief kiss on her eager lips.

"You know I'm crazy about you, don't you?" he asked.

Renee smiled and nodded. "I have that general impression," she said.

"I don't ever want anything bad to happen to you again, Renee. I can't tell you how sorry I am that you had to go through that, but I am glad as hell that you had the courage to get past it. I always knew you were special in so many ways, but now I know how really amazing you are. You are a wonderful woman, Renee, and I am very lucky to have you in my life," he said simply.

Renee was so overcome with emotion that she just turned her head into his shoulder and stood there basking in the warmth of his arms. And he thought he was lucky! She had never felt so wonderful in her life. It was a heady, frightening feeling, and one that she wanted more of. She was about to tell him that when he realized how late it was.

"I'd better get you back so you can get ready for the to-do at Alan's house. This has been the longest weekend of my life, I admit it. Pop is having a ball, though. Maybe when I have a fiftieth anniversary of some kind to celebrate, I will be that geeked, but right now, I am just tired," he said as they were pulling into the alley behind the house.

After one more brief kiss he was gone, with the promise that he would see her later. Renee floated back into the house and picked up the giant bouquet to take up to her room. As luck would have it, Bennie's redoubtable aunt Ruth was emerging from her guest room as Renee hit the landing. She braced herself for a long chat, but Aunt Ruth was a woman on the move.

"Ha! Looks like there's going to be two weddings around here," she said wickedly. Before Renee could ask for clarification, Aunt Ruth answered her. "Well, Bennie and Clay, that's fairly obvious. And you and Andrew. You'll be next. I know you and I know my nephew. It's about time, too," she added as she sauntered down the stairs.

Renee opened her mouth to protest but decided against it. What was the point, after all? Aunt Ruth would never admit she was wrong about anything and this was one time that Renee was rather inclined to agree with her. After the previous night and that morning, anything was possible.

All things were possible but apparently not probable. Since the tumultuous weekend when Renee had clobbered Andrew and then told him all the next day, he had been treating her like a display of Kosta Boda glassware at an expensive department store—he looked with reverent appreciation but did not touch. He acted as if she were so precious and fragile that she would shatter with the slightest pressure. Renee had tried and tried to convince him that she was not only resilient but healed, only to be given the sweetest and most loving look, followed by a gentle hug or squeeze.

"I don't want to rush you, Renee. We'll both know when it's time," was all he would say.

Renee had told Yolanda everything in her last session, and Yolanda was once again full of praise and encouragement for Renee. She also posed a few questions for her.

"Renee, it sounds as though Andrew cares for you very much. And it would seem that you return that feeling. Are you sure that you're ready to take that next step and move into a physical relationship with Andrew?" she probed gently.

Renee was emphatic in her insistence that yes, she was ready. "Yolanda, I had forgotten how exciting and romantic it feels to really *be* with a man! I was never particularly fond of a lot of kissing, even before the rape. I just didn't like anyone up in my face, you know? And frankly, it didn't seem all that hygienic, if you ask me," she said, making a face. Then she smiled dreamily.

"But kissing Andy? Oh, my goodness, it's like a little piece of heaven, it really is. I love the way he feels, the way he tastes, the way that beard feels on my cheek. . . ." She turned glassy eyes to Yolanda. "Did I mention that he has a beard now?" she asked irrelevantly.

Yolanda covered her mouth to hide a grin. "Yes, Renee, I believe you mentioned that several times. And I think that you are experiencing a long-awaited sexual reawakening, which is wonderful. I caution you, though, to be very sure of your feelings as you enter into this new phase of your life. I do not want anything to befall either you or Andrew, who sounds like a wonderful man. As I said, he seems to care for you very much and I want you to ask yourself if you could have the same feelings for him."

Renee had mulled those words over carefully and thought about how far she had come in the last few months. Just a few weeks ago, words like that from Yolanda would not have been necessary. There was no one in her life that fit into that category, for one thing. And if she had brought up something like that, Renee would have jumped out of her skin from anxiety. Now she was just as cool as a cucumber about the whole thing.

She was completely ready to start another phase of her relationship with Andrew. She knew that he cared about her and she returned those feelings wholeheartedly. How could she not, when Andrew was the kindest, sweetest, most endearing man she had ever known? There was nothing to dislike about him. He was smart, skilled, dedicated, family oriented, funny and affectionate. He was a wonderful dancer and he could even cook. And he could iron better than she could; he admitted to doing the ironing when they were growing up. He did have a temper, and she had witnessed it firsthand. But his was a rational anger, if there was such a thing. He only lost it when he was pushed to the wall.

The only thing that she could fault him on was being too patient and considerate when it came to their affair. And she was about to take care of that little detail herself. Renee had tried being demure, seductive, flirtatious and coy to no avail. Andrew seemed to have it in his head that she was some kind of fragile flower that needed delicate handling now that he knew that she had been assaulted. Yolanda assured her that this was not uncommon.

"Just remember, Renee, you have had ten years to cope with this, plus about eighteen months of expensive therapy. Andrew is just finding out about it. So give him a little time, he will come around soon enough. And it is an entirely appropriate reaction—he does not blame you, he cherishes you and wants to protect you, which is actually quite sweet."

After a couple of weeks of sweet, though, Renee was ready to pop. They had many sweet, romantic dates that ended with a passionate kiss and hug, and that was it. Andrew seemed oblivious to the fact that he was driving her crazy. And he truly was driving her out of her tiny little mind. The scent of him, the taste of him, the sheer beauty and sensuality of him, was all she could think about. She wanted nothing more than to follow one of those hot, sizzling kisses to its logical conclusion and wake up the next morning wrapped in Andrew Cochran and nothing else.

And since he wasn't cooperating, it was up to her to get the ball rolling. The tennis ball, to be exact.

The next day, she and Andrew were fishing up a game of tennis at the center where she customarily played. Andrew was as strong as she was, so he gave her a good game. They each won three games and were more than willing to call it a day as the skies darkened and it looked like it was about to storm. They went into the clubhouse to shower and change, agreeing to meet in the juice bar afterward.

After he and Renee left the athletic club, he suggested lunch at Fishbone's, one of their favorite restaurants. Renee docilely agreed, then remembered that she had left her purse at home.

"Can we run by the house to get it?" she asked sweetly. "It'll only take a second."

Andrew assured her that she did not need her purse, but if she wanted it, fine. They got to the house in a few minutes. Andrew noticed the absence of Bennie's car and was told that she was in Atlanta with Clay. Since they announced their engagement the day after Big Benny's party, she had been back and forth to Atlanta constantly.

Renee left Andrew downstairs while she went in search of her purse. He made himself comfortable in the living room and was listening to a CD while perusing a newsmagazine. He became absorbed in an article about some medical development and did not notice the passage of time. The room grew darker as the promise of rain came to fruition; he noticed that it had started raining quite hard. He went over to the stairs to ask Renee if she still wanted to go out in the rain.

He called up to her and she took her time answering. He was about to repeat his question when she finally spoke.

"Actually, Andy, I'm not terribly hungry right now. But something is broken up here, can you come take a look, please?" she asked.

Andrew ambled up the stairs and entered Renee's sitting

room. He stopped in midstride as he realized that something was very different about the room. He had never really paid any attention to it before; he thought it was pretty and that was about it. It was a very seductive room, which looked a lot like Renee—soft, feminine and modern. The pinks and grays gave it a French feeling, like an Impressionist painting. And there were fresh flowers everywhere, as well as soft, seductive music playing.

"It's in here, Andy—are you coming or what?" Renee asked softly.

Finally Andrew was able to walk across the parlor and enter Renee's bedroom. If he could have breathed, he would have issued a deep, heartfelt sigh of pure pleasure. As it was, he had trouble holding on to the little air that was in his lungs.

The centerpiece of Renee's bedroom was a huge four-poster bed with a canopy frame. There was sheer fabric draped over the head of the bed in lieu of a canopy. The shimmering length was sprinkled with fragrant blossoms, as was the bed itself. Fragrant candles were burning on the bedside tables as well as floating in a glass bowl on a stand near the French doors that led to her tiny balcony. Next to her velvet chaise longue there was a stand that held a frosted ice bucket with a bottle of champagne chilling in its icy depths. And there was Renee, leaning against one of the thick posters at the foot of the bed, wearing the most incredible thing Andrew had ever seen.

Renee had on an amazingly sheer teddy made of silk georgette and lace. It was a deep, soft pink that was almost mauve. She had on a matching peignoir that had slipped off one shoulder and she looked indescribably desirable. She stood there for a moment with her hands behind her back, leaning against the bed's poster. She didn't say a word, but she was smiling. She started to walk toward Andrew and did not take more than one step before he started walking toward her.

Andrew pulled her into his arms and kissed her with

all the ferocity and passion that he had been trying to control. He lifted his head long enough to look into her eyes and whisper, "Thank you."

Those were the last words that either of them spoke for some time. Andrew let her out of his arms long enough to behold her beauty in the incredible lingerie. While he was watching her watch him, he was also taking off his clothes. In what seemed like seconds he stood before her as bronzed and magnificent as she remembered him, the only difference being his powerful arousal. In the meantime she had let the filmy robe drop to the floor and was about to divest herself of the teddy when Andrew stopped her. That was a pleasure he wanted for himself and he slowly removed the delicate garment as he walked her backward to the waiting bed. With one sweep of his hand he turned back the coverlet to reveal her Porthault linens bought specifically for this occasion; finally they sank onto the mattress together.

She was shaking all over and he stroked her velvety length while saying her name.

"It's okay, Renee, it's okay. I've got you, baby, it's okay," he murmured. Soon the trembling stopped and was replaced by an incredible heat that coursed through her body.

"Andy. Oh, *Andy,*" was all she could say.

She didn't need to say anything else; their bodies were doing the talking. Everything that Andrew was feeling, every tender word he had ever wanted to say, every erotic dream he had ever had about Renee, translated into the motion of his body and his hands. By the time he was ready to join their two bodies, Renee could have picked him blindfolded out of a room of thousands, just by the touch of his hand. Her hands never stopped moving, either. She matched Andrew stroke for stroke, caress for caress. Just when she thought there couldn't be anything more sensual than the way he was touching her and kissing her, Andrew stopped moving completely. Renee's eyes flew open and without a word she slipped her hand under the pile of pillows at the head of the bed and drew out a box of latex condoms. The look of relief on Andrew's face was priceless; so was the speed with which he slipped on the protection. And this time he brought their intimacy to its most passionate end as he entered her body. Her eyes closed and a cry of fevered bliss escaped her lips.

As she was getting used to the incredible sensation of being filled like she had never been before, she felt Andrew's hand on her cheek.

"Open your eyes, baby. Look at me, Renee," he pleaded.

Renee looked directly into Andrew's dark eyes, which were smoky with passion. Her hands were stroking his shoulders and he was connected to her in the most powerful and intimate way possible and she was spiraling off into a fiery cloud that she never knew existed. But with every stroke, every push, she knew that she was where she should be. The adoration that was in Andrew's eyes was staggering, even in her state of erotic euphoria. Andrew was giving her everything he had. He was holding her hips and telling her in every way possible that he loved her. Finally, when he sensed that she was on the brink of ecstasy, he pulled her even closer to his body and whispered in her ear.

"I love you, Renee. It's always been you, baby, only you. I love you." He groaned before joining her in the explosion of stars that made him hers.

It was still raining by the time they were able to breathe normally. The French doors were open, allowing the moist, fresh smell to mingle with the scent of the expensive candles and the earthy smell of love. Andrew had turned on his back and held Renee against his heart and they clung together holding hands and not speaking. Finally Renee lifted her head long enough to kiss him on the neck and murmur, "Thank you," with a soft sigh.

"The pleasure was entirely mine," Andrew said sleepily.

They fell asleep in each other's arms while the storm continued. They did not sleep long; the urgent hunger that they felt for each other was not to be so easily satisfied.

Renee woke up to find Andrew gazing down at her with his heart in his eyes.

"Renee, are you okay, baby? I wasn't too rough, was I?" he asked softly. "I tried to be gentle," he said, "but you are so damned incredible that I couldn't slow down."

Renee loved the way he was stroking her face and turned her head to kiss his palm.

"Andy, honey, do I look unhappy?" She smiled lazily, knowing that she must look totally content.

He had to admit that she looked very satisfied. "But, Renee, it had been so long for you, and you were so small, I didn't want to hurt you with my impatience. I wanted this to be the most incredible night of your life," he admitted.

By way of answer, Renee stroked his face and kissed him with all the fire that she was feeling. She pushed his shoulder gently so that he would roll onto his back. Once he was where she wanted him, she began stroking him from his hips to his shoulders. When he let out a soft sigh of contentment, Renee lowered her head and began kissing his nipples in the same manner that he had kissed hers, which made him wild. Knowing that she had total control of him, she boldly slid her hand down to his throbbing manhood and caressed it slowly and surely.

Andrew choked back a cry of passion and immediately reversed their positions.

"Baby, I want to make this special for you and I can't do that if you drive me out of my mind," he groaned.

Renee smiled and slid her hands down his strong, muscular back, which was damp with perspiration. She grasped his buttocks and moved her hips sensuously at the same time.

"Andy, this *is* special, sweetheart. Everything about this is special. And this *is* the most incredible night of my life. Besides, it's hardly begun," she whispered. "Look out the window."

Amazingly, despite the rain, it was still not totally dark outside. The cool, rain-scented air drifted over them as they loved each other over and over through the night.

Eleven

The next time that Andrew awoke, he saw Renee re-entering the bedroom with a large tray. He watched her through his barely opened eyes, enjoying the view. She had put the filmy robe on and it did little or nothing to obstruct his view of her body. She set the tray on the needlepoint-covered bench at the foot of the bed and turned to the ice bucket to retrieve the bottle of champagne that was chilling there. It was actually a second bottle; the first one had been consumed sometime before.

Renee was so intent on her tasks that she did not pay any attention to the fact that Andrew was watching her. By now, he was fully awake and sitting up, propped on the great pile of pillows arranged at the head of the bed. Finally, as she turned around to retrieve the crystal flutes they had been drinking out of earlier, she noticed that he was no longer asleep. With a ravishing smile she leaned over and kissed Andrew, who promptly pulled her back into bed.

He immediately divested her of the robe, saying, "You have on way too many clothes. Besides, that doesn't really cover anything up, you know."

Renee shrugged and agreed. "But who likes to get a present that isn't wrapped? Are you hungry?"

"For food? Kinda. For you? Always," he answered.

They kissed again and again, which made Renee almost forget that she had gone down three flights of stairs to prepare him something to eat.

"Mmmm, stop it. Those stairs are not conducive to breakfast in bed, so you'd better enjoy this now. Who knows when I will do this again," she said frankly.

Andrew released her temporarily, but his eyes roved over her with a ravenous look of desire. "I'll fix breakfast for you next time, how about that? That seems fair," he murmured.

He could not take his eyes off Renee's lissome body as she arranged the tray on his lap so that she could feed him. The sight of her dark, smooth body next to him with nothing covering her but the afterglow of their lovemaking was amazing.

"You know what," he said before accepting the strawberry she held out to him. "I have been dreaming about this since I was eighteen."

He bit into the strawberry and licked the resultant juice from her fingers. Renee ate the other half and looked at Andrew demurely.

"Oh, really? Do I look the same?" she asked, arching a brow.

Andrew looked her over seriously before answering. "Yes and no. You're slimmer than you were in college. You're more toned, I guess. All that tennis. You have to understand, I fell in love with what I saw that day, Renee. Especially one part of you in particular. And now it's gone," he said ruefully.

"And just what part would that be?" she asked in surprise.

Andrew sighed. "You had the cutest tummy in the world. It was round and sweet like a baby's and now it's flat like a model's. Which is fine—I'm not about to complain or anything. You are still the most beautiful woman I've ever seen," he added hastily. "I actually memorized a poem after I saw you," he confessed.

Renee looked at him with total disbelief. Andrew saw her look and raised his right hand.

"I did. It's the only poem I ever memorized, and this is from a child who had to have a crib sheet for every church pageant; Bennie can verify that. Want me to say it for you?"

Renee nodded slowly and Andrew cleared his throat.

He looked at her fiercely and said, "Don't you laugh at me—this is serious. Okay."

With a look of total surrender he began speaking softly:

> "She walks in beauty, like the night
> Of cloudless climes and starry skies;
> And all that's best of dark and bright
> Meet in her aspect and her eyes;
> Thus mellow'd to that tender light
> Which heaven to gaudy day denies."

Renee was so touched that tears leaped to her eyes. Andrew leaned over and kissed away the tears.

"That wasn't supposed to make you cry," he said gruffly. "I must not recite very well."

Renee kissed him back, very gently. "Oh, no, Andy, you did it just right. You're so sweet; I don't think I deserve you," she said softly.

Andrew swallowed hard to get past the lump in his throat. "Well, I don't know about all that. But I know I deserve to eat. You worked me hard, woman. Feed me so I get my strength back," he said comically.

Renee kissed him once more and then did as he asked and fed him the tray of fruit, cheese and croissants that she had prepared. He moaned his appreciation as she fed him a piece of canary melon wrapped in prosciutto. His eyes lit up as she offered him a raspberry Bellini to follow the saltiness of the Italian ham; raspberries were another passion that they shared.

"You know, Renee, I could get used to this kind of treatment and want it all the time," he warned her. "What would you do then?"

Renee had gotten out of the bed to remove the tray and put it back on the trunk. She turned to look at Andrew, whose arms were crossed behind his head and who was wearing an extremely happy expression and nothing else.

"Well, I guess I'll cross that bridge when I get to it," she said with a smile. "In the meantime, how about the only bubble bath you may ever get in this house?" she asked over her shoulder as she walked toward the bathroom.

Andrew was out of the bed before she finished the sentence.

The next few weeks were as sweet and rhapsodic as anything either of them could have imagined, although not nearly as discreet. By some tacit agreement they still had not revealed their relationship to the world at large. It was still much too new and tender to be subjected to scrutiny, although various family members found out bits and pieces here and there.

Donnie discovered the truth of their relationship. The occasion was a cookout at Bennie and Renee's the day after Bennie's shower. Bennie was outdoors watching Alan and Andre grill the meat. Renee was in the kitchen arranging vegetables on kabobs to grill after the meat was done. Andrew was entering the kitchen with Donnie when Donnie got a wicked gleam in his eye. He picked up a dishtowel and wrapped it around Andrew's hand and doused the hand with a bottle of hot sauce that was on the cooking island. Before Andrew could protest, Donnie picked up a large knife and put it in Andrew's other hand.

Renee's back was to the two men and she was not paying them a bit of attention until Donnie's dramatic announcement.

"Damn! Renee, Andrew cut his hand!"

She whirled around with a look of total panic on her face. She had turned as pale as the French vanilla walls of the kitchen. Covering her mouth, she ran to Andrew.

"Oh, my God! Oh, baby, are you hurt? Donnie, call an ambulance, *now!* Oh, Andy, baby, let me see," she implored, trying to remove the dishtowel.

Andrew threw daggers at Donnie and took the towel off.

"Renee, sweetheart, it's just hot sauce. I'm not hurt; Donnie was just trying to be funny, that's all. I'm sorry, baby, really I am," he said gently.

Renee's relief was audible as she sighed heavily and wrapped her arms around Andrew's neck. She stayed there until her heart stopped pounding while he stroked her back with his clean hand. They stayed in each other's arms murmuring to each other and doing a lot of kissing, forgetting that Donnie was in the room.

Donnie was totally dumbfounded. Andrew's voice caught him before he could leave the room.

"You can apologize later, Adonis, but just make sure you keep this to yourself, okay?"

It was getting harder and harder to keep the relationship a secret from Bennie. Bennie was so wrapped up in wedding and moving-to-Atlanta plans that she hardly noticed what was going on around her, of that Renee was sure. But it was such a delightful secret that it was killing Renee not to confide in Bennie. She couldn't wait to see the look on her best friend's face when she found out her best friend and brother were a couple. But the timing wasn't quite right for Renee—she didn't want to distract Bennie in any way from the monumental tasks ahead of her. So she bided her time and thought she did a great job of keeping it under wraps.

Her entire staff at Urban Oasis was well aware that something incredible had happened to their boss. Renee had always been a pleasant person to work for and with; now she was a veritable goddess of joy. She floated into the salon in the mornings, she was charming and vivacious all day long and she was constantly thinking up things to show her staff how much she appreciated them. She would bring lunch in that she had prepared herself, or she would order out for everyone. There were added incentives, too, in the form of bonuses for outstanding performance. Urban Oasis was now

An important message from the ARABESQUE Editor

Dear Arabesque Reader,

Because you've chosen to read one of our Arabesque romance novels, we'd like to say "thank you"! And, as a special way to thank you, we've selected four more of the books you love so well to send you for FREE!

Please enjoy them with our compliments, and thank you for continuing to enjoy Arabesque...the soul of romance.

Karen Thomas
Senior Editor,
Arabesque Romance Novels

Check out our website at
www.arabesquebooks.com

SPECIAL OFFER!
4 FREE BOOKS

ARABESQUE ®
A PRODUCT OF
BET BOOKS

3 QUICK STEPS
TO RECEIVE YOUR "THANK YOU" GIFT
FROM THE EDITOR

Send this card back and you'll receive 4 FREE Arabesque novels! The introductory shipment of 4 Arabesque novels – a $23.96 value – is yours absolutely FREE!

There's no catch. You're under no obligation to buy anything. You'll receive your introductory shipment of 4 Arabesque novels absolutely FREE (plus $1.99 to offset the costs of shipping & handling). And you don't have to make any minimum number of purchases—not even one!

We hope that after receiving your books you'll want to remain an Arabesque subscriber. But the choice is yours to continue or cancel, anytime at all! So why not take us up on our invitation to receive 4 Arabesque Romance Novels, with no risk of any kind. You'll be glad you did!

Call us
TOLL-FREE
at 1-800-770-1963

THE EDITOR'S "THANK YOU" GIFT INCLUDES:

- 4 books absolutely FREE (plus $1.99 for shipping and handling)
- A FREE newsletter, *Arabesque Romance News*, filled with author interviews, book previews, special offers, and more!
- No risks or obligations. You're free to cancel whenever you wish... with no questions asked.

BOOK CERTIFICATE

Yes! Please send me 4 FREE Arabesque novels (plus $1.99 for shipping & handling). I understand I am under no obligation to purchase any books, as explained on the back of this card.

Name _____

Address _____ Apt. _____

City _____ State _____ Zip _____

Telephone ( ) _____

Signature _____
Offer limited to one per household and not valid to current subscribers. All orders subject to approval. Terms, offer, & price subject to change. Offer valid only in the U.S.

Thank you!

AN013A

Accepting the four introductory books for FREE (plus $1.99 to offset the cost of shipping & handling) places you under no obligation to buy anything. You may keep the books and return the shipping statement marked "cancelled". If you do not cancel, about a month later we will send 4 additional Arabesque novels, and you will be billed the preferred subscriber's price of just $4.00 per title. That's $16.00 for all 4 books for a savings of 33% off the cover price (Plus $1.99 for shipping and handling). You may cancel at any time, but if you choose to continue, every month we'll send you 4 more books, which you may either purchase at the preferred discount price. . . or return to us and cancel your subscription.

THE ARABESQUE ROMANCE CLUB: HERE'S HOW IT WORKS

ARABESQUE ROMANCE BOOK CLUB
P.O. Box 5214
Clifton NJ 07015-5214

PLACE
STAMP
HERE

the most sought-after salon in town as a place to work as well as a place to be royally pampered.

"I told you—hot and steamy does the trick every time, doesn't it?" Valerie said sagely one day.

"Hell yes," Renee said promptly. She did not even pretend that she did not know what Valerie was talking about.

They both cocked their heads in the often-used nod that meant "I-ain't-mad-atcha-witcha-bad-self" and started laughing. It was plain that Renee's emotional boundaries had been brought down by Andrew. And it was about time.

Andrew knew that Renee cared for him deeply—it was apparent in the way she talked to him, the way she treated him and the way she looked at him with her heart in her eyes. He didn't think he would ever get over the idea that he and Renee were a couple. The time that they spent together was like a gift to him, one that he had not had much time to enjoy lately. The military precision with which his sister's wedding arrangements was unfolding was terrible and fascinating to behold. Not to mention the fact that Bennie would be moving to Atlanta at the end of it all. As her housemate and best friend, Renee was naturally in the thick of these plans and did not have nearly as much free time as Andrew would have liked. Plus, she was going to have to use some of that precious time to visit her mother in Cleveland, something that Andrew was trying to be adult about.

"Andy, it's my mother's birthday, so of course I have to go," she said reasonably. "And you will be at that medical conference, anyway. So really, it couldn't have worked out better," she pointed out.

They were sitting on Andrew's huge leather sofa, rather, Renee was sitting and Andrew had his head in her lap. A cooling breeze came in through the open windows, and Jill Scott was playing softly. Only candles lit the room, and everything would have been perfect if they had been planning a weekend getaway instead of separate trips. Andrew said as much to Renee without even opening his eyes. He was too comfortable, for one thing, and he did not want his eyes to betray how much he was going to miss her for another. They were only going to be apart for a couple of days, but it was looming like a separation of months to Andrew. He took a deep breath and inhaled Renee's unique fragrance before drawing her head down for a long, lingering kiss.

As they pulled apart, he abruptly got up from his reclining position and stood, pulling Renee up with him. Without a word they began dancing, and before Renee could utter a word of protest, he had danced them up the stairs to his bedroom. Not that she would have said no—Andrew had her completely under his spell. Renee was still overwhelmed by the act of love as she experienced it with Andrew. He was gentle, passionate, inventive and energetic, everything that she had never had in a lover. In Andrew's arms she truly understood what it was like to be a fulfilled woman.

Andrew's eyes bored into hers as they removed each other's clothing, piece by piece, until they were completely naked and ready for each other's love. Andrew was the happy owner of a huge, heated water bed, a type of furniture Renee had never appreciated until the first time she lay down with Andrew in its warm embrace. With the pliant heat of the mattress underneath her and his firm, hot body on top of hers, it was like being suspended in ecstasy. This time was no exception as she felt herself surrounded by his arms. As he began tracing a line of kisses down her neck, Renee felt like she was being stroked with a mink glove. The moist heat of his tongue and lips was so profoundly sensual that she was lost in the exquisite pleasure that was building inside.

Renee was conscious only of the sweet fire that had overtaken her; it did not dawn on her exactly what Andrew was about to do until he reached the springy curls at the apex of her femininity. When she realized the depth of the intimacy that she was about to experience, she tried in vain to be nervous or embarrassed and discovered that all she felt was desire. Andrew was touching her with such desire and reverence that she lost the ability to think—she could only feel.

And what she felt defied description as wave after wave of hot, consuming passion rolled through her, leaving her weak from sensation. By the time Andrew had kissed his way back up her body to her lips, she was almost spent from the encounter. But then his lips touched hers and she was again wakened to ecstasy from his touch.

"Andy, that was . . . wonderful." She was too honest to hide her eyes; she looked directly at him so that he could see the happiness and desire shining out of them. Andrew did not respond right away—he was too taken with the love in her eyes. Finally he spoke.

"Do you know why it was so good, Renee?" He waited for her to shake her head from before he told her. "It's because I love you completely," he whispered.

Renee smiled and kissed him sweetly before urging him to turn over on his back so that she could straddle him with her long legs. She was poised over him like an African goddess with an incredible expression on her face while she stroked his chest with both hands.

"I'm going to give you something equally incredible, Andy. And do you know why? My darling Andrew, you are everything to me. You are my joy, my heart, my greatest treasure. I have never felt like this before and no one could ever make me feel this way again. I love you so much that when we are apart, my heart breaks hour by hour until we are together. You are my every thought, my every desire, and I love you with all my heart," she whispered in French.

Renee continued to stroke his muscular chest in preparation for her exploration of his body. She was smugly pleased that she had just told Andrew how much she adored him without his understanding a word of it. She spoke French to him every time they made love because it was easier than pouring out the overflowing emotions that she felt. Love and trust were still quite new to her, after all. So it was quite shocking when Andrew began to speak to her in a low, confident voice full of adoration.

"My darling Renee, to hear you say those words makes

me happier than you can imagine. I feel as though I have loved you my entire life. I don't think I really began to live until the moment that I met you. You are everything to me, now and forever. I adore you and I cannot conceive of any part of my life without you."

Renee was frozen from shock. Not that Andrew had spoken such loving words to her, but that he spoke them in perfect French. Oh, my, the jig was well and truly up now. She stared at him for a long moment and he smiled and shrugged.

"President of the French club for four years. Guess I forgot to mention that, huh?" he said with a guileless smile.

Renee couldn't help it; she started laughing. She should have been furious or embarrassed or something, but she wasn't. All she felt was joy at that particular moment. She collapsed on his chest amid the giggles and felt him laughing, too. Finally she was able to control herself long enough to roll over to his side and prop herself up on her elbow. She looked at the man she loved so dearly and sighed.

"You should be dreadfully ashamed of yourself, you know? There is nothing that you won't pull on me, is there?" she inquired. She was trying to look stern but was failing miserably.

"You're right. I should be ashamed, but I'm not. You volunteered the information, you know. It's not my fault if you were unaware that I could understand what you were saying. You wanted me to know that you love me, or you wouldn't have told me," he pointed out.

They kissed for a long time after that, until Renee's questing hand found irrefutable proof that there was much more to be done in the way of intimacy that evening.

"I still think there was something underhanded about it," she murmured. "But right now, there is something else I'd rather do with my lips than waste time losing an argument with you," she whispered.

Andrew moaned aloud as he realized just what she meant by that cryptic statement. This time it was Andrew who cried out a passionate message in French for Renee's ears only. They spent the rest of the night speaking a different kind of French with their hands and bodies as well as their hearts and minds.

Twelve

Renee loved visiting home so much that after a couple of hours she couldn't wait to be gone so that she could look forward to another visit. The anticipation of seeing her mother and sisters was often the most enjoyable part of any trip home, and Renee had learned over the years to space her homecomings wisely. Kemp women were characters—strong, formidable, delightful and lovable. And when all four of her sisters were together, plus their indefatigable mother, it was indescribable. Renee had a high tolerance for feminine foibles after working in the beauty industry for so long, but the Kemp women could wear her down fast.

Strictly speaking, they were not Kemps anymore, with the exceptions of her mother, Pearlie Mae, and herself. All of Renee's sisters were married to men whom Renee liked but did not understand. Of course, it was not her job to understand her brothers-in-law, but she had a time understanding why her sisters stayed married. Frankly, years of observing her sisters' courtships and marriages had left Renee feeling like a good marriage was somewhat like herding cats: theoretically possible but unproven.

Her oldest sister, Helena, a banker, was married to Sam, a quiet, docile man. Sam was so quiet and docile that Renee had at first thought he was a mute. He found disfavor with Renee because he was such a complete and utter doormat. Helena walked over him and wiped her feet daily, and Renee could not see that as being an integral part of any marriage that she would be party to.

Yet, Sam was preferable to Gloria's husband, Fred. Fred was loud, opinionated and bombastic. His motto seemed to be that if you can't be right, be wrong at the top of your lungs. Fred committed the unforgivable sin of being a Republican who was proud of the fact. He would spend hours espousing his conservative politics to anyone who would listen and was a true "bootstrap" brother in that he firmly believed that everyone should pull themselves up by their own. The fact that many people did not have shoes, much less boots with straps, seemed to escape him totally. How Gloria, a communications executive, had put up with years of his fundamental "Man is the head of the house" ramblings, Renee could not fathom, but she made it a point to avoid Fred whenever possible.

Then there was her sister LeeAnn, a teacher, who lived in New York. Renee was often glad that their paths did not cross more often, since she and LeeAnn did not sit horses on a lot of issues. LeeAnn thought that Renee needed to get married and settle down. Renee thought that if LeeAnn were any more settled, she would be a statue. She looked at the plump, dowdy woman that her vibrant sister had evolved into and placed the blame squarely on the shoulders of LeeAnn's husband, Gordan, who owned a talent agency and was constantly surrounded by beautiful, flashy people at beautiful, flashy events. He dressed out of Barney's and Bloomingdale's and places of that nature. LeeAnn looked like a frump in comparison, which Renee thought unforgivable.

And then there was her youngest sister, Karen, who owned a bakery. Karen had moved out to Hawaii sometime before to get over a heartbreak and moved back home with a new husband. A big, strong, blond surfer of a husband, thank you very much. Tim was not stupid or cruel; he was just so totally foreign that he seemed alarmingly out of place in the family. This liaison had truly frightened Renee, but it showed no signs of abating.

Renee looked at all of her sisters around the dining-room table in her mother's house and sighed with happiness. She loved each and every one of them, no matter how much they got in her business and tried to tell her and one another what to do. They were her family and she adored them, even now while they were fighting over the assortment of hair care products she customarily brought home to them. She was hoping that the friendly bickering would deflect undesired attention from her, and she was partially right. Only LeeAnn, the most perceptive of her sisters, was truly observing her, a fact of which Renee was completely aware. *I'm in for it now. She is going to corner me before the weekend is over,* Renee thought, and she was right.

Renee's mother, the estimable Pearlie Mae Kennedy Kemp, made her way into the dining room from the kitchen, where she had been seeing to the dinner that she customarily prepared for the first night of Renee and LeeAnn's visits, since they were in from out of town. The rest of the time the daughters would be expected to cook—that went without saying. But tonight it was Mama's home cooking, a fact that she was happy to hold over everyone's head.

"Since I've been up since dawn preparing a meal, I would think the least you wild mares could do would be to set the table. Instead, you all come in here huddled over these bottles of gunk like they're full of holy water," she grumbled.

It was a mistake to take Pearlie Mae's gruffness personally; she simply liked being the center of attention and would use whatever means necessary to maintain that position. However, Pearlie Mae had not raised any fools, either, so while Renee mollified her with her own personal shopping bag full of products, the other women cleared off the table and got the table set with a quickness. Their mother had perfected the art of keeping them off balance with her temperament and there was no point in risking a real scene.

"Now, Mama, you make sure you actually use these products and don't just keep them for show. And don't give them away to the girls, either, they have plenty of their own," Renee reminded her. "The girls" were her teenage nieces who could wrap their grandmother around their little fingers.

Pearlie Mae looked over each bottle and jar and sniffed them but made no promises about the use of the contents. She patted her thick, luxuriant hair, which had just a few strands of white, and sighed. "Well, since you're so ashamed of my hair, I guess I'd better make an effort to use this stuff. I certainly wouldn't want to embarrass you in public," she said in a hurt voice.

Renee took a deep breath and counted to ten. This was just another variation of her mother's mind games. To say "Gee, thanks for the hair stuff!" would be just too much like right. Instead of a simple thanks, there always had to be a mini passion play staged to demonstrate how Renee had somehow failed her as a daughter. But not today. She was saved from comment by LeeAnn's entry into the living room, where she and Pearlie Mae were seated.

LeeAnn was also immune to her mother's games by virtue of being the second oldest and living so far away. She had too many years of their mother's theatrics under her belt to be impressed by any of Pearlie Mae's machinations. And as she often told Renee, having children of her own more or less put the cap on it for her. It gave her both a better understanding of her mother and a greater intolerance for her carrying on. She joined her mother on the sofa and watched her try to wheedle a necklace away from Renee.

"Oh, baby, that sure is a pretty necklace. Let Mama try it on," she said sweetly.

Renee did not make a move to unfasten the necklace the way she normally would have. All she did was look at her mother with her long-lashed golden eyes and say, "No."

Pearlie Mae squinted as though she had not heard her daughter correctly. Before Mount Pearlie erupted, Renee smiled nicely and said that she never removed the necklace, as it had been a special gift from a special friend. She said this without a glimmer of regret, too. Most galling of all, she did not attempt to change the subject or leave the room, she just sat there as if to dare her mother to ask again.

Pearlie stared at Renee and lowered her gaze to the necklace again. It was a big teardrop-shaped South Sea pearl in a rare shade of pink that was completely natural. The pearl was crowned by an eighteen-karat braided cap suspended from a thick gold chain that was long enough to just touch her cleavage. It was obviously very expensive and very rare, and Renee was willing to risk her mother's wrath to guard it. Pearlie was not to be denied, though. She was just about to get really dramatic about it when LeeAnn intervened.

"Mom, we need a few things from the store, so Renee is going to drive me over there. Be back in a few," she said, and hustled Renee out of there fast and in a hurry.

Renee was full of admiration for her big sister. "That was slick," she said gratefully. "Although I think I could have taken her. Maybe."

LeeAnn looked at her and they burst out laughing. Renee and Karen at five-ten were the tallest of the five sisters. LeeAnn, Gloria and Helen all hovered around the five-eight mark. They all resembled each other with their hourglass figures and golden toffee complexions—all but the chocolate-colored Renee. Their personal styles all varied, but the one thing they shared was the fact that they had all outgrown the diminutive Pearlie Mae, who was a mere five-five. But their mother was feisty enough to beat them all until their legs "roped like okra," something she would periodically point out, to the sisters' chagrin. Today, however, marked a turning point in Renee's relationship with her mother.

"You know, that is the first time I ever saw you turn Mom down when she asked you for something," LeeAnn remarked as they wheeled the cart around the grocery store. "That necklace must have come from the man who has made such a difference in your life," she added sagely.

Renee stopped the cart and stared at her sister. She had

not said a thing about Andrew so far, so how did LeeAnn presume to know that Renee was involved with anyone? LeeAnn answered her unasked question.

"Renee, honey, it's all over your face! You are *happy,* for one thing. You don't have that tense and edgy look that I have come to associate with you. You aren't bragging about those excursions you used to take with those geriatric gigolos. You touch that necklace about every three minutes, and every third time you smile like Ed McMahon just handed you *the* check and you sigh," LeeAnn pointed out. "You're in love, little sister. *True* love, and don't you even try and deny it! I know you, girl. I used to change your diapers. So you'd better dish, girl, or I'll make up something really ugly and tell Gloria."

Renee laughed but looked puzzled. "You mean tell Mama, don't you?"

"No, chile, I mean tell Gloria. You know the girl is like an old refrigerator—she can't keep nothin'. And she'll run to tell Mom and make it even worse. So get to talkin'."

Renee was happy to unburden herself and talk, *really* talk, about Andrew for the first time with someone other than Ceylon. While she and LeeAnn shopped, she told her everything about her romance with Andrew, leaving out only a few of the more intimate details. There were, after all, some things that a sister shouldn't know. She was happy to tell how Andrew had surprised her with the fabulous necklace, though.

They were about to leave her house one evening and Andrew had patted his pockets absentmindedly. He fished out the small jeweler's box and presented it to Renee without any kind of fanfare, just saying, "Here. This reminded me of you."

Renee had opened the box curiously and then stared at the contents for so long that Andrew had gotten worried. When she finally found her voice, she murmured, "Andrew, this is the most beautiful thing I have ever seen. It's astounding," she said in a voice choked with emotion.

He had sighed in great relief. "Don't do that to me! I thought you didn't like it." Without waiting for a response from her, he took the necklace out of the box and put it around her neck. He stepped back and looked at the lustrous pearl resting just at her cleavage and smiled.

"Now, that is beautiful. Your neck, not the necklace." He leaned over and kissed her quickly. "It suddenly hit me one day that I had never bought you a present. And I saw this, and I thought that it was like you. It is unique, one of a kind, miraculous and natural, and it is very, very lovely. And so are you."

Renee was so overcome that she wanted nothing more than to have a good cry and spend several hours kissing, but Andrew kissed her tears away and dragged her out the door.

"That's dessert. I want food and I want it now!"

Renee and LeeAnn had returned to their mother's house by the time Renee was finished telling her all about Andrew. LeeAnn hugged her hard and told her how happy she was that Renee had found someone like Andrew.

"I know it is rude of me to say this, but I was getting worried about you, Renee. You had become so haughty, so self-involved and stuck-up that I was afraid you were doomed to a life lived alone. I am not saying that everyone in the world has to get married," she said hastily. "But I think it is essential to most people's nature to want to have a loving relationship with someone special. I was afraid that the sweet, loving, adorable little sister I knew had turned into a hard, unloving woman who would never know that kind of joy. And now I see it all over your face, and I am glad."

Renee blinked several times. She wasn't quite sure of what to make of that statement, and she did not have time to fathom it since it was clear that dinner was ready to be served. She and LeeAnn quickly put away the groceries they had purchased and washed up. By the time they entered the dining room, the sisters and Pearlie Mae were already seated. Her nieces and nephews were not in attendance— this was strictly sisters and Mama. After grace was said, everyone got busy passing dishes and chattering a mile a minute.

Renee looked around at her sisters as if they were a sorority that she was thinking about pledging. Was she ready for the kind of permanency that each of them had opted for? Marriage—a huge step and a huge word. And kind of beside the point, anyway, since no one had mentioned it besides LeeAnn. But for the first time the idea of marriage did not cause her stomach muscles to clench and her ears to ring. In fact, it made her think of something—someone—else altogether. Renee was so mesmerized that she ignored the platter of baked chicken that Gloria was trying to pass to her. Lost in thought, she stroked the pink pearl with her fingertip.

After the celebration of her mother's birthday, Andrew made a solemn vow that Renee was not getting out of his sight again. It was just too taxing. He had missed her more than he thought possible in the three days they had been apart. He said as much to her when they were back in each other's arms and she was suitably pleased with his words. Although, she was practical as usual, reminding him that she and Donnie were driving Bennie's car down to Atlanta after the honeymoon.

"So I will be gone for a few days in October. Do you think you will live through it?" she teased.

Andrew looked at her with all seriousness and said, "No. I think I will have to go with you instead of Donnie. I'll miss you too much." He kissed her with great passion, which silenced both of them for a while. Then he felt compelled to comment on her living arrangements for the tenth time.

"I just don't like the idea of you being in this big mausoleum of a house all by yourself after Bennie moves to Atlanta. I mean, I understand her not wanting to sell it right now, and your continuing to live here is a good solution, I guess, but this house is so big and I just don't like the idea of you being here alone," he said worriedly.

Renee lay in his arms, savoring his warmth and concern. Andrew was so genuinely sweet that she couldn't bear it sometimes. She loved the way he worried about her safety, but she didn't want him fretting unnecessarily.

"Andy, love, I am a big girl, for one thing. For another, how often are you actually going to leave me here alone? You will be here or I will be at your place a lot of the time, if you stop and think about it. And one of my nieces is thinking about coming to Wayne State for the winter semester and she will live here with me. So stop worrying, okay? I will be just fine," she promised, nuzzling his neck contentedly.

They were in Andrew's living room enjoying the last moment or two of solitude they would have for the next few days. Bennie's wedding was in three days and chaos was about to reign, despite everyone's best efforts. There were so many people involved and so many out-of-town guests that it boggled the mind. Renee had struggled to keep overnight guests from flooding the big Indian Village house, but it was inevitable that there would be a few people underfoot. She sighed a deep and heartfelt sigh at the thought of it.

"You aren't tired of me already, are you?" Andrew joked.

Renee closed her eyes and leaned closer into him. "No, darling, I'm not. Never will be. I'm just thinking about all those people that will be swarming around this weekend, not the least of whom will be Her Majesty Queen Pearlie Mae. She thinks I'm up to something illicit with you, and the fact that she's right is absolutely no reason for her to be so vigilant, but that's Ms. Queen for you. I will never escape her, you watch."

Andrew laughed as he stretched out so that Renee was lying on top of him. "Don't worry about a thing, sweet Renee. Let me take care of Ms. Queen."

Over the next couple of days, Renee forgot her apprehension over her mother and concentrated on getting her friend married. Bennie's brothers and Clay's went off for an evening of gambling in the casinos of Greektown, in downtown Detroit, and Windsor, Ontario, the Canadian city right across the river from Detroit. It was a much less harmless bachelor party than a night of debauchery at what Bennie referred to as a "booty bar," although Windsor was full of those establishments, too. Bennie was not about to object to the guys having fun, but she did pull Andrew aside and assure him that her beloved had better come back in the same condition he left.

"Not a scratch, Bunchy, or else. I'm putting my baby in your hands, so you have to be the designated sane grownup for the night," she said sternly.

Andrew swore to protect Clay with his life, and the evening went off without a hitch. Clay was even thoughtful enough to win a few thousand dollars at baccarat, which he gave to Bennie for mad money on their honeymoon.

While this was going on, Renee had a special spa day for all the wedding participants. From the flower girls to the bride, they were manicured, pedicured, coiffed and pampered until everyone was radiantly lovely. Clay's mother was especially pleased with the results. She was not only seeing her oldest son married to a wonderful woman, she was doing some serious courting of her own with Bump Williams, whose band was providing the music for his goddaughter's reception.

"Oh, Renee, I love this new hairstyle!" she exclaimed, looking at herself in the three-way mirror. "Bill Williams is not going to know what hit him," she said confidently.

Renee couldn't help but smile—love and affection were flowing as freely as spring water in a French aquifer and it felt wonderful to be a part of it all, even if Mrs. Queen was trying to put a damper on it. She had done her mother's hair earlier in a separate appointment because she knew Pearlie Mae might have some pithy and unkind things to say about the institution of marriage—and she did.

"You know, Renee, you are the only one of my children who has any sense. Why someone wants to tie herself down with a husband is beyond me! You have the right idea, daughter—stay single and stay smart. Don't be a fool like your sisters, and please don't follow my example. Just keep doing what you're doing and you'll be just fine," Pearlie Mae intoned.

Renee did not say a word throughout this diatribe; she just smiled a little catlike smile. *You are so right, Mama dear—I fully intend to keep doing just what I'm doing,* she thought. Of course, her mother had no way of knowing that what she was doing was loving every minute of being in love with Dr. Andrew Bernard Cochran Jr. LeeAnn was still the only one of her sisters who knew the truth of the situation, and Renee saw no reason to share the information at that particular time. She just wanted to get through the wedding and see Bennie and Clay off on their honeymoon without any added theatrics.

When the day of the wedding finally dawned, it was pouring rain, which thrilled Bennie because some bit of wedding folklore suggested that this was a lucky omen. By the time the wedding party left for the church it was sunny and bright and perfect. Renee was thoroughly impressed with Bennie's serenity—nothing seemed to touch her. She was beatific and calm and radiant, and when she was finally adorned in her amazing custom-made gown, she was beyond beautiful.

Renee could feel tears welling up in her eyes as she put the final touches on Bennie's hair. This was the natural culmination of the love that Bennie and Clay shared. This was the logical next step for them, for most people who were as much in love and as committed as they were. And despite what her mother felt, despite what she had always felt about marriage, Renee realized at that moment that this could be the next step for her and Andrew. It was an epiphany for Renee, a flash of insight that was staggering. Hoping that her face did not reveal what she was feeling, she squeezed Bennie's hands tightly before hurrying to take her place in the processional.

Even though Andrew was not a big fan of weddings, he

had to admit that his sister's was beautiful. Truthfully, he didn't observe too much after Renee wafted down the aisle as the maid of honor; her beauty mesmerized him as always. She looked indescribably pretty in a bronze dress made out of some shimmery stuff that made her eyes glow and her skin look like velvet. He was so taken with her beauty that he almost missed the moment that his sister entered the church on the arm of their father.

Andrew had to swallow hard to handle the huge lump in his throat as he watched his beloved sister enter the church. He had always been thankful that Clay had plenty of brothers to act as groomsmen because it meant that he wouldn't have to be in the wedding. If all the Cochran and Deveraux men had to be in it, it would have been a carnival-size affair. So he got to watch his sister go to meet her husband and got to see all the joy on her lovely expression. He also observed the passion and love all over Clay's face. They looked like lovers in a Renaissance painting, flushed with adoration and contentment.

At that moment Andrew knew that this was a journey that he wanted to take with Renee. Not on this scale, certainly, but with this much love and commitment. Andrew knew as well as he knew his name that this was what he wanted for himself and the woman he loved.

The reception was spectacular, but to Andrew and Renee it was much too long. They wanted to be alone with each other, something that seemed virtually impossible. Renee danced with every single person there, it seemed to her—Bennie's father, all of Bennie's brothers and all of Clay's, with the exception of Martin, who claimed he did not dance. Martin and his identical twin brother, Malcolm, were next to Clay in age. This was the first time Renee met him, since he was rather reclusive as the result of a tragedy.

Some years earlier, Martin had been in a terrible car accident, which caused him to be rather badly scarred on the left side of his body. His wife had left him upon seeing the extent of his injuries; as a result he was not the most trusting of men. As well, he had a handsome identical twin to remind him daily of what he had lost. Martin was friendly enough but aloof, Renee thought. What Ceylon thought was another matter entirely. When she laid eyes on Martin, she was struck dumb, which for someone like Ceylon was saying something. She stared at the tall, brooding man with the eye patch and tried to catch her breath.

"Renee, who is that beautiful man over there?" she whispered.

Renee looked around, mystified. "Ceylon, honey, you have to be more specific. There's, like, three thousand good-looking men in here at last count," she said, laughing. Ceylon did not hear the teasing in her friend's voice, so mesmerized was she with Martin's overwhelming masculinity. "I mean, that gorgeous man with the patch on his eye. Who is he? If he's married, I swear I'll open a vein right here in this ballroom," she vowed.

Renee looked at Ceylon and saw she was quite serious. "That's Clay's brother Martin. And he's not the most sociable person you are going to meet tonight. But no, he's not married," she confirmed.

Ceylon smiled sweetly and her index finger stroked a curl of her short, silky hair. "He's not married now, but he will be soon. To me." She started to walk toward him and Renee stopped her.

"Do you want me to introduce you?" she asked.

Ceylon just smiled again. "Thanks, but no. I can handle this all by myself," she purred.

Renee stared after her bemusedly. Ceylon was certainly not afraid to go after what she wanted. She just hoped that Martin's bitterness did not make him lash out at Ceylon. *Then again, knowing Ceylon, Martin is the one who needs to look out,* she thought. The thought of the stern and unyielding Martin pursued by the passionate and effervescent Ceylon put a big smile on her face, which Andrew observed as he joined her at a secluded table. "I hope that big, beautiful smile is for me," he said softly as he reached for her hand under the tablecloth.

"This smile and everything else I have. It's all for you, Andy," she said in an equally soft voice as their fingers entwined. She loved the look of raw passion that came over his face as she spoke. She just loved him, period. And she wanted to be with him so badly that she felt as if she were on fire.

As if he could read her thoughts, Andrew responded: "I have a surprise for you, Renee. Come with me." He rose from the table and took her hand. Before they could make their escape, however, it was time for Bennie to throw her bouquet and Clay to throw the garter. Of all the silly things to have to put up with now, this was the silliest. Renee was so intent on sneaking out of the ballroom unnoticed by her mother or sisters that when the bouquet left Bennie's hands, she was paying it no attention whatsoever. When it landed in her arms, Renee was as thrilled as if someone had handed her a live chicken.

Andrew had whipped out his ever-handy cell phone to make an urgent call and was trying to keep an eye on Renee at the same time. So when the champagne-colored garter with the tiny cerise rose landed on the antenna of his phone, he was understandably startled. While everyone laughed, he immediately tossed it away from him like it was a large insect. Finally the hubbub died down long enough for him to grab Renee's hand and make tracks.

They were seated in his Bentley heading for Birmingham and the Townsend Hotel, a lovely establishment that looked as though its only purpose was to serve as a trysting place for lovers. Before Renee could utter a word of protest, Andrew assured her that everything was under control.

"Your mom is going to have quite the hangover tomorrow, but your sister LeeAnn, who likes me a lot—thank you very much—is going to keep her fine and mellow and out of your hair for the next twelve hours or so. And she is more than happy to play hostess in your absence, so we don't have to go home until tomorrow morning. And someone is taking all my calls, so we are totally on our own," he finished happily.

Renee just stared at him. "You mean to tell me that you and my sister conspired to get my mother drunk so that you and I could have an evening of hot, unbridled sex under her very nose?" she said in a voice of indignation and righteousness. "I wish I'd thought of that. You're good. Very, very good," she praised. As they pulled to a stop at a traffic light, Andrew leaned over and planted a big, noisy kiss on Renee.

"That's not the only thing I'm good at. I have a few more talents that I can't wait to place at your disposal," he said with a wicked grin.

Renee returned the kiss with one of her own and slid her hand up his thigh to a crucial juncture. As he moaned with pleasure, Renee informed him that the light was now green.

"Let's go, Andy. I wouldn't want any of your talent to go to waste," she murmured as she stroked him harder.

They were at the hotel and checked in five minutes later.

Thirteen

Even days after the wedding Renee was still glowing. It had been such a wonderful celebration of love and happiness for Bennie and Clay that her heart was completely warmed. Besides, it had proven to be quite a turning point in her relationship with Andrew. The cat was well and truly out of the bag now; everyone knew that they were in love. Andrew had always said that they would know when the right time came to let everyone know, and he was right. The timing could not have been better.

As it turned out, Andrew was right about a lot of things concerning Bennie's wedding. For one thing, Renee's mother did indeed have a tiny hangover the next day. But Pearlie Mae did not mind that minor inconvenience. She had seen what everyone else at the wedding had seen— that Renee and Andrew were truly a couple. For some unknown reason, she decided that she was okay with that development, much to Renee's surprise.

Renee had quite honestly been holding her breath when her mother had come face-to-face with Andrew; one never knew what gems the lovely Pearlie Mae would retrieve from the "archives," as Renee and her sisters referred to Pearlie's store of witticisms. One thing that was in Andrew's favor was the fact that he was not a stranger. He had met all of Renee's family on many occasions over the years and had always left a favorable impression. At the reception Pearlie Mae was, for her, effusively glad to see Andrew.

"Well, young man, I see that you are looking no worse for the wear," she intoned while looking him up and down. "In point of fact, you are looking quite well. Well enough to dance, one might hope," she added with a steely glint in her eye.

Andrew got the rather broad hint immediately and escorted her out onto the dance floor, where they danced a few numbers together. Pearlie Mae's expression changed from distant to warm to downright bubbly, right in front of Renee's amazed eyes. Gloria and LeeAnn could not resist needling her in the tradition of older sisters. They sat together at one of the big round tables and watched their mother flirt outrageously with Andrew while Renee grew more and more apprehensive. *What is she saying to him? And, more importantly, what is he saying to her?*

"You're just dying to know what they're talking about, aren't you?" Gloria teased. "Well, just remember the hoops of fire that she had our boyfriends jumping through. It's your turn, little sister. She's probably asking him how much he makes per annum right now." Gloria laughed boisterously.

Renee moaned and pressed her fingers to her temples. LeeAnn saw no reason to alleviate her suffering; she chimed right in after Gloria.

"Oh, no, girl, she's probably asking him for his last AIDS test and his credit rating. Then she'll ask what his intentions are concerning her *spinster* daughter. She might even ask for a motility count to see if he can still father children," LeeAnn pointed out.

Stifling a shriek, Renee reached for a glass of champagne on the tray of a passing waiter. After watching her down it in one swallow, her sisters relented. It was plain that Andrew and Renee meant a great deal to each other and Renee's sisters hastened to assure her that even the original Ms. Queen would not say or do anything untoward, at least not today.

"She likes to bide her time," LeeAnn said truthfully. "She has the rest of your lives to meddle, so she'll pace herself. Now, after you and Andrew get hitched? It's *on*, sister, so watch your back." The three women looked at each other and burst out laughing.

It was such a relief to be able to be open and honest about their relationship that Renee was almost giddy. And it wasn't like it was such a big surprise, anyway. Even Andrew's father had some inkling that Andrew had more than a passing interest in his sister's best friend. Big Benny was happy to inform her of that while they were dancing.

"So. You and Andrew finally decided to act like adults, did you? It's about time. I was wondering if you two were ever going to get over that foolishness and see that you were meant for each other," he said affectionately.

Renee blushed deeply. She and Big Benny had always gotten along like a house afire—he was, in fact, known to refer to her as his other daughter from time to time. Still, it was rather touching to have his obvious approval. She smiled up at him sweetly and was about to speak when he added a bit of wisdom.

"All I can tell you is to take care of each other and love each other. And for God's sake, *elope*. Damned weddings cost too much," he grumbled.

Renee took a lot of pleasure in telling Andrew some of the milder things that had been said regarding their new status as a couple. Andrew had taken it all in stride, acting as though he had known all along that their liaison would be greeted with cheers.

"Renee, sweetheart, when are you going to realize that I am the smartest man in the world, especially when it comes to us?" he asked rhetorically.

At the moment that he made his pronouncement, they were sitting before the fireplace in the living room of the Indian Village house. It wasn't really cold enough for a fire, but the evening was cool and rainy and autumnal and they both felt the need for a cozy backdrop. Renee took her time in answering—she was curled in his lap with her cheek resting against his chest and she was perfectly content, except for one thing. Finally she spoke.

"I know you're the smartest man in the world, darling. That's why you were asked to be on that surgical team. I am still in awe over that," she confessed.

Andrew sighed briefly. He had been asked to participate in some groundbreaking surgery that was going to be extremely complicated and had never been attempted before. A set of twins was born conjoined in such a way that if they were not separated, death was certain for both of the babies. They were joined at the head and shared parts of their skull as well as brain matter. Until very recently, no one would have attempted this kind of surgery, but a world-renowned neurosurgeon who had done amazing things with intercranial surgeries was going to make the attempt. Andrew was his first choice for the facial maxillary surgery that would also take place. Both babies would lose an eye, but there was a very good chance that both would live.

Renee turned her face to Andrew when she heard his sigh. "What's the matter, honey? Is all the notoriety of this case getting to you already?" she asked with concern. As much as they tried to keep the procedure under wraps, the media was already hounding the family of the children as well as the doctors for interviews, thus turning the case into a tabloid feeding frenzy.

Andrew assured her that was not it. "I'm not crazy about all the attention, that's for sure. I want to do this, Renee, for a lot of reasons. There are a lot of people who can be helped if this works. And this is the perfect case for the new polymer replacement material I have been developing. I'm really looking forward to getting started on this and doing our best to save both of those babies. I just wish the timing were better, that's all," he said glumly.

Before Renee could ask him what he was talking about, he reminded her that he wanted to go to Atlanta with her to take Bennie her car and her cat. "It's just not going to be possible, Renee. I'm sorry, but I just can't leave town right now," he said ruefully.

Renee kissed him sweetly and passionately then, forestalling any further conversation. Andrew brightened up immediately.

"I don't know what that was for, but I'll take as many of those as you have on hand," he quipped.

Renee stroked his face and smiled. "It's because every time I think I can't love you any more, I fall in love with you all over again. Here you are on the brink of one of the biggest cases of your career and you are concerned about taking me on some little trip. You are the sweetest man in the world, you know that?"

Andrew was considerably more cheerful by now. "Yes, I am," he agreed without shame. "Let's see—I'm the smartest and the sweetest. . . . Tell me I'm the best-looking and I'll run for office. Ouch!" He winced in fake pain as Renee punched him lightly in the arm.

"You're quite crazy, you know." Renee tried to look stern but failed miserably. Andrew was happy to agree with her, though.

"Damned right I am. Crazy for you," he replied, growling before pulling her down on top of him and showing her just how delightful crazy could be.

Despite Andrew's absence, Donnie and Renee had a great old time on the way to Atlanta, Aretha less so. She was not fond of riding in cars, particularly when she was confined to her despised carrier. But left to her own devices, she liked to drape herself across the steering wheel or ferret her way between the driver's legs and other dangerous activities. So she was tidily caged up on the backseat, where she made her displeasure known with periodic snarls. Renee tried talking to her for a while but was rebuffed.

"Well, just remember, it was this or drugs. I was trying to do you a favor, and this is how you act. Suit yourself, cat."

Donnie looked at Renee out of the corner of his eye. "Uh, Renee? Are you under the impression that she can understand you?"

"Of course she can. And I have heard you talking to those ruffian retrievers of yours just like they are children, so don't you even go there," she reminded him.

"Yeah," Donnie agreed, "but they're *dogs*." The implication of course was that dogs could understand human talk and behavior whereas cats could not. They argued amicably over the various merits of dogs and cats and talked about different kinds of music, the latest movies and everything else they could think of as the car ate up the miles to Atlanta.

Donnie and Renee had always shared a special rapport. They both loved Bennie devotedly and, perhaps because of that love, accepted each other in a sibling role. Donnie was particularly pleased that Renee and Andrew had found their way to each other. He, like everyone else, had sensed that there might be something behind all their bickering and dislike, although he couldn't understand how they could have let it go on for so long. "I just hope that I am smart enough to know when I have met the right woman, and lucky enough to have her feel the same way about me. The one thing I do not want is a lot of drama," he said sincerely.

Renee smiled at him fondly. "Well, sometimes the getting there is half the fun. Although with Andrew, I must say that *being* there is even better." She sighed. "And what about Miss Aneesah? I thought she was pretty much your girl for life," Renee teased.

Donnie smiled sheepishly. "Okay, now you've quit preaching and gone to meddling, as Aunt Ruth would say. You know I'm crazy about Aneesah. But she wants to go to Stanford after she finishes her M.B.A. She says she's not stopping until somebody calls her Doctor Shabazz. Which is cool, I applaud that. She's smart as hell and she's ambitious. But I'm not leaving Detroit and the business is going to be expanding, so we are going to have as much fun as we can until she leaves next summer. End of story," he said matter-of-factly, but with genuine regret.

They continued to talk and enjoy each other's company until their arrival in Atlanta. Renee was bowled over as usual by the sight of Bennie and Clay's majestic house. Nestled in a wooded area on the outskirts of Atlanta, it was perfect for the couple. Unique and well proportioned, it was exquisitely furnished with a combination of their furniture and some new pieces that Bennie had purchased right after the honeymoon. It was always a pleasure to visit in the beautiful house, but it was a greater pleasure for Renee to see her best friend. Especially now that she could talk about Andrew, something that she had been dying to do for months.

"Bennie, girl, I have to tell you that you are just radiant. Radiant! Marriage certainly agrees with you, my dear." Renee could not get over how Bennie was fairly glowing with happiness. She was so blissful she *sparkled.*

Bennie raised an eyebrow as she looked at her friend. They were seated in the cozy breakfast room to one side of her cavernous kitchen. She poured a cup of Renee's favorite tea, Lapsang souchong, and offered her a plate of imported crumpets. Renee took one and remarked that she liked them much better than English muffins because of their density. Bennie narrowed her eyes and offered to pour the homemade marmalade over Renee's head if she did not talk.

"Girl, if you do not cut the small talk, I will hurt you! You know that I am dying for details about you and Bunchy and you just keep sidestepping the issue. Now, I am *slow,* I will grant you that. But I am not *blind,* and I saw you two at the reception looking like you had just invented love. What happened? When did it happen? How did he? . . . When did you? . . . Where were you? . . ." Bennie had so many questions that she couldn't get them out fast enough.

Renee was laughing so hard by this time that she could barely speak, but she managed to hold up her hand.

"Okay, okay, you win. But please understand, I did not want to tell anyone anything until we knew that it was real, and it would last more than a couple of days," she said sincerely. And to Bennie's delight, she went on to tell her the whole story of their courtship. Even after all this time, Renee hated to open up that wound with Bennie. She believed in her heart that she had built a bridge and gotten over it, so there was no sense in rehashing it for time immemorial. Besides, the bridge's name was Andrew, at least half of it was.

To say Bennie was delighted was an understatement. She was absolutely thrilled with the news.

"Ne-ne, I have wanted you two to get together forever! I never brought it up because I knew that you would have me committed if I did, but I always thought you two would be divine together. I always sensed that Bunchy had some kind of interest in you, but he would never confide it all the way. But I still knew, in my heart, that you would be perfect for each other." She sighed happily.

"Bennie, what horse doody! You had to keep us from killing each other half the time!" Renee protested. Bennie's joy was sweet, but there was no need to glamorize the earlier relationship between Renee and Andrew.

Bennie demurred, however. "Unh-unh. That wasn't true enmity, you know. It was all that pent-up passion and unfulfilled desire that made you two act the way you did. You know that twins have this psychic bond and know what the other is thinking. With Bunchy and me it goes deeper, though—we can feel physically what the other one is feeling. Like, if you were to hit me, Bunchy would feel it," she said offhandedly.

Renee grew pensive for a moment. "You mean, if I were to pinch you, he would feel it?" she asked slowly.

Bennie nodded. "Yes, and get the bruise, too."

Bizarre things started forming in Renee's mind. "So, does that mean that every time we . . ." She puckered her face up in an expression of disgust and could not finish the thought.

" 'Fraid so," Bennie agreed with a sigh. "It's one of the drawbacks of being a twin."

Renee's face was frozen in horror. "You never told me that before. . . . It's . . . *unnatural.* It's weird! You have got to be making that up!" she said desperately.

Bennie smiled sadly. "I am. Gotcha!"

Renee looked relieved enough to weep and Bennie almost felt bad for teasing her. *Almost.*

"That's what you get for keeping secrets from me! And I have more of the same for my darling twin. Oh, Renee, I am so, so happy about this! My best friend and my best twin are in love." To Renee's delight, she started singing Chanté Moore's song in their honor, about Renee having a man at home.

All Renee could do was smile idiotically because she often hummed the same tune to herself when she thought she was alone. And why not? Andrew was her man and her home was wherever he was.

After a few days of Bennie and Clay's hospitality, Renee was more than ready to get back to Detroit and Andrew. Donnie was staying over an extra day to go over some business deal that he was in with Clay and The Deveraux Group, Clay's media conglomerate. Renee just wanted to get back home. Urban Oasis needed her, and so did Andrew. Bennie took her to the airport and insisted on getting her some reading material from a newsstand. Renee was just making sure that her boarding pass was handy and that her carry-on bag was at the ready when her attention was caught by something in the crowded area leading to the concourse.

Even days later, she was not sure what made her turn her head, but whatever it was, it seemed to signal the end of everything for which she had worked so hard. Her peripheral vision revealed a tall, fair-skinned man of medium build with distinctive brown hair cut in a timeless rather than trendy cut. He was dressed conservatively and expensively and moved with the absolute assurance of someone who is welcome everywhere he goes. Although she could not see his full face, what she saw was enough.

It was the face she had seen often enough in her nightmares to have memorized the exact number and placement of every pore of his skin, every hair of his mustache. It belonged to Donovan Bailey, the world-famous journalist, author, lecturer and *rapist*. It was the face of the man who had nearly destroyed her.

Fourteen

Bennie returned from the kiosk loaded with magazines. "I got you *Marie Claire* and *Essence,* and of course I got you *Image;* we must support out Deveraux Group," she said cheerfully. She stopped speaking immediately when she got a look at Renee's face, which was now a sickly gray.

"Ne-ne! Honey, are you sick? Sit down here and let me get you some water!" Bennie exclaimed.

Allowing Bennie to seat her, Renee brushed aside her offer of water.

"I'm . . . I'm fine," she got out. "I just got a little dizzy, that's all. It's a little hot in here," she finished lamely.

Bennie looked at Renee carefully. The grayish color was giving way to Renee's normal complexion, but a faint sheen of perspiration coated her brow. Bennie couldn't help herself—she went there.

"Um, Ne-ne? You couldn't be toting a niece or nephew of mine in there, could you?" she asked hopefully while looking at Renee's stomach.

That did the trick as Renee sat bolt upright, put her hands on her hips and swiveled her neck as if to say that Bennie had lost her feeble mind. Luckily, her flight was called and Renee did not have to protest her virtue for too long.

"Looky-here, sister-girl. When I am anticipating, you will be the second person to know, right after Andrew. Until then, keep your mind off my innards. You know babies are like those people you don't really care for—talk about them and presto, there they are at your door. Last thing I need is my mother dreaming about fish," she said dryly.

They hugged each other tightly as they laughed and said their good-byes. Renee also decided to take her own good advice once she was aboard the plane. There was any number of light-skinned black men with sandy hair in the world. What were the odds that she would run into that creature at Hartsfield Airport? Especially since he had been in Europe for many years as international bureau chief for one of the cable news networks. She had to be mistaken, that's all. And if she kept dwelling on it, she might conjure him up for sure.

Still, she could not sleep on the long flight, nor could she concentrate long enough to read any of the magazines Bennie had bought her. She just stared out the window as the afternoon faded into twilight. What did she care about her flights of fevered fancy? She saw a man who resembled that bastard, that's all. And she was not about to let all her good work crumble in the face of that. Besides, Renee had a man at home . . . and that's just where she was going. She could not wait to be in his arms again.

Emerging from the plane, Renee scanned the crowd anxiously for Andrew's handsome face and was disappointed but bemused. A man in a chauffeur's uniform was holding a placard with her name on it. She slowly walked toward him with a slight smile. What was going on here?

"Ms. Kemp, Dr. Cochran arranged for me to drive you home," the man said politely. "If you will be so good as to follow me," he continued as he took her carry-on luggage and her magazines. He led Renee to a splendidly appointed yet understated limousine and held the door for her to enter. Inside was an exotic bouquet of orchids and roses and stargazer lilies, all in incredible shades of pink from the palest to the deepest. There was also a martini shaker, chilling in a bucket of ice, that contained an expertly blended Absolut martini. Best of all, there was caviar, soft music and a smooth, almost motionless ride.

Renee forgot whatever had been troubling her as she basked in the comfort Andrew had provided for her. She blinked several times because she could feel herself getting mushy with love.

They arrived at her house in short order and Renee was escorted through the front door, which she never used, into a bower of flowers, candlelight and music. She was presented with a note from the ubiquitous chauffeur, who tipped his hat and left discreetly. Renee immediately read the note:

> *Hello, darling. I trust you enjoyed the ride. Please go upstairs, take one of your special bubble baths and then join me for dinner. Clothing is optional, but there is something on your bed that you might fancy.*

Renee dashed up the stairs and went directly to the bedroom of her suite. She had moved her things to Bennie's old suite of rooms on the second floor, so everything had a fresh appearance and appeal. Plus, Bennie's old rooms were larger than the upstairs suite. Across the bed was a sinfully lovely silk jersey lounging gown. It was slit up to the hipbone on one side and had a plunging neckline with a deep cowl front and back. The elongated sleeves puddled a bit around the wrists, making her slender hands seem even smaller and more delicate. The material was luscious and felt like a summer breeze on naked skin. Renee raced through her bath and toilette so that she could slip it on over her scented body. The color, a soft peony pink, was perfect for her dark skin. She took a final look in the mirror and descended the stairs in search of her not-so-mysterious benefactor.

Andrew was waiting for her in the living room; he had an odd look on his face. He rose to greet her with a quick kiss but did not take her in his arms the way he normally would. By way of explanation he said, "You look exquisite, by the way. They told me you would like it."

Renee looked at her beloved Andrew. "Who told you what? And why are you standing like that?"

Andrew was resplendent in a beautifully tailored suit, but his arms were crossed in a rather odd fashion. Before he could explain, a tiny head popped out of the front of his jacket. It was a little terrier puppy, with round shiny eyes and a happy doggy expression. Renee raised her eyebrows.

"And who might this be?" she asked.

"That's Chaka," Andrew said, and grimaced as another small head made its way out. "And this is Patti. Or whatever you want to call them. *They* told me you would like the gown. They're here to keep you company," he added anxiously. It suddenly seemed to occur to him that surprising someone with two puppies was not necessarily the brightest thing in the world. He need not have worried, though; Renee was enchanted with the little dogs.

They were black and shiny and had the high spirits of good health. They also seemed to recognize Renee as "Mama" and took right to her. She lifted them out of Andrew's jacket and cooed over them like he had given her the crown jewels of England. After sitting down with them on the sofa for a few minutes, she turned her attention to Andrew.

"You are truly the most thoughtful man in the world. You knew I would be missing that silly cat of Bennie's and you went out and got me these adorable little dogs. And the limo and the gown and just everything. On top of all you have been doing, you do this for me." She sniffed, but she couldn't help it. Tears were running down her face freely by then.

She stood and was hugging him around the neck with everything she had and telling him how much she loved him and missed him and needed to be with him. Meanwhile, the puppies were amusing themselves by stalking the deadly throw pillows on the sofa. Their excited barks punctuated Renee's declarations of love, and Andrew was touched to his very soul.

"Is this what it's going to be like when we have kids, Renee? Barking, whooping and hollering every time we try to be romantic?"

Renee smiled through her tears and nodded. "Only worse, I'm afraid, because I think I want a lot of your babies," she confessed.

Andrew was overcome with the enormity of what she had just said. He just held on to her without saying a word. Finally he said, "Well, we'd better get in some intimate moments before this house is filled with infants. Come on, woman, I'm dying for you."

He had her upstairs and naked before she could utter a sound. Much, much later, after they had finally eaten the meal he had arranged to be catered and the puppies were put to bed in their crate, they were back in bed, safely wrapped in each other's arms. Andrew had one more point to make to Renee before they went off to sleep.

"That is positively the last time you are going anywhere without me. I can't stand being away from you," he murmured.

"Me either," she said softly.

"So that's the deal. No more trips apart. Period." He yawned and used the rest of his strength to kiss Renee again before they both fell into a deep and dreamless sleep.

Renee still saw Yolanda about once a month, more to chat than anything else. This month, however, Renee felt a real need to talk with her therapist. After their usual greeting, Yolanda could see that Renee had something on her mind, something that she did not hold back.

"Yolanda, I was in the airport in Atlanta, and I thought I saw him," Renee confessed.

"Him?" Yolanda probed gently.

"Him. The one. The bastard who raped me, Donovan Bailey," Renee said in a monotone. She didn't say anything else for a few minutes and then she looked at Yolanda with a shaky determination.

"That is the first time I have spoken that name since it happened. It was as if saying the name would make him appear somehow. Donovan Bailey. Donovan Bailey. Do-no-van Bai-ley. Oh, look, lightning didn't strike me or anything," she said hoarsely. Her bravado was fooling no one; this was obviously difficult.

Yolanda urged her on gently. "What happened when you saw him, Renee? When you saw the man whom you thought was Donovan Bailey?"

"I froze," Renee said quietly. "I couldn't move, couldn't speak, couldn't blink. Then I got nauseous. If I hadn't been so stunned, I probably would have made a huge, ugly scene right there in the terminal. I just felt dizzy and queasy and sick to my very soul. But Bennie was there and they called my flight, and when the plane landed here, I was fine."

She went on to tell Yolanda all of the wonderful things that Andrew had arranged for her as a welcome-home surprise. Yolanda was once again impressed with the playful and sweet relationship that they were enjoying. She couldn't help but ask a pertinent question, though.

"Did you tell Andrew what you thought you saw at the airport?" Yolanda said quietly.

"No, I didn't," Renee said in an equally quiet voice. "I wasn't sure about what I had seen, and I didn't want to give it energy in any case. It all happened a long, long time ago. It's over. I have a new life and a new love and he can't touch any of that," she said confidently.

Yolanda let that statement settle and watched the determination on Renee's face. "One last thing, Renee, and then we will have some tea and relax. If you were to encounter Donovan Bailey, if you were to come face-to-face with him, how would you handle it?"

Without hesitation Renee answered, "I would try to kill him." She drew in a sharp breath as she realized what she had just uttered. *But I'm not taking it back.*

In the awkward silence that followed her outburst, Renee had a moment to reflect that perhaps she was not quite as well adjusted as she might like to think. *But it's not like I'm going to Europe to gun the man down. I'm not supposed to forget what he did to me.* It was really a moot point, she told herself. It was just a bizarre variation on word *association,* although part of her was a bit piqued that Yolanda had sprung it on her like that. They had a quick cup of tea and Renee used the puppies as an excuse to dash home.

By the time she got her charges walked, fed and had given them an outing in the backyard, she was feeling much better about the session. She was, after all, in control of her life and was enjoying every minute of it. There was nothing that creature could possibly do to her, nothing at all. She was free of him and of his specter. As far as she was concerned, there was no such creature.

Renee saw a marked change in Andrew over the next few weeks, due solely to his involvement with the surgical team. He was obsessed with eliminating every possible chance that either baby would perish in the attempt to separate them. His usually immaculate house became a forest of articles and books on every aspect of the development of and treatment of conjoinment. He was at the hospital for incredibly long hours, as he was still caring for his regular patients. "Free time" was nonexistent, as he spent every waking hour at the clinic, in meetings, in conference or on his computer doing research.

Renee was a demon researcher, given her broadcasting background, and she was able to scrounge up obscure information in a heartbeat, for which he was profoundly grateful. She was happy to do it, since it meant that she was helping him in some way. On some days it was her only link to him, but she truly did not feel neglected. She knew that she could not articulate what she was feeling without Andrew becoming terribly embarrassed, but she felt privileged to be a part of his life right now. In her secret heart she thought that Andrew was the most selfless, noble man she had ever known. But she couldn't say those words to him; he was so self-effacing that they would have had the opposite effect.

Andrew, on the other hand, felt terribly torn by the amount of time that he had to put in on the case. It was ultimately going to be worth it, in terms of saving two lives and contributing to medical science, but Renee was still his major priority and he knew she was getting the short end of the stick.

"I am going to try, as soon as this is all over, to make this up to you in some way," he promised.

His large, beautiful eyes were troubled as he looked down at Renee. They were in his office late one night. Renee had insisted on bringing him a hot meal instead of the cafeteria food or fast food that he had been ingesting. She absolutely melted at the expression on his face.

"You," she said, tapping him on the chest with her index finger, "do not have anything to make up for. I knew who you were and what you did long before we fell in love. You do not ever have to apologize to me for doing what you do. You concentrate on doing your best for those babies, and when it's all over, we'll be back on track. Now kiss me and eat this or I will give it to you intravenously," she threatened.

Sighing with gratitude, Andrew held Renee as tightly as he could for a long moment. "This would be so much more difficult without you, Renee," he murmured. "I don't care what you say, when this is all over, we are going to some island somewhere and disappearing from the rest of the world for about a week so I can remind you how much I love you."

Renee kissed Andrew with a gentle sweetness that was as comforting as it was stimulating. "Baby, I already know," she assured him.

It was now the middle of November and Thanksgiving was looming near. It had been decided long ago that Big Benny, Martha, Donnie, Adam and Renee would visit Bennie and Clay in Atlanta, with Andrew, of course. It simply was not going to be possible, though. The surgery had been postponed twice, once to allow the babies to recover from an infection and once so that they could gain a few more precious pounds before the trauma of the surgery. Now it was going to take place the Monday before the holiday and that made travel impossible for Andrew. Renee wanted to stay with him, but he would not hear of it.

"Look, baby, this cannot be all about me. I cannot have you putting your life on hold indefinitely because of my career choices. I want you to go with the family and see Bennie and Clay. You know she is dying to see you, especially since she's pregnant now."

Andrew and Renee were curled up on the soft gray sofa in her suite, basking in front of the fire that was burning fragrantly in the fireplace. Renee set her cup of hot cider down on the end table so that she could make a point to Andrew. Taking both of his hands, she clasped them to her.

"Andrew, for the last time, this is not a sacrifice. Over the course of our life together, there are going to be times when we compromise, when one person's needs take precedence over the other. I do not have a giant scoreboard in the basement somewhere where I tally up our count or something. We decided that we did not want to be apart anymore. And now you are pushing me out the door. Honey, there is no place that I would rather be than here with you for the holiday. This is our first big holiday as a couple, and even if you are at the hospital most of the time, I still want to be with you."

Andrew's eyes were full of love and passion as he heard her out. "Damn, you're sweet. You're just sweeter than anything I can think of and I love you for it. But," he cautioned as he began kissing her, "I am not going to change my mind."

They exchanged a few more sweet, hot, little kisses before he pulled away and looked directly into her eyes.

"My sweet Renee, I realize that this is our first big holiday together, but I will be so concerned about you that I won't be able to concentrate on my work. Please go with the family to Atlanta, and I will make a vow that I will not willingly be separated from you again. After we're married, you'll get sick of me, I'll be so close to you."

Renee opened her mouth a couple of times to protest and then gave up. She did bring up another topic, though.

"So was that a formal proposal?" she asked sweetly.

Andrew thought about his last few statements. "Hmm. I didn't mean to ask you like that. I meant to do it romantically, and sweep you off your feet or something," he admitted with a frown. "But I can't take it back. I love you more than my life and I can't possibly live without you. I want to share my whole life with you and make some beautiful babies and take care of you and make you happy," he said sleepily. "So you have to marry me, Renee. You're mine."

Renee kissed him softly and laid her head on his shoulder. "And you are mine."

Thanksgiving wasn't nearly as bad as Renee thought it was going to be. In fact, it was wonderful. She and Bennie cooked together and had a chance to really catch up, something they had not done since before Bennie's marriage, really, since Renee had been keeping her relationship with Andrew on the down low. Now she couldn't shut up about it. And Bennie could talk about her pregnancy and all of the wonderful plans she and Clay were making for the future.

There was a huge gathering for Thanksgiving dinner; even Clay's sister, Angelique, made an appearance. Angelique was not cut from the same cloth as the rest of the Deveraux family—she was stuck-up and rude, despite being extraordinarily gorgeous. She and Donnie had crossed swords in the past and it took about thirty minutes for a rematch, after which she slammed out of the house. Donnie shuddered as she left and made an exaggerated face of fear.

"Renee, if Bennie's kid takes after Evilene, they're going to have to chain it in the backyard and throw meat at it," he predicted.

Renee tried not to laugh, but Donnie looked so serious that she couldn't help but snicker. She was relaxed, happy and full of family feeling. Her mother was safely in New York, as it was LeeAnn's turn to host her for the holidays. She had spoken with all of her family and had even talked briefly to Andrew, who had surprised her with a call. It was just a pleasure to bask in the bosom of her friends, who would soon be her family. Renee smiled a secret, happy smile as she looked at the people who would soon be her in-laws. Before long, she and Bennie, who were as close as sisters, would really be sisters-in-law. And Big Benny, who had referred to her as his other daughter, would truly be her father-in-law.

She had not told anyone that she and Andrew were getting married; there was plenty of time for that. And for the most part, everyone seemed to assume that it was a fait accompli. The same alchemy that had let everyone know that she and Andrew were meant for each other had shown that they were in it for life. No one would be at all surprised when they announced their engagement, she thought happily. It was just the next logical step, like putting up the Christmas tree the day after Thanksgiving.

And that was exactly what they did. The next day, Clay and Donnie went off with Bennie and Renee to get the perfect Christmas tree, braving the pandemonium of the holiday weekend to get Christmas decorations. It was Clay and Bennie's first Christmas, after all, and they were establishing traditions that would last their lifetimes and be passed on to their children. Renee got a little teary when she thought of the enormity of what they were doing, but she did not speak of it, she just couldn't. She just hugged Bennie really hard when they went into the kitchen to make lunch for everyone after the shopping expedition.

And Bennie seemed to understand what Renee was trying to convey.

"You know what, kiddo? I have a feeling that this time next year it will be you who is decorating your house for the first time in your married life. But that is all I am saying on the subject," Bennie said with a big smile.

Renee didn't even bother to look coy; she just smiled in return. She and Bennie made lunch while the men set up the enormous Christmas tree. After eating, they all pitched in to decorate the tree—at first. One by one, the men deserted to the family room to watch football. Clay was the only one who stayed until the project was finished, and that was mainly to keep Bennie off the ladder. He was terrified that she would do something to injure herself or the baby she was carrying. Renee was struck afresh with the love and devotion the newlyweds shared; she said as much to Bennie.

"Honey, I have never seen a man so crazy about a woman before in my life! Clay truly adores you, you know that?"

Bennie smiled dreamily and looked over at her handsome husband, who was putting ornaments on the uppermost branches of the tree. "Yes, he does. And I adore him in return. But you have never seen a man as crazy in love as Clay because you don't see my brother look at you when you are unaware of it. Trust me, Ne-ne, Bunchy is completely, truly-madly-deeply in love with you, too."

This time Renee tried to look coy but failed. Her face wreathed in smiles, she beamed. "Yeah. Ain't love grand?"

Renee was quite ready to head back to Detroit the next day, but Bennie prevailed on her to stay. There was some huge dinner dance that held some kind of significance to The Deveraux Group and it was sure to be a splashy gala event.

"One of the sororities sponsors it every year as a means of raising scholarship money. The Deveraux Group is a big contributor. In fact, they are receiving some kind of recognition for it this evening. So please stay, won't you? I promise you, I will have you on the next thing smoking out of here on Sunday morning. Swear," she vowed, holding up the fingers of her right hand like the Girl Scout she once was.

Renee sighed and capitulated. Martha and Big Benny were all for this evening, as was Donnie, so she did not want to be the lone voice of dissent. And it gave them a chance to shop, anyway, since Renee had not bought anything that dressy with her. Bennie had of course offered Renee full run of her closet, but Renee demurred, wanting to get something new that would boggle Andrew at a later date. Then she told Bennie about the wedding reception and the "Incident of the Pink Dress."

"Did I ever tell you that I borrowed your dress? The one you had made for Clay?" she began.

On their way to the mall she regaled Bennie with the story of how she had knocked Andrew's socks off and put Ms. Dana "Safari Barbie" Pierson firmly in her place with one fell swoop. "I tell you, that dress has *powers,* girl. We just have to use them for good, not evil."

While she was not looking for anything as risqué as the pink dress, Renee nevertheless came up with a frock that meant business. She found a hot little Herve Leger in pewter with gray pearl beading that fit her like a glove. In the manner that the designer was known for, the dress made her luscious figure look downright scandalous without revealing a thing. It had a relatively modest surplice neckline and a rather chaste midcalf hem, but everything in between was incendiary.

Renee actually felt as good as she looked, because the party was much more fun than she had imagined. The shimmering ballroom held the crème de la crème of Atlanta and parts beyond; there was an amazing cross section of society. From the luminaries of show business to the academic elite, athletes to doctors, shining stars to rising stars of the business world, everyone who was anyone was there. Including, to Renee's delight, their old friend Ceylon, whose presence Bennie had kept secret. Ceylon was actually one of the headliners of the program—there, as she delicately put it, to "separate people from their money for a good cause."

"Oh, my dear, that dress is amazing," Ceylon commented after effusive hugs and kisses. "I would ask to borrow it, but my fanny would look like two bulldogs fighting under a blanket in something that form fitting." She sighed as she ran her daintily manicured hand across her generous derriere.

Renee looked sideways at Ceylon before answering. Who was Ceylon kidding? Every inch of her was drop-dead gorgeous—whether she was a size 6 or 16. She was wearing a midnight navy Marc Bouwer that made her bronze skin absolutely sparkle. Renee chuckled. "Well, don't look now, hon, but there are six men staring at that rear end like it was made of candy, so don't go there, okay?"

Ceylon did not miss a beat as she replied, "If one of the six is that gorgeous Martin Deveraux, he can have a bite. If not, they'll get over it."

As she spoke, her eyes lit up—across the room was Martin Deveraux in the flesh. This was a truly rare occurrence in the social annals of Atlanta—Martin had shaken the dust off his tuxedo and joined the living. Murmuring something to Renee, Ceylon made a subtle but determined beeline to Martin. Laughing to herself, Renee went back to the Deveraux Group table that Clay had purchased for the tidy sum of $5,000, which did not include the $500-per-plate dinner or the generous donation that he was making later. The after-dinner speeches that preceded the dancing were about to start.

Renee was busy greeting various people whom she knew—she even saw a few of her personal clients from Urban Oasis. Between socializing and telling Bennie about Martin and Ceylon, her attention was captured, so she did not see Donnie approach the table behind her. She did hear his voice, however.

"Everyone, I want to introduce you to someone who is going to be an integral part of Cochran Communications and The Deveraux Group. After we hammer out the details with Clay, some amazing things are going to start happening at both organizations," Donnie said with an animated authority.

Renee turned her head just in time to see the face of the person Donnie was introducing.

"Everyone, I'd like for you to meet Donovan Bailey."

Those were the last words Renee heard for some time.

Fifteen

Somehow Renee managed to get away from the table without causing a scene. There was so much handshaking and exchanging of names going on that she could make a mad dash for the ladies' room without attracting undue attention to herself. She wouldn't have cared if someone had noticed her—she was so overcome with nausea that she had to get to a toilet immediately. Luckily, the room was deserted. Renee bolted for the first stall just in time for the racking waves of sickness to overtake her. It was thousands of times worse than the flu; she was shaking all over and cold sweat was pouring off her forehead.

When the painful heaving ceased, she rocked back on her heels and tried to stop trembling as she flushed the toilet. It was minutes before she was able to stand, and when she did, she almost fell down again with the sudden onslaught of dizziness. All the while she tried vainly to compose herself, to think clearly. *It* was *him.* . . . *It was that sick bastard. It* was *him at the airport; it was him all along. Oh, my God, he's here in the same place with me, with my friends.* . . .

Renee almost started heaving anew when the realization hit her that Donovan Bailey was in the same room with her dearly loved friends and family-to-be. It was as though she feared he would somehow taint them with his presence or . . . *Oh, my God—he might say something. He might remember me.* . . . *He might tell.* . . .

Renee was seized with the need to flee the ballroom, to get as far away from there as possible. She rinsed her mouth and used her linen handkerchief to blot away the moisture on her face. Dispassionately she tidied her hair and placed an Altoid in her mouth. An eerie calm had taken over her; she was governed by one principle right then and that was her overwhelming need to get out of there without causing a disturbance. But how?

She left the ladies' room and started toward the front of the huge hotel. She was walking with the insouciance of someone who knows exactly where she is going, when nothing could have been further from the truth. She would decide what to do when she got outside—there had to be a cab service or hotel limousine or something available. Renee was concentrating so assiduously on her escape that she did not hear Ceylon call her name. She stopped at the front doors, trying to remember if it was cold outside, if she had a coat, if she remembered Bennie's address.

She jumped like a startled Burmese cat when Ceylon touched her arm. Ceylon looked alarmed. "What in the world is wrong with you? I have been trailing behind you, calling your name like a crazy woman . . . Renee? *Renee?*

"Renee, angel, what happened? Oh, never mind, I'm taking you home, okay? I will take you right back to Bennie's and get you into bed," she said soothingly. She led Renee to a nearby banquette and looked around for the concierge or a valet so that she could send for her limo. As luck would have it, she saw Martin, who was slipping out for a cigar, or just cutting out early. She called his name once and he responded immediately.

Taking one look at Renee's ashen face, he surmised that she was not well. Ceylon asked him to wait with Renee while she found her driver, but Martin brushed aside that suggestion. "I'll get my car and have her home in a few minutes. Are you sure we shouldn't go to the hospital?"

Hospital seemed to be a word Renee recognized and she recoiled. Ceylon put her arms around Renee and assured her that they were going right back to Bennie's house. "I'll fix you some tea and a hot bath and we will have you feeling better in no time flat," she promised.

Ceylon was so concerned with Renee that she did not even register the fact that Martin, that reclusive and nonsocial Deveraux, was driving a silver Rolls-Royce. She surely would have had some flirtatious remark to make, had she been aware; as it was, all she could think of was Renee, who had yet to utter a sound. Ceylon had enough presence of mind to call Bennie on Clay's cell phone. Ceylon made Renee's sudden collapse seem like a touch of flu or an allergic reaction, since she did not want to panic the expectant mother.

"Oh, honey, she'll be fine. That big, handsome Martin is driving us to your house, and by the time you get there, she will be just fine. But make some noise when you come in—Martin and I might be *busy*," she added merrily. Realizing what she had just done, she turned to Martin with a sheepish look on her reddened face.

"I was . . . trying to make light of it. . . . I wasn't, umm . . ." For once, Ceylon was at a loss for words.

Surprisingly, Martin seemed to understand. He reached over and squeezed her hand, something that would have ordinarily had her heart pounding. This time, though, it was just sweet comfort. Her thoughts were completely centered on her friend in the backseat.

After a ride that was much shorter than it actually seemed, they were at Clay and Bennie's house. Without consulting anyone, Martin swept Renee up into his arms and carried her up to the house, handing Ceylon the set of keys Clay had given him for emergencies. She quickly opened the door and disarmed the burglar alarm according to his instructions. Martin took Renee up to the bedroom where she was staying and left her to Ceylon's ministrations.

Ceylon got Renee out of the beautiful dress and into a robe, chatting to her in a low, comforting voice. "I'm going to go and make you a cup of tea with lots of honey and lemon in it, the way you like it. And probably a little shot of brandy, too. Brandy is good for just about everything; it will take the edge off. And when I come back upstairs, I am going to run a hot bubble bath for you, if you want one. You just lie down and rest, okay? I'll be right back," she assured her. Renee never responded.

When Ceylon went downstairs to the kitchen, she found that Martin had already started the teakettle and had taken out a variety of teas. "I have no idea what she'd like, so I thought you could pick one," he said in his deep voice.

"Lapsang souchong is her favorite. Or Earl Grey," Ceylon said quietly. She got down a mug and a small plate from the cupboard. Then she stopped and stroked the bridge of her nose with her index finger, a sure sign that she was upset. She could feel tears surging to her eyes and blinked rapidly to prevent them from falling. The last thing Renee needed was some big ol' drama-queen scene.

Suddenly the most unexpected thing happened—Martin turned her around and settled her next to his heart for a big hug. Enfolded in his arms was the last place she ever expected to find herself, but she did not fight it—his arms felt too good and she was too distraught to question what was going on. She just let him hold her and she clung to his strength while he whispered comforting words to her. After several long moments the teakettle noisily reminded them that it was full of boiling water. Ceylon reluctantly drew away from Martin and prepared the tea.

"So what happened tonight, Ceylon? I can see that it's not just a case of being ill. She looks traumatized," Martin said quietly.

For some reason Ceylon was not surprised by his perception. Nothing about Martin really surprised her, not his moodiness, his unexpected kindness or his potent masculinity. She looked up into his beautiful, scarred face and sighed.

"I'm not sure what happened, but you're right—she had some horrible shock. There is only one thing I can think of that would do that to her. I just hope she can talk about it. Would brandy help, do you think?"

Martin found a bottle in Bennie's pantry and added a small amount to the tea. Ceylon put some homemade shortbread on a small plate and put everything onto a tray. "Sugar helps when you're in turmoil. I have no idea why, but it does," she said. She picked up the tray to go upstairs, only to have Martin take it from her. She led the way to Renee's room and Martin placed the tray in her hands.

"I'll be downstairs until Clay and Bennie get home," he said in response to her unasked question. "I will also cancel your limousine—I'll take you to your hotel."

Before she could react to that, he leaned over and kissed her—it was too close to her mouth to be on her cheek, yet too far on her cheek to be on her mouth. Ceylon did not doubt that he had deliberately placed it there. But she couldn't afford to get all gooey—she had to see to Renee.

Renee had rolled herself up into the smallest ball possible; her golden eyes were dull and listless, but wide open. Ceylon set the tray down on the dresser and went to Renee, stroking her hair.

"Sweetie, I want you to drink this tea, okay? Just sip a little of it and maybe you will be able to tell me what happened." She went to the dresser to get the tea and was encouraged by the fact that Renee stopped rocking back and forth and sat up. She was even more encouraged by the fact that Renee spoke to her as she was handing her the mug of tea; at least she was until she heard the words Renee whispered.

"Ceylon, he was there tonight. The man who raped me was at the dinner."

Before she realized what she was doing, Ceylon gasped in sheer horror. She immediately tried to compose herself, but she could not help the expression of pain that flitted across her face. To some extent she was expecting the words—she knew of nothing else except the unexpected death of a loved one that could make someone as strong as

Renee collapse like that. But to hear them in those soft, measured tones was dreadful. She wanted Renee to get it all out, but she wasn't sure that she would be able. But after a few sips of the steaming, brandy-laced tea, Renee continued to talk. She talked until she was all talked out, but she wasn't able to sleep for a long time. When she finally drifted off, Ceylon went downstairs to see if Bennie and Clay had come in.

It was only Martin, who was in the family room pretending to read a book while the stereo played softly. He was leaning back on the big sofa and looked too good for words with his tuxedo jacket removed and his band-collared shirt opened at the neck. Ceylon stood in the doorway, stroking her nose again. Martin held out his arm to her and without hesitation she joined him on the sofa, nestling into his side and cradling her head on his shoulder. They sat quietly like that until Martin could feel the moisture from Ceylon's eyes dampening the front of his shirt. That was when he pulled her into his lap and held her as close as he could so that she could cry out her pain for her friend. It was a little bit after that when he kissed her, and there was no doubt about where this one landed.

Renee was on her way back to Detroit before noon the next day. It took an Academy Award–caliber performance to convince Bennie, Clay and the others that she was fit to fly, but she carried it off. She made a great show of light-heartedness and chalked her anxiousness up to homesickness for Andrew. It was only a partial lie, she told herself.

"Now, Bennie, it's been three days since I have seen my beloved. And my babies—don't forget I have two puppies waiting for me, too. It was just a little touch of the flu, is all. I will be just fine when I get home. After all, Andrew is a doctor, for heaven's sake!" she said lightly.

While she was selling this happy tale to Bennie, she was also packing rapidly. It didn't really matter what Bennie or

Clay or Big Benny or anyone else had to say on the matter—she was getting the hell out of Atlanta that day, even if she had to walk.

It would not have been possible to convince Ceylon, but then again Ceylon knew the whole truth of the matter and was in agreement that Renee needed to get home to Andrew as fast as possible. She said as much to Renee on the telephone as Renee was about to leave for the airport.

"Okay, dear heart, you get back home to Detroit as quick as you can and tell Andrew everything. The sooner he is aware of what is going on, the quicker you two can work it out," Ceylon said confidently. "Everything is going to be fine, Renee, you'll see. You are not alone in this anymore. You have me and Andrew and Yolanda, and nothing bad is going to happen while we have breath in our bodies, okay?"

Renee was so overcome with emotion that she could barely reply. Ceylon seemed to sense it because she immediately switched to a more neutral topic—the elusive Martin.

"He's a perfect gentleman, damn him." Ceylon sighed dramatically. "He could have taken advantage of me last night, but no, he stayed with me until I fell asleep and then he disappeared into the night. But I've got news for Mr. Man—I'm not that easy to lose," she murmured in her husky, silky voice.

Despite the tears clogging her throat, Renee managed a chuckle. Ceylon did have a way of making her laugh, even while she was in turmoil. Still, she was thoroughly relieved to be on board the plane, where she could have the privacy to deal with the horror show her life was becoming. The plane was crowded due to holiday traffic, but Renee was glad; the hordes gave her the luxury of anonymity. No one knew her or paid any attention to the beautiful woman whose icy demeanor was betrayed by the rapid movement of her fingers. As always in moments of stress, she was rapidly counting her fingers with her thumbs—*One, two, three, four. . . . One, two, three, four. . . .*

* * *

Renee's homecoming wasn't quite what Ceylon had predicted, but anything was better than being in Atlanta. Contrary to what she had told Bennie and Clay, Renee had not alerted Andrew to her travel plans. She could not have dealt with seeing him right away. She had no idea what she would say to him, how she would explain what happened, how he would react. . . . Her mind was in such chaos that all she could do, the long ride home from the airport, was stare blindly out the window of the taxi and count silently. *One, two, three, four. . . . One, two, three, four. . . .* The tears didn't start until she was safely inside the house.

The sense of relief that she was expecting when she entered the big house evaded her completely. It was warm and familiar and oddly welcoming, but there was no release from the tension that had held her in its grip since the night in Atlanta when it all began. Despite being safe at home, the miasma of rage and terror still engulfed her. She wasn't safe here any more than she was in Atlanta; being home only made her face the fact more clearly.

A sound from the mudroom reminded Renee that she was not alone in the house. She hurried into the room off the huge kitchen and let the little dogs out of the carrier, where they spent their days until they were thoroughly housebroken. Andrew had promised to see to them in her absence and he had done an admirable job. She was gratified to see that her little pets had not forgotten her in the few days that she was gone. On the contrary, they made their adoration known with barks, wet doggy kisses and the legendary "wee-wee of joy," as Andrew irreverently referred to the tiny puddles they made when excited.

It was that bit of normalcy that popped the bubble of calm Renee had vainly been trying to float. The tears started rolling down her cheeks unchecked and she finally sank to her knees and let go with the huge, racking sobs she had been holding in. Renee wept until there was no more breath in her body, until her throat was raw from sobbing. The room grew smaller and smaller and the darkness pushed in on her until there was nothing but inky black surrounding her.

Sixteen

When Renee's eyes opened, she felt no better. She was stiff from her awkward position on the floor and she was cold. Mostly, though, she was thoroughly disgusted with herself. How could she have let herself fall to pieces like that? For God's sake, what had the last ten years of her life been about, if not keeping insanity from her door? What had all that hard, painful work with Yolanda been about if she was going to fall to pieces like an overwrought teenager with an eating disorder?

Renee sat up abruptly and rubbed her eyes with her fists, something she never, never did because it could wreck the delicate skin. *What a mess, what a mess. What am I going to do? How am I going to tell Andrew that his brother is about to go into business with the man who raped me? How am I going to face Donnie? Or Clay? Or anybody else? And why am I sitting in a puddle of puppy pee crying like an idiot?*

The absurdity of her current position made her move, finally. She stumbled to her feet and hastily cleaned up the small puddle left by her excited puppies. After taking them for a much-needed walk, she came back into the house and took her luggage upstairs. While she unpacked, she tried to keep her mind clear and focused on what she had to do next. It was clear that she had to tell Andrew everything. Just being able to express her pain and confusion would lessen the agony; she knew this in her heart. But what the proper words were, she had no idea.

Hi, honey, missed you, had a great time, your brother is going into business with the man who raped me. No, it just didn't play. Somehow, though, she had to find a way to tell him, the sooner the better. The afternoon passed in a blur—as keyed up as she was, Renee could not sit still. She busied herself by doing needless cleaning and straightening, which proved to be rather unrewarding, as the house was always immaculate. After rearranging the objects on her dressing table a third time, she decided to prepare a big meal. Cooking would occupy her mind as well as her hands, she decided.

When Andrew walked in the back door of the house to check on the puppies, he was amazed. Not only was Renee home unexpectedly, but she had prepared a magnificent meal for him. It was simple food, comfort food—meat loaf, macaroni and cheese and a special sautéed cabbage that only Renee could prepare. But the meal was one of Andrew's favorites and he was touched that she had gone to so much trouble, in addition to being thrilled that she was back. He found her in the dining room arranging a romantic table setting for two. In seconds he had her in his arms.

"Baby, what are you doing here?" he asked happily. "Did I get my days mixed up or something? I thought you weren't coming home for a couple more days."

Despite his surprise at seeing her, it was plain that Andrew was ecstatic to have her where she belonged. His gentle embrace was just what Renee desperately needed after the turmoil of the past hours. She returned his sweet, gentle kisses and allowed the pain and anxiety to flow away as she adjusted to feeling his strength flow through her body. Finally she began to speak.

"Well, I had a . . . a slight stomach virus and . . . I just knew I would feel better here with you. So I came home," she hedged.

There was plenty of time for him to hear the whole sordid story—for now, she just wanted to look at him and assure herself that he was real, that this was her real life and nothing ugly could intrude on her happiness. She stepped away from him so that she could adore him with her eyes and was reassured with what she beheld. He was rumpled and tired-looking, but there was an air of peace and happiness about him, too. Before she could ask him about his eating and sleeping habits, he took her hands and drew her into the living room and they sat down on the big sofa together.

Andrew gathered her as close to him as possible, kissing her again before speaking.

"Damn, I'm glad you're back!" he admitted. "Renee, the surgery went well. It went better than 'well,' actually. So far, everything has gone perfectly and the babies are holding their own," he told her with obvious pride.

Renee was stricken with guilt for a moment. She had been so caught up in her own world of misery that she had almost forgotten the complicated case that had kept Andrew in Detroit while she went to Atlanta. She tried not to let her shame show as Andrew went on to explain to her what had occurred during the surgery and after.

"I've been spending most of my time at the hospital monitoring the babies, which is why I look so bad. In fact, I just came home to see about the dogs and get some clean clothes. There's a press conference tomorrow morning and I didn't think I would have time to come get a shirt and tie or something. But now that you're home, I think I'll stay here for a few hours." He ended this statement with a huge yawn.

"Oh, baby, I had no idea how tired I was. I've just been going nonstop and I think it all just caught up with me." He excused himself while he yawned again.

Renee swallowed hard to get past the huge lump in her throat. *Bad timing, bad timing.* There was no way she was going to bring Andrew down now; she would just have to wait until the time was right. In the meantime, there was something she could do for him.

"Why don't you go upstairs right now and take a hot bath? I'll run it for you and I'll even scrub your back. Then after you have had a nap, we can eat dinner, how does that sound?" she offered sweetly.

The look of gratitude on Andrew's face was worth any price to Renee. They disentangled themselves from each other and Renee preceded him up the stairs. She dumped lavish amounts of mineral salts into the tub and filled it with hot water. The clean, green scent of pine and horse chestnut filled the room as Andrew walked in naked as a jaybird. He gave a great sigh of pleasure as the blue-green water surrounded him and Renee adjusted a bath pillow behind his head.

"I'll be back in ten minutes. Don't fall asleep," she cautioned.

Andrew assured her that he would manage to stay awake. "Just don't be too long. I seem to remember something about getting my back scrubbed; I liked the sound of that very much," he added.

Renee managed a cheerful little smile before closing the door behind her. She stood in the hallway for a moment with her head down and her hands balled into fists so tight that her nails pierced her skin painfully. She took a deep, shuddering breath as she descended the stairs, with her fingers working in their familiar rhythm: *One, two, three, four. . . . One, two, three, four. . . .*

A week had slipped by and Renee had still not found a way to approach Andrew with her dilemma. She simply could not find the words to tell him that his brother had somehow formed a liaison with the man who had raped her years before in Newark. How Donnie had managed to dig up the one person in broadcasting that she had cause to hate above anyone in the world, she would never know. To be honest, she still did not know the details of their partnership. All she knew was that it was something involving Clay's company, The Deveraux Group, and the Cochran family radio conglomerate, Cochran Communications.

Under normal circumstances this would be a really big deal, something to celebrate and rejoice in; after all, Donovan Bailey was a name to be reckoned with in broadcasting. This was quite a coup for Donnie, something akin to getting Bryant Gumbel to be the anchor on a local radio station. Whatever the plans were, they were sure to bring in a ton of money for all concerned. *As long as you don't mind working with a rapist,* she thought bitterly.

Renee was in her office at Urban Oasis, ostensibly making plans for the annual Christmas party she threw for her employees and patrons. What she was really doing was trying to avoid anything and everything that would remind her of Donovan Bailey and the fact that such a creature existed. She made neat stacks of all the pertinent papers on her desk, mostly invoices and holiday greetings. Keeping her hands busy seemed to lull her into a neutral state, but only for a moment or so. She rubbed her temples in small circles, trying to relieve the headache that she suffered with constantly since that horrid night in Atlanta.

A discreet knock sounded on her office door, and before she could speak, Valerie, her manager, entered with a look of concern on her face. She handed Renee a cup of Earl Grey tea and a headache powder, saying, "Don't even pretend like you don't need this, 'cause I can tell that you do." She then stood over Renee like a sentry until the powder was dispatched and a good bit of the tea had been consumed.

"Renee, I don't know what's wrong, but I can tell you feel like hell. Why don't you take off today and get some rest? I can handle everything here—it's why you pay me the big bucks, remember?" she added, hoping her lame joke would make Renee smile a little.

Valerie's concern was not misplaced; Renee did not look good. Her normally vibrant skin color was rather ashen and she was obviously not sleeping well, if at all. She apparently was not eating, either, as she had lost enough weight for it to be noticeable. And Valerie's kind words seemed to push her over the edge—to Val's horror, Renee's eyes filled with huge tears. Valerie had never, ever seen Renee in such a fragile state.

She immediately went around the desk and swooped her arms around Renee. Rocking her back and forth, Valerie begged her to share her pain.

"Renee, what is it? Are you and Andrew having problems? Is something wrong with your family, what? Honey, you can tell me anything; you know you can," she coaxed. "You need to try and talk about this so we can make it go away," she said persuasively.

Renee sat up and gently extricated herself from Valerie. "That's just it, Val. It won't go away," she muttered. "Not unless I make it, and I don't know how, not yet." She took a deep, shuddering sigh and almost laughed at the look on Valerie's face.

"I know I'm not making sense. Nothing makes sense right now. But"—she glanced at her wall clock before continuing—"I am going to take care of that right now. I hope. I'm taking your advice—I won't be back today."

Renee stood and gave the still-shocked Valerie a hug. "Thanks for caring about me, kiddo, it means a lot."

Renee gladly handed Valerie the list of things that still needed doing for the Christmas party, then put on her Calvin Klein topcoat and left by the back door. If Yolanda couldn't help her get back on track, no one could.

After refusing Yolanda's offer of tea, Renee started doing what she normally did when she was trying to avoid an unpleasant topic—she started fidgeting. She meandered around the large, homey room staring at familiar objects as though they were displayed under glass at the Detroit Institute of Arts. She gave quiet, monosyllabic answers to Yolanda's remarks until even she couldn't stand it anymore. Suddenly she turned to Yolanda with her fear etched broadly across her face.

"Yolanda, that *was* Donovan Bailey that I saw at the airport. I saw him again in Atlanta. And what's worse, he is going into some kind of business with Andrew's family and with Clay Deveraux's company," she said quietly. Barely pausing for breath, she told Yolanda the whole unpleasant story.

Yolanda's reaction was plain—she could not keep the horror from her expressive face. "My God, Renee! What happened when you told Andrew how you knew this man? I am surprised that his brother would even consider a business arrangement with a creature like that!"

Renee confessed that she had not yet told Andrew that Donovan was the man who had raped her. "Yolanda, when I got back here, I was going to tell him right away. But he was so tired from the surgery and there was all that follow-up and hoopla afterward—that it just didn't seem fair to dump my troubles on him. Everybody who is anybody has interviewed him, did you know that? Not just Andrew, of course, the whole surgical team. They're going to be written up in *People* and *Time* and they're going to be on the Discovery Channel and some other things; I can't remember them all," she finished.

Renee could tell that Yolanda wasn't buying it, and her first words bore out this theory.

"Renee, it is wonderful that the surgery went so well and that Andrew is getting this much-deserved admiration and recognition. But you matter, too! You are making decisions for Andrew about his priorities, and that is something that you are not equipped to do. I know that you are concerned about his time and you appreciate the stress under which he has been operating, but you have to let Andrew decide what he can and cannot deal with; you can't play God for him," Yolanda said gently.

Instead of reassuring her, Yolanda's words had the opposite effect on Renee. She leaped from the couch, where she had finally perched, and resumed wandering with a vengeance. She was making minute adjustments to every object on every surface she came to, still letting the sound of Yolanda's voice wash over her.

"From what you have told me of Andrew, your well-being is of paramount concern to him. The longer you put off discussing this with him, the more confused and hurt he is liable to be. Besides, it may very well be that if you wait, his brother and Bennie's husband will find themselves in a business arrangement they cannot get out of."

That got Renee's full attention, and she swirled around to face Yolanda. "But, Yolanda, the only way they would not go through with this is if they know the whole story of what happened between me and that creature, and I don't know if I could handle them knowing. I know it seems irrational after all this time, but I just don't know if I could stand for them to know what happened," she admitted.

Yolanda sighed, and asked Renee to come back and sit down, which she did. After she was seated, Yolanda joined her on the couch and took Renee's hands in her own.

"Renee, you know that Bennie's family feels as though you are a part of them. Her brothers, with the exception of Andrew, view you as another sister. Andrew loves you and wants to marry you. Do you think for a moment that these people would willingly enter into a business agreement with a man who has harmed a member of their family? Do you not think that you should at least give them the opportunity to decide on their own what their course of action should be?"

Renee had to take back her hands to dash away the hot tears she felt forming. Yolanda made it all seem so simple, and maybe it was. . . . But maybe it wasn't. She knew, though, there would be no peace for her until she confided everything in Andrew.

"I know you're right, Yolanda. I know you are," she murmured. "I just haven't been able to find the words to say to him. I know that every day I hesitate is making it harder,

but I just have not been able to find the way to tell him."
She sighed aloud. "God, I am such a coward! After all this
time you would think that I wouldn't be such a ninny, and
look at me. I'm the one who was going to try and kill him,
remember? I can't even *tell* on the bastard, much less seek
revenge." She ended with a snort.

Yolanda reached over and took her hand again. "And as
long as you cannot articulate it, he has power over you. Remember how old folks used to say, Tell the truth and shame
the Devil? That's what you've got to do, Renee. Take the
power away from him. You have me and Andrew and Ceylon and everyone else on your side. You may not believe it
right now, but you do. Take the power away from him, *now.*"

Yolanda's words continued to pound through Renee's
aching head the rest of the day. She knew that Yolanda was
absolutely right—by not exposing Donovan Bailey for the
creep that he was, she was giving him power over her life.
The same power that he had taken away from her so many
years ago. There was only one way that she could free herself from this trap, and that was to tell Andrew that
Donovan Bailey was her rapist and that through some
bizarre twist of fate Donovan was about to begin a business enterprise with Andrew's family's business.

Logically, this was the only way that she could regain
the ground she was losing, but logic was not known for
having a pretty taste or sound. The words would not be
easy to say or pleasant to hear, but they were necessary. By
the time she reached home, she was steely with resolution.
She and Andrew were going to have that much-needed talk
tonight, as soon as he got to her house. She glanced at the
clock on her dashboard as she pulled into the garage. She
had time enough for a hot shower and a change of attire,
something that was akin to donning the armor of a samu-
rai in her estimation.

After tending to the little dogs, she ran upstairs to prepare for the evening. Her phone started ringing as soon as

she got into her sitting room, but her irritation turned to happiness as she realized it was Andrew.

"Listen, sweetheart, I want to take you out for dinner tonight. I'm at the station taping an interview, so why don't you come by and we will leave from here. Unless you'd rather I picked you up," he added.

Renee agreed that meeting him was more expeditious and they set a time to meet.

"Andy? I love you," she whispered. She could actually hear his answering smile over the telephone.

"Baby, every time you say that I get. . . . Well, I'll show you tonight," he promised. "And I love you, too, more than you know," he said softly before ending the call.

By the time Renee had showered, perfumed and pampered her way into a red cashmere sweater that was one of Andrew's favorites, she was feeling much better. She noticed that her black leather jeans were much looser than they should have been, something that ordinarily would have elated her but was rather depressing. *Just another service of that bastard, Donovan Bailey—loss of appetite.* The brief observation just fueled her determination to tell Andrew everything.

She got to the station, parked in the underground structure and had just left the elevator that opened onto the floor where the studios were when she spotted Andrew. His interview over, Andrew was chatting amiably with some of the station personnel. His face lit up when he saw Renee and he started toward her. He had, in fact, just reached her side when his brother's voice came floating down the corridor.

"Andrew, wait a minute. I want you to meet someone. Oh, hey, Renee, I'm glad you're here, too, since you didn't get to meet this guy in Atlanta."

Adonis was beaming with pride as he gestured expansively with his right arm. "Donovan Bailey, I'd like you to meet my brother, Dr. Andrew Cochran. And this is Renee Kemp, who is practically part of our family. Andrew, Renee, this is Donovan Bailey, who will be an integral part of both Cochran Communications and The Deveraux Group in a very short while."

With nothing that even resembled shame, Donovan Bailey's handsome face broke into a wide grin. "I hate to correct my new boss," he said in his mellifluous voice, "but Renee and I go back a long way."

The only things that kept Renee from slipping to the floor in a dead faint were the towering rage that she felt about to burst from her soul and Andrew's arm around her waist.

Seventeen

"Dr. Cochran, can I borrow you for just a few minutes?"

The request from the station's news director made Andrew turn his attention away from the introductions his brother was making, but not before he sensed a slight change in Renee.

To the casual observer, she was as regal and composed as ever, but there was something amiss there. Andrew went into a nearby office with Tawny, the news director, and chatted with her for a few minutes. After giving her the information she sought, he accepted her thanks with one eye on the scene a few feet away. Something just wasn't right, but he couldn't put his finger on what it was.

Renee was drowning. *Oh, God, how can this be happening?* She kept her hands out of sight under the coat she was holding—not for anything in the world would she shake hands with that creature. She could feel her heart pounding like a pneumatic hammer under her red sweater and the only hope she had of not screaming was to refrain from speaking. It was difficult to hear what was being said, because the combination of fear and rage was causing a sound in her ears like rushing water. But she did hear, as from a very far place, the voice she heard in her nightmares for so long, the voice she prayed she would never hear again.

"Renee Kemp. Well, it's been ages. You're looking fabulous, I must say. But then you always did," he said in his silky broadcaster's cadence.

He was actually going to try and embrace her, something that she warded off by dropping her purse, which he gallantly retrieved, totally missing the look of loathing she shot at the back of his head. He didn't look any different, really; he didn't seem any different, still the same handsome, likable chap who won fans by the droves with his charisma. But the fact remained that he was the same monster who had almost destroyed her life.

Donovan had just explained to Donnie that he and Renee had known each other in Newark some years before when Andrew returned to her side.

"Sorry about that. Listen, Renee and I were about to go out for dinner, so we won't linger," he added with a sidewise look at her.

Donnie immediately suggested that he and Donovan tag along so that he could fill them in on the new developments at the station. "Hey, there are a lot of things I haven't had a chance to tell you two; we can get acquainted and catch up at the same time," he said.

Andrew was about to ask Renee if she minded, when he sensed rather than saw her retreat even further. Renee, who was the most gracious and outgoing woman in the world, was not saying a word. She was so contained, so frozen, that only someone who was very, very close to her would have realized that she was about to explode. Donnie was so animated by his announcement that he missed it entirely. Donovan Bailey was so egotistic that he never noticed the icy calm that had taken over Renee. But Andrew knew that something was wrong.

Renee had gone from soft and yielding to brittle and still, and her respiration was shallow. Her eyes were the muddy brown that only came on when she was very angry or upset and her skin had an unhealthy gray edge to it. Without drawing attention to Renee's condition, he gracefully extricated them from Donnie's plans.

"Look here, this is the first time my lady and I have had time for romance in a long time. And the last thing I want to do is share her with you two hard-legs. So y'all will have to excuse us, but we have other plans for the evening," he added with a smile, a smile that did not quite reach his eyes.

As they entered the elevator to the parking garage, Andrew looked at Renee carefully. He took her pulse and felt her skin, which was clammy and cool.

"Renee, I'm taking you to the emergency room. I want someone to take a look at you, because it's obvious that you're not well. Why didn't you say something earlier?" he asked gently.

Renee responded immediately, although not in the way he was expecting. "No hospitals, no emergency rooms!" she insisted. "I'm okay, Andrew; I'm just . . . tired. Just take me home, okay? I'll be fine, really."

Andrew wasn't buying it, but she was so insistent that he capitulated. He seated her in his car, both of them forgetting that she had also driven to the station. When it dawned on her halfway home that her car was still at WWCC, Andrew shrugged it off.

"I'll take care of it later. Let's just get you home and comfortable," he said.

And shortly they were home and she had taken off her coat and sat down on one of the tall stools in the kitchen. "Why don't you go upstairs and lie down and I'll bring you some tea or something. I know when there's something wrong, so don't try that 'I'm okay' stuff with me. I'm a doctor, remember?" he teased gently. Seeing her wan smile at his lame joke made his heart cry. He kissed her softly on the lips before taking the puppies for a quick walk.

Renee heard, rather than saw, him close the door because she was too distracted to truly focus on her surroundings. *Oh, Jesus, help me. Help me.* She was cold, unbearably cold, and she couldn't move from the stool. She couldn't cry because she couldn't get enough air around the huge lump in her throat. Her entire body started trembling and she dropped her head into her hands. *I have to tell him. I have to tell him now.* The time for hesitation was over. She had to tell Andrew everything, now before things went any further.

Andrew could not get past the idea that something was terribly wrong with Renee. As he gamely walked the energetic little dogs, which were trying to sniff every rock, tree, twig, paving stone and dead leaf they encountered, Andrew thought about Renee. She had been distant and quiet since she returned from Atlanta, but in his preoccupation with the conjoined-twins case, he had put it down to the mild stomach virus she claimed to have contracted. But there was more to it than that. He tried to sift through the guilt that he was feeling for neglecting her over the past weeks to get at solid bits of evidence.

Point one, her early return from Atlanta. She claimed to have a slight virus, but wouldn't that make a person prolong a trip and not truncate it? Who wants to risk air travel with a touchy stomach? Point two, her distance and reticence since her return. Yes, Renee had in the past been cool and self-contained, but not once since they had acknowledged their mutual love did he have cause for complaint in that area. Renee was open and direct with him about everything, or at least she had been up until she got back from Atlanta.

He was so deep in thought that he almost tripped over Chaka, who had wound her leash around his leg without him noticing. "Hey," he said as he disentangled himself, "you guys would tell me if she was upset about something, wouldn't you?" They panted happily at the question and continued their trot.

"Okay, Cochran, this is bad news. You are talking to dogs to ask them what's bothering the woman you love. You have been completely wrapped up in yourself and you have put your career ahead of your relationship, which is exactly what you said you would never do. And you're talking to yourself. Prognosis: you have lost your rabbit mind," he muttered.

He was about to head back to the house when something struck him hard. Renee had been fine that evening until she encountered Donovan Bailey. And Donnie had said something about them not meeting in Atlanta, which meant that they had been in Atlanta at the same time. *She never told me what his name was. . . . I never asked. But I swear to God, somebody said 'Newark' tonight. I swear I heard it—Newark. Why else . . .*

He did turn then, scooping up the startled little dogs and making for the house on a dead run.

He was barely winded when he blew in the back door. Renee was still in the same position, rocking back and forth with her face in her hands. Andrew knew then that he was right—the final piece fell into place with a sickening logic.

"That was him, wasn't it? That Donovan Bailey—he's the bastard who raped you, isn't he?"

All the color left Renee's face and she slid off the stool in a dead faint so quickly that Andrew almost didn't catch her.

"Oh, damn, baby, why didn't you tell me?" He groaned as he pulled her into his arms.

When Renee came back to herself, she was lying in her own bed, wearing a favorite nightgown. She blinked several times as she slowly sat up, trying to determine how she got into bed. Andrew was sitting motionless across the room from her, a dangerously neutral expression on his face. Finally she felt able to speak.

"What happened?" she asked softly. "How did I get up here and undressed?"

Taking the easy question first, Andrew answered her in a deceptively calm tone. "I carried you up here, Renee. I undressed you and put you to bed because you fainted." His eyes raked over her, assessing her as though they had just met.

"You *carried* me up here? You're quite the he-man,

aren't you?" Renee said lightly, although she could tell from his expression that she was not going to get off easily, and she did not.

"You fainted when I asked you if Donovan Bailey was the man who raped you," Andrew said coolly. "He *is* that animal, is he not? He is the reason that you went into shock at the station tonight and he is the reason you rushed back here after Thanksgiving. How long were you going to keep this a secret, Renee? Just when did you plan to tell me that the bastard had come back into your life?"

Renee recoiled at Andrew's obvious anger. She almost did not recognize his beloved face, distorted as it was by pure anger. Defensively she said, "I would hardly call this 'coming back into my life.' By some cruel twist of fate, your brother and Clay pick the one man I have reason to hate to enter into business with. I had no control over that whatsoever. And when I encountered him the first time in Atlanta, I was so taken aback that I had no idea what to say or do," she said heatedly.

"But why didn't you tell me? It seems to me that would have been the first thing you would do, tell the man who loves you, the man you say you are going to marry. We're supposed to be a team, Renee. What affects you affects me. What hurts you hurts me. And yet, when something like this happens, you don't say a word. I can't believe this, Renee; I really can't."

Andrew's hurt and anger caused his voice to escalate to a degree that Renee had never, ever heard in all the years she had known him. He had long since gotten out of the chair and was pacing and gesturing widely as he walked. Feeling at a distinct disadvantage by lying in bed, Renee rose quickly and put on a robe. She turned to face him with a growing anger of her own.

"Andrew, I had planned to tell you when I returned from Atlanta. I was not deliberately trying to hide anything from you. But when I came back, you were so involved with the case that I just couldn't dump it on you then. Yes, what affects me affects you and I could not run the risk of distracting you just then." To her surprise, those placating words served only to make him angrier.

"Renee, that's just not good enough. I don't care if I was in the middle of doing open-heart surgery on the president, you still should have told me. How can I protect you, take care of you and love you if you're going to close up on me and decide what I should know and when I should know it? Who decided that you were in charge of this relationship?" he demanded.

Before she could react, he went on. "Besides, there are other people involved here besides you and me. Do you think for a minute that Donnie would do business with a rapist, especially one who violated *you?* He loves you like a sister! Do you think that Cochran Communications and The Deveraux Group would actually consider going into a contract with a low-life bastard like that? Donnie and Clay need to know so that they can pull out of this business with Bailey before it goes any further. Your keeping silent could have very well pushed them into a very awkward corner," he said with finality.

By now, the blood vessels in Renee's temple were about to burst. Shock, rage and horror warred with each other for precedence, and rage, for the moment, won.

"No! No! I don't care what you think of me or what happens, you can't tell anyone about this! No one, do you understand? That's why I didn't say anything! I can't go through this again—I *can't*, I tell you! You don't have to protect me, you don't have to take care of me, you don't have to love me, but you do have to respect my privacy," she railed.

Heedless of the hot tears that were coursing down her face, Renee crossed the room and grabbed a startled Andrew by his shirtfront. "I won't go through that pain again, I won't. This is my business, nobody else's. It's mine, do you hear me? I took care of it before and I'll take care of it now. Just leave me alone, just go away and . . . and . . ."

Before she could finish her last sentence, Andrew's

arms were around her and he was holding her as close as he could while his own tears dampened her hair. *What kind of an idiot am I?* he thought savagely.

"My God, Renee, I don't deserve you—I swear to God I don't. I'm sorry, baby, I'm so sorry; I was wrong, I'm sorry," he murmured over and over as he led her over to the bed.

He held her in his lap and continued to stroke her and murmur soft words of apology. "Renee, please forgive me. I was being stupid and arrogant and macho and every other stupid thing you want to call me. I know why you felt like you couldn't say anything; I was just so damned mad at that son of a bitch that I wasn't thinking. You didn't do anything wrong, baby—it was me."

Renee did not say anything for a while; she was adrift in her turbulent emotions. Finally she raised her head off Andrew's shoulder and smiled sadly. "The irony is that I was going to tell you everything when you came back in the house. I finally realized that I couldn't keep this to myself anymore," she admitted.

Andrew gave a heavy sigh, and was about to start excoriating himself again, when Renee put her hand over his mouth. "No more, Andy, not tonight. Please. We'll figure everything out in the morning. Just keep holding me, okay?"

Andrew was more than happy to oblige her in anything she wanted, but he knew that things were far from settled. *He's going to pay for this. That son of a bitch is going to pay.*

The next morning, Renee felt somewhat better, although things were far from settled between her and Andrew. They had talked during the night and some things had been laid to rest, although the larger question of the business affair between Donovan Bailey and Cochran Communications was still up in the air. Renee could not rid herself of the horror of exposing her past to Andrew's family.

"I agree that no, they probably won't want to do business with him," she finally conceded, "but can't you just tell them that you know of someone that he abused in the past? I mean, how specific does it have to be?"

They were having coffee in the kitchen, sitting close to each other on the tall stools at the work island. Andrew had made a huge breakfast of which Renee was barely able to partake. Her eyes could not meet his—rather, she stared into her coffee mug as though it were an oracle with the hidden answers to her problems. Andrew longed to tell her that everything would be fine and that he would handle it all, but he knew that would prove impossible.

"Renee," he began, putting his finger under her chin to force her to look into his eyes, "I know how much this means to you. I know that you have kept this secret for so long that to dredge it up again will be painful and extremely difficult. But, sweetheart, it's like Yolanda told you—if you don't let go of it, then he still has power over you. Let's take that power away from him."

Renee looked into Andrew's eyes so full of love and concern for her and trembled slightly. Everything he was saying was true, but she didn't know at that moment if she had the courage to deal with it. And as she pointed out to Andrew, she did not want Bennie to be upset by any hint of the news.

"Andy, Bennie is pregnant and for her to hear this now would be just terrible. She would blame herself for not being here with me. How can you tell Donnie and Clay without her finding out?"

Andrew moaned. It was so like Renee to be concerned about his sister, a concern that he normally would have thought was loving. Right now, though, it just seemed martyrlike. "Renee, Bennie is a strong woman. Her only concern is going to be for you. And not telling her now, that's just another secret that is going to end up causing you more pain."

He could see from the glint in Renee's eyes that she was about to start on another stubborn track to prove her point, so he capitulated. "Okay, okay. We won't say anything to Bennie. Even though I think my sister can handle the news—she's pregnant, not feeble. But if that's the way you want it, fine. But"—he looked at her closely as he spoke—"we have got to get this out in the open as soon as possible."

Renee took her half-full mug over to the sink and carefully rinsed it out. She could not look at Andrew because she knew that he could talk her into anything. With her back to him she began to speak slowly and softly. "All right, Andrew. I will think about discussing this with Donnie and Clay, okay? I guess they have a right to have all the information before signing anything. I'll think about it. And when I have made up my mind, we will talk to them. But not today, okay? I have a killer headache and I want one peaceful Sunday before all hell breaks loose."

She turned to face him then, unaware that her drawn face was etched full of pain. "Just one peaceful Sunday with you and my puppies is all I ask," she said plaintively.

Seeing her so unhappy and withdrawn stoked the fires of the dormant rage that Andrew still felt toward Donovan Bailey. But he let none of that show as he went over to embrace her.

"Anything you want, baby. Anything you want," he vowed.

The last thing Adonis "Donnie" Cochran was expecting on a Sunday morning was to find his oldest brother and two squirmy terriers at his front door.

"Come on in, Bunchy. What brings you out so early?" he asked mildly. It was clear that his brother was upset about something and it did not take him long to find out what it was. Luckily, his two golden retrievers were in their dog run in the back, so there was no chance of a dog massacre in his living room.

"Sit down, Adonis. We have a lot to discuss and it isn't going to be pleasant."

Eighteen

"You have to call off this deal you're getting into with Donovan Bailey," Andrew said without preamble. He waited for the shock to register on his younger brother's face and then went on. "The man is bad news. He is the worst kind of trash there is, and if you knew all the details, there is no way in hell you would be involved with him. So, please God, tell me that you haven't signed any contracts and you can get out of whatever it is you're into with him," he finished.

"Wait just a minute, Andrew. This 'whatever it is' is a *very* big deal for Cochran Communications and The Deveraux Group. You expect me to just walk away from the biggest thing I have done in my working life just on your say-so? Let me explain just what it is that we are doing here," Donnie said calmly.

He went on to explain that Clay's company, The Deveraux Group, was about to launch an all-news cable channel, much like CNN, with Donovan Bailey at the helm. Plus, Cochran Communications was about to turn several of its AM stations into a talk/news format that would be in partnership with the television news. This was a groundbreaking move on the parts of Donnie and Clay—one that would prove lucrative in the extreme, as well as set an industry precedent for years to come.

"This is an idea whose time has more than come, Andrew. This can pave the way for so many more things—I don't have to give you a grocery list. You can just imagine what this is going to mean to African American broadcasting and how many jobs it is going to create. All the groundwork has been done and it has all been done with the idea that Donovan Bailey is going to be our executive in charge as well as being the main anchor. That man has credentials coming out of his ears! All that work that he did in Europe over the years is just the experience we need, and you're asking me to tell Clay that we just walk away from it? On a whim? What the hell have you been smoking?"

Donnie had worked himself up from his normally laid-back persona to what for him was molten rage, and even then he had not raised his voice. As the youngest of six he had learned other ways to get his point across. He waited expectantly for Andrew to explain himself.

Andrew, in the meantime, was sprawled on the sofa with his head back and his eyes closed, almost as though he weren't listening. Finally he opened his eyes and looked his brother full in the face.

"Donovan Bailey"—he spat the name—"is a rapist. Some years ago when he was still working in the States, he took a colleague home from work and molested her in her apartment. No charges were brought, even though the woman filed a report. There was considered to be insufficient evidence to pursue the matter and he got off scot-free," Andrew said in a quiet, deadly voice.

Donnie looked shocked at both the words he was hearing and the look on Andrew's face. Then he shook his head as if to rid himself of the effects of those words. "Look, Andrew, that's a pretty nasty story. But if it happened all those years ago and there were no charges brought, how do you know the woman was even telling the truth? You know as well as I do that there are a lot of women out there who cry 'rape' when they take a notion for a whole lot of reasons. How do you know this isn't some kind of urban legend brought to life?" he asked reasonably.

Andrew sat up and leaned forward, resting his elbows

on his knees. He looked at the floor for a long moment before answering his brother.

"Because the woman told me herself. The woman was Renee," he said softly.

Donnie's face went pale and his eyes seemed unnaturally dark in contrast. He swallowed several times before he could speak. "That son of a bitch. That sick, low-down son of a bitch. Last night he stood grinning in her face like a Cheshire cat, talking about how they used to work together in Newark. That sleazy mutha. . . . Oh, damn, Bunchy, how is Renee? How did she take seeing him?" At once, all of his concern was for Renee.

Andrew explained the whole situation to Donnie, and was surprised and touched to see tears come to Donnie's eyes. Donnie and Renee had always enjoyed a very special relationship. It was Donnie's turn to explain as he poured them both a scotch.

"See, Renee was like a big sister, but she was better than a sister because we weren't related, you know? She always treated me like an adult, something that a gawky teenager does not get from his family," he said fondly.

He went on to tell Andrew how he and Renee often had long talks about things that were bothering him, usually about girls. "She would take me out to lunch or to dinner, just like we were the same age or something, and let me just piss and moan about Sheila or Tonya or whomever. And then she would give me great advice," he said with a laugh. "You might not know this, but Renee went to the prom with me," he added.

This was news to Andrew. At his dumbfounded expression Donnie nodded.

"Yep. You were in med school and I, as you recall, had not reached the full pinnacle of my masculine beauty," he said with a wink. "But I worked up my nerve and asked the prettiest girl in my class to the prom. Everything was all set. We were going to double-date with Briscoe and his girlfriend and we had gone into hock to rent a limo and go out to dinner, the whole shot. And at the last minute, Charisse—that was her name, Charisse—backed out. It seems that she got a better offer from the captain of the basketball team.

"Man, I was *crushed*. The embarrassment and the heartbreak—you are talking about some serious teen angst here. And Renee was in town that weekend and tells me not to worry, she'll be happy to go to the prom with me. And she did. It was the best night of my entire life, bar none. She had on some foxy designer dress and she danced every single dance with me and made me feel like I was, like, twelve feet tall instead of an overgrown, gangly kid. That's the kind of person she is," he said reflectively.

"And that bastard put his hands on her. Son of a bitch," Donnie swore, and continued to swear for a few minutes. He had reached the point where he wanted to get his hands around Donovan Bailey's throat, something that Andrew had to talk him out of.

"Believe me, I know where you're coming from. But the problem right now is how to get out of this deal without letting Bennie know about Renee's past. Remember, Renee does not want anyone knowing, especially Bennie and the family. That's why she went through this all by herself for so long. She's going to kill me if she finds out I told you, but I didn't know what else to do. I knew you wouldn't want to have anything to do with the slimy rat bastard and I didn't want to wait until you had put something in writing."

Donnie was on the phone to his brother-in-law Clay Deveraux in Atlanta. After stressing the need for utter security on the matter, he told Clay the deal had to be nullified and explained exactly why. With no hesitation Clay agreed.

"We still may be put in a position to defend why we brought him along to this point and dropped him, but you've got two lawyers in your family and I have one—so between them, we'll be okay. Rotten son of a bitchin' asshole—I just hope his ass survives long enough to do some time. You know, don't you, that if he did it to Renee, he's done it before and has done it since. And I agree with Renee, Bennie does not have to know this right now," Clay said gruffly once Donnie put him on speakerphone.

"There is plenty of talent out there. We can find another person to put in that spot. Just get rid of Bailey and take care of Renee," he added. He spoke to Andrew for a few minutes before hanging up.

Andrew looked at his watch and groaned. "I told Renee I was going to get the *New York Times* about an hour ago. I gotta get back over there before she knows I did exactly what she told me not to do," he said glumly.

Donnie took his brother's arm. "Hey, Bunchy, you did what you had to do. There was nothing else you could have done under the circumstances. The important thing now is to get him out of our lives completely."

The rest of Sunday went, more or less, according to Renee's wishes. During Andrew's absence she took a long, long bubble bath and tried to erase the events of the past weeks from her mind. By the time Andrew returned to her house, she was in a much calmer state; it was as though she had crossed a mental bridge to a more hospitable environment.

Andrew did his best to make sure she stayed relaxed and happy the rest of the day. They talked quietly and listened to music while they did the crossword puzzle; Renee was moved to prepare a nice Sunday dinner of Cornish game hens and wild-rice stuffing. They spent the night in each other's arms, sleeping soundly.

That day of rest was just what Renee needed. She was at Urban Oasis earlier than usual on Monday, and she was actually able to give herself over to her myriad tasks. The holiday season was in full swing, which meant Christmas weddings, cotillions, dinner dances and a plethora of other activities would require head-to-toe beautification of her clients. Renee always welcomed the attendant hubbub because of the magnificent increase in sales figures; now she welcomed it for another reason entirely. As long as she was busy, she couldn't dwell on Donovan Bailey.

She was going over the Christmas-card list to make sure that everyone who had visited Urban Oasis in the past year would receive holiday greetings; this was the kind of special treatment that made the salon such a standout. Vaguely she heard the door to her office open and assumed it was Valerie.

"Val, did you get the final menu for the party to the caterer? We may need to increase the quantities, since we are inviting sales reps. You know how some of those reps can eat!" she said without looking up.

"Well, if you invite me, I'll be sure to come with a hearty appetite," a male voice replied.

Renee forced herself to maintain a semblance of calm, although the nausea that was now familiar had overtaken her. She stood and slowly turned to face Donovan Bailey, who was standing in her doorway wearing a smile that said, "I know you're glad to see me."

Before she could ask how he found her and how he got into her private office, Donovan casually entered the room and explained his presence.

"Donnie Cochran told me that you owned the premier day spa in Detroit, so of course I had to drop in. I hope you don't scold Valerie, but I told her that I was an old friend and that I wanted to surprise you, so she brought me back," he said with a smirk.

Renee was amazed that she could stand, but she found that she was able to, albeit with her arms crossed tightly over her chest. In a deceptively calm voice she asked him point-blank, "Why did you lie to her?"

"Valerie" . . . *like they are just the best ol' buddies in the world,* she thought. Donovan always did have a way of getting the female of the species to grant him special favors. Like he was God's gift to women. And in truth, if you did not know the ugliness that lived inside the shell, he was quite a package.

Six feet tall, with the muscular build of an athlete, he

was fair-skinned, with brown wavy hair that was always cut impeccably; his hazel eyes always twinkled and his lips were nicely shaped, although a bit on the thin side. And he sported a dimple that would flash with any provocation, especially when he was trying to be endearing, like now.

"Renee," he said charmingly, "how did I lie? I did want to surprise you and we are old friends, after all. We go back a long way, you and I, just like I told Donnie last night," he added confidently.

Before Renee could give him the blistering retort that was on the tip of her tongue, he went on: "I have to tell you again, Renee, you are looking absolutely fabulous. Fabulous. And this place . . . it's magnificent! Who would have ever dreamed that this is where your real talents lay? You have come a long way from Newark, Renee. I lived in Europe for many years, but even in Paris, Rome, Milan and Amsterdam, there were not many women who could rival your beauty and style," he said, looking her up and down.

He was so busy taking in the picture Renee made in a smoke gray Missoni sweater and leather Prada skirt that he did not notice the look of total incredulity on her face. The pashmina stole she had been wearing in the chilly back office was flung over her desk as she finally found her voice.

"Either this is a nightmare, or I'm in hell. It can't be a nightmare because I'm awake. So this must be my personal version of hell, since you're in it. What has gone wrong with your mind that you think you can come into my place of business and pass yourself off as a friend of mine when nothing can be further from the truth? And what makes you think that you can throw a few compliments my way and all traces of what you did to me will disappear—*poof*—like it never happened?" she snarled.

Donovan's poise began to crumble and he raised his hands to placate Renee and stave off any further vitriol, but it was too late.

"How dare you speak to me of my 'talent lying elsewhere'—my talent was in the newsroom, you yellow bastard, and you well know it. My talent, my skill and my training were all about television, and that little rug got jerked out from under me, thanks to you, you animal. Well, guess what, I still rose like the phoenix from the flames and I will keep on rising, which is none of your F-ing business.

"I don't know what you think you are playing at here, but I have to warn you that you are on very dangerous ground. I am not a safe woman for you to be around, Bailey. I have already been through the fires of hell at your hands, so I have no real fear of death. I am not afraid of you, Bailey."

She stood still for a moment as the realization of what she said sank in. It was true. At that moment she had no fear of the man. She looked at him and all she saw was a pampered, spoiled man who got his kicks out of hurting women. She took a few steps toward him, and sure enough, he backed up a few steps.

"So answer my question. What the hell do you want here? 'Cause if I were you, I wouldn't trust me with a sharp implement in my hand—this would not be a good place for you to get a trim," she advised.

"Renee, I feel terrible about that misunderstanding we had so many years ago. . . ."

Renee gave a short, harsh laugh. "Don't go there, Bailey. I understood what you did back then and you understood it, too. It was rape and you got away with it."

By then, Renee was less than a foot away and she dared him to make a move with every tensed tendon and sinew in her body. Just then, she could have taken him apart with her bare hands; he seemed to realize it, too.

"Look, Renee . . . a lot has changed since then. I did a lot of things I regret, and I can't tell you how desperately I want to make amends for them. But"—he hesitated and, like a novice soap-opera actor, he morphed into an "I'm sincere" face—"I don't see how rehashing the past can get any of us anywhere. I had no idea that you were a friend of the Cochrans, but . . . you probably know the time and money spent in developing the new cable network."

Renee's narrowed eyes and alert posture told him that he had hit pay dirt.

"There has been a tremendous outlay of cash on the part of your friends the Cochrans, and if anything should happen to abort the deal, I am in a contractual position to cost them even more. So it would seem that we derive a mutual benefit in keeping the past in the past, if you know what I mean," he said with a smug smile.

Renee's eyes betrayed her emotions—they immediately turned muddy and unfocused—and like the animal of prey that he was, he went for the kill.

"I don't think you've ever made a stupid move in your life, Renee, and now is not the time to start. I think we understand each other perfectly." He smirked and he showed himself the door. He turned and looked around once more before leaving.

"Oh, and this really is a nice place you've got here," he added with a wink.

Nineteen

"So it's settled then. No contract was signed; therefore he has no contractual basis for a lawsuit. We just tell the bastard he's out and move forward."

Donnie leaned back in his big leather armchair and surveyed the men assembled around the table in the conference room of WWCC. Present were his brothers Alan and Andre, who were attorneys in charge of all legal affairs pertaining to Cochran Communications, Andrew, who was as tired as he looked, and surprisingly, the next to youngest Cochran son, Adam.

Adam was an architect and land developer and not strictly involved with the business of Cochran Communications. But like his brothers, he had a vested interest in Renee and this was a business decision that could ultimately affect the whole family. He felt that he had a right and an obligation to be there, which he did.

Alan spoke next, in the measured tones that attorneys use when looking at all aspects of a situation. "Not completely. True enough, nothing has been finalized and no contracts have been signed. But Bailey could make a case for misrepresentation on our part. This deal has been in the works for some time and he has every reason to expect that he will get the position for which he had been considered, at the salary that had been quoted. For us to pull out now could constitute a breach of an *implied* contract, and he could sue, successfully, I might add," he informed the table.

Andrew's immediate reaction was explosive. "I don't give a happy damn what he thinks was implied and what he tries to do in court. The bottom line is that the deal has to be off. That's it, period, no questions asked or answered."

Andre held up a conciliatory hand. "Hold on, Bunchy. Alan is just looking at all the angles. He might threaten a suit and he might even attempt one. But I doubt seriously that it will get that far. You realize that Clay is completely correct in saying that his behavior with Renee is in all probability not an isolated incident. There are all kinds of ways to find out all kinds of things about him, things that he would not like to see in the morning paper. Which is exactly where that kind of information will inevitably end up," he advised.

Andrew ran his hand over his once perfectly styled hair. "And that's exactly what can't happen. I have told you over and over that this is exactly what Renee has been trying to avoid. She is not going to be the toast of the tabloids over this. Hell, I will buy out his damned nonexistent contract to prevent that! There has got to be another way to go on this."

Adam, who had been silent through most of this, offered a solution. "I've got a big ol' truck that can make him into a speed bump in no time flat. Range Rovers can handle roadkill way bigger than that sack of shit." Adam was the wildest and most unorthodox of the Cochran men. Like all of them, he was well over six feet and broad-shouldered, but there was an almost feral quality that set him apart from his brothers. He was daring, iconoclastic and intensely loyal to anyone he gave his allegiance to, and that included his future sister-in-law.

Andrew looked at him bleakly. "I told Pop to quit sending you to those damn wilderness camps. If I didn't know you were serious, I'd almost think that was funny."

Andre and Alan forestalled further comment by getting back to the legalities of the situation. They were identical twins, exactly alike in appearance, manner and voice, so much so that you had to be looking at them to determine which one was speaking.

"What you have to remember is this: no matter how rotten a human being he is—and he is a bona fide critter—that does not mean that he is not qualified to do the job he was courted to do. This is what a court of law may very well decide; the fact that he is a rapist does not mean that he won't be a fine executive for a cable network. Hell, it might even qualify him," Alan said glumly.

Before gloom could descend, Andre pointed something else out. "On the other hand, if he *is* a criminal, and he is, there is the matter of several felonies. If he is doing time in the big house, he is not going to be available to take up any new duties of any kind, except maybe laundry detail and running from Big Bubba in the shower room. Like it or not, we are going to have to do some digging into his background."

Now it was Donnie's turn to burst out in sheer frustration. "What the hell are you saying? Can we go forward or not? Are you saying we're stuck with this raping bottom feeder or what?"

Alan and Andre exchanged a look of satisfaction. "Oh, we'll get out of it, all right. Without Renee's past coming to light, without Grizzly Adam making road stew of him and without a court case. We not only went to Harvard Law, we went to *class*. But"—Alan paused dramatically—"I don't think we'll get through it without Pop finding out about it, and you know what that will mean."

Just then, the conference room door crashed open and there in all his septuagenarian splendor stood the patriarch of the Cochran clan, Andrew Bernard Cochran Sr. And he was not happy.

"What the hell are you boys up to, and what is it that you're trying to keep from me?" he demanded.

Total silence was his only response.

* * *

Once again, Renee found herself taking solace from Yolanda. This time, though, she was more able to speak freely about what had been happening to her. After apprising Yolanda of the events of the past few days, she concluded, "You were right, though, he has power over me and I want it back. I want every single bit of it back. I don't want that evil, twisted, night-crawling, scum-sucking bastard to be able to control one iota of anything that has to do with me and anyone I care about. But, Yolanda, I don't know what to do. I just don't, short of blowing his head off."

She took a deep, quivering breath to calm down and Yolanda was able to get a word in edgewise.

"Renee, from what you told me today, it would seem that you have taken a huge step in making that happen. Not the shooting part, certainly, but you faced him down, you confronted him and you spoke your mind. That is a far cry from hiding in the ladies' room and going into a mild state of shock," she reminded Renee.

Renee slumped down into the pillows of Yolanda's familiar, comfortable couch and stared up at the ceiling for a moment.

"Yes, but, Yolanda, he could ruin Andrew's family. He could destroy them financially. They have put out massive sums of money to make this talk radio and cable network thing happen. And he could sue them for the rest if anything happens to make it not go through, or to put him out of the executive spot. You see? This is what they mean by a rock and a hard place. Even if I could say 'Yes, Andrew, tell your brother that his newest executive is a rapist,' it wouldn't ultimately make any difference because if they try to pull out, he can sue them. How could I possibly let that happen?" she asked frantically.

Yolanda spoke quietly. "Renee, you are making a lot of assumptions. Number one, they can countersue. If he has grossly misrepresented some aspect of his background, any contract can be nullified. Number two, I don't know a lot about the media, certainly, but it seems to me that any English-speaking human trained in that kind of work can do that job. I doubt seriously that the whole project hinges on one night-crawling scum sucker," she said, enunciating each epithet carefully.

Renee surprised herself with a teary snort that was almost a laugh. Encouraged by her response, Yolanda continued.

"Always remember what everybody's granny always told them when they got too big for their britches: 'One monkey don't stop no show.' I will bet you they have more résumés than they know what to do with. They can replace him, so they are not going to lose those dollars they have shelled out. And number three . . ." She paused dramatically to make sure she had Renee's full attention.

"Number three, what makes you think this man is telling the truth? He is a liar, a cad, a rapist and a bounder, so why would he suddenly turn to the truth as his holy beacon?"

Renee sat up straight on the sofa and stared at Yolanda in awe.

"Yolanda, I think I know what I need to do now. Something I should have done a long time ago."

As soon as Big Benny Cochran entered the conference room, there was no doubt about who was who. Despite the fact that he had just turned seventy, Big Benny was still the undisputed king of WWCC. It was easy to see where his sons got their looks—he, too, was over six feet tall, but his wavy head of hair was silvery white, as was his mustache and goatee. He still dressed like a million bucks, even though he no longer worked every day. He had retired completely from the day-to-day activities of the station and other business concerns, but he still knew everything that went on within the walls of the building and certainly within his family. To try to get something past Big Benny's eagle eye was tantamount to nailing Jell-O to a tree—it could not be accomplished by mere mortals.

He surveyed the group with little pleasure, gesturing with his unlit stogie to Donnie. "Get up from there, boy. And somebody better tell me what the hell is going on around here," he said with a grunt as he usurped the big leather chair at the head of the table.

"Look, Pop, we were just discussing the possibility of restructuring the merger with The Deveraux Group, that's all," Alan began—or maybe it was Andre.

One look at Benny said that would not wash. He leaned back and looked at each son in turn. "I am not going to ask you all again. What has arisen to occasion all five of my sons, two of whom have no connection whatsoever with the operations of Cochran Communications, to meet in this particular boardroom on a Monday afternoon? This is by no means a normal procedure for this family and do not insult my intelligence by pretending that it is," he said, his voice rising with every sentence. "Now, must I repeat myself or has someone's memory come back?"

Andrew, now that he could get a word in, braced himself to explain the events leading up to the council of war that his father had invaded. In truth, it was out of consideration for his health and his love for Renee that none of them wanted Benny to know what was going on. He had already had a couple of heart attacks, which made them want to protect him from stress—plus the fact that Big Benny was not a man known for patience or prudence. Back in the day, Benny had learned to dispense his brand of justice from some of the highest men-about-town; some were even legitimate businessmen.

"Listen, guys, leave me and Pop alone for a few, okay?" Andrew rose and his brothers quietly left the room.

Andrew moved to the head of the conference table and brought his chair around to face his father. Big Benny, sensing the gravity of the situation, leaned forward to meet his oldest son. Speaking in a low, tight voice, Andrew told Benny that the woman he loved like a daughter, the woman that would be his daughter-in-law, had been violated some years before by a man who was ironically about to become a part of the family business.

Big Benny's head dropped for a moment, and Andrew braced himself for the worst. He was shocked but somehow not surprised to see tears in his father's eyes. His fondness for Renee went back as far as her friendship with Andrew's twin sister. He had always thought she was a hell of a woman and was proud as could be that she would be a Cochran.

"Goddamn it to hell. Goddamn it to hell," Benny muttered. "So what the hell are you doing about it, Andrew? How do you plan to take care of this situation?" he demanded.

"Pop, I told you; we are severing all ties with the man. He will not work one day for Cochran/Deveraux and he will not see a penny of money. . . ." Andrew stopped speaking when his father slammed his big hand down on the conference table.

"Don't give me that shit! I don't give a good Goddamn about all of that—what I want to know is how are you going to take care of him? This man hurt your woman; he almost destroyed her. And you're talkin' about severing ties?" Big Benny's face was vermilion with rage and he began loosening his collar.

"What kind of man have I raised? If a man had put a hand on my Lillian, we wouldn't be talkin' about nothin' except what time to be at the funeral home, you can damn well believe that!" Benny roared.

"Pop, Pop, calm down. You think I don't want him dead? You think that there isn't an hour that goes by that I don't want to see him beaten bloody because of what he did? I can't go there, Pop, because I'll go crazy if I do," Andrew admitted. He stood abruptly and walked over to the window, which displayed the fading sun over the Detroit skyline.

"I have to think about Renee. She kept all of this bottled up for so long because she was afraid and ashamed, and it wrecked her life for a long time. The last thing she needs is a lot of turmoil about it. I want him to pay, all right; I want him to suffer just the way she did; I want him to bleed; I want him to feel every bit of her pain," he said slowly. "But, Pop, it is *her* pain. I can't make it better for her; I can only be there for her. I can't take a magic wand and make it like it never happened, and I can't fix the bastard who did it without going to jail. And I won't be much good to her there. If she even knew I had told you and the boys, she would . . . damn, she would raise hell and put a chunk in it. And then she would kick my livin' ass and I would have to take it because I knew that this was not what she wanted. But it had to be done, Pop."

At the end of this speech, Big Benny stared at Andrew for a long time. "Son, the only thing I agree with is that you have to protect Renee. The rest of that hogwash . . . I guess I've just lived too long. When the time has come that a man can't take care of his own, I guess that's something I just don't know how to deal with," he said quietly.

He looked at his son again and he had to honestly ask himself what he would do in Andrew's circumstances. "Son, get me a ginger ale, would you? My throat is dry from all that damned yelling," Benny said ruefully.

"Sure, Pop. Be right back," Andrew said as he left the room to get the Vernor's that was always in the small refrigerator in Big Benny's old office.

No sooner had the door closed than Big Benny grabbed the telephone and punched in a number he had long ago committed to memory.

"It's me. Meet me at the usual place at seven. I got some work for you."

By that evening Renee's plans had been finalized. Valerie could take care of Urban Oasis for a couple of days while she took care of some long-overdue business. She was going home to Cleveland to have the talk with her mother that should have taken place years before. She was surprised at the mild reaction that she got from Andrew when she told him that she was going home for a couple of days, but she was equally relieved that he did not press for details.

Her confrontation with Donovan Bailey had given her the knowledge that she could indeed wipe the slate clean. All it took was guts and she seemed to have found hers. The drive to Cleveland took about four hours, during which time she forced herself to think only about the up-coming holidays and the mammoth amount of shopping she would be doing during the next few weeks. By the time she turned onto Chateau Avenue, the street where she had grown up, she felt almost lighthearted. Of course, one wrong look from her mother could change all of that.

But Pearlie Mae was effusively glad to see her. "Ooh, look at my baby, looking just like a china doll! Ooh, it's so good to see you!" she exclaimed as she hugged Renee tightly.

The two women went into the kitchen for tea and some of her mother's special tea cakes; Renee was soon basking in the glow of being at home with just her mother for company. With four sisters, it was hard to find a moment alone with either parent, so times like these were always special. And for some reason, Pearlie Mae was always so much more mellow in a one-on-one situation. After laughing at an anecdote about one of her mother's church groups, Renee felt bold enough to say that very thing.

"You know, Mama, I always loved it when it was just the two of us. We always seem to have better times when we're all alone. Why is that, I wonder?"

Luckily, her mother did not take offense. "Honey, all you girls tell me the same thing. I guess my nerves were so shot from having five of you mares that when there's not a bunch of you underfoot, things just flow better. It is nice like this, isn't it?"

They chatted and caught up on family gossip and Renee prepared dinner for her mother. And unlike most meals that came from hands other than her own, Pearlie Mae did not find anything amiss with the meal. Renee had braced herself for one of her mother's usual stunts, like taking a deep sniff of the contents of her fork, eyeing it closely and then tasting it like it contained known carcinogens. A raised eyebrow and squinted eye would follow, then a comment like, "Was that *turmeric* you put in there? Tastes kinda off, is all."

But not tonight—the meal and the company were superb, the kind of thing Renee had often wished she could do with her mother. Pearlie Mae even asked about Andrew.

"You know, he really is a lovely man. He's just right for you. You know, it's hard to believe, but all my daughters married well," she said with satisfaction.

Renee could feel her mouth opening and closing like a tropical fish, but she could not seem to formulate a proper response.

"Oh, stop gaping like a guppy! It's true, although I know I never said it before. All of those men, despite their flaws, are very good men. Nice men and they love your sisters very much. They are good husbands," she said with every appearance of sincerity.

"Okay, Mama, what kind of drugs are you on? Are you taking those blood thinners again?" Renee asked with concern. "Because this is the most surprising thing I have ever heard you say. Since when have you become a fan of your sons-in-law? And a proponent of marriage? This is . . . not you, I must say."

The real Pearlie Mae reared up for a moment. "And why would I not be in favor of marriage? Do you think I want my children living in sin?" she countered indignantly.

Renee narrowed her eyes at her mother and widened them just as quickly. "Well, Mama, you have said that very thing on many occasions after Daddy left. You said that a woman who tied herself to a man was a fool and that it was better to live in sin than be shackled to a jackass, and that is a direct quote," Renee reminded her.

Like most mothers, Pearlie Mae hated it when her children used her own words against her, but at least she acknowledged that she might have said such a thing.

"Oh, I was just out of sorts. I was going through the change and I wasn't terribly rational. And for your information, missy, your father did not leave me. He asked me to go with him and I refused." She looked sideways at Renee, whose delicate jaw had dropped. "Close your mouth before something flies in it. I have told you girls how unladylike that is."

Finally she relented and told all. A General Motors plant, which had moved its operations to Doraville, Georgia, employed Renee's father. Rather than take a forced retirement on a partial pension, her father was transferred to Georgia to finish his working years so that his retirement package would be intact.

"He wanted me to move down there and I wouldn't go. I told him when I came to Ohio that I was never living down South again and he didn't believe me. But I meant it from the bottom of my heart. I tried to get him to take an early retirement, but he was determined to work those last ten years so we would have more money for our golden years. I told him if he did that, he would do it alone. And he did," she said defiantly.

Renee jumped from the love seat and stared at her mother with huge, angry eyes.

"Mama! You told us that Daddy had left you for no good reason and we have been treating him like a stranger ever since! You had us all traumatized and upset and made us think the worst of our own father! How could you do that? You . . . I . . . Mama, this is unbelievable!" she ranted.

Her mother was just this side of contrite. "I was an awful, selfish woman, I know," she admitted. Thoughtfully she added, "I think it was the menopause. I had such a hard time with it; it made me really crazy at times."

Renee had to leave the room to keep from throwing something at her mother. *Lord, today. That woman is the very limit. Talk about more nerve than a brass monkey. . . .* She stuck her head back into the living room to ask her mother if her sisters knew about the situation.

"Well . . . they will pretty soon, I guess. You father's retirement has come at last and he is moving back up here. With me."

Twenty

Oddly enough, that bizarre conversation with Pearlie Mae somehow made it easier for Renee to reveal her dark secret, that she had been a victim of rape some years before. The fact that her mother had been sitting on a time bomb of her own helped Renee find the words to tell her about Donovan Bailey and his recent reappearance in her life.

Pearlie had wept and raged and sympathized, and when she had calmed down, she agreed with Andrew that the truth had to come out. She also wanted a few of Donovan's body parts to be detached in the most painful way possible. She went so far as to dig out a pistol that she kept in the linen closet behind the guest-room sheets.

"Ma! Where did you get that thing? Get it away from me; you know how scared I am of guns!" Renee protested.

Her mother squinted an eye as she pointed the gun out the back door in a position that was a dead-on Cleopatra Jones stance. "Well, *I'm* not scared of guns or of low-down raping dogs. It's probably a good thing you never told me, Renee. I'd probably be just coming up for parole," she said in all seriousness.

She lowered the pistol and looked at Renee sadly. "To think that you couldn't even come to me, your own mother. All these years you've been carrying this around inside you like a big sack of poison. It shouldn't have been like that, baby. I have been a terrible mother to you." She sniffled aloud.

Renee hugged Pearlie Mae tightly, which was rather awkward as Pearlie was still holding the dreaded pistol. "Mama, you were and are a wonderful mother. Scary, yes. Unorthodox, certainly. But I wouldn't trade you for anyone. Now could you please put that thing away?"

Pearlie looked at the offending piece of weaponry with reverence. "Okay, I'll put it up. Just remember, it's not too late for some down-home justice. What is Andrew going to do about this sorry-ass bastard?"

"All I know is he won't be doing business with Chochran/Derevaux. He'll be hurting where he lives, right in his wallet. Losing that money will hurt him worse than anything."

Her mother did not look impressed in the least. "Back in the day, when a man messed with somebody's woman, he paid in blood. *Money?* You can't buy back nobody's honor with money," she spat.

Renee sighed deeply. "I'm going to get some wine. Would you like some wine? I think you need some," she said firmly.

She turned to go to the kitchen to get the libations. "My honor is totally intact, Mama. Andrew loves me, respects me and treats me like an adult. He communicates with me and honors me in every way possible. Nothing Donovan Bailey can do or say can change that in any way. This is not like the Wild West, where men had to have showdowns for the virtue of their womenfolk," she said over her shoulder. "He honors me by letting me handle things in my own way."

She did not hear Pearlie Mae snort and mutter that a pistol whipping was still a wonderful idea for the slimy pig who molested her daughter.

On Wednesday morning there was yet another meeting in the WWCC boardroom, but this time there was a slightly different group of attendees. Present were Clay Deveraux, CEO and president of The Deveraux Group, accompanied by his brother Martin Deveraux, chief counsel of the corporation. They had flown in from Atlanta the night before for this special gathering. As CEO of Cochran Communications Adonis Cochran was of course present, as were the firm's attorneys, Andre and Alan Cochran. Donovan Bailey was pleased to see all these key players in one room. It made the plans that had been discussed at length seem that much closer to reality; the dream job of a lifetime was about to be his, as soon as he signed on the dotted line.

A man of less confidence would have felt intimidated by this group; they were towering men, all inches taller than his own six feet. Being the shortest man in a room full of tall, impeccably clad men, all of whom had enough personal wealth to buy him and sell him six times over, would have made most people feel a bit out of their depth, but Donovan Bailey was not most people. He was relaxed, convivial and in actuality felt like he was in his true element with the movers and shakers, the men of power who could make things happen in the world. He was *home,* as far as he was concerned. He glanced around at what he felt was his new universe, pausing a bit only when his eyes fell on Martin Deveraux.

The eye patch and the long ponytail were just a bit much for Donovan, especially with that—*ugh*—big, ugly scar running down his face. *It's called plastic surgery; look into it,* he thought. But Martin was just counsel. It wasn't like he would have to deal with the dude personally. He would be dealing with Adonis Cochran and Clay Deveraux for the most part. And he already had the young Adonis eating out of the palm of his hand. *God, I love it when things come together,* he gloated silently. *This is going to be the biggest money I will ever make in my life. And the easiest. These people think I'm God.*

Just then, the young, impressionable Donnie Cochran called the meeting to order. The slight clink of coffee cups being returned to saucers was the only noise in the room, other than Donnie's voice.

"Clay and Martin, I'm glad you were able to make it up here on such short notice. I wanted to get this over with as quickly as possible so that we can all enjoy the approaching holidays," he began. Looking directly at Donovan Bailey, he spoke quietly and confidently.

"Donovan, the purpose of this meeting is to tell you that we have decided to go in a slightly different direction with the news network. We appreciate your time and input, but we have decided at this point to keep our options open before making permanent staffing decisions. We're sure that a man of your stature and reputation will have no trouble finding the right niche within the industry and we wish you the best with that."

Astonishingly, that is all he had to say. Donovan Bailey blinked a couple of times and tilted his head slightly to the side as if to allow the words to flow more easily into his thick skull. He started to speak and instead opened and closed his mouth a few times before anything would come out. When he was able to verbalize again, his first words indicated that he had not quite grasped the situation.

"New direction? We're changing the format, changing the production timeline, what? I'm sure that I can accommodate any changes that you deem necessary to the success of the project, Donnie. My background lets you know what I am capable of in these matters," he said in what he hoped was a suave and unshaken manner.

Donnie looked at his brothers and then at Clay and Martin before answering. He took his time about it, too. He leaned back and examined his fingernails briefly and said in what was almost an aside, "Donovan, the only thing that we are changing is our choice of executive vice president and anchor. That would be you. Everything else will remain the same, including the projected air date."

This time there was no mistaking the tone or the dismissal. "You're telling me that I'm out? I don't understand! We have practically signed the contracts! You all but assured me that the position was mine. I can't believe that this is the way that you people do business. My attorney will certainly have something to say about this . . . this . . . cavalier treatment." Donovan's face had turned pasty and damp with trickles of perspiration. His fury was evident in the scarlet patches that mottled his fine bone structure and his voice, which was rising with each word.

"I'll sue you, Cochran, for every penny you have. You people don't know who you're dealing with, apparently. You better ask somebody," he ground out.

Clay was beginning to tire of the spectacle. "We did ask somebody, Bailey, and they said you weren't shit. We concur. You are out. Cochran/Deveraux does not require or desire your services in any capacity, including that of janitor. You can threaten all the lawsuits you want, but the fact remains that you have no legal basis whatsoever to pursue it." Clay leaned forward and growled in a voice that was several octaves lower than Barry White, "In other words, you ain't got nothin' comin' here."

The look on Donovan's face went from rage to comprehension when Clay made his pronouncement. He got to his feet and looked at the assembled men incredulously.

"It's because of that woman, isn't it? What did Renee tell you? She's lying, whatever she said. Yes, we used to work together in Newark, but it wasn't the way she said it at all," he said hotly. He took out a silk pocket handkerchief and wiped sweat that was still pouring off him. In his expensively tailored suit and his expensive haircut, with the smell of his expensive cologne mixed with the stench of pure fear, he looked like a prize pig caught in a snare.

He loosened his tie and was stammering something else out when Alan interrupted him. Or Andre, it was impossible to tell from the crisp legal tonality of the voice.

"I have to ask, Bailey: If nothing of an untoward nature transpired between you and Ms. Kemp, why would you even mention her name? My brother informs you that you are no longer a candidate for a position with Cochran/Deveraux and your first response is to deny that anything improper took place between you and Renee Kemp."

Donovan's face became even more mottled as rage overtook him completely. He stared at the Cochran retainers as if they were speaking some complicated Slavic language, but he was managing to understand a word or two.

"I GET IT! I understand now! That lyin' wench told you I did something to her. Look, we may have kicked it, but we were both grown. What damned difference does it make? What is she to you?" he cried in the voice of a man who does not know he is sealing his own fate.

He was moving around anxiously in an adult version of the shuffle that little children demonstrate when they have to go to the bathroom. "Look, you know and I know that I am the best man for this job. You are going to risk the success of this whole enterprise over that bitch? Come on now, those black bitches are a dime a dozen, but there is only one Donovan Bailey."

"And it's a good damned thing that there is only one," a voice said behind him. "It makes you a lot easier to eliminate."

Donovan whirled around to see Andrew Cochran looking like the very wrath of God, accompanied by Adam Cochran, who wore no expression at all but looked more dangerous than any man in the room, including the scarred and silent Martin.

Donnie and the twins were not particularly happy to see either man. "Andrew, you aren't supposed to be here—this is nearly over with. Adam, get him out of here."

It had been agreed that these two would not be anywhere near WWCC when this meeting took place because Andrew's stake in the matter was too high; he had reason to want to do bodily harm to Donovan Bailey. And Adam was wild enough to welcome a physical fight, something that was clear to every man in the room, despite Adam's relaxed, almost casual posture.

His brother may as well not have been speaking for all

the attention Andrew paid him. "I may not be a lawyer, but I understand slander when I hear it. If you ever, in word or deed, malign my fiancée again, you will regret it," he snarled, pushing Bailey in the shoulder.

Adam, his face still impassive, grabbed his brother's arm to prevent more of the same. "Hands, Bunchy. You're a surgeon and you need them," he noted. His tone suggested that he would be more than happy to use his own fists.

Donovan finally grasped the danger that he was in. He looked around frantically at the imposing figures facing him down and he knew true fear for the first time. He tried to make his way to the door, bluffing as he went.

"It's my word against hers," he insisted. "You can't prove anything, so it's all just hearsay. Just a frustrated woman who couldn't have me, so she tried to bring me down, that's all it was. . . ."

Andrew's hands around his throat cut off his words. The men who weren't already standing came to their feet to pull Andrew off, but once again Adam prevailed. Using all his strength, he jerked his brother's hands away and let Bailey collapse to the floor.

"Bunchy, it's not worth it. Leave it! Come on, man, it's not worth it," he urged as he led him away from Bailey, who was giving every appearance of knocking on death's door. Adam walked over to the man and actually helped him stand.

He helped him straighten his jacket and handed him the handkerchief that had fallen to the floor. Speaking in a deceptively calm voice, he suggested that Bailey leave the building while he was able.

"You know, these men are all reasonable, respectable members of the community, which is why they are so civilized. But I"—he grinned and looked truly lethal for the first time—"am not a respected, world-renowned surgeon, or the head of a corporation, or an officer of the court. I am self-employed and answer to no one, and I would take great personal pleasure in rearranging that cute face of yours," he offered quietly.

Donovan had backed up to the door of the conference room by then and was frantically grabbing for the knob. When he felt it, he turned it as quickly as his sweaty palm would allow and jerked it open.

"You people are crazy! You're all crazy. You can't threaten me! I'll sue—I'll sue every single one of you crazy bastards! You think you can threaten to do harm to me and get away with it? I warned that bitch—I told her what would happen if she messed with me! Now she's gonna pay and you're gonna pay," he swore.

That was enough to get Andrew into action. When he heard the word *bitch,* he pushed his way through the assorted Cochran and Deveraux men. His fist connected with Bailey's jaw as soon as he stopped speaking. Bailey hit the floor and Andrew stood over him, flexing his hand.

"Go near her again and I will kill you," he said murderously. Heedless of the crowd of employees who had responded to the noise from the conference room, Andrew left with Adam close on his heels. The fact that Adam's booted foot connected with Bailey's leg as he struggled to a sitting position was in all likelihood an accident.

The reception that Renee had planned for Andrew that night was no accident, however. She returned to Detroit on Wednesday. Arriving in the early afternoon, she had just enough time to put her plan into action. She was filled with a sense of purpose and renewal; the power was hers again. Yolanda was right, and Andrew had been right also. There was nothing to be gained by continuing to hide behind the past. Telling the truth, no matter how painful, was curiously liberating. Telling the truth would indeed shame the Devil, and that was precisely what she was going to do.

She took the girls out for a brief constitutional and truly enjoyed their antics for the first time in a long time. After racing home with the eager little dogs, she got her bag from the car and unpacked rapidly. Tonight would be one of relaxation, conversation and passion for Andrew, she had decided, and it was long overdue. Along with a few other things, she mused as she looked around the house. Here it was, the second week of December and she still did not have one bit of holiday decoration anywhere. Well, that could be remedied rather quickly.

There was a huge artificial tree in the basement that she and Bennie had used for several years. There were also boxes of ornaments and other trimmings at the ready. Glancing at the clock, she realized that she did not have time to emulate Martha Stewart *and* create the perfect evening for Andrew, but she could get some flowers and a couple of wreaths and at least get some kind of holiday feeling going. And she could have a casual tree-trimming party that weekend with Andrew's nephews and niece. They would love it, and it had been far too long since she had hosted his family. With that settled, at least in her mind, she went into overdrive.

Throwing on her coat, she bade good-bye to her startled doggies and dashed to the car. In two hours she was back, laden with packages and feeling like the "Queen of the World."

"I'm back," Renee sang out. The little dogs were, as always, happy to assist with whatever their human was up to, and she was happy to inform them.

"First we are going to put these lovely wreaths on the doors. See? Nice, big burgundy velvet bows, aren't they pretty? And then we are going to set these poinsettias out. I like the pink ones best, don't you? So much more sophisticated, yet traditional."

Patti and Chaka barked their approval as Renee arranged the flowers and quickly dispatched the wreaths to their new homes.

"Now we are going to fix a lovely dinner for Andrew. We are having deviled crabs for a first course, then red-pepper bisque and a nice little filet mignon with those tiny red potatoes and spinach salad to follow. Doesn't that sound yummy?"

It sounded way better than Puppy Chow, apparently, as the eager terriers tried in vain to beg some of the food from Renee. She ignored them as she quickly put the meal together. It had the dual advantage of being a beautiful and tasty meal as well as one that could be prepared ahead. While she cooked, Renee put several albums of Christmas songs on the stereo system's multidisc carousel and sang along.

The feeling of release and freedom had also imbued her with a sense of joy, which she had not felt in a few weeks. She felt so blessed in so many ways; she had a man who loved and supported her, friends and family who cared for her and her well-being, and a career that was exciting, fun and rewarding. She had been so bound up by guilt and fear for so many years that she had forgotten what was really important in her life, in anyone's life—love, friendship and family.

Well, I won't be forgetting again, she vowed. *I will have that attitude of gratitude that makes for a grateful spirit. I am a lucky woman and I am going to make Andrew feel like a* very *lucky man tonight.*

But, as the poet once said, the best-laid plans can often go awry and tonight was no exception. Whatever Renee had been expecting, it was not to see her handsome Andrew leaning on his brother Adam in the kitchen doorway. He was wearing an extremely silly expression and was obviously three sheets to the wind.

Renee raised an eyebrow and looked to Adam for an explanation.

"Well . . . we had a kind of a, well . . . I guess we were celebrating," he offered lamely. "Andrew will explain everything tomorrow, I'm sure."

Meanwhile, Andrew had transferred his weight from Adam to Renee and was trying to kiss her when he could get her face in focus. "I can explain now," he said grandly.

"I'm not as think as you drunk I am," he added in the precise, lofty speech of one who is not used to heavy drinking.

"Ye gods and little fishes," Renee said with asperity. Her lovely reconciliation dinner would have to wait; plus, here was her poor fiancé sloshed to the gills. "Well, take him upstairs, Adam; he can't sleep on the sofa, his back would be in knots. And I certainly can't get him up there by myself."

With a bit of bobbing and weaving, they managed to walk Andrew upstairs and deposit him on the bed in Renee's room.

After assuring him that she could handle things, Renee walked Adam downstairs. She looked at him carefully to make sure that he was sober before turning him loose.

"Renee, I only had one, and that was hours ago. And I have a feeling that Andrew is going to feel like hell in the morning, since he really doesn't drink. But tonight, well, he. . . . He'll explain everything tomorrow," Adam said for the second time. Adding to her mystification, Adam suddenly grabbed her and hugged her hard. He gave her a big kiss on the cheek and said, "Love you, sis," before leaving.

Renee stared at the back door for a few moments before putting away the food from the postponed dinner. *Things are getting stranger and stranger around here. What was all that about?*

Twenty-one

The next morning, Andrew was almost sure he was dead. His head seemed to be encased in cement, and sharp pains were stabbing him all over his chest. Worse yet, he was apparently bleeding from unseen head wounds, as he could feel a warm, wet stickiness over his face. He moaned loudly, which caused keen yipping sounds to penetrate his thudding eardrums. A final warm, wet swipe dangerously near his mouth was the thing that made him force his eyes open. He peered into the happy smiles of Chaka and Patti and groaned. Their little toenails provided the stabbing chest pains and their drooly little tongues accounted for the wetness on his face.

"How did you two get in here? Where is Renee? And what happened to my clothes?" he asked plaintively as he realized for the first time that he was naked under the rumpled bedclothes.

Renee appeared in the doorway, the answer to his prayers and his questions.

"I sent them in here to wake you up. And I took off your clothes when Adam brought you home last night, drunk as the proverbial skunk," she said cheerily. She was carrying a tray, which she sat on the upholstered bench at the end of the bed. "Drink this," she said briskly, with no apparent concern for his fragile state. She thrust a glass of Alka-Seltzer at him, and the look in her eyes dared him not to consume it.

He pulled himself to a sitting position and drained the

glass, grimacing at the horrid taste. Handing the empty glass to Renee, he noticed that she was dressed for work. And she looked fabulous, as always.

Her hair had grown quite a bit over the past months and soft tendrils caressed her neck and face, while the rest was artlessly arranged in loose curls. She was wearing a festive red angora tunic over a midcalf red wool skirt with an enticing slit up the back. Just the sight of her made him drool; he was about to compliment her when the seltzer kicked in and the result was a huge belch. He was terribly embarrassed, which was sweetly endearing to Renee.

"Renee, I am sorry. Please forgive me," he began, stopping when he was cut off by a wave of her hand.

"I appreciate the apology, Andy, but bodily functions are a fact of life and something we have to get accustomed to from each other. I plan to stay married to you until the last breath leaves my body, so I am sure that you will have occasion to see me in a state that is somewhat less than my best," she said graciously.

She neared the bed and made as if to kiss him, but he pulled away hastily. "Dog spit," he explained, wiping at his cheeks. "And some lethal halitosis. My mouth feels like I've been licking the bottom of a hamster cage."

"Well, you'd better go brush before you drink this," she suggested, holding up a big glass of tomato juice. The juice was as vibrant as her outfit, and the mere thought of it made Andrew squirm.

"Oh, you will drink every drop," Renee assured him silkily. "This will put you right back on your feet. And perhaps when I return from work, you can give me an explanation for last night's performance, amusing though it was. I've got a long day at the salon, and since I have been gone for two days, I have a whole heap of work to catch up on."

Blowing him a kiss, she returned the glass of tomato juice to the tray and was about to leave the room when Andrew remembered the reason for his drunken tear.

"Renee, there's something I have to tell you. It's about yesterday and it's something you need to know now," he said uneasily.

"Baby, it's gonna have to wait—I have got to get to the salon. I'll be leaving there at about eight tonight and I'll come straight home. Unless you want to meet at your place." After Andrew agreed to come to the house, she made another passionate kissing sound at him and was gone before he could protest.

Andrew lay down with a groan and stared at the ceiling. After the confrontation with Donovan Bailey, he and Adam had gone to their favorite dive bar and he had proceeded to get roaring drunk—something he never, ever did. By instinct, Donnie knew where they would be and he brought Clay and Martin, as well as Andre and Alan, and they had made quite a party of it. Adam had thoughtfully stayed sober to play chauffeur and had apparently brought him to Renee's the night before, although Andrew was fuzzy on those details.

One thing was clear, though. He had broken his word to Renee and she was going to have a raving, screaming fit when she found out. Regardless of her anger, though, he knew he had done the right thing. It had to be done; someone had to derail the Donovan Bailey express. It was a moot point now—it was all over but the shouting—and when Renee calmed down, she would be able to see it that way. At least he prayed that she would.

Glancing at the bedside clock, Andrew groaned and threw his long legs out of bed. He had to shower and get to the hospital. With a truly contrite heart he drank the tomato juice laced with lemon and Worcestershire sauce. He shuddered and gasped, but by the time he got out of the hot shower, he really did feel better. If Renee could cure his hangover, she could do anything, including forgive him. *God, I hope so.*

* * *

It was the kind of day Renee loved at the salon; the customers never stopped coming and the sound of Christmas music added an air of festivity and warmth to the atmosphere. Renee was running her legs off as she always did during these harried days—roller setting patrons, combing out others, shampooing when a stylist was getting backed up and even helping out the nail technicians. Renee's skills were never rusty—thank goodness—as this was the time of year when everybody just had to have sparkling nails in red and gold and platinum. Naturally, a few wanted some cute holiday design airbrushed on a nail or two.

She made sure there was a catered lunch every day during the busy season, since it would have been next to impossible to leave for a lunch with so many customers. In fact, she was leaving to make a run to the bakery for more of the tiny holiday cookies to which her patrons were addicted. She took off her smart smock, which protected her clothes, and was giving Maurice, the evening manager, a few last-minute instructions before she scooted out the back door.

"Mrs. Henley should be dry in about five minutes. Sabrina is running late; her baby is sick and she has a color and a relaxer coming in. Someone can section them off. . . ."

She stopped speaking when Maurice took her by the arm and guided her to the door. Maurice was somewhat of a rarity in the business—big, muscular, arrow-straight and a genius when it came to hair.

"Renee, we can handle it. Just get those cookies and get back here before these women take a bite out of me. You've got them so spoiled that they think everything in here is edible," he said cheerfully.

Renee was still laughing when she reached her Mercedes, but the laughter died when she was grabbed from behind.

"You dumb black bitch," a familiar voice whispered. "You stupid, ignorant black bitch! I warned you to keep your mouth shut, but you couldn't, could you? You had to shoot off your goddamned mouth, didn't you?"

Donovan Bailey had a grip on Renee's throat, cutting off her breath. Her handbag fell to the ground as she clawed frantically at his hands, to no avail—the leather gloves she was wearing protected him from her fingernails.

"I told you to keep your mouth shut and everything would be fine, but you had to shoot your mouth off, didn't ya, bitch?"

Renee could not get a sound from her constricted throat and was beginning to slip into unconsciousness; then she heard a loud grunt from somewhere and, miraculously, she was free. The sudden loosening of his hands made her lose her balance and she would have fallen, but a strong pair of arms caught her. It was Maurice, who had been wondering why her car had not left the lot.

"Maurice," she gasped, "thank God you came. Oh, God, he could have killed me!" she whispered in horror.

Maurice continued to hold her as she tried to control her breathing. "I'm not the one you should be thanking, Renee. If he hadn't come up when he did, it might have been too late."

Renee turned puzzled eyes to the stranger who was standing over Donovan Bailey's unconscious body. He was tall, about six-four with oddly exotic features. He had short, coarse dark blond hair and olive skin that was taut across his high cheekbones. His eyes were an eerie dark gray-blue. His features seemed distinctly Caucasian, but when he spoke, his ethnicity became a bigger puzzle, due to the deep richness of his voice. He might not look like a brother, but he sure sounded like one. In answer to her unasked question, he told her his name was Titus Argonne.

"I'm here to keep an eye on you, ma'am. I think you need to go inside and get warm. I'll take care of this," he said with a nod to another man who seemed to appear out of nowhere.

Renee had no choice but to reenter the salon, especially after Titus said he had contacted the proper authorities. Maurice's large body shielded her from the view of any patrons or employees. In minutes she was shivering uncontrollably in her private office while Maurice made her a cup of Earl Grey tea. Maurice was raging about carjackers and muggers and fuming about how they might need a security guard after all, despite the relative safety of the neighborhood, but his words were falling on deaf ears.

The authorities. Good God, does that mean police? Renee had her hand on the phone to call Andrew when she was distracted by the television. It was tuned to E, the entertainment channel, and there was some late-breaking story that was of earth-shattering importance, to judge by the animated Barbie doll delivering the news.

"A ripple that could be measured on the Richter scale went through the annals of the cable industry today when word got out that the new cable news network forming in Atlanta has fired its newest executive," the chirpy newsbunny trilled.

"For months now, the buzz has been that Cochran Communications, based in Detroit, and The Deveraux Group, headquartered in Atlanta, are forming a partnership to produce an African American cable news network. With Donovan Bailey as the executive vice president, there was no way it could fail, given the expertise of the principals. Now we have received word that they plan to go ahead with the network, but without Mr. Bailey. This is a move that can only mean that the entire enterprise is on shaky ground," she purred. "Neither Cochran Communications or The Deveraux Group would offer any comment."

Renee was sickened to her heart. Not only by the obvious thrill that the little skank was getting from spooning out such delicious gossip, but also by the sure knowledge of why it had come about. Andrew told. He had told them everything. The thin china cup dropped from her hands and crashed to the desk, spilling its contents. Renee never heard a thing.

* * *

When Andrew arrived at Renee's house, he found her sitting quietly in the living room. The little dogs were asleep on the throw pillow next to her, and she was as motionless as a statue. Having gotten a phone call from Martin, he knew that the jig was well and truly up; there would be no sidestepping of the issue. In fairness, he did not know that Martin had hired the private investigator to keep an eye on Renee while he dug up dirt on Bailey, but he was profoundly glad he had when Martin informed him that there had been an incident. The words that Martin had spoken to him were still echoing in his head.

"Look, Andrew. Titus Argonne just called me. He's a private detective that I hired to protect Renee as well as dig into Bailey's background. And it's a damned good thing I did. The bastard waylaid her in the parking lot of her salon today."

Andrew almost dropped the telephone, but instead he cursed a blue streak.

Martin could sympathize completely. "Titus and I go back a ways. He's the best there is and he and his men will make sure nothing happens to her. But it's obvious that this isn't over. I have a feeling that Bailey has leaked something to the press, so you'd better be prepared when you see Renee. We all know you did the right thing, but I doubt that she is going to see it like that."

The two men talked a few more minutes; then Andrew checked in with Donnie before heading over to Renee's. He stood in the doorway to the living room, watching her for a moment before making his presence known. It seemed as though he could feel her pain from across the room. He entered the room slowly and went to stand in front of the fireplace.

"Renee, I doubt that it will do any good for me to say that I'm sorry, but I am. I just didn't see any way out of this except to let Donnie and Clay know what Bailey had done. I don't suppose you will be able to forgive me, but I was trying to protect you," he said quietly.

In an equally quiet voice Renee responded, "So now you're thinking for me, too? I don't even have to open my mouth and you know what I'm going to say? That's some medical degree you've got there, Andrew." The sarcasm and anger were evident in her tone. And so there would be no mistake about what she meant, she stood and crossed the room to stand in front of him.

"How dare you come in here looking like a whipped dog and tell me how sorry you are? There was one thing I asked you not to do and it appears to be the first thing you did. I do not really care at this juncture what your motivation was; the fact remains that you betrayed my confidence. You told them my personal, private business! You knew how much it meant to me and you just waded in there with both feet, didn't you?" Renee's voice was shaky with rage and she was tensed all over.

"Renee, listen to me. It wasn't like I was just blabbing my mouth off for no good reason. Donnie and Clay wouldn't have gone into business with that rat bastard if they knew what kind of slime he was. They were on the verge of signing a contract with him! How would it have made them feel if they had been legally tied to the bastard?" he reasoned.

His conciliatory tone did nothing to assuage her anger; in fact, it seemed to stoke her fire. She tightened the belt on her ivory robe and lit into him once again.

"It might interest you to know, Andrew, that I had come to that very same conclusion before you opened your mouth. I did not get a chance to tell you last night, since you came in here like a backslider from AA, that the reason I went to Cleveland was to talk to my mother and let her know what was going on. I came back here yesterday intending to tell you that you were right and it was time to get rid of Donovan Bailey once and for all," she stormed.

Andrew's mouth dropped open, and before he could speak, she flung up a hand to stop him. "But no, you had to take over. And with disastrous results, I might add. If you hadn't taken matters into your own hands, this might not have happened," she threw at him as she opened the neck of the robe to expose the dark bruises surrounding her neck.

Despite her rage, Andrew grasped her arms and pulled her into the light. "That rotten, miserable son of a bitch, I'll kill him! Oh, my God, baby, I'm so sorry," he breathed as he anxiously stroked her neck.

It had been so long since she and Andrew had shared an intimate moment that Renee could not help the sensations that overtook her. For a moment all she wanted to do was let him hold her and draw strength from the warmth of his body, and for a moment she did. He held her like he would never let her go, stroking her hair and murmuring words of endearment. She was about to succumb to his touch when she remembered how angry she was and pulled away from him.

"No you don't, Andrew Cochran. Oh, no you don't. This is not something that you can kiss and make better! You betrayed me and I am not about to forget that! How can you act like nothing has happened?" she accused, her eyes dark and flinty.

Exasperated, Andrew ran his hands through his hair and stared at her. "Renee, I am not trying to make it seem like nothing happened. I acknowledge the fact that I jumped the gun and shot off my mouth. But what the hell was I supposed to do? You're my woman and it's my job to protect you. Did you think I was going to sit around until doomsday and wait for it to all blow over? Hell no," he said angrily, answering his own rhetorical question. "It was past time for talking, Renee. Somebody needed to take some action and I did. So I was wrong, so sue me! I was trying to take care of you, that's all."

Their angry voices awakened Chaka and Patti, who were more than willing to add their voices to the melee. Ignoring the excited yips of the terriers, Renee planted her hands on her hips.

"I'm your *'woman'*? You have to 'protect' me? First of all, I am nobody's property. And if this is any indication of your brand of protection," she spat, pointing at her neck, "it's a damned good thing I'm not. Because it seems to me that all your big talk just got me in deeper—it didn't solve a damned thing," she said with disdain.

Andrew's face paled, indicating his fury and hurt. "Well, excuse me, Miss Thing, I just can't seem to do a damned thing to please Your Highness," he said nastily.

"Well, you've finally gotten something right tonight. Perhaps you *can* be taught," she said with narrowed eyes.

Andrew was stunned into silence. Further conversation, if that's what this shouting match could be called, was fruitless. He stared at Renee for a long moment before abruptly leaving the room. Before Renee could say another word, she heard the back door open and close. It was worse, in a way, than if he had slammed it shut. Still standing in the middle of the room, she covered her mouth with her shaking hand and felt the hot tears spill over onto it.

Unknown to her, Titus Argonne and one of his men were drinking coffee in a midnight-colored van parked across the street from her house. If she had been aware of their presence, she wouldn't have felt so all alone. As it was, the very walls seemed to be crushing her with their collective weight. *How could I have said all those horrible things?* The fact that she meant them on some level wasn't reason enough for her to lash out like that. She finally moved to the kitchen to prepare some tea with a big jolt of brandy. No, bourbon. She needed to sleep that night and there was no way that she could, feeling the way she was.

Ungrateful, stupid, hateful wench, that's what I am. She castigated herself in French while waiting for the kettle to boil. Suddenly she laughed at herself, scorn ringing in every ragged peal. *That "attitude of gratitude" lasted about twelve hours, didn't it? You don't deserve to be happy, you stupid wench.* Her near-hysterical laughter quickly turned to sobs. She was crying so loud that she did not hear the door open or even feel the cold air that blew in with it.

Suddenly Andrew's arms were around her and he was holding her the way she needed to be held.

"Andy. Oh, Andy, I'm so s-sorry." She sighed as she clung to his strength.

"Baby, so am I. I really, truly am," he said softly.

Taking a last hiccuping breath, she turned her face to his for the tender kiss they both needed so badly. Even after the kettle started wailing, they continued the sweet, healing kiss.

Twenty-two

After their rapprochement in the kitchen, Andrew and Renee were able to talk about the events of the past few days. Renee went first, explaining what had transpired on her momentous trip to Cleveland. Andrew was astounded to hear about her mother's machinations regarding her father.

"Oh, yes, Andrew, I apparently come from a long line of high-strung, erratic women. All this time while I was thinking my father was 'Dog Emeritus of the Canine Brothers,' the gold standard by whom all other dogs will be measured and found wanting, he was in Georgia working his fingers to the bone for that harridan. And, Andy, I haven't even begun to deal with the guilt," she added ruefully.

Andrew did not pretend that he did not know what she meant. She and her sisters had all but ignored their father's existence over the past eight years out of loyalty to their mother. To find out that he was in fact the injured, innocent party was to call into question their own humanity. It would take a lot of healing and a lot of love before any of them felt right about it. He nodded understandingly and pulled her closer. They had moved to the sitting room of her suite and were cuddled up on her sofa under a pashmina throw.

"Baby, I am truly sorry you, your sisters and your dad got such a raw deal, but I think you will be able to work it out. Just talk to him and reopen the lines of communication, that's all you can do to get back on track," he said reasonably.

Renee sighed and then went on to tell him of Pearlie Mae's "pistol-packin' mama" act, which made him laugh out loud.

"So Pearlie Mae thinks I should defend your honor, huh? I would have loved to have seen her with that gun," he cracked, thinking of Renee's dainty, impeccable mother with a sidearm.

"No, Andy, you would not have enjoyed it a bit. She might have taken a shot at *you* for not taking a shot at the slime bucket," she reminded him tartly.

That was when Andrew had to enlighten Renee on the events of Wednesday morning, when Bailey was given his walking papers. Renee was more interested in the reactions of his brothers and Clay to the news of her molestation.

"Andy, I know it's ridiculous, but it makes me feel dirty and ashamed, even today. I just don't want your family to think any less of me," she murmured, looking down at her lap.

Andrew immediately turned her face to his so that he could look directly into her eyes. "Baby, they think *more* of you, not less. I told you that Pop figured out that something was up and barged into the meeting we had last week. And I had to explain everything to him," he began.

At her gasp Andrew touched his lips to hers very gently. "Baby, he cried when I told him what had happened to you. He loves you, just like Donnie and Alan and Andre and Adam and Clay and Martin, too, as near as I can figure. He plays it pretty close to the chest, but he is genuinely fond of you. Martin was the one who had the foresight to hire that detective," he reminded Renee.

"And by the way, I didn't know you went with my baby brother to his prom," Andrew remarked.

Renee's eyes grew soft at the memory. "I had forgotten all about that," she said softly.

"Well, *he* didn't. He adores you, Renee. My whole family does. Everybody thinks that you were extremely brave and one hell of a woman to go through all of that alone.

And every single one of them wants a piece of that scum bucket's ass. Especially Pop. Man, back in the day, he would have had him bumped off in a New York minute," Andrew said reflectively.

"Andy! You're exaggerating!" Renee admonished him, but she derived deep enjoyment out of the idea that his father cared about her.

Andrew just raised an eyebrow and said, "Okay. Believe what you want to believe. But remind me to tell you about Pop back in the day," he said mildly.

Suddenly Renee remembered something. "Andy, that detective Martin hired. . . . What did he do with Donovan Bailey?"

Andrew snorted. "As near as I can figure, he told him to get the hell out of town. Told him that Detroit was an extremely unhealthy place to be and suggested he get on the next thing smokin' outta here. He didn't call the police because he knows how important it is to keep a low profile on this, but I have to say I wish he had. At least there would be a police record if anything else happens."

Renee took his face in her hands and assured him that nothing else would. "Donovan Bailey is not *that* crazy. After getting pimp-slapped from behind, I think he will turn tail and leave. He always was kind of a sissy," she said confidently.

Later, although she would not have thought it possible, she fell deeply asleep wrapped in Andrew's arms. Andrew lay awake for some time, contemplating the difficult days that lay ahead. But he knew without question that he would do it again, if he had to. *In a New York minute.*

The next day, it was apparent that things would not blow over easily. The wire services had picked up on the story and it seemed everywhere one turned, there was another story about Cochran/Deveraux and their seemingly high-handed treatment of the beloved Donovan Bailey, the golden boy of the media. There were varying reactions within the concerned parties. Andrew and Renee were furious, but Donnie was remarkably sanguine about the whole thing.

"Look, we have a dossier on Donovan Bailey about two inches thick and he is going to keep his mouth shut about this or be very, very sorry. Some very unsavory things can come to light about his past, which is something he will want to avoid at all costs. Clay's people are getting ready to do some spin doctoring that will make us come out smelling like a rose garden in June, so don't worry, okay?"

Renee was sitting in her private office while Donnie was outlining his plans. The fact that he seemed so cheery and energized was unnerving to Renee and she told him so.

"I am just not used to my baby acting like some ruthless corporate shark," she admitted.

Donnie—*darn him*—just beamed. "Yeah. Ain't it cool?" he said happily.

Men. They got excited over any old macho thing, her sweet Donnie included. Andrew was just as agitated as Renee. He did not want her to be continually concerned and upset about the mess, and it seemed that every time a television was turned on, there was a clip of that slime bucket in his prime, plus some pious newscaster adding his two cents. The reports that really galled him were the ones that included pictures of Bailey with his perfect family, including a sweet-faced wife and some children, who, Andrew thought privately, looked rather snivelly. He kept that to himself, as he knew it was only his own unreasoning prejudice.

He was in his father's study in the big Palmer Park house he had grown up in. In answer to his father's question, he assured him that Renee was fine.

"She was mad at me for telling everything, as I knew she would be, but we're talking at least. She's concerned about how you all feel about her now and she's really nervous about facing everybody tomorrow night. But she's fine," Andrew assured him.

Renee had already invited the family over to decorate

the tree and was loath to cancel the party, although she was a bundle of nerves. It angered Big Benny to think of her in that state and he once again offered his opinion that Bailey needed to be shown once and for all that he couldn't mess with a Cochran woman.

"I'm telling you son, the man needs killin' bad. I couldn't sleep a night on this earth if somebody laid a hand on your mother. Or Martha. I wish a son of a bitch would touch my Martha," Benny grumbled, fuming.

"Pop, your blood pressure," Andrew reminded him. Luckily, Martha, his father's lovely fiancée, came into the study with a tray of tea.

"Ben, I could hear you all the way down the hall. Try to stay calm, baby. The boys are taking care of everything. Just drink this tea and listen to Andrew for once," she scolded gently.

"I hear him, I hear him," Big Benny said irritably. Sniffing at the tea, he reluctantly took a sip. Tea was his least favorite beverage, especially the herbal variety, but Martha would never let him drink in the afternoon.

Andrew grabbed the remote control and switched the station as yet another sensational blurb pealed out regarding Bailey's ouster. "Okay, that's my cue to leave. I've got to get back to the clinic for a few hours. See you both tomorrow."

"Give Renee my love," Martha said as Andrew kissed her good-bye.

As soon as she left the study to see Andrew to the door, Benny snatched up the cordless phone and hit speed dial.

"It's me," he barked. "What the hell is taking so long?"

"Uncle Renee! Uncle Renee!" The arrival of Alan and Andre with their wives and children momentarily erased the anxiety Renee had been suffering. The children were devoted to her, especially little Drew.

"Where you been, Uncle Renee? You ain't been to see me in a long, long time," he accused as he accepted her kisses. Renee gulped and was about to try to answer him when his mother, Faye, stepped in.

"You *haven't* been to see me," she corrected with a smile. "And get down off poor Uncle Renee before you break her neck."

Drew reluctantly loosened his death grip on Renee's neck and allowed her to set him on the floor, but he did not budge from her side. He looked up at her with such adoration that she got a lump in her throat. Just then, Andrew appeared next to Renee and put his arm around her waist.

"Hey, shorty. You aren't trying to steal my girl, are you?" he said seriously.

Drew looked to be considering the matter. He loved his uncle Andrew, but he was crazy about Renee. "Well," he said slowly as he eyed his favorite uncle and beloved Uncle Renee, "we can *share* her, I guess." He was obviously loath to give up that much, but sharing was something most little children understand, albeit with reluctance.

So the three of them made their way over to the Christmas tree and watched as Alan and Andre put on the last strand of lights. This was the job everyone hated and they did the best, primarily because they did it fast, accurately and considered their contribution over. For the rest of the night they would do nothing but eat like young horses and sequester themselves in the basement with ESPN. The hard work, as they called it, was taken over by the other guests.

Donnie had brought his usual date, Aneesah Shabazz, who was home for the holidays from Stanford. She was a beautiful full-figured woman with an elaborately braided hairdo and incredible dimples. Adam's date was his business partner and best friend, Alicia Fuentes, a stunning African American and Puerto Rican woman with a numbingly high IQ and a great sense of humor. She and Adam were busy tying on the myriad brocade bows while the children doggedly hung ornaments at their eye level, which would give the tree a lopsided effect that Renee and Bennie always corrected after the kids went home. While everyone was busy trimming and gossiping, Renee went into the kitchen, ostensibly to check on some food-related issue. In reality, she was going just to get away for a moment.

She leaned against the work island in the middle of the kitchen and took a deep breath. Everything was going surprisingly well; she had anticipated being awkward and ill at ease among the Cochrans now that her deepest secret was practically known to one and all. But she had felt nothing but affection and support from the moment the guests had started arriving. With a profound sense of gratitude for being with such understanding people, she was about to make sure that the buffet was well stocked when first Faye and then Tina entered the kitchen. She did not have time to wonder what was up when they each took an arm and led her into the breakfast room.

"Renee," Tina began, "we are not going to pretend that nothing has happened. Obviously, the Cochran men have told all," she said ruefully. "But we wanted you to know that we are here for you. I know, better than anyone, how you must be feeling, and all I can tell you is it will get better."

Renee stared in amazement at Tina, a slender, dark-skinned, curly-haired woman. *How can you possibly know?*

Tina made a slight grimace and sighed. "I know because it happened to my sister when she was a freshman in college. The circumstances were quite different—she was accosted by a stranger and beaten quite badly, but the result was the same."

The women's hands clasped tightly as Renee tried to recall what she knew of Tina's vivacious younger sister, who was now married with two children. Before she could speak, though, Faye added something even more poignant to the conversation.

"My best friend was raped, Renee. It was a horrible experience for her, because like you, she knew and trusted the man who did it to her. She was so traumatized that she . . . well, it was a long time before she was able to come to grips with it. But she did. And I have to tell you, having been through it with her, I am amazed and grateful that you have been able to cope as well as you have. But you don't have to be superwoman about this. We are here for you whenever you need anything. Don't feel like you have to slog through this all by yourself," she said with just a bit of a tremor in her voice.

Renee was stunned by the emotion she felt. Looking at Faye's fair face surrounded by auburn waves, she felt positively humbled. She had always liked Alan and Andre's wives, but she had never been particularly close to them. She had precious few women friends outside of Bennie and Ceylon, and she suddenly realized what she had been missing. She said as much to the two women and they all got a little teary-eyed for a moment. The ever-practical Tina pointed out that it would not be this easy when Bennie found out that this was being kept from her.

"You're going to have a lot of explaining to do, you know. Pregnant or not, she's going to feel like she should have been there for you."

Renee's sigh came all the way up from her toes. "Yeah, well, I was going to wait until she has been up all night breast-feeding a crying baby before I dropped it on her. She couldn't possibly have the strength to go upside my head then," she said with a weak attempt at humor. "But you know how Bennie is. She knows everything. Clay forgot how addicted Bennie is to news. Bennie would watch CNN in her car if she could figure out a way to steer. She called me up and let me have it big time for not telling her myself." Renee shuddered delicately, remembering the level of decibels Bennie's displeasure had reached during that particular phone call.

"She eventually forgave me after I promised to name my first child after her and keep her kids *all* summer *every* summer regardless of how wild they turn out to be," Renee added. "Actually, I think I got off light, considering the fact that she can still take me even though she's pregnant!"

The three women laughed together, and when Andrew entered the room, they tried to look as though nothing of importance had occurred. Their attempt met with limited success, as Andrew could see that this was a momentous occurrence, but he chose to ignore it. Tina and Faye hastily took their leave so that the two of them could be alone, which was how Renee found herself sitting in Andrew's lap at the breakfast table.

He put one arm around her and held her tight while he fished around in his pants pocket with his free hand. Renee watched him bemusedly without saying a word. Finally he found what he was looking for and smiled triumphantly.

"Ah-ha, there it is. I didn't want to wait until Christmas to give you this, and now seemed as good a time as any. And remember, you already said yes, so this is a formality," he reminded her as he slipped an engagement ring on her finger.

Renee could not utter a sound as she stared at the ring. It was a huge emerald cut stone with three one-quarter-karat diamonds on either side. The stone itself was remarkable; it caught the light and showed bronze, golden and amazing bluish highlights with every turn of her hand. Andrew spoke into the silence.

"I wanted something as rare and beautiful as you are," he said softly. "That's an Alexandrite, from Russia. All those colors seemed to match your eyes and it just looked like something you could stand to keep on your hand for the rest of our lives."

Renee still had not said a word. She finally raised her tear-wet eyes from the amazing ring to her beloved's sweet, handsome face. She locked her arms around his neck and kissed him with every bit of love and passion she had.

"Andy, you will never know in a million years how much I love you," she expressed with a sigh.

He looked into her eyes for a long time and smiled the smile of a very happy man. "I do know how much you love me. You love me as much as I love you now, as much as I'll love you forever, as much as I have loved you for seventeen long years, Renee DeShawn Kemp."

Then he kissed her back, a long, sweet, wet kiss that spoke from his very soul. It had been much, much too long since they had shared the act of love, something that he planned to remedy that very night as soon as possible.

"Let's go tell everybody and then get rid of them," he pleaded. "I need to be alone with my future wife and I need it now."

Renee could not have agreed more. She stood on shaky legs and Andrew got up with her. They held each other tightly and exchanged one more hot, passionate kiss before making their way back into the living room. Just as they neared the front door, the bell rang several sharp rounds. Renee jumped out of her skin before she could collect herself to open the door. Then she froze. Her mouth opened and closed several times before she could make an intelligent utterance. Finally she found her voice.

"Daddy?"

Twenty-three

Renee sat curled in the corner of the huge leather sofa in Andrew's living room. His home had become her refuge since her parents' unannounced visit to Detroit. For most of that time she had walked around with an expression that the witty Valerie referred to as her "Lucy, you in big trouble" look, meaning she looked just like Lucy Ricardo when she had done something that Ricky had forbidden. Her eyes were almost always wide open and her smile just a bit forced. Andrew had nothing but sympathy for her.

"It's not that I'm not glad they're here, Andy, I really am," Renee said for about the tenth time. "It's just that everything feels so . . . so *surreal*. It feels like a Fellini movie in blackface," she said in a voice that begged for contradiction. Unfortunately, Andrew could not offer her the denial she so desperately wanted.

From the time she opened the front door to find her normally diffident father and her always-voluble mother on the front porch, her life had not been her own. And it was, as she said, not because she wasn't glad to see her father, she was thrilled. She had hugged him with the ferocity of someone welcoming a loved one back from the dead, which was in effect where he had been. She couldn't stop hugging him or holding his hand all night, and her father, bless his heart, seemed to know exactly from where all the emotion was pouring. He was too much the devoted husband and father to bear a grudge; as Pearlie Mae had often said during the early years of their marriage, John Kemp had gone back for a second helping of humble because the line was so short.

Pearlie had actually been on her best behavior during the party. She was the engaging social maven who could charm the very songs from the larks when she chose, the one who could make everyone feel that they had been graced by a queen when she smiled on them.

While they were guests in her daughter's home, she was gracious, effervescent and delightful to Renee's everlasting relief. As coats began to be donned and sleepy children carried out to cars, though, Renee could sense her mother's real character shining through. Sure enough, as the last guest made his way to his vehicle and Andrew was bringing in the Kemps' luggage, the sea change began. Pearlie Mae placed her hands on her hips and the look she gave Andrew made him wish that she actually had a gun instead of just her rapier tongue and her laser glare.

"Young man, I expected better of you, I really did. Why did you allow this to happen to my daughter, and why is that man not in jail or the morgue, where he belongs?"

Andrew did not let the fact that his future mother-in-law had just impugned his manhood enrage him. He had been pretty much expecting this and was prepared to answer on his behalf, but his future father-in-law preemptively spoke up.

"Pearl, now enough is enough. From what you told me, Andrew here was as much in the dark as everyone else about this situation. Our daughter, for whatever reasons, chose to keep this to herself, something that I regret." John Kemp's handsome face showed that exact emotion along with a range of more subtle feeling.

"Since he found out, Andrew has done exactly what he should have done to protect and take care of Renee as best he can, and that is all we can ask of him. The whole reason I am here is to see with my own eyes that my daughter is all right and she looks fine. So please stop carrying on like some vigilante mother on one of those cable movies and calm down."

There was a finality in his tone that even Pearlie Mae did not question. Amazingly enough, she didn't speak, although not without a couple of well-placed "hmmphs" to let him know her spirit wasn't broken. To Renee's shock, the rest of the evening went well, although it was a brief one due to the lateness of the hour.

Andrew and her parents sat in the living room and chatted while she made them herbal tea and prepared a guest room. There was really no time for her to question the whole situation; she went into hostess mode with a vengeance and had the elder Kemps all settled in for the night before she realized that her evening with her fiancé was now torpedoed by subatomic machine gun Pearlie Mae.

The living room was unnaturally silent, as the little dogs had willingly gone to their kennel to sleep off a night of chasing and being chased by small children. Her parents were safely upstairs and she and Andrew were facing the fact that any amorous pursuits were going to have to wait until another time. Renee tried not to let her disappointment show too much as she walked Andrew to the door. Andrew was also trying to take it in stride, but looking down at Renee's velvety skin, her luscious lips and all her glorious curves made it truly difficult for him. Especially since they had reaffirmed their abiding love for each other just a few hours earlier.

Renee stared at her lovely ring and sighed. "You know, we didn't even get to make our announcement tonight. But, honey, it's just as well we didn't. Mama would have pitched a side door fit if we had said something before we told her. God help us if we had said one mumbling word before speaking to her!" Renee shuddered at the thought.

Andrew was cheered immensely by Renee's words. "Look, baby, everything is going to be fine. We'll take your parents and Dad and Martha out to a fabulous dinner and spring it on them then. Or I'll ask your father for your hand or post the banns or whatever will make them happy. Who cares? The important thing is you and me and our life together. Nothing can stop us now, Renee. We're almost home free."

He pulled her into his arms and kissed her thoroughly with the air of a man deeply in love with nothing but time on his hands. And at that moment he was. It took a couple of hours for reality to sink its teeth into his butt.

That had come the next day when he did indeed ask Renee's parents for her hand in marriage, something that sounded romantic and sweet but instead opened up avenues of unspeakable horrors as far as Renee was concerned. Her parents were thrilled to the extent that Pearlie Mae actually got it into her head to act as a duenna for Renee until the nuptials. The news of the impending marriage coupled with the recent news that her daughter had been raped made Pearlie Mae exceptionally protective. Like a middle-aged lioness with an unexpected and much loved cub, she wasn't letting her baby out of her sight until she was safely married. Which was the main reason that Renee was now sitting in Andrew's living room looking shell-shocked.

"Andy, she is driving me nuts," Renee confessed. "I got rid of her this afternoon by sending her and Daddy shopping at Somerset. I claimed I had to be at the spa, which was kinda true, but really I just needed to be away from them for a while. If they do not go back to Cleveland soon, I'm going to be sitting in a corner, strumming my lips, and my eyes will be spinning around like pinwheels!"

Andrew brought her the steaming mug of tea he had prepared and sat next to her. He pulled her legs into his lap and started rubbing her feet, something that ordinarily would have her purring with enjoyment, but she was beyond noticing his ministrations.

"Well, how about calling your sisters? Surely they could prevail upon her to come home," he said reasonably.

Renee snorted inelegantly. "Those harpies are ganging

up on me. They're all pissed because I kept the dark secret from them in the first place. They feel like the Kemp girls should have issued out some Cleveland justice back when it happened and I wouldn't be going through all of this now. The only one with any sense about it is LeeAnn and she's the only one in New York—too far away to help."

Renee's brow lowered as she remembered the long and colorful conversations she had with each of her sisters, who each berated, consoled and condemned her before the talks ended. "They were also not too happy that I kept the news about you on the downlow—it's a Kemp tradition that all the sisters celebrate engagements and I had not let them know that things were this serious between us, so I must be punished at least for a while. Those heifers won't lift a finger to help me." She sniffed, clearly put out at the betrayal by her aces in the hole.

Andrew tried not to look amused, but he couldn't help but be delighted that Renee was being so thoroughly distracted by her folks. At least the Bailey business had taken a backseat to the goings-on at hand. Suddenly their attention was drawn to the television, which they had been ignoring while Renee ranted. A special bulletin was forming before their eyes.

"This just in: In a bizarre turn of events, prominent media personality Donovan Bailey was found near death in his Southfield hotel. He has apparently been badly beaten and shot. He was taken to Beaumont Hospital, where he is currently undergoing emergency surgery. There are no further details at this point."

The only sound in the room was Renee's empty mug hitting the oak floor.

The next hours were some of the most confusing that Renee had ever had the misfortune to recall. What with the telephone ringing and various family members checking in, it was as though a huge circus had arrived from the ninth circle of hell with Satan as the ringmaster. All Renee knew for sure was that she had nothing to do with Donovan Bailey's plight, nor did Andrew. After that, all bets were off. They continued to monitor the televised reporting with a macabre fascination. A competent, dispassionate female reporter was giving yet another update on what was being referred to as the "bizarre shooting of the highly respected newsman."

"The police can only speculate about the events leading up to the shooting of Donovan Bailey. Mr. Bailey, who recently returned from Europe, was residing in a hotel while the contract negotiations for his new position were finished," she said as she gracefully indicated the building behind her.

"As you will recall, the deal with Cochran Communications of Detroit and The Deveraux Group, based in Atlanta, was abruptly broken off recently and it was announced that Mr. Bailey was to be replaced. Neither organization has had any comment to make about his dismissal, which has led to rampant speculation as to the circumstances behind the parting of the ways.

"It appears that Mr. Bailey was surprised by an assailant or assailants and was severely beaten. The extent of the injuries is unknown at this time, but he was shot at close range by a small-caliber handgun." The woman stopped speaking abruptly and placed a hand on the headset that was feeding her information from the studio.

"Mr. Bailey has just been taken to the recovery room after emergency surgery, which appears to have been successful. He will be placed in intensive care in critical condition, and at this point that is all we know. Further details will be available as they are known. I'm Rhonda Sampson with Channel Five News."

The newsroom reappeared on the screen as Andrew clicked the remote to silence the endless bulletins and updates. He looked over at Renee, whose fingers were flying in her usual distress pattern. *One, two, three, four. . . . One, two, three, four. . . .* Andrew frowned and grasped the hand closest to him to reassure her.

"Hey, it's okay, Renee. I know you're shocked, and this

is . . . ironic to say the least, but it doesn't involve us. This has nothing to do with us, honey. Don't look so scared," he said soothingly.

Renee's face was blank with distress. "Andy, it's just that I wished, hell, I even *prayed* so many times for something bad to happen to him. And now, something terrible *has* happened. And I know that I didn't do it, and you didn't do it, but who's to say how it happened? That small-caliber handgun? That pretty much describes the gun that Mama had stashed in the linen closet," she fretted aloud.

Andrew slid closer to her in the corner of the sofa. "Renee! Don't even go there! Your mother could no more shoot a man than she could flap her arms and fly to the moon! You're being crazy, baby, and it's understandable, but don't go off the deep end on me now."

Renee buried her head in the crook of his neck and allowed him to stroke away some of her fear. Then she gave a soft, laughing snort. "You don't know for a fact that my mother *can't* fly. You have never seen her in action. And believe me when I tell you that you don't want to see Ms. Queen on a tear. But let's go over there and make sure that they're okay. I'm sure they've heard the news by now and I don't want Daddy's pressure going up."

When the news first broke, Renee's parents were not reachable, as they were still out shopping, so going back to the Indian Village house seemed the logical thing to do. But even when she could see her parents with her own eyes, Renee was not completely relieved. Pearlie Mae seemed a bit nerved up and giddy, and her father wasn't much better. The reason for their state was soon out in the open. Pearlie Mae announced that they had heard the news bulletins while in the car.

"I'm a Christian woman and I wish I didn't feel like this, but I am glad it happened to the rotten son of a . . . *gun*. You know, God doesn't love ugly and what you do in the dark will eventually come to the light," she said in ringing tones of self-righteousness.

Renee had nothing to add to that statement, nothing whatsoever. She went into the kitchen, where her father was making a pot of coffee for Irish coffee—his usual cure for what ailed one. She wanted to be appalled at her mother's callousness, but she understood exactly where her mother was coming from. Donovan Bailey was a first-class dog and she knew that better than anyone. But somehow, in the face of all Renee had gone through to get rid of the specter of his presence in her life, it seemed wrong to do a happy dance over his shooting. *What would Miss Manners say about this situation? How does the well-brought-up rape survivor react upon hearing that her rapist has been bludgeoned and shot?*

Renee's conflicted feelings erupted in a strained laugh that was more like a bark; it made Mr. Kemp start patting her on the back and offering her water. Renee shook her head in refusal and studied her father's concerned face carefully.

"I'm fine, Daddy, really I am. I'm more concerned with you right now. This has been a lot to take in for you. How are *you* doing?" she asked solicitously.

John embraced his daughter tightly and assured her that he was fine. "My pressure is right where it should be, if that's what's worrying you. And everything else is where it should be, too," he said obliquely, although Renee got his message.

He meant that he understood the reluctance of his daughters to be close to him over the years, that he accepted it and bore no ill will. Renee could feel the tears that never seemed to be far away these days making a comeback, and she tried to will them away.

Her father sensed her distress and sat her down at the work island for a cup of coffee. "Look here, Renee. As much as I want to be with you right now, I think I need to take your mother back to Cleveland until things calm down around here."

As if to underscore his words, the phone rang for the

fourth time since Renee had entered the house. This time, though, it was someone she wanted to speak with, Ceylon.

"Oh, Renee. Dear heart, how are you holding up? I saw the news this morning and I know you must be going through hell. On the one hand, no one deserved it more, but on the other hand, it's a terrible thing to have happened to anyone, even that . . . creature," Ceylon comforted.

Renee relaxed for the first time that day. "Ceylon, you hit the nail right on the head. I am all at sixes and sevens here. I wanted something horrible to happen to him for so long, and now that it has, I feel guilty as hell," she admitted.

"See? I knew it! Renee, honey, you have no reason to feel guilty, none whatsoever! Get Yolanda on the phone and she will tell you the same thing! He was a bad person and something bad happened to him, but it wasn't your doing. You were not responsible for what happened to Donovan Bailey, not at all!" Ceylon exclaimed indignantly.

"But Ceylon, suppose . . . just suppose that I *was* responsible?" Renee whispered.

Even her conversation with Ceylon could not rid Renee of a sense of evil about to descend. With the fascination of a rubbernecking bystander at a five-car collision, she kept taking surreptitious glances at the television to get more information about the Donovan Bailey situation. She and Andrew had bid farewell to her parents, despite Pearlie Mae's vociferous objections. It had taken much persuasion to cleave her from her daughter's side, persuasion that had come in the form of repeated assurances from Renee and Andrew and a final "Get in the car and let Andrew do his job, woman," from John Kemp. Finally they were on their way and peace of a sort was restored.

That is, if repeated phone calls from every male Cochran and Deveraux could be ignored, along with messages from Ceylon, Yolanda, *all* of her sisters and everyone who had reason to be close to Renee, especially Bennie, who was being extra protective of her friend. The convergence of Andrew's brothers did little to calm Renee's fear, either. They all showed up at Renee's house in the early evening with an air of conspiracy and confidence that worked Renee's very last nerve. When she noticed a large bandage on Adam's hand, a hand that was red and swollen, she felt her stomach lurch.

"Adam, honey, what happened to your hand?" she asked in what she fervently hoped was a normal tone. His reply did not convey any degree of truth that Renee could discern.

"This?" he replied breezily. "Accident at work, that's all." And that was all he would say on the subject.

Renee looked at the handsome, intelligent men sitting around her breakfast room swilling icy beer straight from the brown Stroh's bottles and was torn between rage and abject fear. She was suddenly gripped with a cold, clammy sensation that was not unlike a sudden onset of flu as she toyed with the idea that someone in that very room could have been driven to do something incredibly wrong, dangerous and felonious on her behalf. She quickly excused herself and fled upstairs to quell the wrenching nausea that accompanied the fear. *I am losing what is left of my mind. This cannot be happening, Lord. One, two, three, four. . . . One, two, three, four. . . .*

Standing upstairs in her bedroom, Renee could barely hear the murmur of voices that was punctuated by laughter every so often. After tossing the meager contents of her stomach into the toilet, she had brushed her teeth three times and tried to gauge how bad her headache was. The implacable black face of the television in her sitting room drew her like a magnet and she succumbed to its lure. She stumbled over to the armoire, which housed the monster, and flicked on the set. Sinking onto her soft gray sofa, she clutched a rose velvet pillow and waited. Sure enough, the screen was filled with the weeping image of the sweet-faced woman unfortunate enough to be married to Donovan Bailey.

"I—I just can't understand this"—she wept softly—"because Donovan is the gentlest, most loving man in the world. For someone to harm him, well, I—I. . . ." Her words trailed off as her tears trickled down her small, pinched face.

The news crew had superbly staged the scene to be just what it appeared, a terrified, grieving wife trying to be brave for her three frightened, innocent children. The sight of this woebegone little family in the hospital waiting room only compounded Renee's massive guilt.

She was about to turn off the television when the scene switched abruptly to the newsroom.

"This just in: While Donovan Bailey fights for his life in intensive care, police report a new development in the case. A woman was seen leaving Bailey's Southfield apartment just moments before building security was alerted to sounds of gunshots. An eyewitness has come forward and an arrest may be made sooner than anyone previously thought." The African American anchor managed to look concerned, informed and satisfied as he delivered his bombshell.

"Police at this moment are very close to identifying the woman from the description given by an eyewitness, whose presence was not reported previously for obvious reasons. Security on this case has been paramount, due to the celebrity of the victim and the brutality of the attack. We at Channel Eight are pleased to be able to bring you the most accurate and most current updates on this serious situation. More details to follow on the eleven o'clock news." He seemed to smirk, fairly sizzling with grandeur.

This time Renee did turn off the television as though in a trance. She could barely believe what she had just heard. A woman was seen leaving Bailey's apartment around the time of the shooting. And that was when she had been with Andrew, and her mother . . . had not.

For the second time that evening, Renee raced to the bathroom consumed with acute nausea brought on by fear. She hated the vomiting; she hated the terror; most of all she hated herself. *What have I done, Lord? And how can I be forgiven?*

Twenty-four

Renee sat quietly in the rocking chair, listening to the Nnenna Freelon CD and deliberately trying to think of nothing. She had been doing only that for the several hours that she had sought refuge with Yolanda. After a tense, sleepless night in which she did not even confide her fears in Andrew, she had gone to Yolanda's brownstone like a frightened child running home to her mother.

Yolanda, bless her heart, had not even blinked. She, too, had been keeping track of the latest developments in the Donovan Bailey situation and had been more or less expecting Renee. She made her strong cups of tea, plied her with toast and honey and let her ramble for as long as she needed. Renee was convinced that Donovan Bailey was at death's door because of her. Finally Yolanda spoke.

"Renee, if wishing bad things would happen to people made them come true, people would be dropping in the street like flies," Yolanda gently pointed out. "Besides, the man betrayed you, violated you and indirectly made it impossible for you to pursue your chosen career at the time you were just getting a toehold in the business. Why *wouldn't* you think bad things about him? What were you supposed to do, hope he wins an Emmy, a Peabody and a Pulitzer?"

Yolanda's gentle irony was just the medicine Renee needed. Impossible as it would have seemed a few hours before, Renee almost smiled. Then the gravity of the situation returned in full force and she turned a somber face to Yolanda.

"It's not just that, Yolanda. Neurotic as I seem to be lately, even I don't think that I have that kind of power. What I mean is, thanks to me opening my big mouth about this whole situation, there were a lot of people gunning for Donovan Bailey. I mean that literally, *gunning* for the man. When I heard on the news that there was a woman seen, I immediately thought of my mother. She has a gun, she is apparently *not* afraid to use it, she wanted him dead and she was right here in Detroit when it happened and I have no way of accounting for her whereabouts," Renee emphasized.

"And then there is the matter of Adam and his hand. Now, he says he had an accident at work, which he has never done in all the time I have known him. But remember, Bailey was beaten as well as shot—who is to say that Andy's brothers did not take a notion to have a good ol' Detroit-style beat down/blanket party and knock the hell out of him?" Renee's eyes were huge and a dull pewter color from anxiety.

"And then, Andrew says his father . . ." Her rapid words were cut off by a wave of Yolanda's hand.

Yolanda put her right hand into her long braids and shook them rapidly as if to clear her head of Renee's frantic line of reasoning. "Renee, honey, you have got to slow down here. Take a breath! You are about to drive yourself crazy with all kinds of wild suppositions and fears when you have absolutely no basis in fact for any of this! And let's drop that business about your 'big mouth,' okay?"

Yolanda leaned forward and grabbed both of Renee's icily cold hands to make a point. "You were *supposed* to tell what that man did. Your family, your fiancé, your friends, are *supposed* to care about what happens to you. You have rights here, Renee. You did nothing wrong. You did nothing wrong, and neither did anyone who loves you and wanted to see him punished. Wanting a thing does not make it so, remember that," she said firmly.

Renee squeezed Yolanda's hands tightly, grateful for their warmth. She looked around the spacious, airy interior of Yolanda's living room with its Afrocentric decor and multitudes of plants and wished she could absorb the serenity that was evident around her. She knew Yolanda was right, but still. . . . Before Renee could give voice to the "but" that was hovering on her lips, Yolanda took control again.

"Renee, you keep forgetting that like you, Donovan Bailey has a past as well as a present. You also keep forgetting that there is every chance that there was someone out there who hated Donovan Bailey as much or more than you and your family and friends. Someone who wanted him hurt, someone who wanted him dead. Evil does not exist in a vacuum, Renee. What are the chances that you were the only person he ever hurt? I would guess that Donovan Bailey injured a lot of people in his time and that one of them, or some of them, caught up with him at last," she said wisely, never breaking eye contact with Renee.

At last the ice that had encased Renee's insides began to thaw a little. Yolanda was another blessing in her life, Renee thought. After seeing that Renee was calmer and more comfortable, Yolanda suggested that she let Andrew know where she was and just stay there for a few hours while Yolanda went downstairs to her office. Renee was so wiped out that she agreed immediately.

Which is how she came to be rocking quietly, listening to the soft jazz and trying to stay calm. Over the past few hours her mind had mutated into a frantic gerbil on a wheel—she could actually hear the little *squeak, squeak, squeak* of tiny feet on a wire surface. Renee glanced down at her lap and widened her eyes. She had indeed been in a spin when she left the house; she was wearing gray sweats that normally never saw the light of day outside the four walls of her house. True, they were DKNY and fashioned of cotton cashmere, but they were sweats, no getting around it. *Lord, today, worrying about that evil man has made me into a fashion "don't."*

For the first time in a good while, Renee actually laughed. She was laughing at herself to herself, which under normal circumstances would not have been indicative of strong mental health, but she wasn't retching and she wasn't sobbing and that was a definite improvement as far as she was concerned. The buzzer by the front door rang to indicate a visitor. Renee made her way over to answer it, feeling less than thrilled about her makeup-free, ultracasual appearance.

"Who is it?" she asked with more insouciance than she felt.

"It's me, honey, Andrew," he answered.

Renee wasted no time in flinging open the door to greet him. Andrew, of course, noticed nothing amiss with her appearance; she always looked good to him. After a deep, hot kiss he walked her over to the sofa and sat her down.

"Renee, they have made an arrest in the Donovan Bailey case. There really was a woman leaving the scene and the eyewitness identified her. It was Dana Pierson."

Some hours later, Renee was in a place she could not have conceived of a few hours ago—warm and cozy in her own bedroom, recently bathed in a bubbly tub full of Annick Goutal, clad in a pink sheer peignoir and completely relaxed while digesting the remains of a fabulous dinner. And she was thoroughly relaxed, both from the excellent wine Andrew had insisted she drink and from the disappearance of the mighty weight she had been carrying. Now all she was was curious, which she freely admitted to Andrew.

"Okay, but this is the last time we are going over this," Andrew said amiably. "Dana had met Donovan Bailey on several occasions while she was in Europe. He had offered her a job on the new cable network, on the strength of his alliance with Donnie and Clay. Now once he was back here in the States, they hooked up to finalize the details of what she felt was a new position on the ground floor of this new network."

Andrew paused in his recital to take another sip of wine,

which earned him a stern look from Renee. "Okay, okay." Andrew sighed and resumed speaking, although his eyes were closed now. Renee looked much too tempting in that gown and he wanted to get this over with so he could get on to other things.

"Well, Bailey's family went to Maryland, where his wife is from, to visit with relatives. Bailey stayed here." Andrew yawned, but he rallied on with his tale.

"So, our little Dana, who had her own reasons for wanting to be in Detroit, took it upon herself to pay him a visit. That visit led to an encounter like the one you had with him in Newark. Which led to her vowing to light him up, to the extent that she procured a gun, went back to his place and popped a cap in his ass. End of story." He finished with a hopeful leer on his face.

"Are you satisfied now, baby? Can we discuss some more important issues?" He pulled her closer to his hot, waiting body. To his utter disappointment, Renee was not quite ready to let go of it.

"But, Andy, she couldn't have beaten him like that! That was the work of some big men or at least one man. . . . Did she arrange for that, too?"

Andrew ground his teeth in despair and sat up. Renee was not going to be happy until she had every single detail. "Well, now, that's where it gets kinda surreal," he admitted. "The beating was a contract job. Someone who had good reason to punish Bailey severely arranged for some wiseguys to beat him within an inch of his life. Hard as it is to believe, there are people who will maim for hire if you know where to look, and this person knew exactly which rocks to turn over, apparently," he said ruefully.

Something in his voice made Renee sit bolt upright and stare worriedly at him. "Andy . . . is this what you meant about your father back in the day?" she said fearfully.

Andrew raised his eyebrows comically and then lowered them. "Well, yes and no. It appears that there were two asskickings scheduled for Donovan Bailey. One was sanctioned by someone who is old enough to know better, and the other one was arranged by none other than Miriam Roberson Bailey," he said slowly, waiting for the name to sink into Renee's consciousness. "Her team just happened to get to him first."

"His *wife?* His wife hired someone to beat up her own husband?" Renee exclaimed incredulously. "Why in the world would she do that? I thought she worshiped the man! And how in the heck did you find out all this, anyway— none of this has come out in the news," she pointed out.

Andrew looked into Renee's beloved face. She was relaxed, animated and totally sexy. He sighed. He was completely in love with her and would be until the day he died, but if she did not shut up, he was going to have to shut her up the best way he knew.

"You remember Titus Argonne, the detective Martin hired? Well, he's still being retained on the case. He has some friends in the detective bureau here and he called in a few favors. So that's how I got the dirt. Now, as to Bailey's wife, she is no fool. She knew the way women know these things that Bailey is a dog, a player, whatever. What-*ever.* What she did not know was the lengths to which he would go and had gone to satisfy his need to . . . well, you know," Andrew said, gesturing broadly with one hand.

"She had laid the law down to him to the extent that if she even heard about him creeping out on her one more time he was going to regret it. And Dana—oh, boy, Dana—does not miss a trick. In addition to blowing a hole in Bailey, Dana informed his wife just what he had done to her. And when Miriam Bailey got that news, she went ballistic. Turns out her daddy had some connections from back in the day—he's a liquor distributor near D.C. So she got the hookup, greased a few palms and got pretty boy beat within an inch of his life.

"Of course, she had no idea that Dana was going to shoot him, and Dana had no idea that Miriam was going to have him dealt with. So that's one of the reasons why

Miriam just fell to pieces over this thing; she really was scared she was going to lose him, as well as scared she was going to get fingered."

It was all a bit much for Renee to take in. She fell back against the softly patterned pillows piled at the headboard and draped a dark, lissome arm over her head. "Scared she was going to lose him," she mused. "Well, I guess she wouldn't want him dead, after all, but why in the world would you want to stay married to a creature like that?"

Andrew lay down on his side and stared at Renee, who had no idea how desirable and desired she was at that moment.

"Love makes you do strange things, I guess. It knocked me out flat seventeen years ago and it continues to lead me around by the nose every day of my life," he said sweetly. "I know all about love," he continued as he pulled Renee out of her reverie and into his arms, where she belonged.

"I know about wanting to be with someone twenty-four hours a day, about wanting to hear their voice, smell their scent, feel their warmth and tenderness, being lonely even if they are only in the next room. I know about someone having only to smile at you and knowing in that instant that you will belong to them until the end of time."

By now, Renee was completely focused on the man she loved, who was making a declaration so sweet and pure that she was afraid to breathe, afraid to break the precious, delicate bond between them. Andrew looked into her sparkling golden eyes and seemed to sense her hesitation; he kissed her until they were both breathless and wild with passion.

"Sweet Renee, this is the real thing, baby. You can't lose me, no matter what. I'm never leaving you for any reason. You are everything in the world that I want, and I am yours, only yours. Don't be afraid of this, baby; those seventeen years were just the beginning of the best that could ever be," he vowed.

And she didn't even have time to wonder how her gossamer sheer gown found itself floating across the room, she only had time to sigh with happiness as they found a primitive, erotic passion that surpassed anything they had yet achieved in making love.

"I love you, Andy. I love you; I do love you." She wept as they loved. When it was finally over, he held her for hours, stroking her and making plans for the most exquisite wedding they could conceive on short notice. At long last, it was time for their real life to begin.

After a night of lovemaking so hot that the memory of it made Renee periodically stop to fan herself and blush, there was even yet something tickling the back of her mind. She managed to rise before Andrew and make him a huge breakfast, which she was happy to feed him in bed, much to his delight. Throwing caution and cholesterol to the wind, she made him delectable scrambled eggs, crisp bacon and his favorite twisted indulgence, chocolate-chip pancakes. His beautiful eyes lit up when he saw this unexpected pleasure. Renee disapproved of them heartily—all that sugar could do nothing but cause chaos in the body, she felt, but he adored them.

Watching him consume this mammoth repast and topping it off with a big glass of orange juice and a cup of Jamaican coffee, Renee breathed a sigh of pure happiness. She wore an expression that she knew would be called sappy by anyone who wasn't as much in love as she was. Besides, Andrew had the same look. But as much as she would have preferred basking in bliss for a few more days, there was work to be done. Andrew was off to the hospital and she to the salon, which her stalwart staff had kept running like clockwork. After a passionate good-bye and a promise to call each other later, she and Andrew went their separate ways.

The salon and spa were humming along nicely with their abundance of customers readying themselves for holiday festivities. For the first time in ages, Renee was able to really enjoy her place of business and feel that warm holiday feeling, which had been knocked completely out of her. It was that as much as anything that kept bringing her back to one thing. Finally she stole a moment and closed the door to her private office. She consulted the phone book and then entered the numbers into the touch tone pad on her office phone. In less time than she would have thought possible, she had the information she sought.

That evening she surprised Andrew by meeting him at his office. He was taken aback, but not to the extent that he did not kiss her thoroughly.

"To what do I owe this singular pleasure, baby? I thought we were meeting at home in a little while," he commented.

Renee walked back and forth in front of his oak desk and fiddled with the few objects on the surface. Andrew did not mind this at all as he had a chance to enjoy the sight of her long, strong legs in her sexy black boots, and admire the way she looked in a midnight navy Calvin Klein suit. He sprawled on the leather settee and waited for her to answer him. Finally she cleared her throat and began.

"Andy, I made a couple of phone calls today and this is what I found out. Dana is being held in the county jail while she is waiting to be arraigned. They will not allow her to post bail because of the risk of flight. Since she is from California and her father is quite wealthy, it seems highly probable to the courts that she would flee this jurisdiction," Renee rattled off in a monotone.

She stopped and looked amused at herself. "That sounded just like something off television, didn't it?" She shook her head to gather her thoughts and went on: "Andy, I think that if I speak to her attorney, it might give him a basis on which to mount her defense. I know what she did was wrong and certainly ill advised, but I know exactly how she felt when she did it. I know how she felt when he did it to her. I *know,* Andy. And even though she is certainly not one of my favorite people, if there is anything I can do to help her, I want to do it. Will you come with me?"

By now, Andrew was sitting straight up, staring at

Renee as if they had just met. He rubbed a hand over his face as if to clear his vision—yes, it was his Renee speaking. Although the words she was saying were a bit beyond his comprehension, it was indeed Renee DeShawn Kemp telling him that she was going to try to help Dana Pierson clear herself of charges of attempted murder.

"Renee, are you sure you want to do this? What did Yolanda say when you talked to her about it?"

Renee looked him in the eye with a great deal of satisfaction and informed him that Yolanda didn't say anything because Renee had not discussed it with Yolanda. "I am talking to you about it because this is ultimately only going to affect us. Somehow I have to put this entire episode into my past and leave it there. I don't know why, but I feel like telling the truth and shaming the Devil is the only way that I can. So I am asking you if you will come with me to the jail to talk with Dana and her attorney and see if I can be of some benefit to her defense. Will you?"

"Renee, darling, you know I would walk over fire for you. But this could get messy," he warned.

"I know," she replied softly.

"This could get a lot of press coverage."

"I know."

"You might have to testify in court or at least give a deposition in front of a lot of people," he persisted.

"Andy, I know all of that, and I am willing to do it so that her life is not destroyed, so that she doesn't have to go to jail. Why should she be locked away for the rest of her life after what he did to her? Who is to say that there aren't some other women out there who might come forward if I speak up? Evil doesn't exist in a vacuum, you know; there could be many other women he has harmed," she reminded him.

Andrew's eyes shone with admiration. "Damn, you're wise beyond your years, aren't you?"

"Actually, Yolanda told me that," Renee admitted. "But I was wise enough to fall in love with you and wise enough to know when enough is enough, and I am strong enough to do this now. Everybody but Chaka and Patti knows everything now, anyway, so who have I got to hide from?"

Andrew rose from the settee and hugged her fiercely. "Okay, baby, if you're sure. But can we have Alan or Andre meet us there? Just to have someone looking after your interests?"

Renee gave him a sultry smile of pride and pure happiness. "That's what you're here for, honey. Always. And they are on the way over there now, so we need to get going."

To say that their holidays were merry was like saying that Bill Gates had a little money. Renee and Andrew had the time of their lives. They spent Christmas Eve with his family and then had a private, romantic and delightful celebration of their own at the house in Indian Village. The next day, they drove down to Cleveland to celebrate with her family and make amends to her formidable sisters for keeping secrets. All was forgiven in the light of their unmistakable joy in each other.

"Girl, girl, girl, if you all don't stop doing all that kissing, the house is going to go up in flames," Lee Ann said good-naturedly as she found her younger sister in yet another sizzling lip lock with her beloved. "I must say, though, I ain't mad atcha. In fact, I think I will find that husband of mine and see if I can't teach him some new moves." She winked as she left them cuddled by the fireplace in the basement of their parents' home.

"She should talk," Renee groused softly. "At least she gets to sleep in the same bedroom as her man. I'm going to be half a house away from you all night," she complained, pouting.

Then she raised her eyes seductively at Andrew and suggested that he might make a late-night call on her. Even though she looked sexy, sweet and delicious, Andrew laughed in her face.

"Your mama still got that gun? You must be crazy, baby.

We are leaving tomorrow morning, and if you want, we can stop at a hotel. But if you think I'm sneaking around in your mother's house, you have lost your mind. I love you, baby, but I want to live," he said, laughing.

"Speaking of living, I hear Donovan Bailey is getting out of the hospital in a few days," Renee remarked. "And there won't be any charges pressed against his wife, because he can't remember a thing about the attack . . . he *says*."

As a result of the shooting and its aftermath, a myriad of information about Donovan Bailey came out in the media, none of it flattering. He went from being the darling of broadcast news to a pariah. In addition to his womanizing, it seemed that he was a chronic gambler who had a taste for cocaine and underage girls. The beautiful part was that none of the information came from The Deveraux Group; it appeared that there were tongues all over Europe that were more than happy to spread gossip that had been carefully tamped down for years.

To Dana's utter surprise and gratitude, Renee did assist her attorney in staging her defense. And as Renee predicted, several more women came forward with similar tales of molestation. Dana had been released on her father's recognizance and was in all probability going to do community service instead of serving time. Dana had been grateful enough to acknowledge that she had come to Detroit to take one more swing at Andrew, something she recognized back in the summer was a lost cause.

With nothing but candor and admiration in her eyes, she confessed to Renee: "I know I was an absolute snot to you and you had no reason in the world to help me, but I am so grateful that you did. And you know Andrew never looked at me twice. Not even once, if you must know. It was all me, throwing myself at him because I was so tired of being on the road," she said ingenuously.

This conversation had come about a week before

Christmas in the offices of Dana's lawyer. The plush Bloomfield Hills office was the perfect setting for Dana, who was so relieved to be away from the county jail that she fairly shimmered with pleasure. As Renee now recalled, before she could say anything, the door had opened and the attorney Dana's father retained to defend her entered the room. Dana's eyes—for once not covered with her gray contact lenses—sparkled like brown jewels as she looked into the smiling, handsome face of David Baptiste.

Renee smiled to herself when she saw the way he was looking at his client. He was about six feet tall, with prematurely silver hair and mustache, and he was utterly charming. As well as being charmed by Dana from the look of things.

Renee sighed happily, remembering everything that had transpired that day at the lawyer's. Andrew nudged her and asked what she was thinking about.

"About Dana and David Baptiste, about Yolanda, our families, about you, about our future, just everything," she said softly. She looked into the face that she would never, ever get tired of seeing and kissed him sweet and hot. "I love you, Andrew, more than anyone or anything in the world. You are the best thing that has ever happened to me, or will ever happen to me. With the exception of our babies. I hope we have lots and lots." She sighed contentedly.

Andrew held Renee as closely and as tightly as he could for a long, long moment. "We'll have as many as you want, baby. As soon as you want them," he promised.

What promised to be an extremely passionate kiss was cut very short by a disembodied voice from beyond.

"You can try to make a baby in here if you want to. . . . Don't forget I still have my gun," intoned Pearlie Mae.

Between peals of laughter Renee informed Andrew that her mother also listened at keyholes and was known to pick up the extension on private telephone calls. "Are you sure you still want to marry me? It's not too late to back out, you know."

"Renee, it was too late for me the day I laid my prying eyes on you seventeen years ago. This, my sweet baby, was meant to be. We have always belonged together and we always will," he vowed. Then he smiled broadly and shouted up the stairs, "Is that okay with you, Mom?"

In a voice of perfect poise and dignity, she answered, "Why, yes, dear, it certainly is."

Epilogue

"Andy, honey, I'm fine. But if you don't get my mother out of here, it's going to be a different story," Renee said sweetly.

Andrew escorted his indomitable mother-in-law into the waiting area and kissed her soundly on both cheeks. "Okay, Mom, you heard her. And right now, she's the boss, okay?"

Pearlie Mae sniffed and tried to look like her feelings were hurt, but she failed miserably. "I just don't see why my baby doesn't want me in there while she has my grandchild. It just doesn't seem right, that's all."

Andy hugged her as he turned her over to her husband for the duration. "Mom, it's not like this is her first time doing this. This is our second time around, you know."

He was headed back to the delivery suite when Pearlie Mae got her last shot in. "But she's never had *twins* before. Twins don't run in *our* family." Sniffing, she made it sound like a highly unnatural and undesirable practice, but Andrew was long gone.

Renee looked absolutely adorable, which is an odd thing to say about a woman about to deliver twins. The birth of their daughter a year earlier had gone so smoothly that Renee was a little embarrassed by it. Andrew, on the other hand, was as proud as could be. As he was happy to tell people, little Andrea Yvonne Cochran shot out of her mother like a football leaving a quarterback's hands. Of course, he only used this analogy when out of Renee's range of hearing, since she did not appreciate the imagery.

But the process of having children certainly agreed with her. If anything, she was even more radiant than the day he married her in a private, secret ceremony on the isle of Mustique on New Year's Day. They simply had to be together as soon as possible after Christmas, and Andrew made it so. There was nothing he would not do for her, even take the pain of birthing away if he could.

She laughed sleepily when he told her this. "Don't be ridiculous. What's a little pain . . . well, a *lot* of pain, when you get a beautiful baby to take home? Besides, it will give me something to hold against them when they're obnoxious teenagers." She yawned.

And they had already made a truly beautiful baby. Little Andie, named after Bennie, was a chocolate beauty who was the image of her mother, right down to the golden eyes and the stubborn streak. Andrew stroked Renee's huge, tight belly as they waited for the new babies to make their appearance. The sex of these babies was a mystery, like Andie's had been, but Andrew felt sure they were boys. Not that he cared. He just wanted healthy babies and a happy, healthy wife and he would feel more than blessed, which he was.

In what seemed an indecently short time, it was all over and Andrew was staggering out to the waiting room, where his father-in-law dozed with Big Benny, Martha and a few other family members. Pearlie Mae, however, was on full alert.

"Well? How is my baby? And her babies? Were they boys or girls? And is everything all right?" she demanded.

"Everything went wonderfully well. My wife is an amazing woman. She is perfect and the babies are perfect. Beautiful little girls. And, Mom, you were right about twins not running in your family. It seems as though someone was hiding from us for nine months. She had triplets," he said proudly.

For the first time in recorded history, Pearlie Mae Kemp was speechless.

Dear Readers,

I want to thank everyone who wrote to me about *Lucky in Love*. I was overwhelmed and humbled by your response to my characters and hope that you enjoyed Andrew and Renee's story as much. Next is the story of Martin and Ceylon; Martin is a man who is long overdue for something wonderful in the romance department, and Ceylon is determined to give it to him!

Please drop me a line at P.O. Box 5176, Saginaw, Michigan 48603, or at MelanieAuthor@aol.com. And by the time this is published, I will have a website . . . finally! It's a real pleasure to hear from you all.

Thanks for your support and I look very much forward to bringing you more romance in the very near future!

Melanie

ABOUT THE AUTHOR

Melanie Woods Schuster currently lives in Saginaw, Michigan, where she works in sales for the largest telecommunications company in the state. She attended Ohio University. Her occupations indicate her interests in life: Melanie has worked as a costume designer, a makeup artist, an admissions counselor at a private college and has worked in marketing. She is also an artist, a calligrapher, and she makes jewelry and designs clothing. Writing has always been her true passion, however, and she looks forward to creating more compelling stories of love and passion in the years to come.